Macbeth

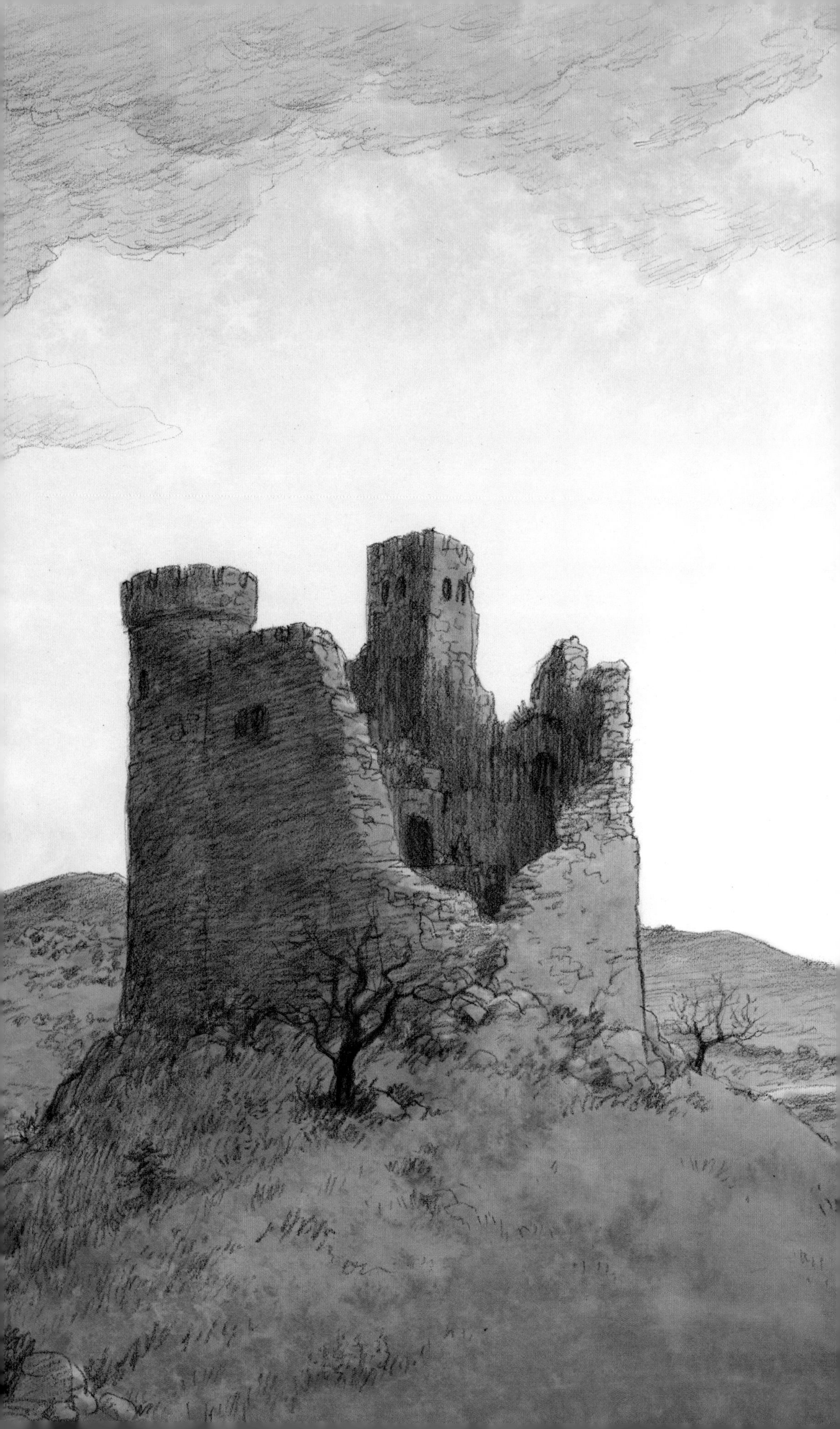

Macbeth

a play by William Shakespeare
adapted and illustrated by Gareth Hinds

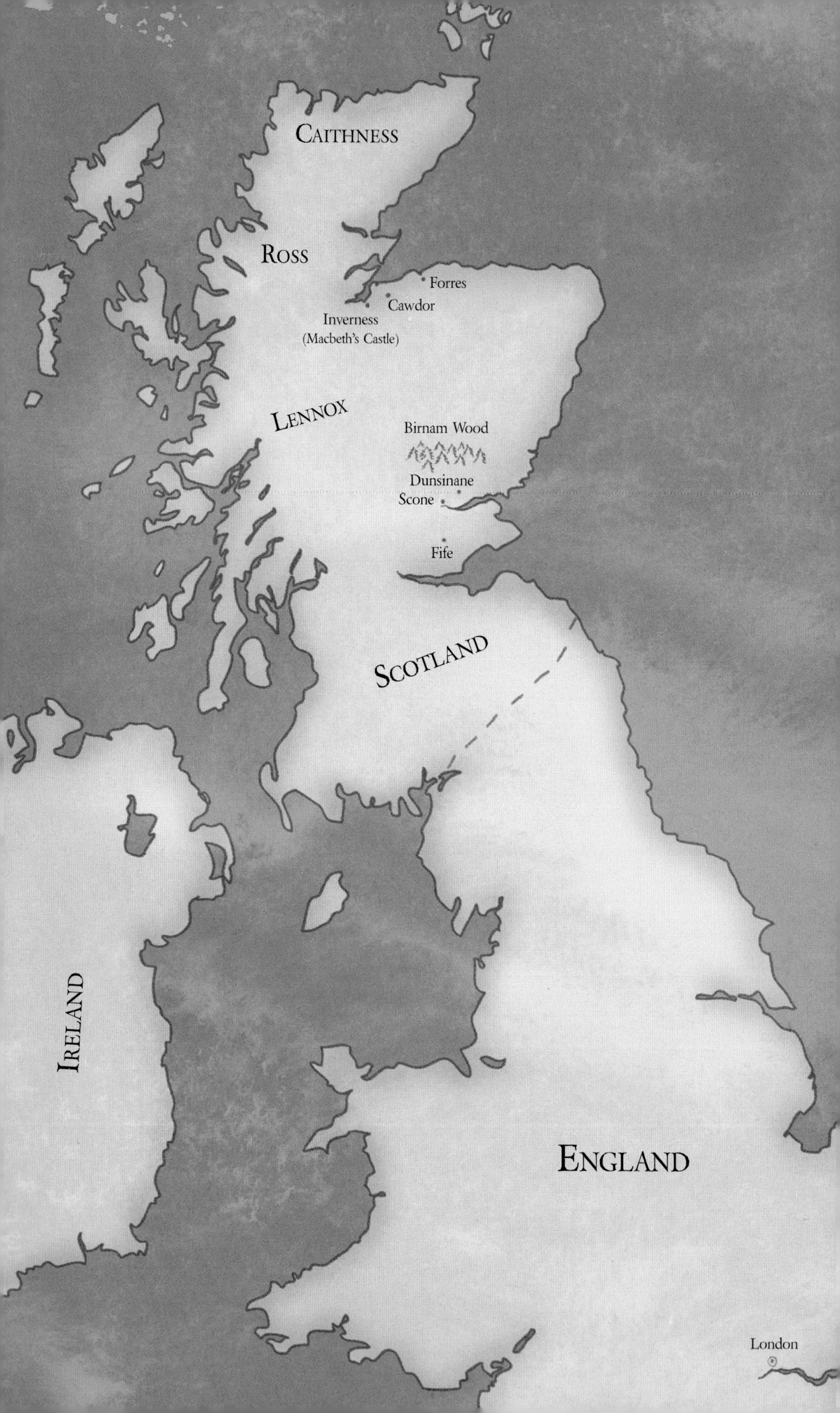
CAITHNESS
ROSS
Forres
Cawdor
Inverness
(Macbeth's Castle)
LENNOX
Birnam Wood
Dunsinane
Scone
Fife
SCOTLAND
IRELAND
ENGLAND
London

Dramatis Personae

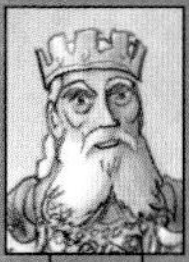
DUNCAN
King of Scotland

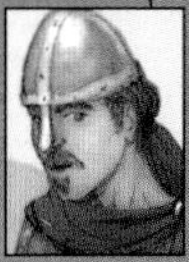
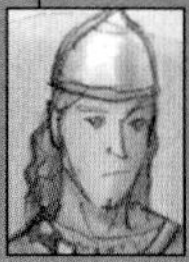
MALCOLM and
DONALBAIN
Duncan's sons

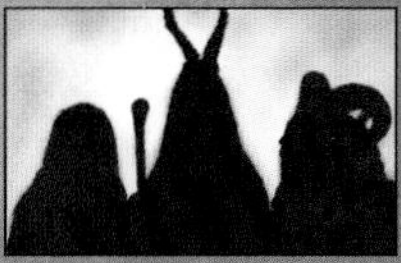
Three WITCHES

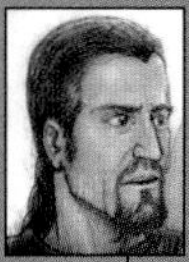
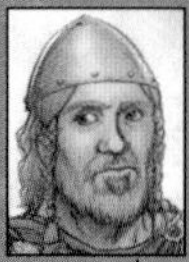
MACBETH and BANQUO
Generals of the King's army

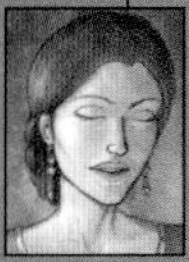
LADY MACBETH

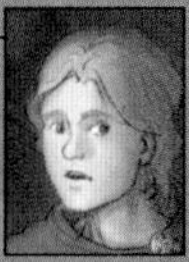
FLEANCE
Son of Banquo

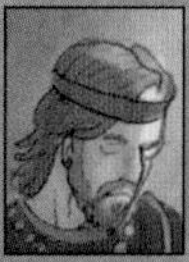
SEYTON
An officer
attending
Macbeth

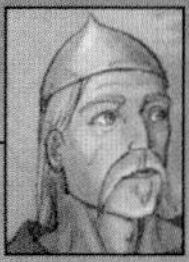
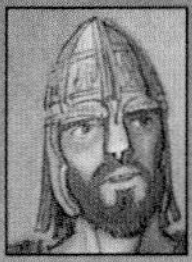
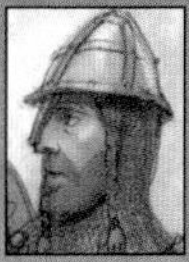
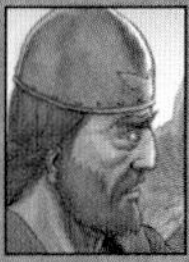
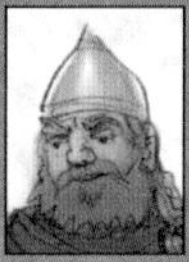
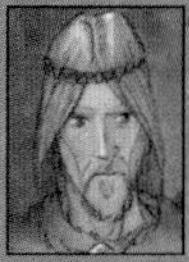
MACDUFF LENNOX ROSS MENTEITH ANGUS CAITHNESS
Thanes (noblemen) of Scotland

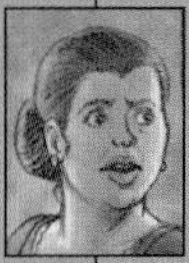
LADY MACDUFF

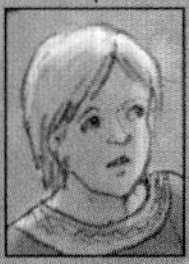
MACDUFF'S SON

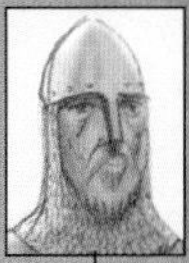
SIWARD
Earl of Northumberland and
general of the English armies

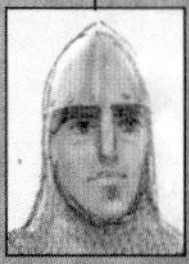
YOUNG SIWARD
His son

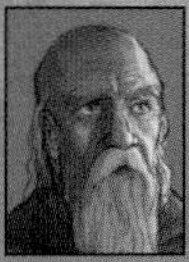
A DOCTOR

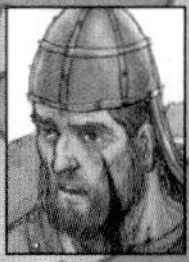
A CAPTAIN

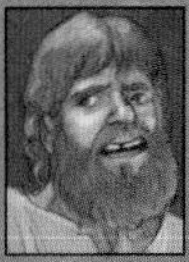
A PORTER

Not pictured: Lords, Gentlemen, Officers, Soldiers, Murderers, Attendants, Gentlewomen, and Messengers; the Ghost of Banquo, and other Apparitions

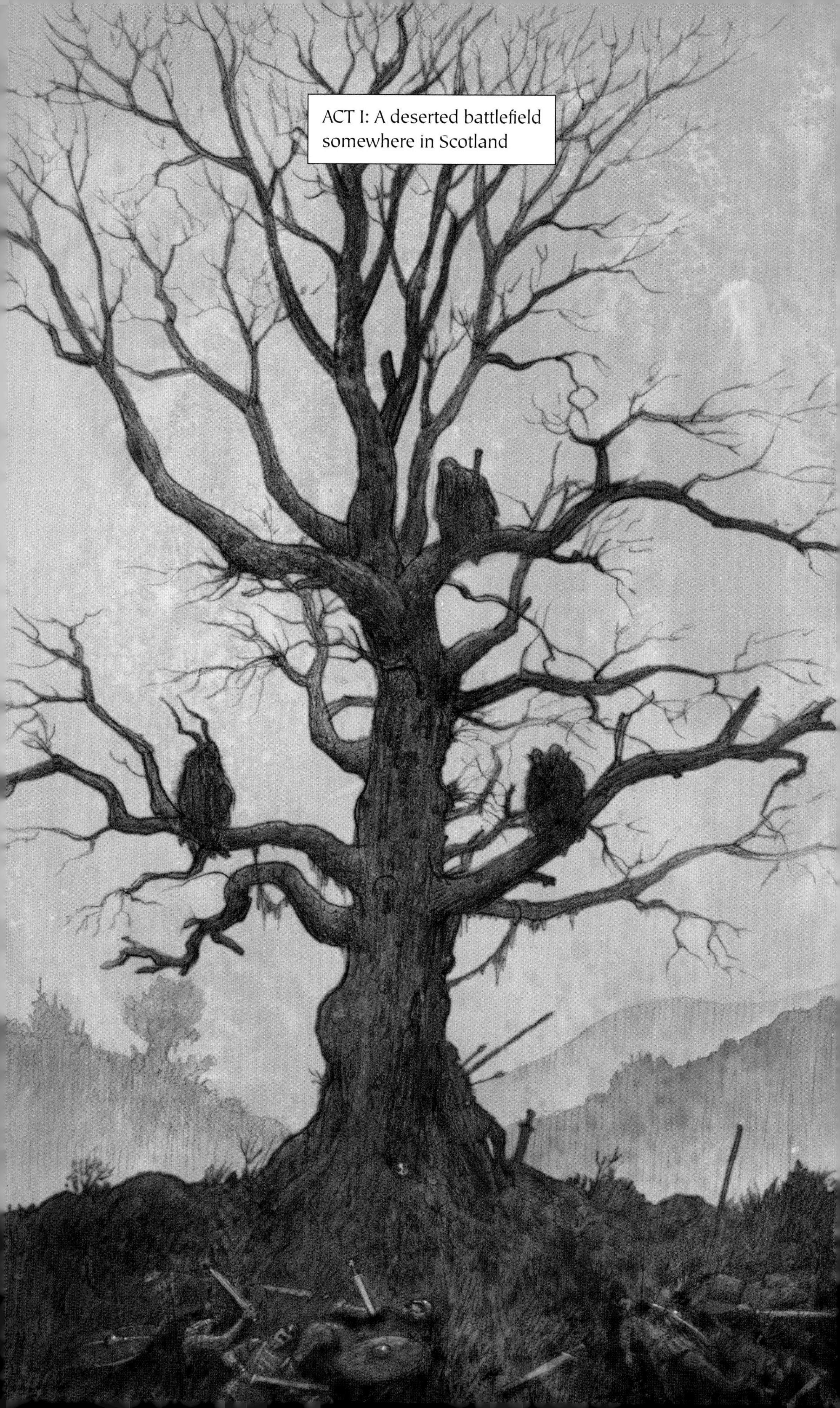
ACT I: A deserted battlefield somewhere in Scotland

When shall we three meet again?

In thunder, lightning, or in rain?

When the hurly-burly's done, When the battle's lost and won.

That will be ere the set of sun.

Where the place?

There to meet with Macbeth.

Upon the heath.

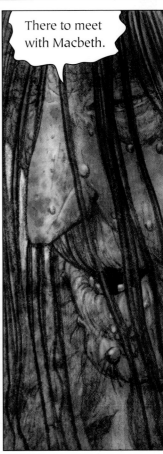

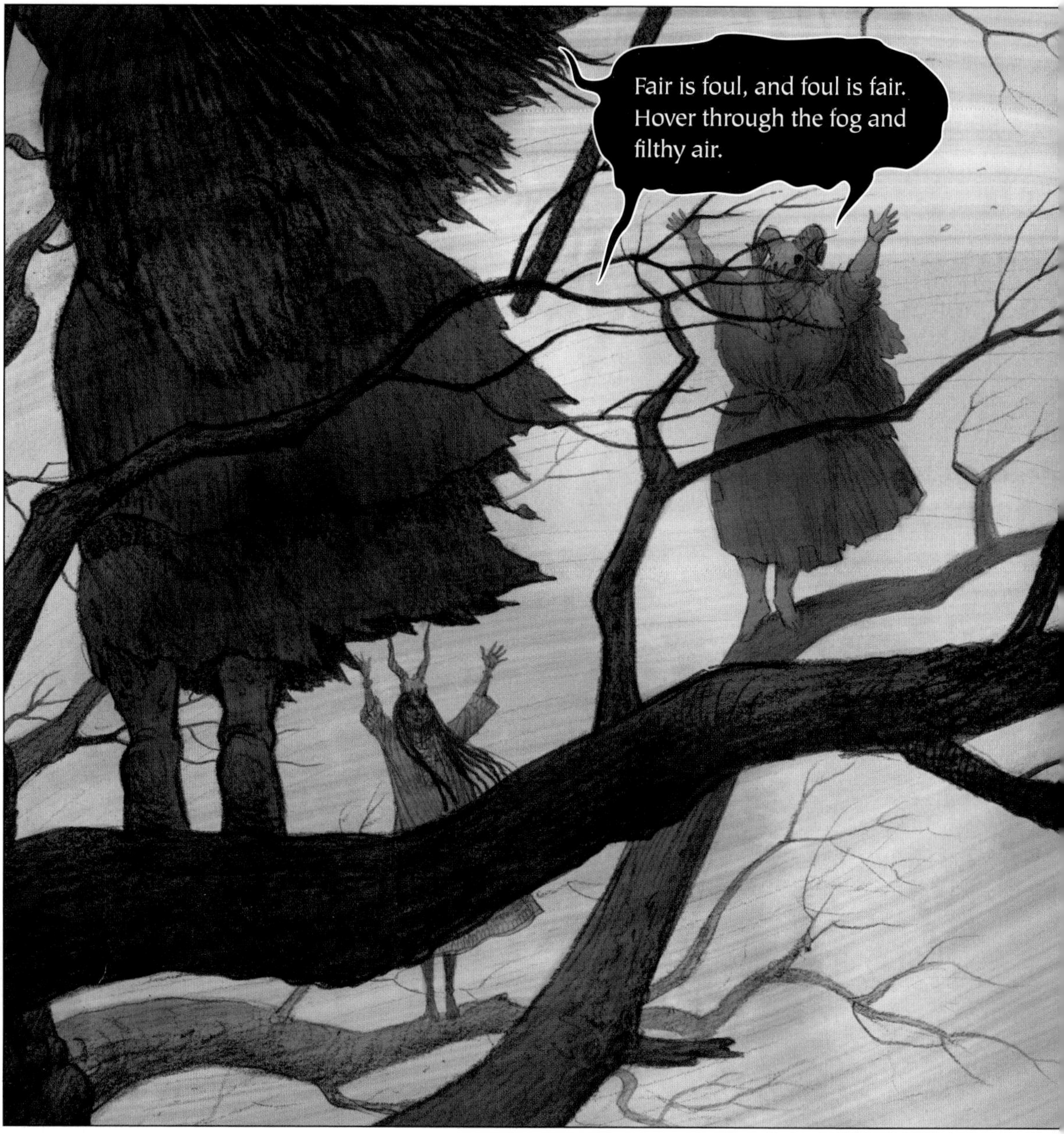
Fair is foul, and foul is fair. Hover through the fog and filthy air.

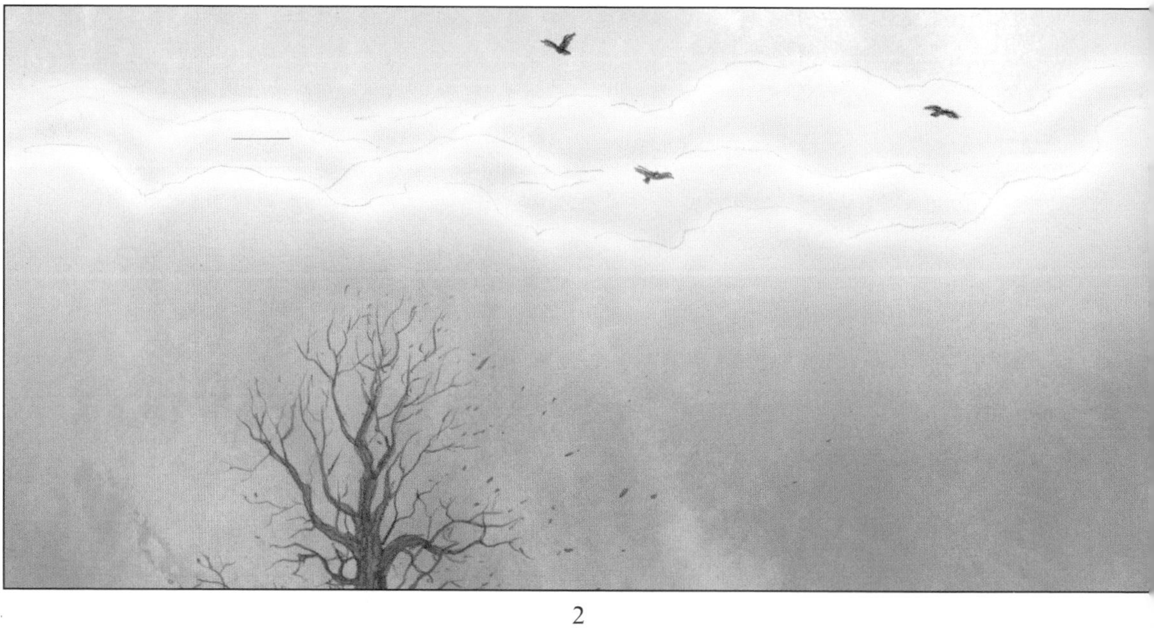

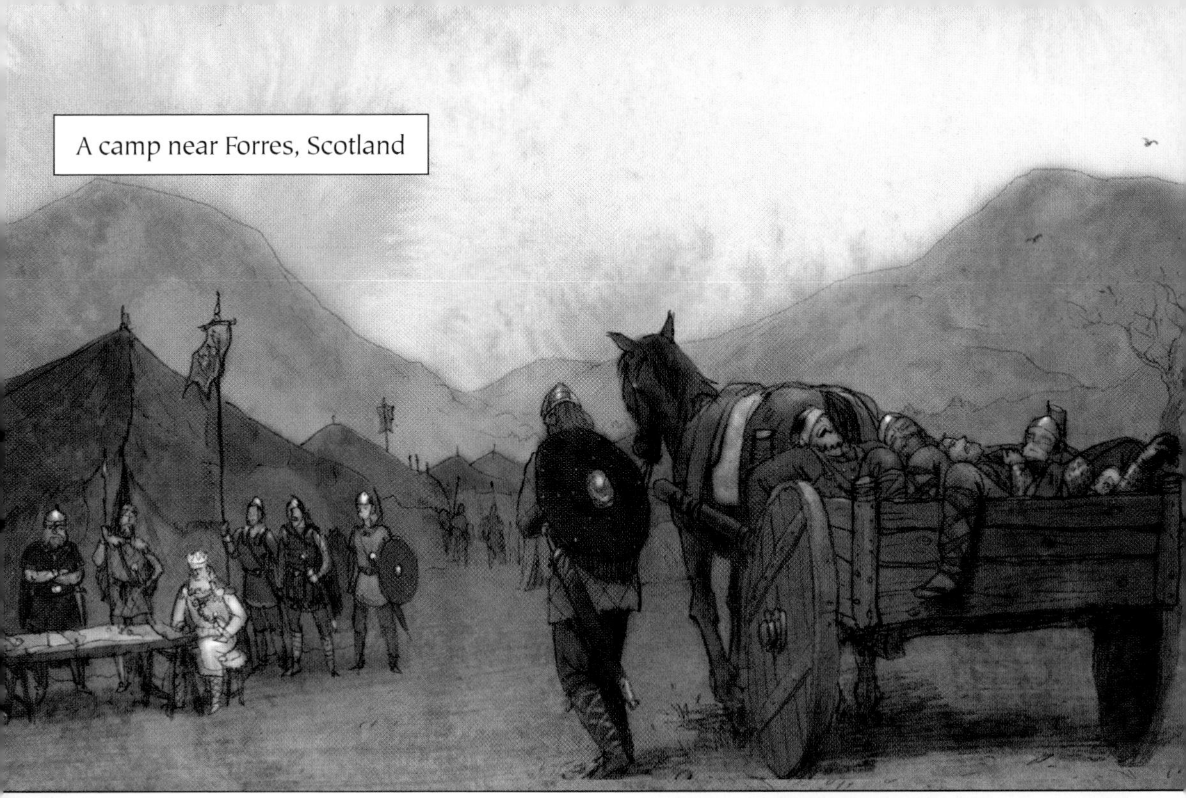
A camp near Forres, Scotland

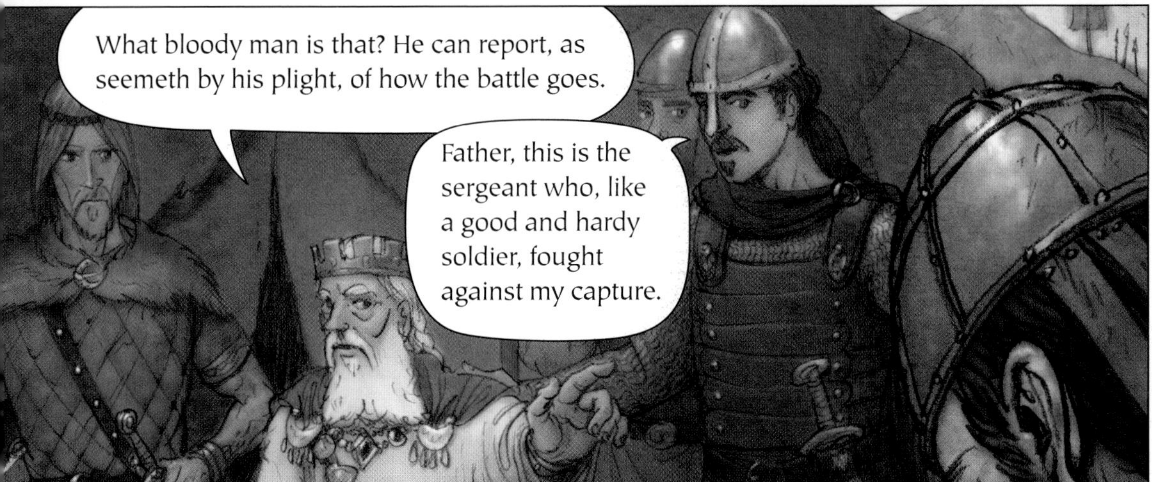
What bloody man is that? He can report, as seemeth by his plight, of how the battle goes.
Father, this is the sergeant who, like a good and hardy soldier, fought against my capture.

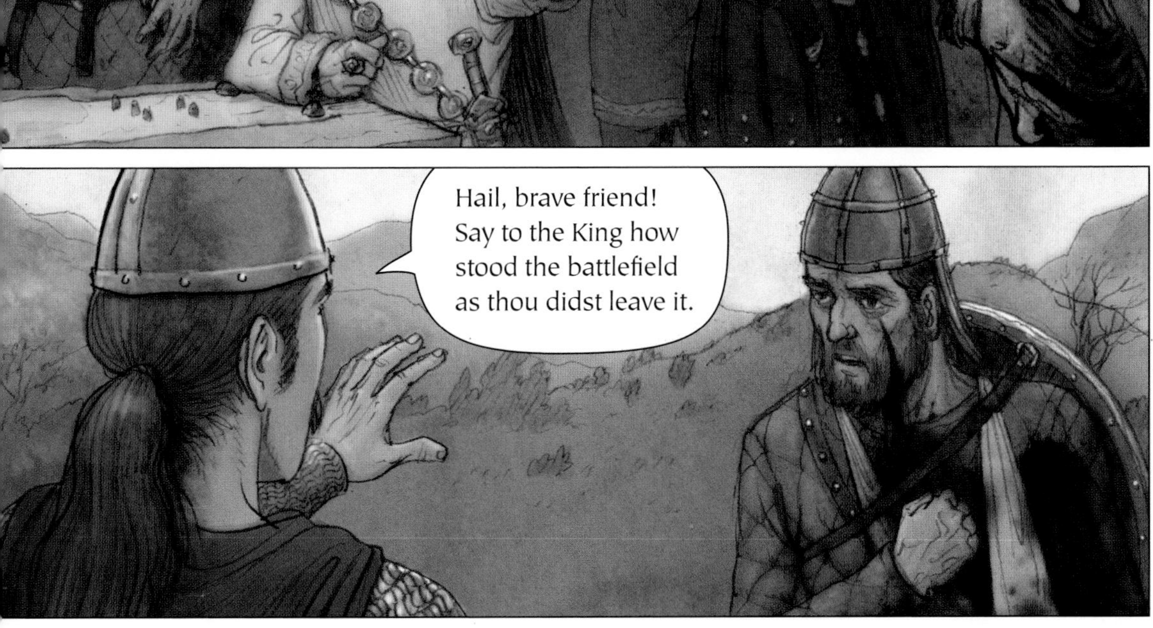
Hail, brave friend! Say to the King how stood the battlefield as thou didst leave it.

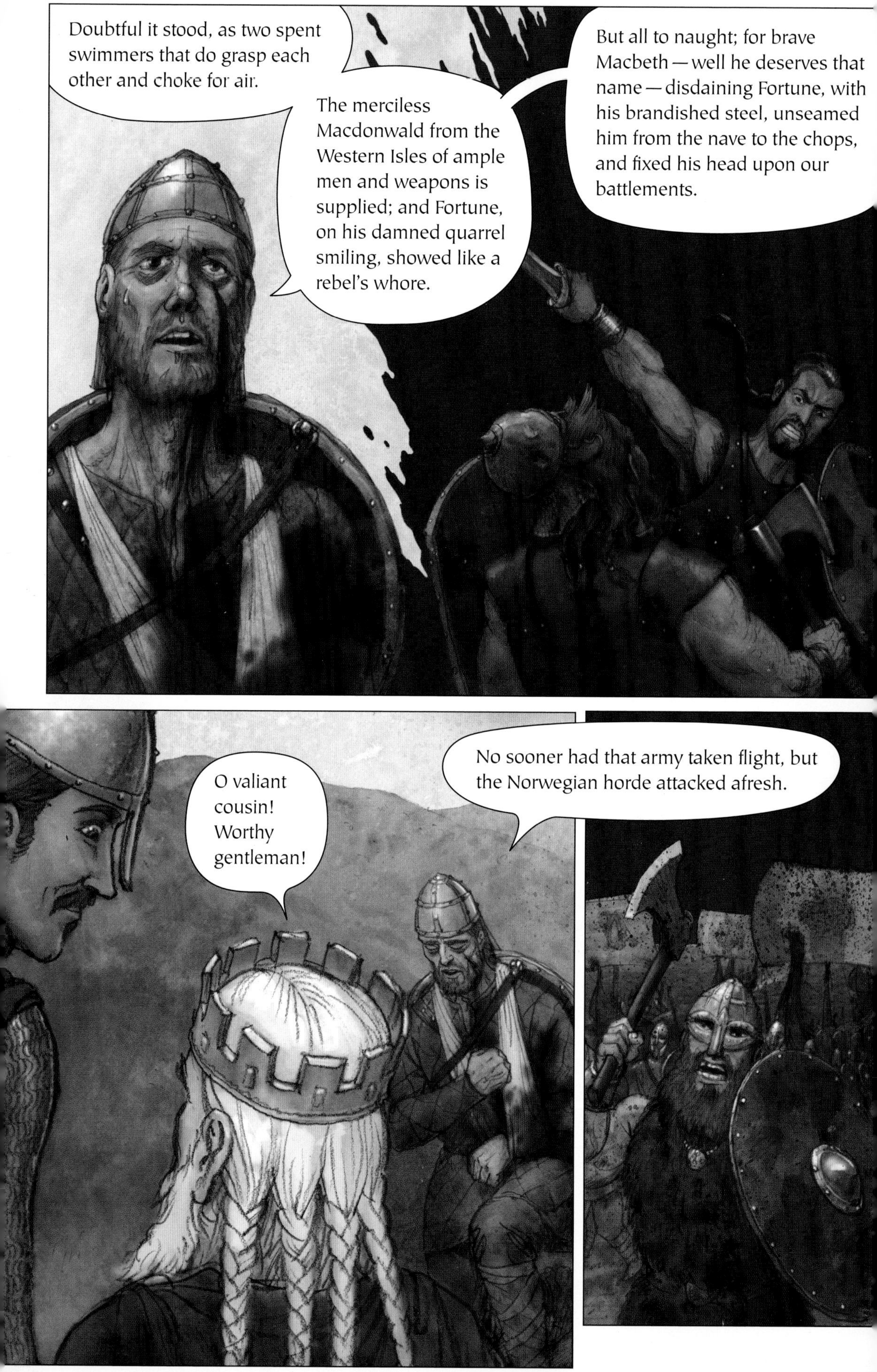
Doubtful it stood, as two spent swimmers that do grasp each other and choke for air.
The merciless Macdonwald from the Western Isles of ample men and weapons is supplied; and Fortune, on his damned quarrel smiling, showed like a rebel's whore.
But all to naught; for brave Macbeth — well he deserves that name — disdaining Fortune, with his brandished steel, unseamed him from the nave to the chops, and fixed his head upon our battlements.
O valiant cousin! Worthy gentleman!
No sooner had that army taken flight, but the Norwegian horde attacked afresh.

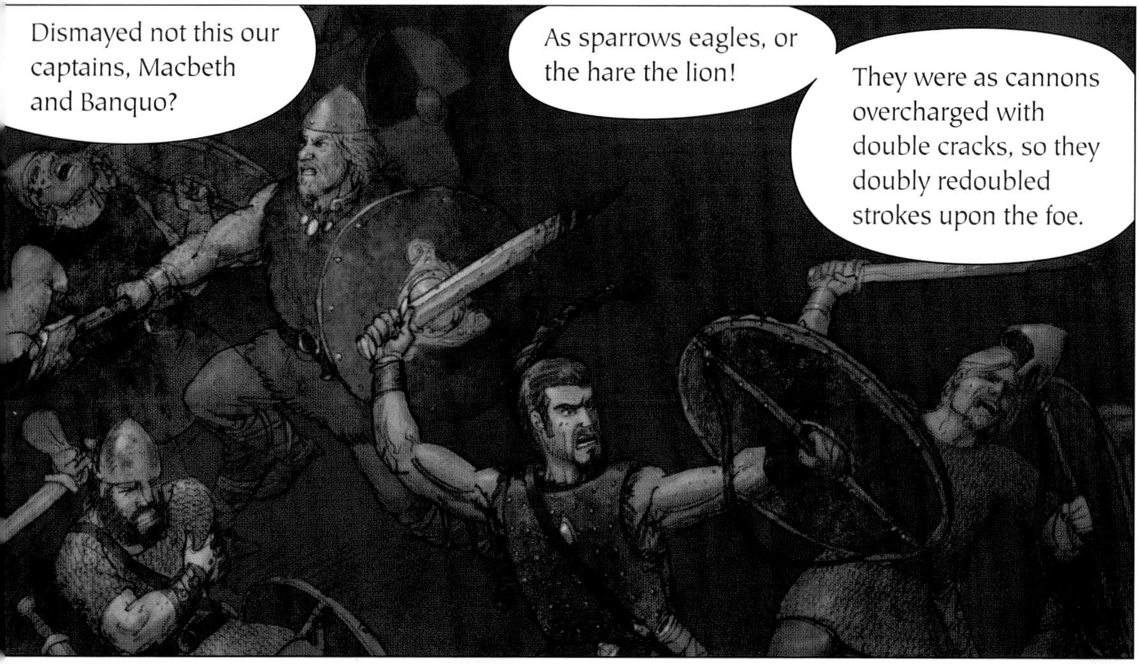
Dismayed not this our captains, Macbeth and Banquo?
As sparrows eagles, or the hare the lion!
They were as cannons overcharged with double cracks, so they doubly redoubled strokes upon the foe.

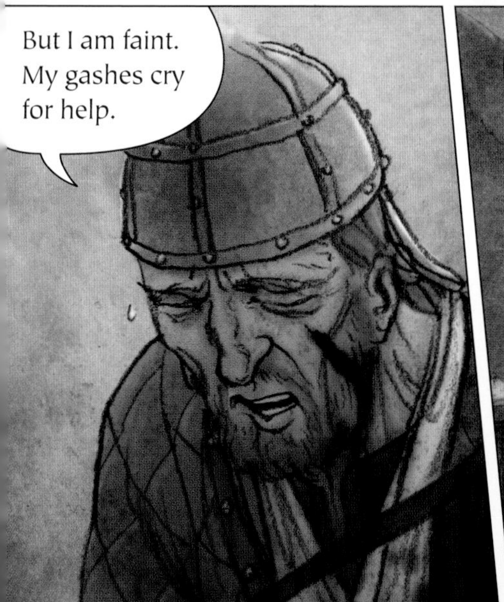
But I am faint. My gashes cry for help.

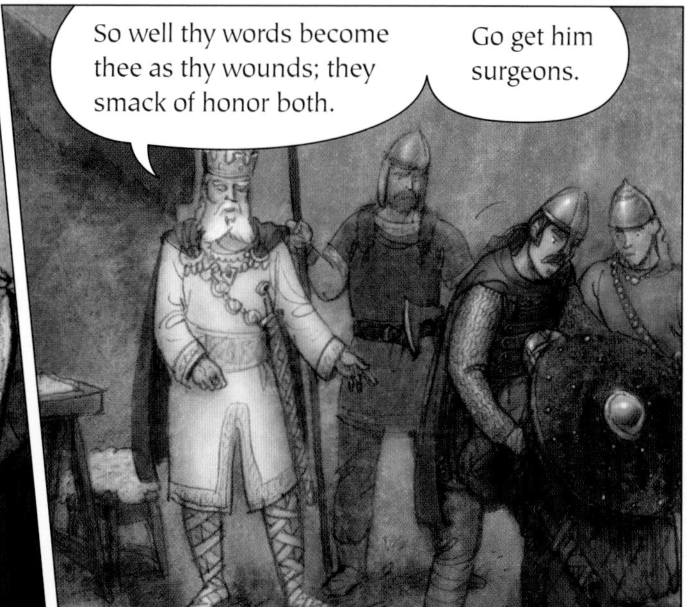
So well thy words become thee as thy wounds; they smack of honor both.
Go get him surgeons.

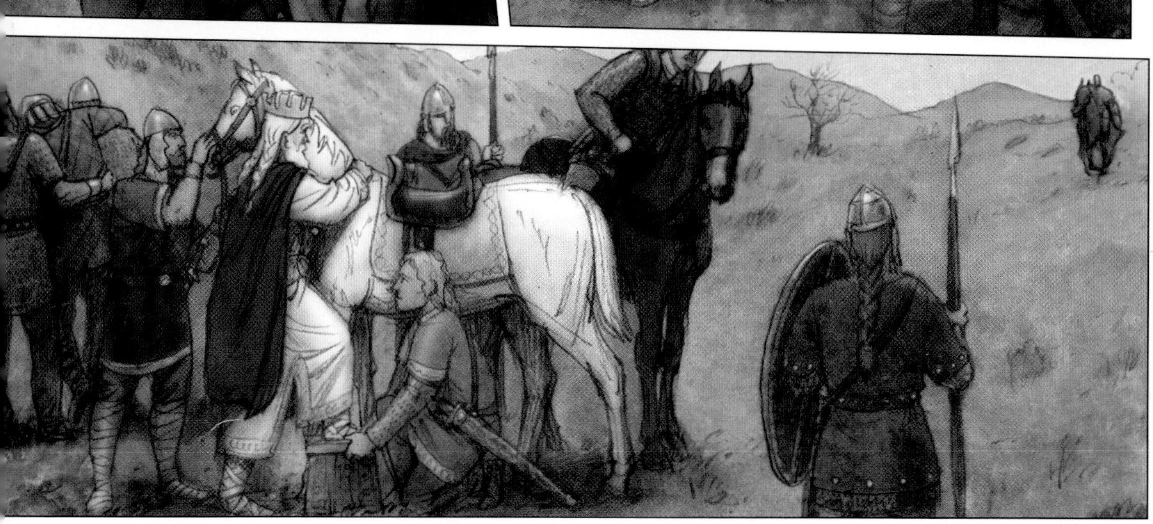

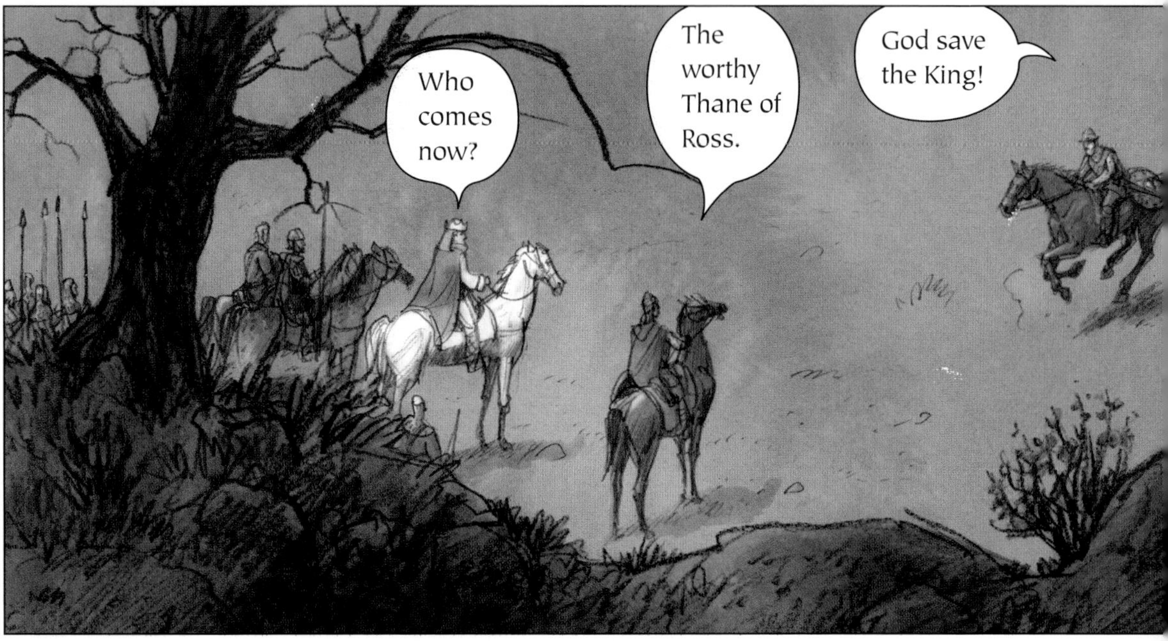
Who comes now?
The worthy Thane of Ross.
God save the King!

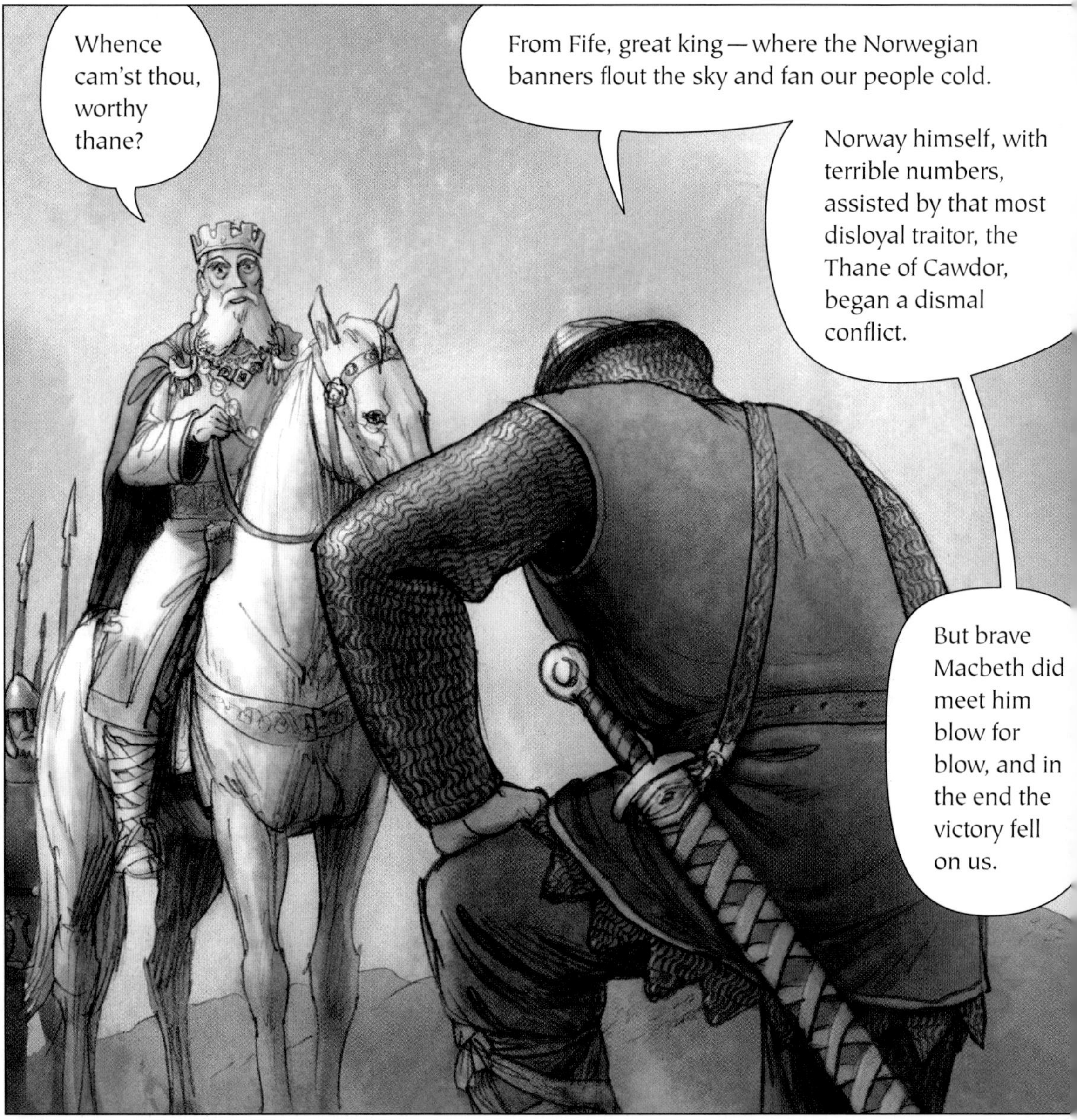
Whence cam'st thou, worthy thane?
From Fife, great king — where the Norwegian banners flout the sky and fan our people cold.
Norway himself, with terrible numbers, assisted by that most disloyal traitor, the Thane of Cawdor, began a dismal conflict.
But brave Macbeth did meet him blow for blow, and in the end the victory fell on us.

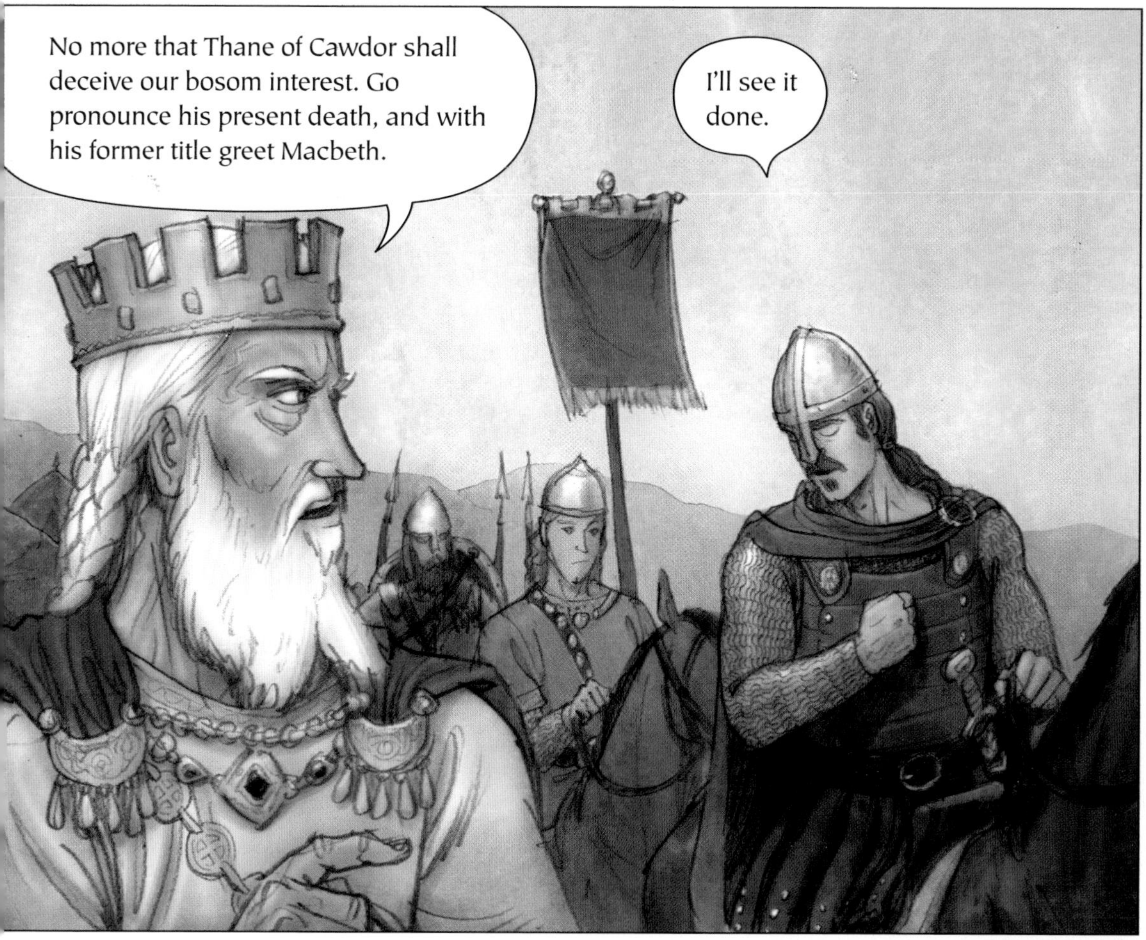
No more that Thane of Cawdor shall deceive our bosom interest. Go pronounce his present death, and with his former title greet Macbeth.
I'll see it done.

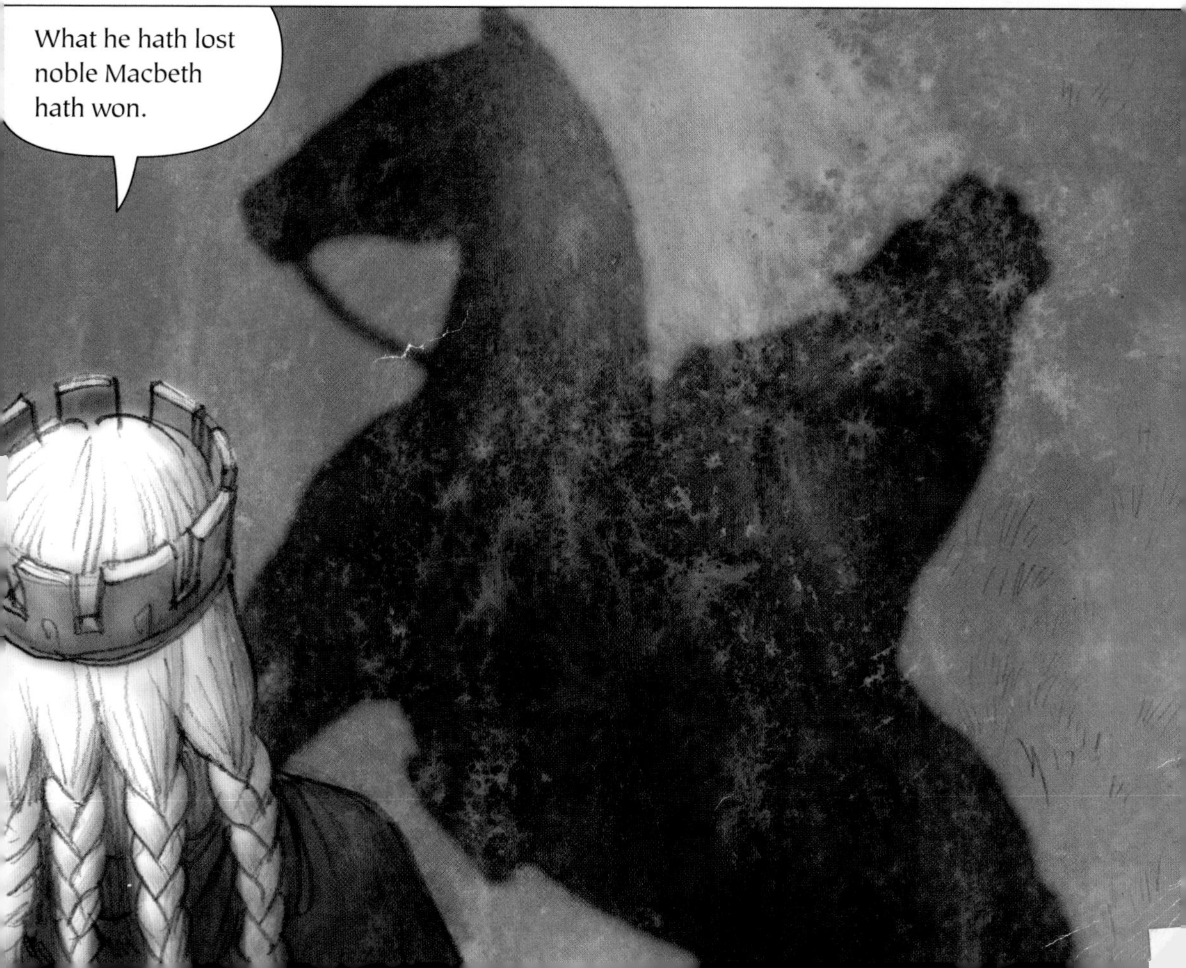
What he hath lost noble Macbeth hath won.

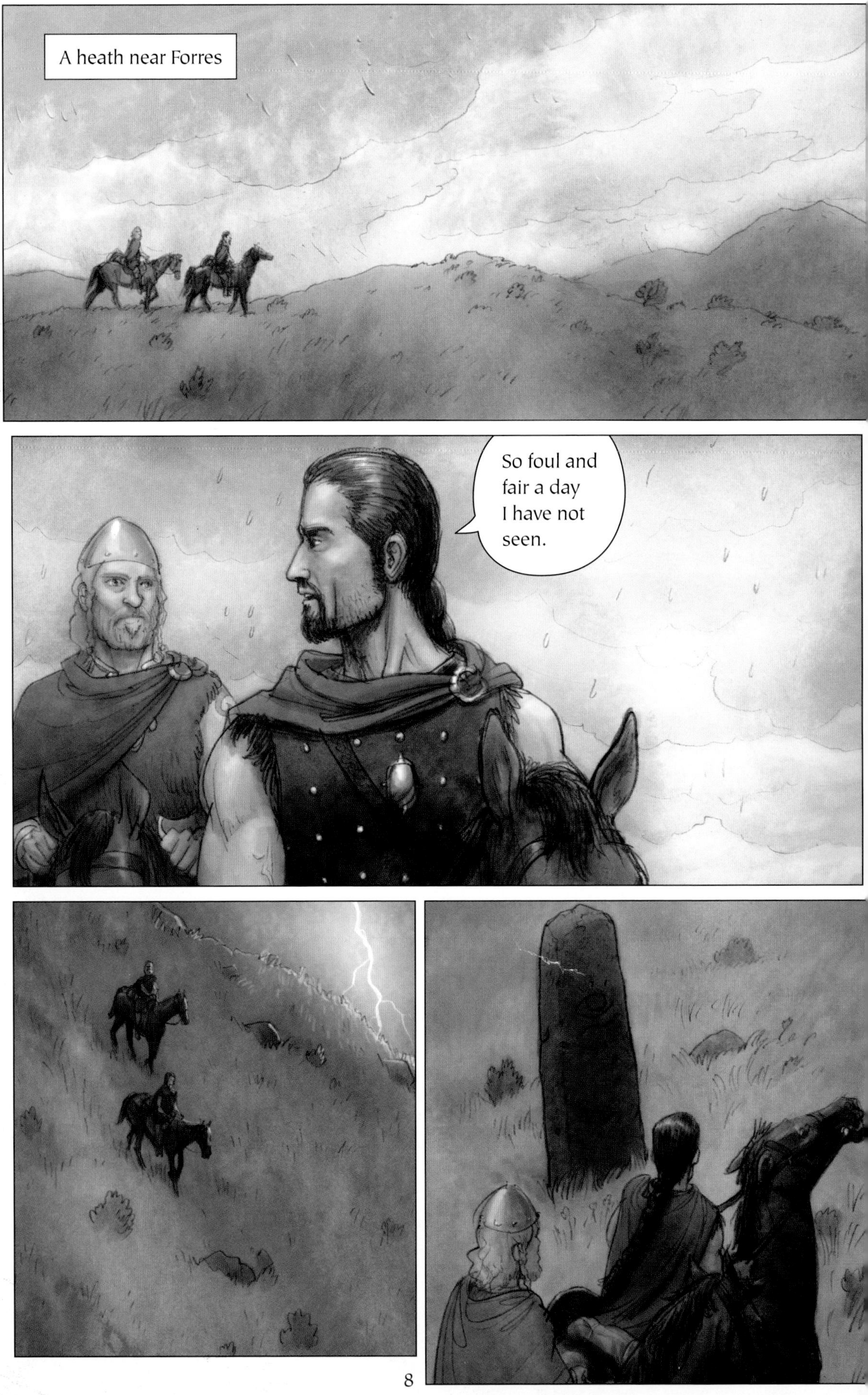
A heath near Forres
So foul and fair a day I have not seen.

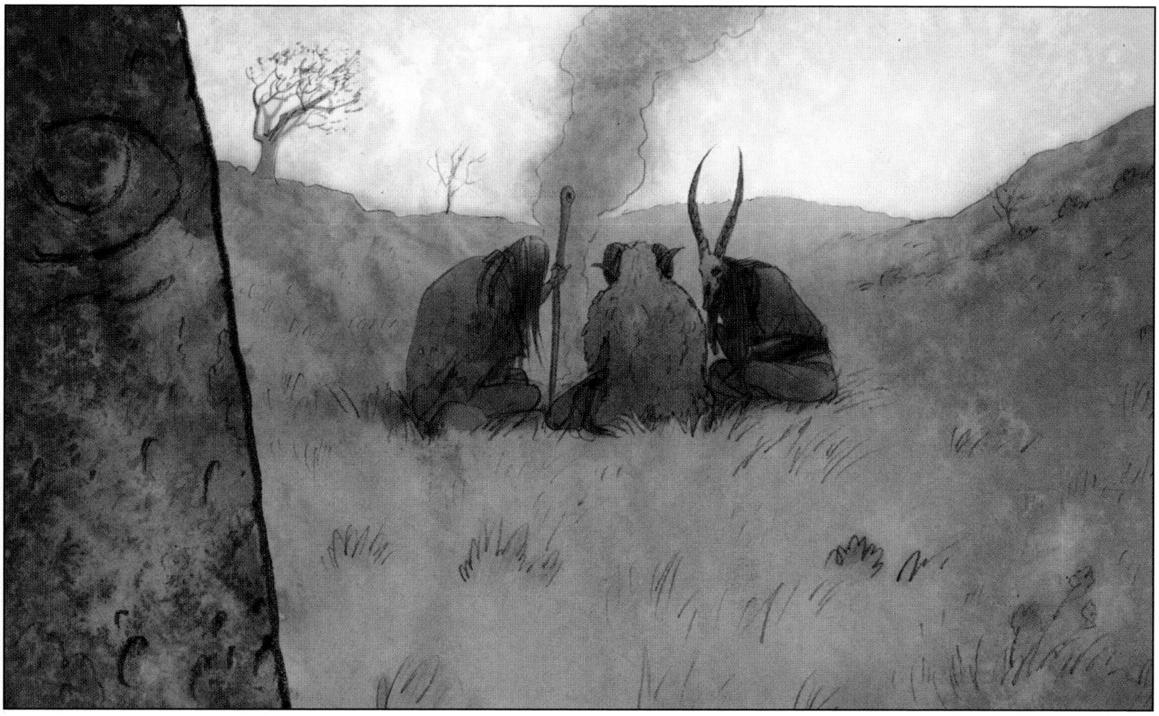

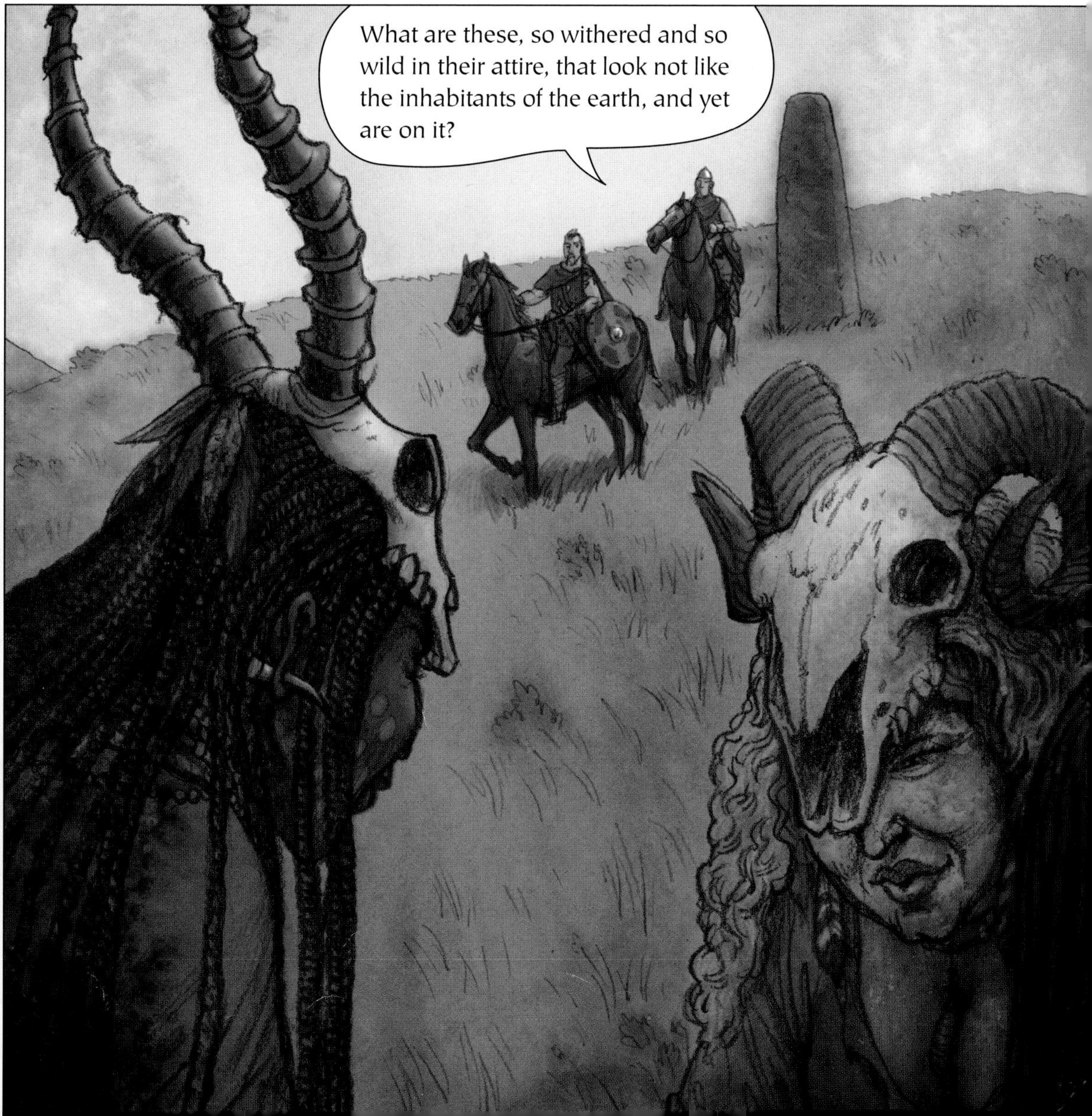
What are these, so withered and so wild in their attire, that look not like the inhabitants of the earth, and yet are on it?

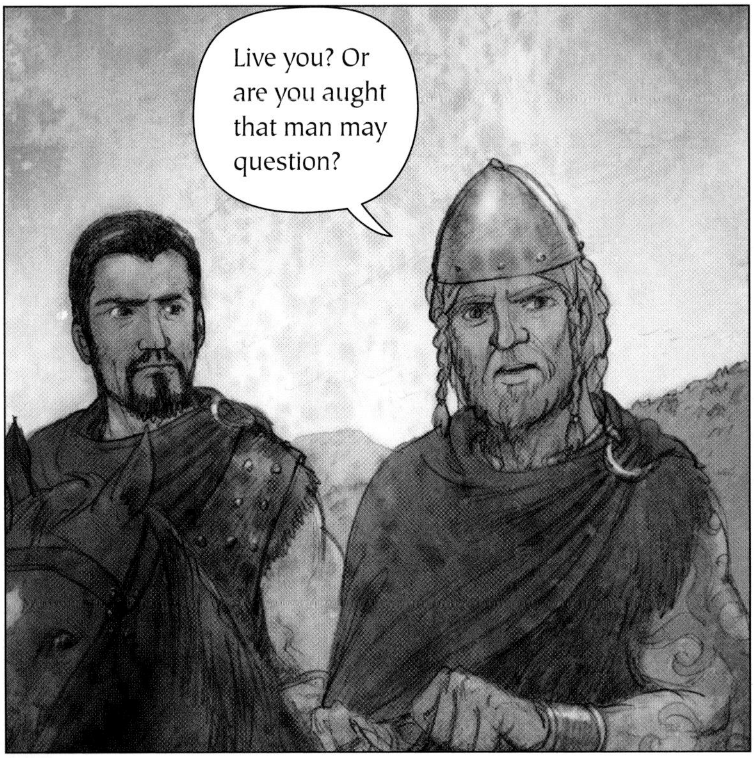
Live you? Or are you aught that man may question?

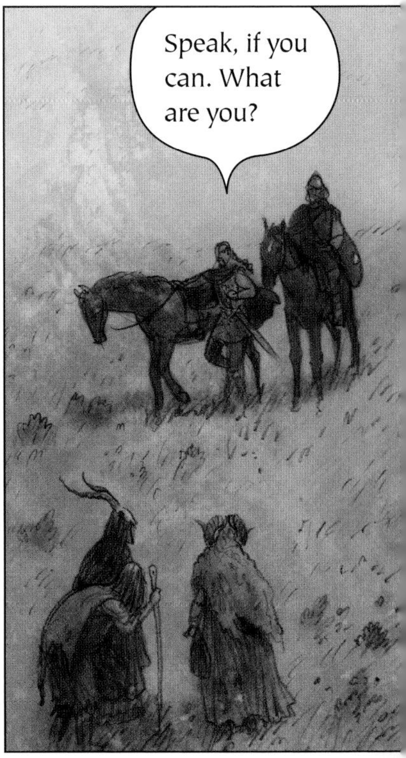
Speak, if you can. What are you?

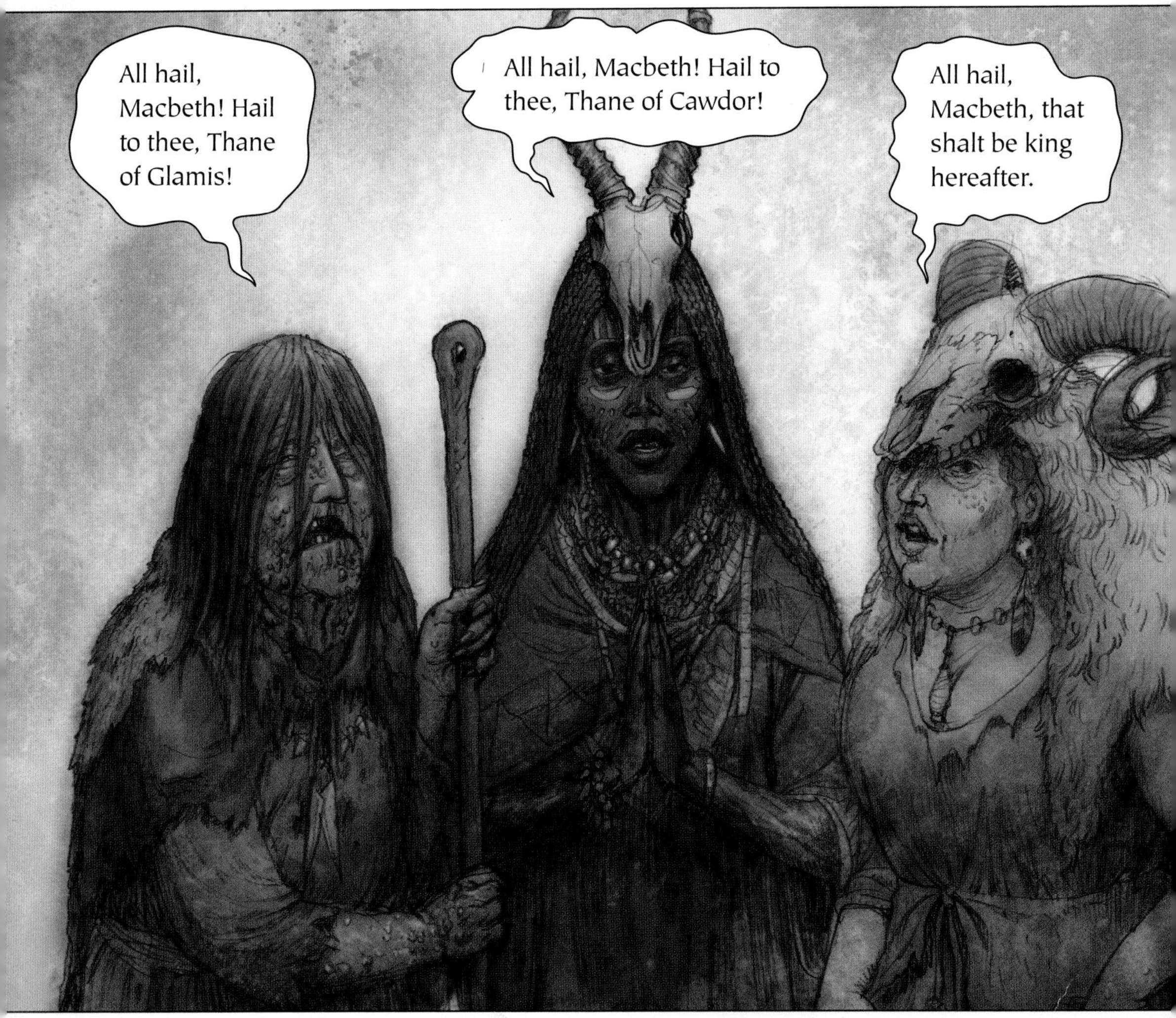
All hail, Macbeth! Hail to thee, Thane of Glamis!
All hail, Macbeth! Hail to thee, Thane of Cawdor!
All hail, Macbeth, that shalt be king hereafter.

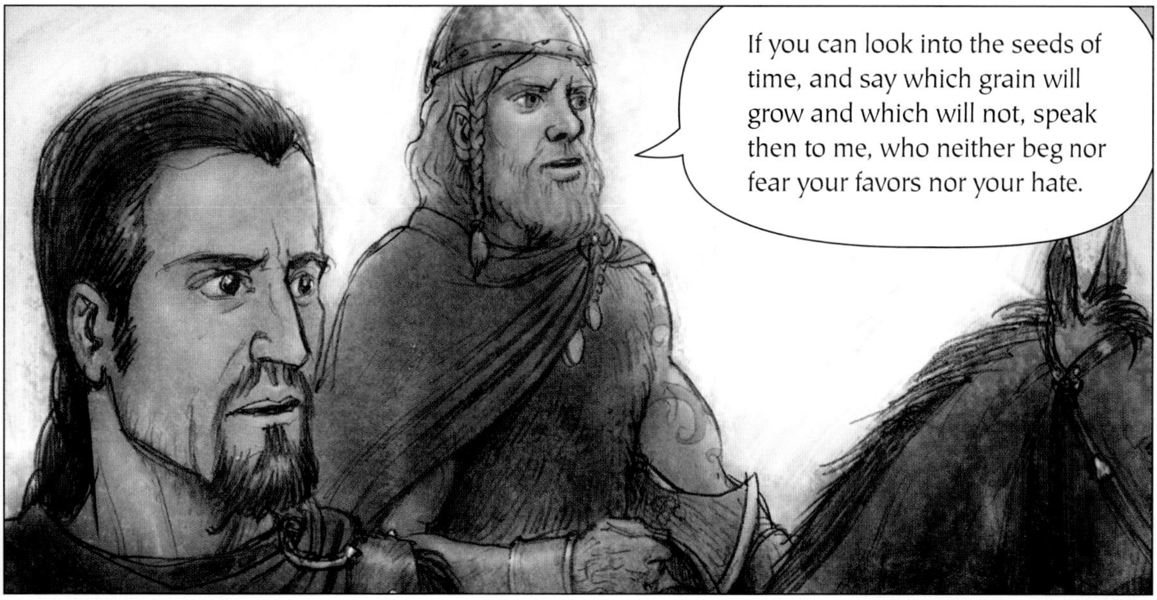
If you can look into the seeds of time, and say which grain will grow and which will not, speak then to me, who neither beg nor fear your favors nor your hate.

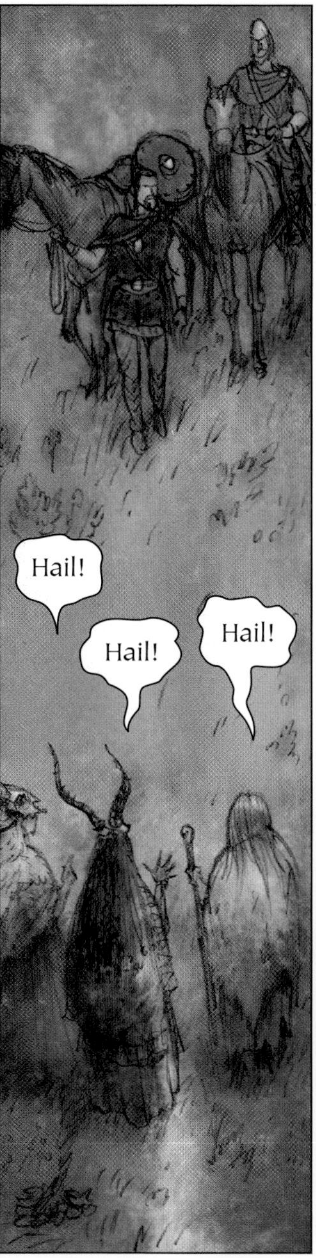
Hail!
Hail!
Hail!

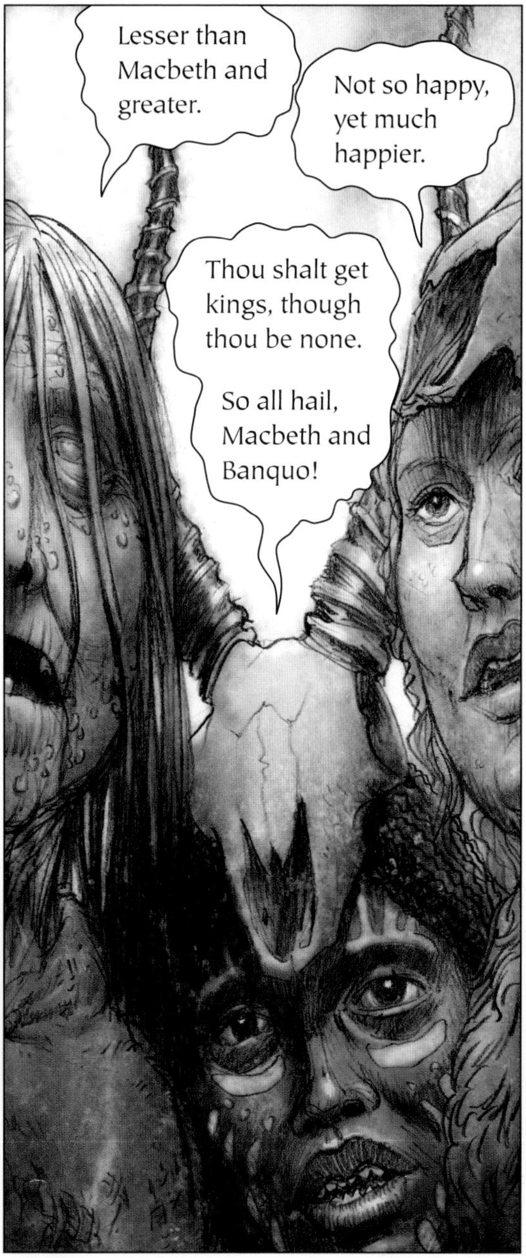
Lesser than Macbeth and greater.
Not so happy, yet much happier.
Thou shalt get kings, though thou be none.
So all hail, Macbeth and Banquo!

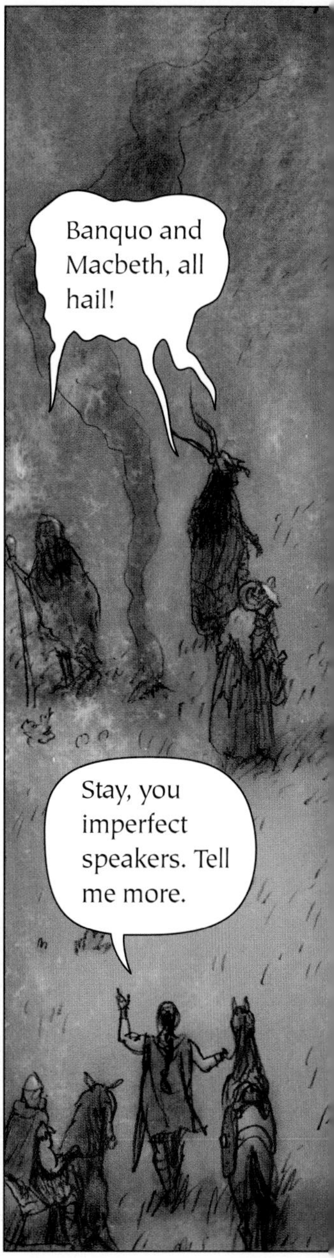
Banquo and Macbeth, all hail!
Stay, you imperfect speakers. Tell me more.

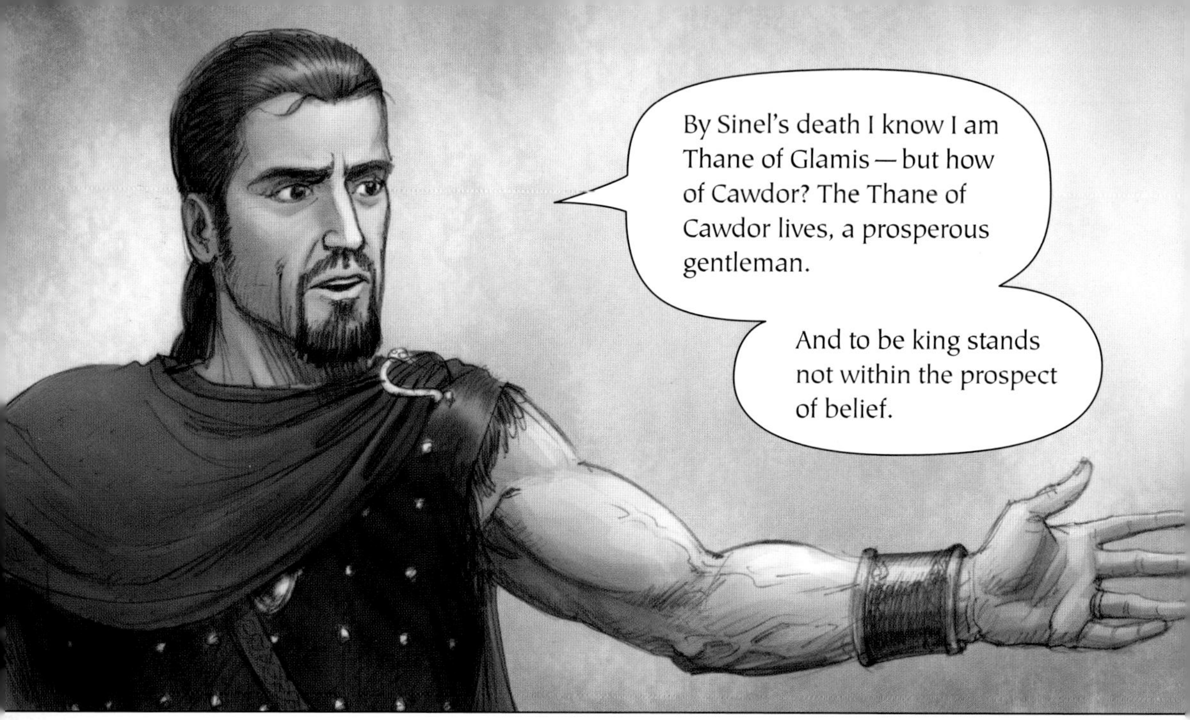
By Sinel's death I know I am Thane of Glamis — but how of Cawdor? The Thane of Cawdor lives, a prosperous gentleman.
And to be king stands not within the prospect of belief.

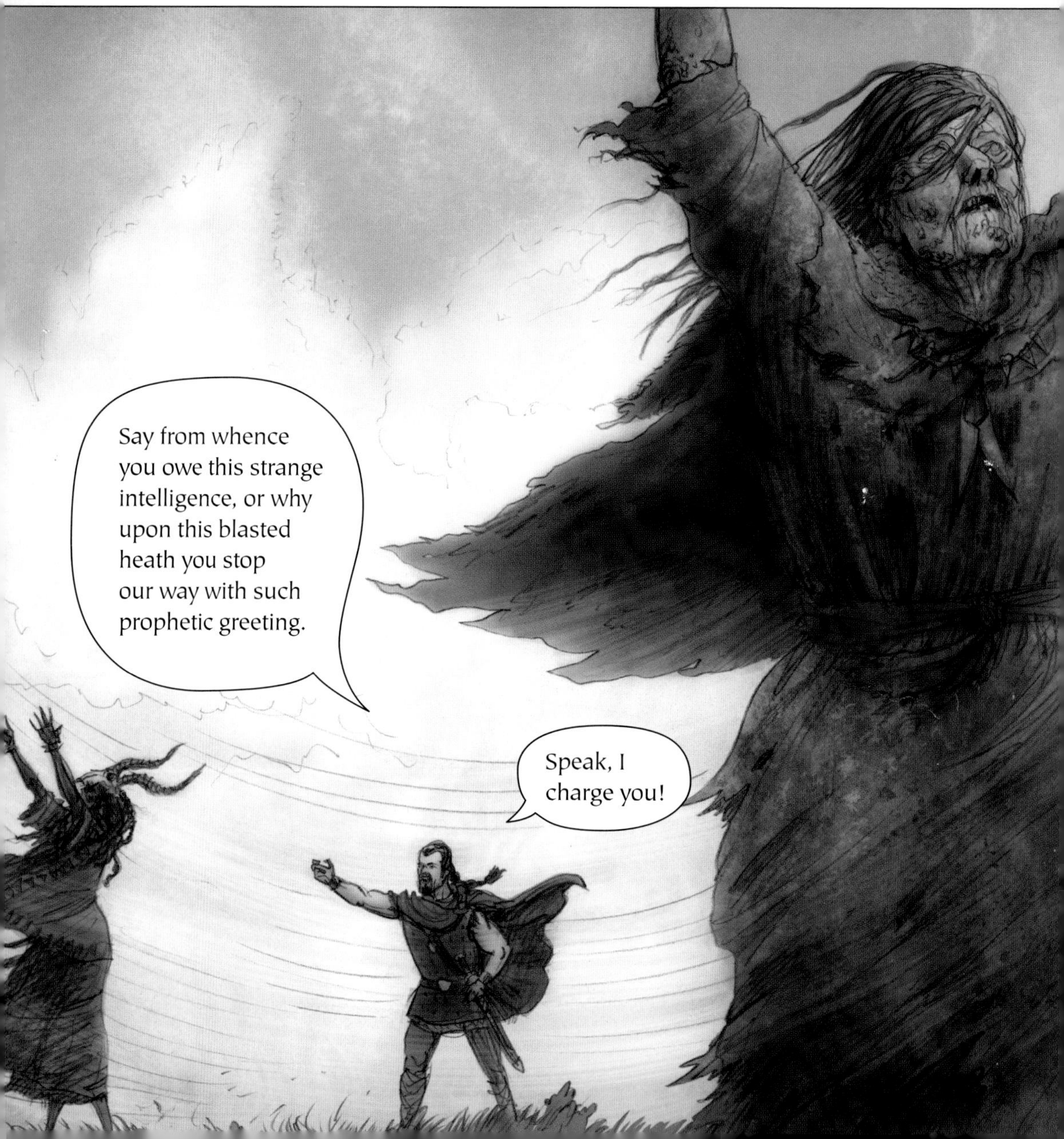
Say from whence you owe this strange intelligence, or why upon this blasted heath you stop our way with such prophetic greeting.
Speak, I charge you!

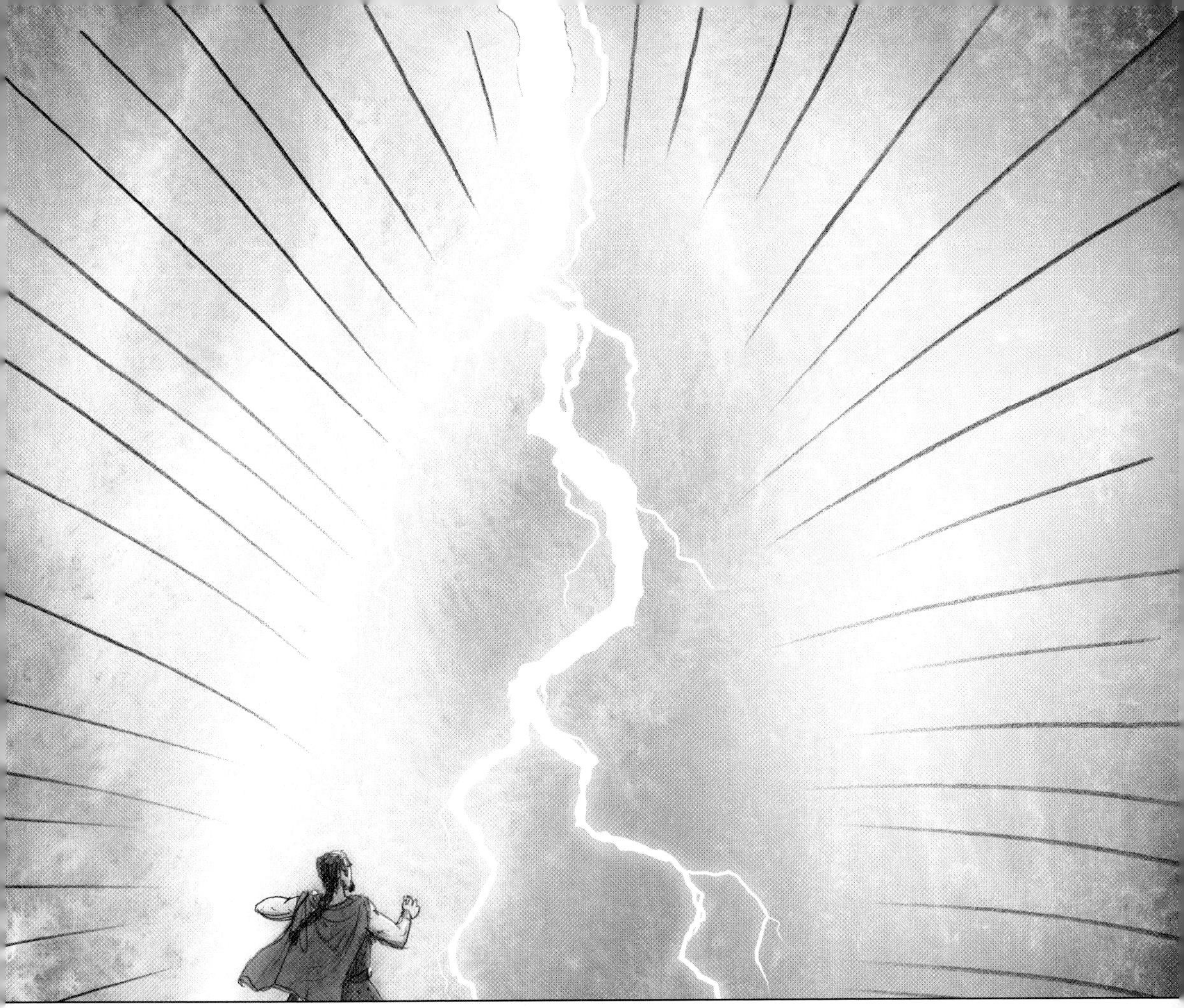

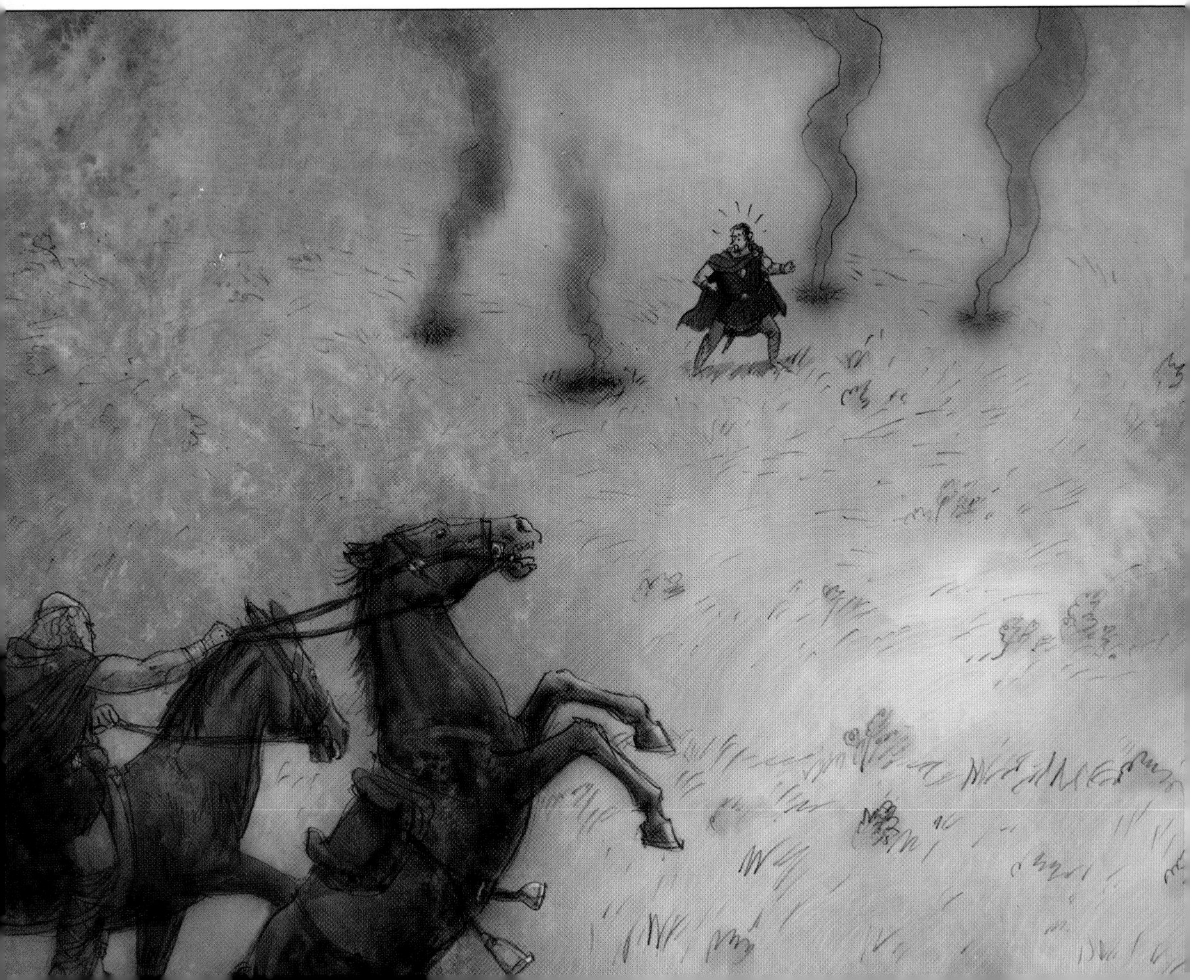

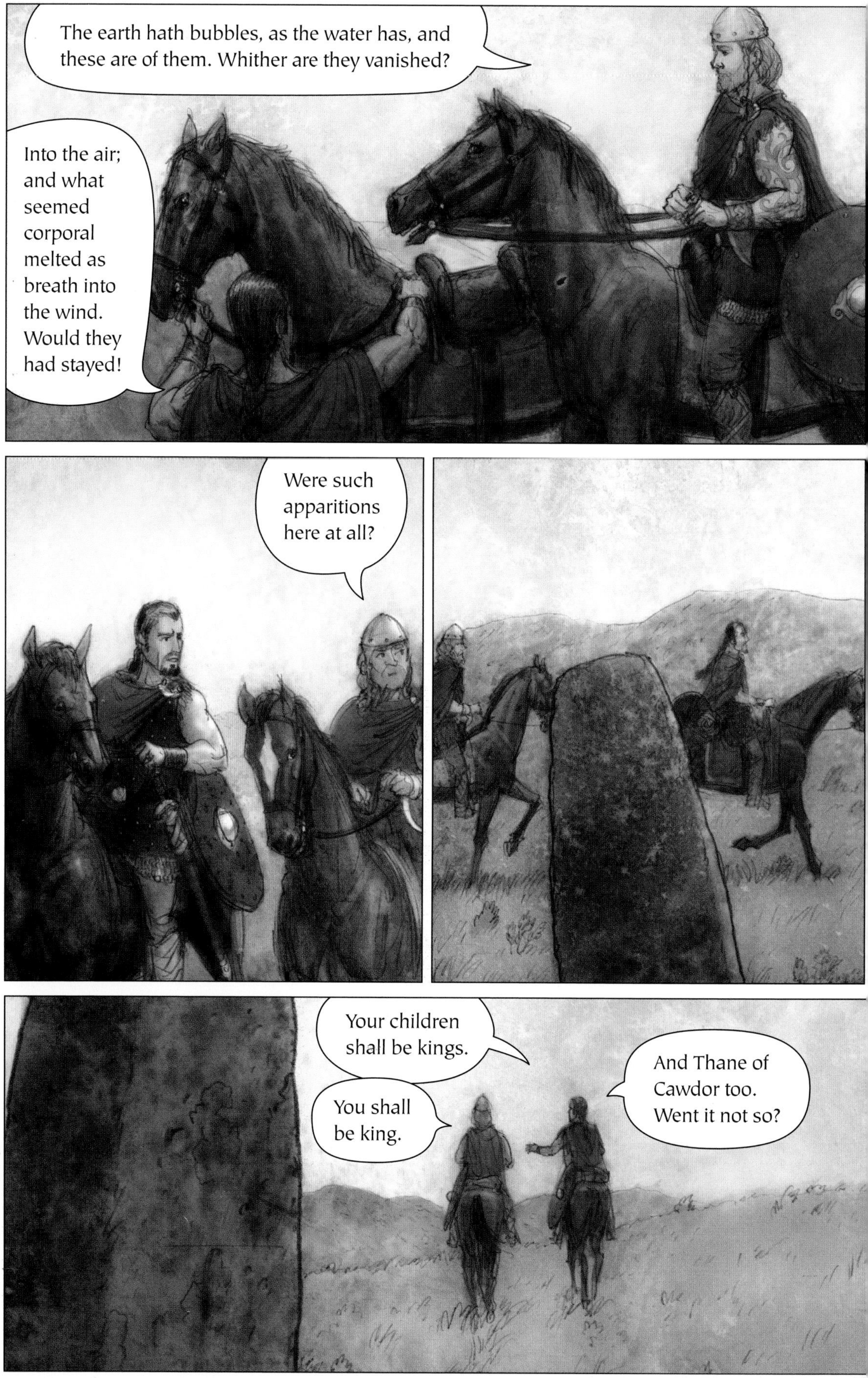
The earth hath bubbles, as the water has, and these are of them. Whither are they vanished?
Into the air; and what seemed corporal melted as breath into the wind. Would they had stayed!
Were such apparitions here at all?
Your children shall be kings.
You shall be king.
And Thane of Cawdor too. Went it not so?

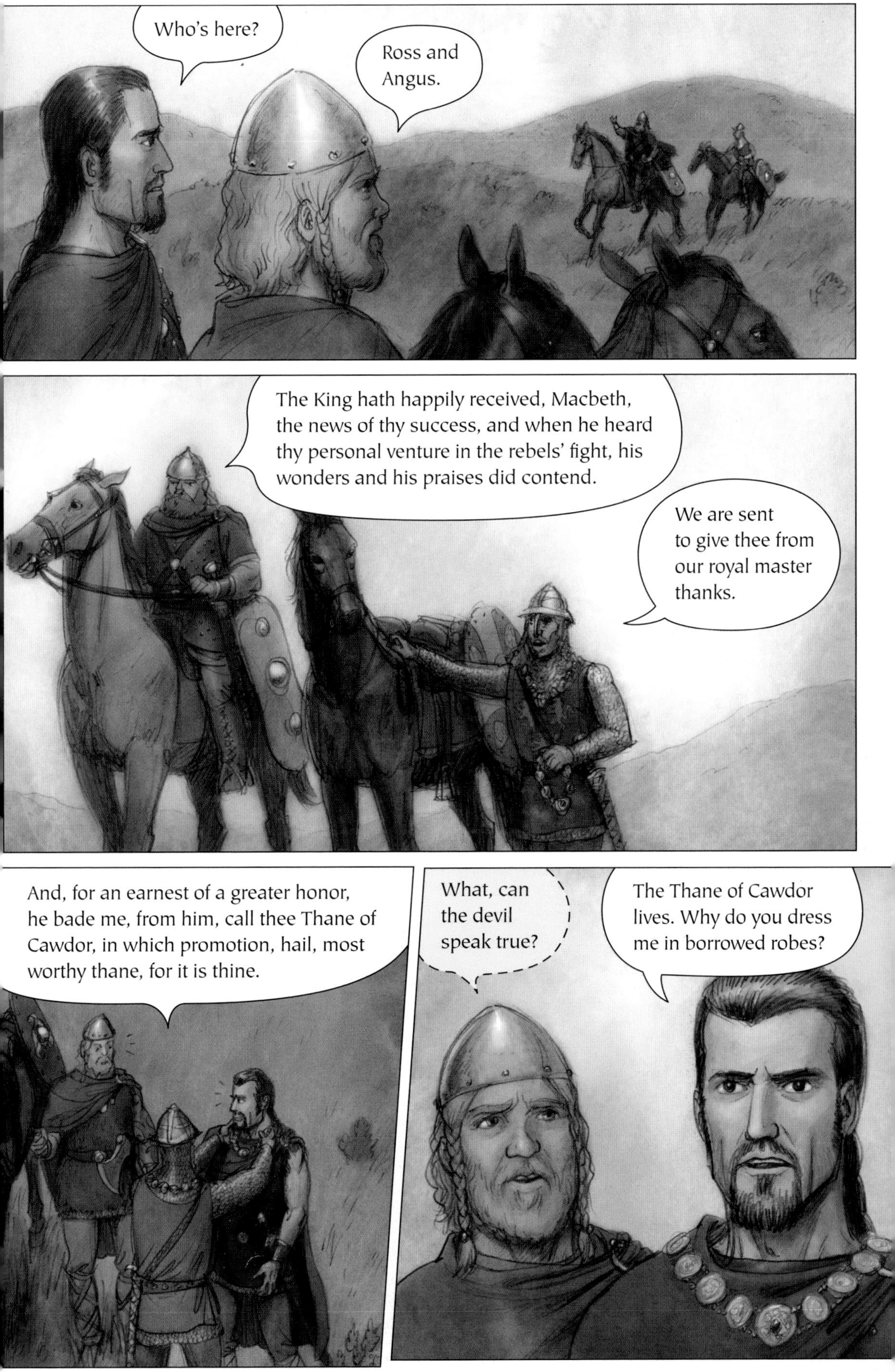
Who's here?
Ross and Angus.
The King hath happily received, Macbeth, the news of thy success, and when he heard thy personal venture in the rebels' fight, his wonders and his praises did contend.
We are sent to give thee from our royal master thanks.
And, for an earnest of a greater honor, he bade me, from him, call thee Thane of Cawdor, in which promotion, hail, most worthy thane, for it is thine.
What, can the devil speak true?
The Thane of Cawdor lives. Why do you dress me in borrowed robes?

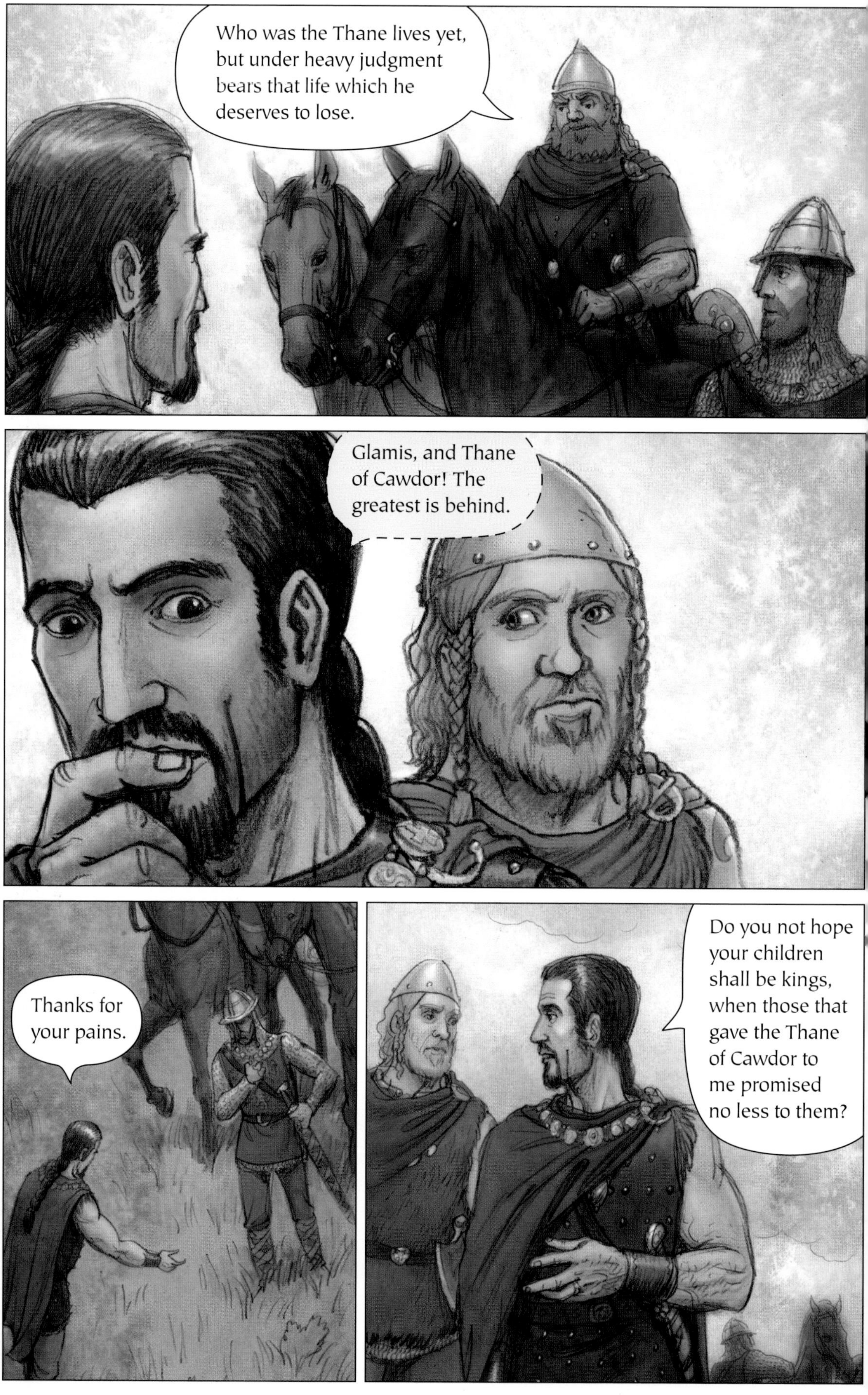
Who was the Thane lives yet, but under heavy judgment bears that life which he deserves to lose.
Glamis, and Thane of Cawdor! The greatest is behind.
Thanks for your pains.
Do you not hope your children shall be kings, when those that gave the Thane of Cawdor to me promised no less to them?

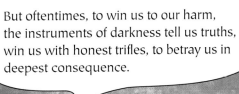

That, trusted home, might yet enkindle you unto the crown.

But oftentimes, to win us to our harm, the instruments of darkness tell us truths, win us with honest trifles, to betray us in deepest consequence.

Cousins, a word, I pray you.

This supernatural soliciting cannot be ill, cannot be good. If ill, why hath it given me earnest of success, commencing in a truth? I am Thane of Cawdor!

If good, why do I yield to that suggestion whose horrid image doth unfix my hair and make my seated heart knock at my ribs, against the use of nature?

Look how our partner's rapt.

New honors come upon him like strange garments.

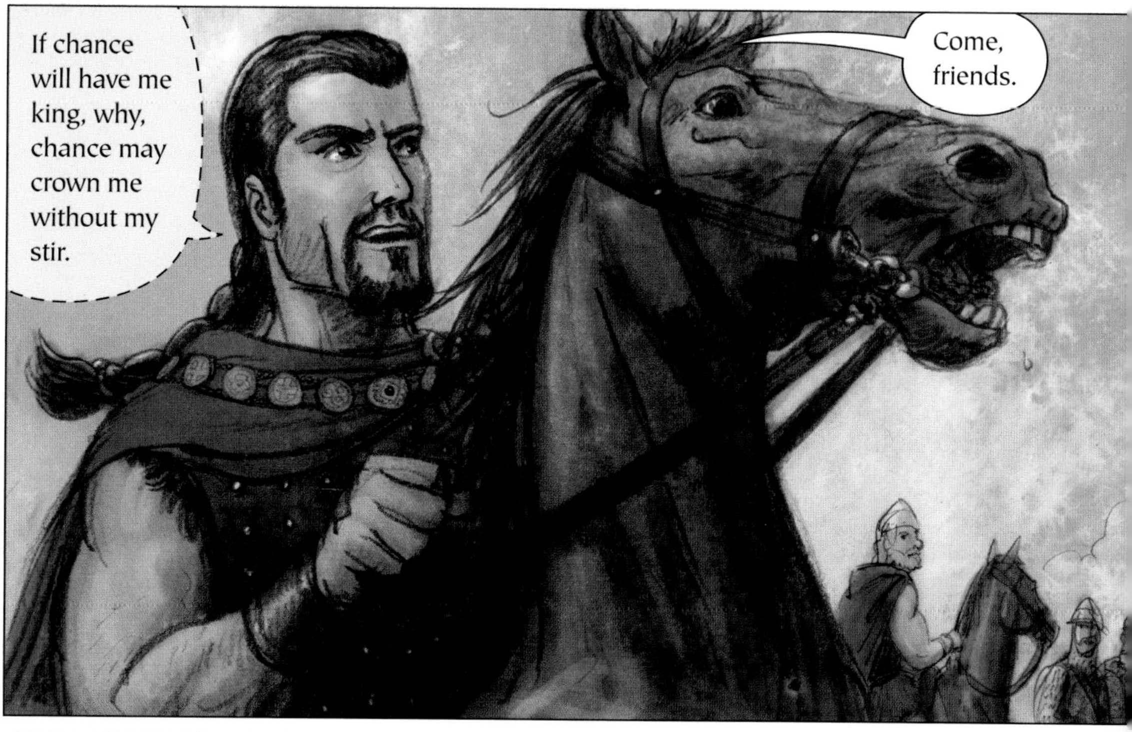
If chance will have me king, why, chance may crown me without my stir.
Come, friends.

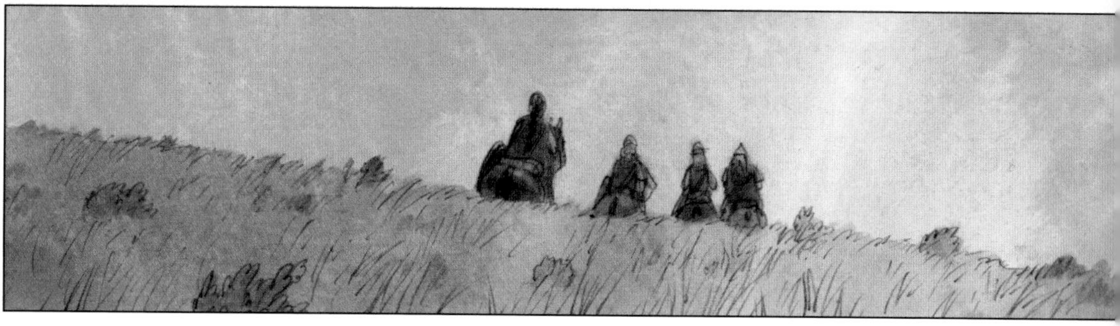

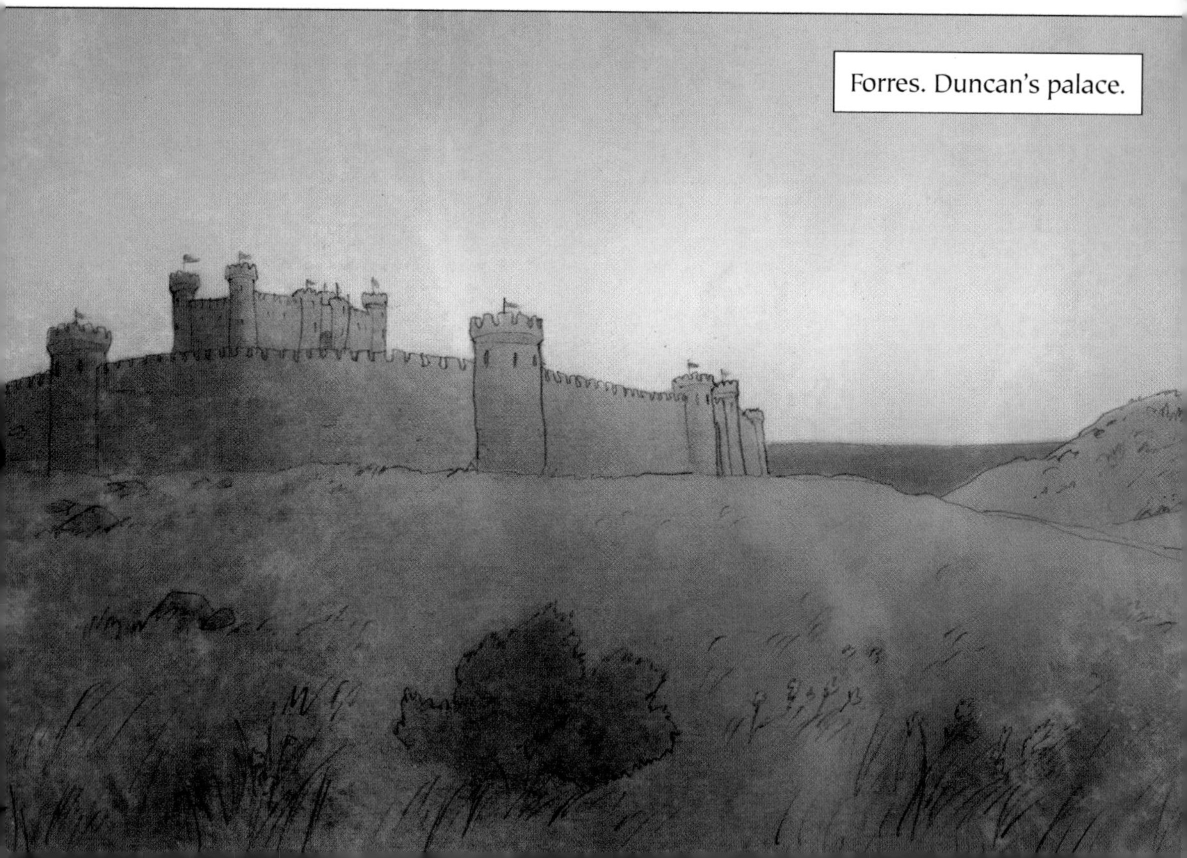
Forres. Duncan's palace.

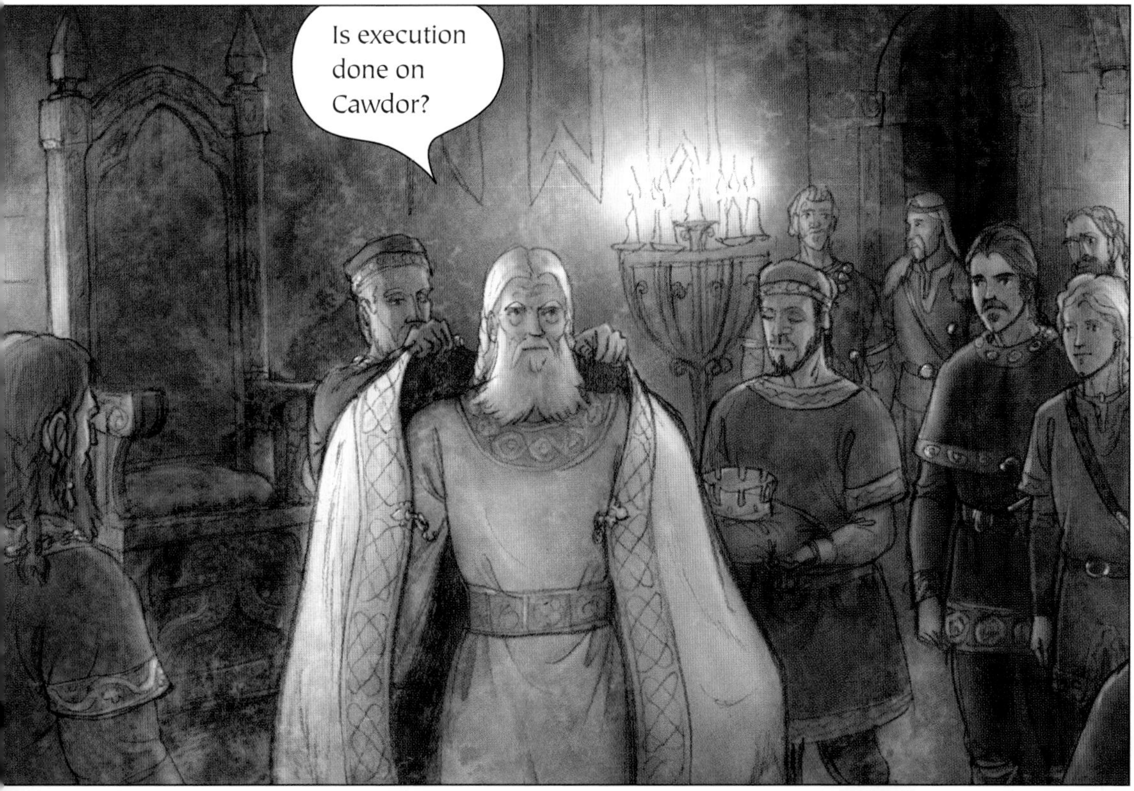
Is execution done on Cawdor?

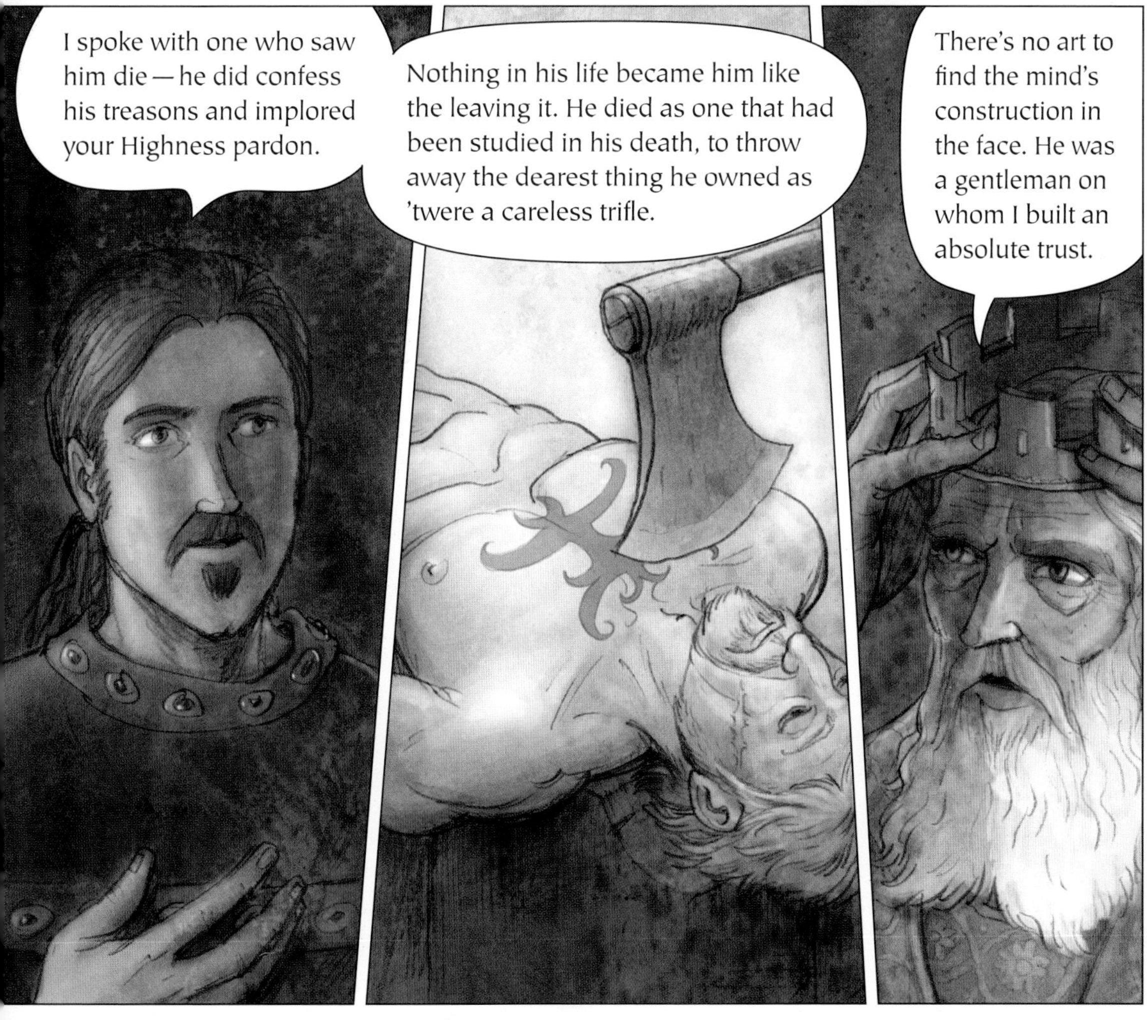
I spoke with one who saw him die — he did confess his treasons and implored your Highness pardon.
Nothing in his life became him like the leaving it. He died as one that had been studied in his death, to throw away the dearest thing he owned as 'twere a careless trifle.
There's no art to find the mind's construction in the face. He was a gentleman on whom I built an absolute trust.

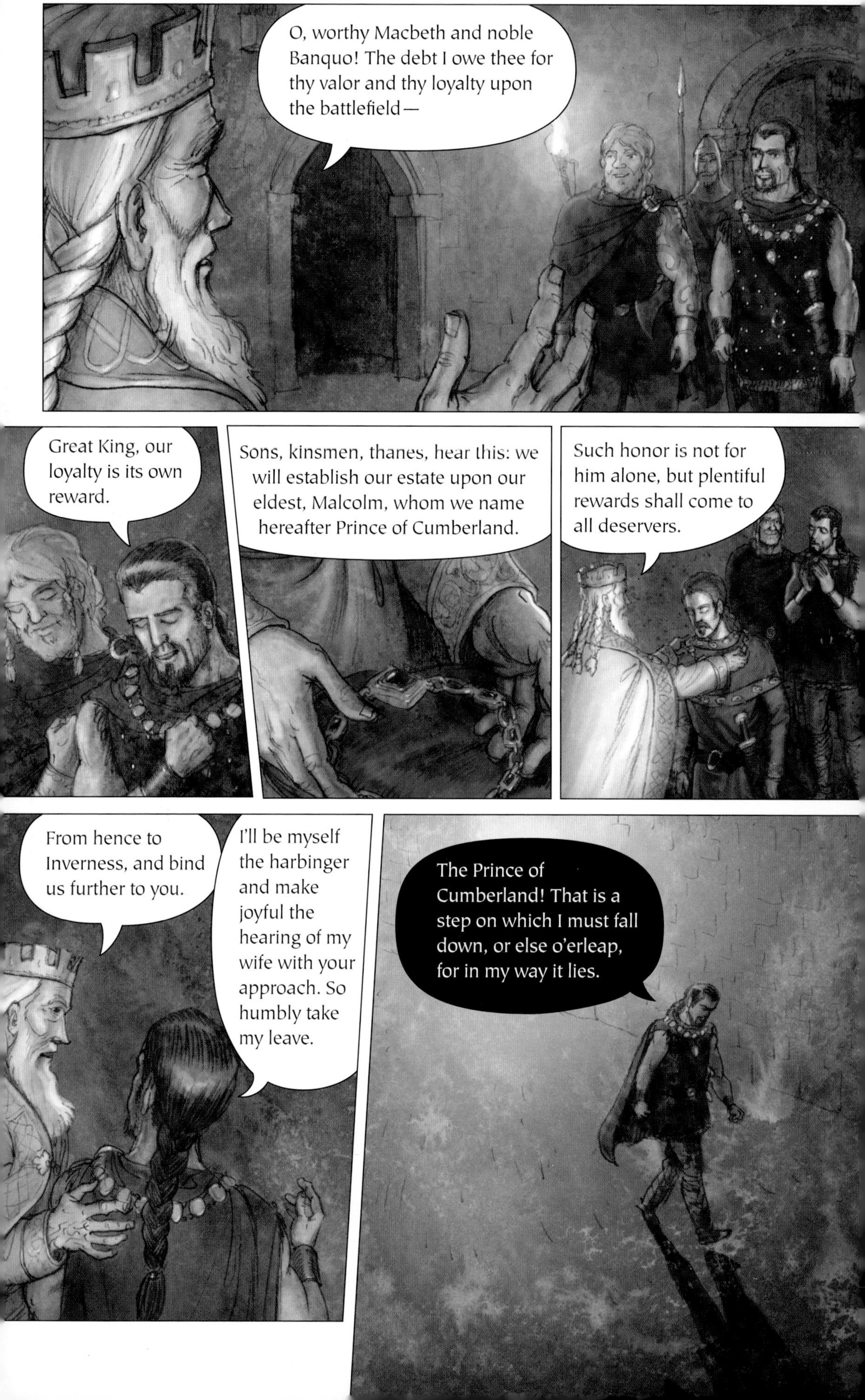
O, worthy Macbeth and noble Banquo! The debt I owe thee for thy valor and thy loyalty upon the battlefield—
Great King, our loyalty is its own reward.
Sons, kinsmen, thanes, hear this: we will establish our estate upon our eldest, Malcolm, whom we name hereafter Prince of Cumberland.
Such honor is not for him alone, but plentiful rewards shall come to all deservers.
From hence to Inverness, and bind us further to you.
I'll be myself the harbinger and make joyful the hearing of my wife with your approach. So humbly take my leave.
The Prince of Cumberland! That is a step on which I must fall down, or else o'erleap, for in my way it lies.

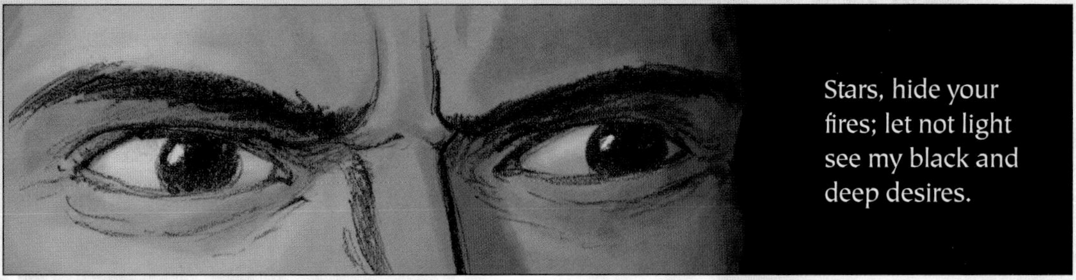
Stars, hide your fires; let not light see my black and deep desires.

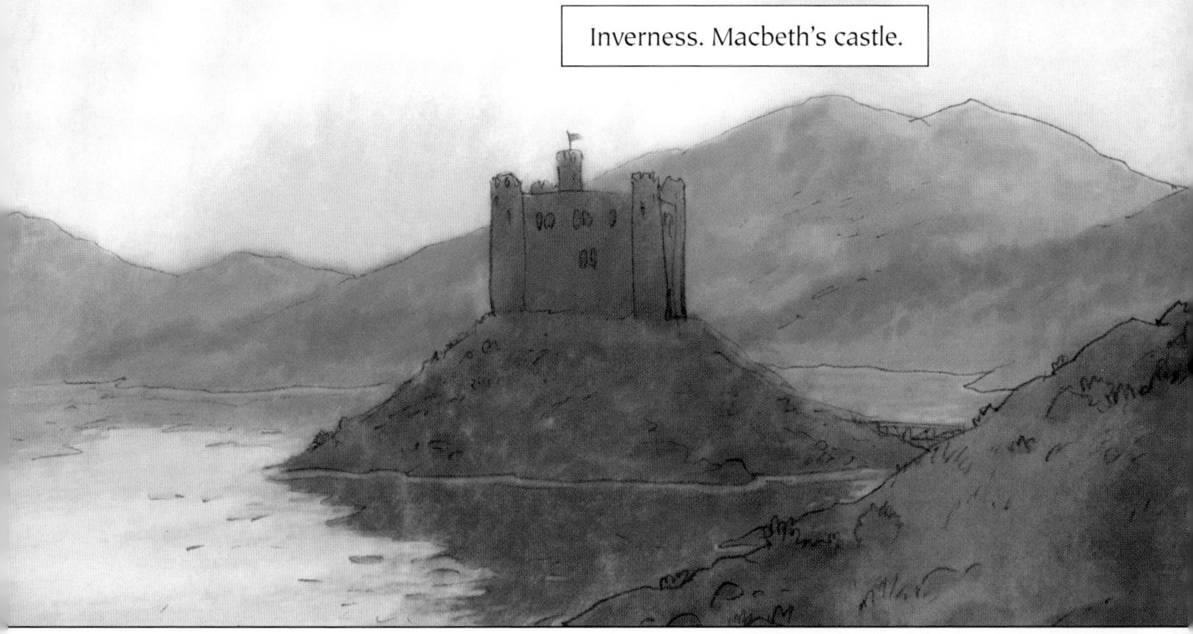
Inverness. Macbeth's castle.

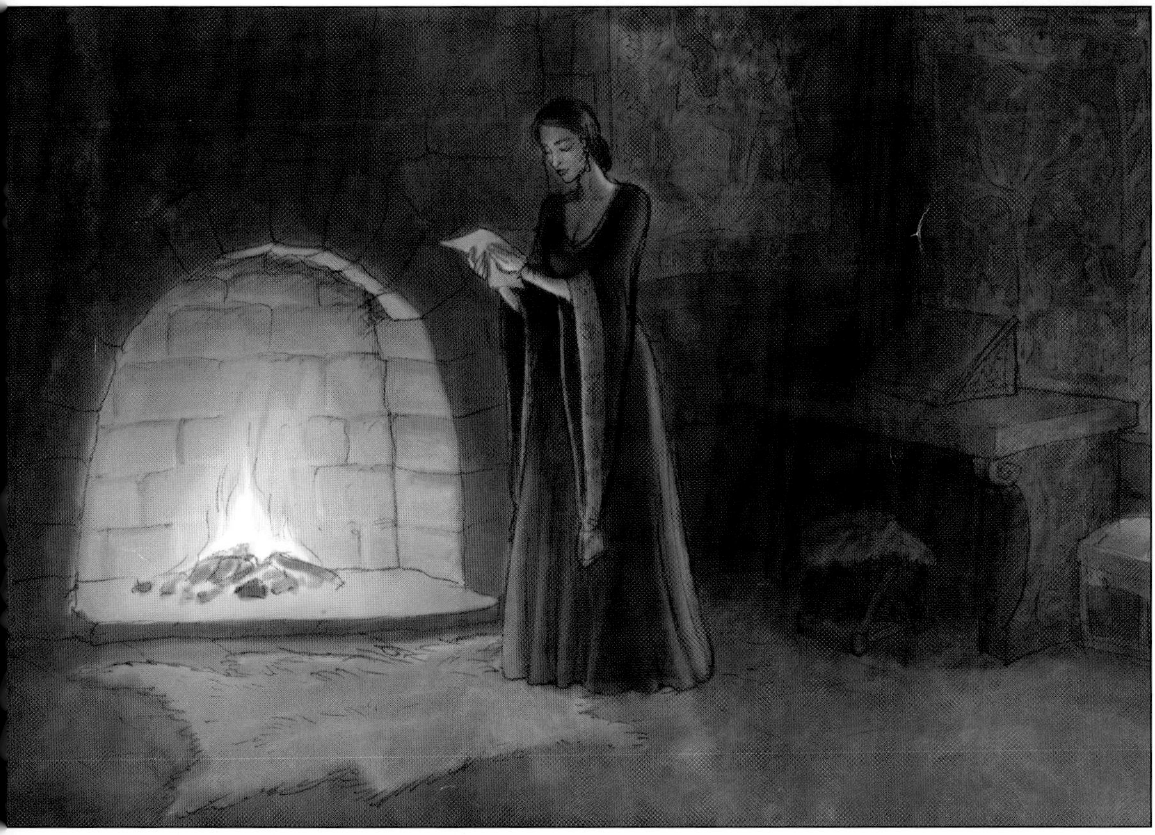

They met me in the day of success. And I have learned by the perfectest report they have more in them than mortal knowledge. When I burned in desire to question them further, they made themselves air, into which they vanished. Whiles I stood rapt in the wonder of it there came missives from the King, who all-hailed me "Thane of Cawdor," by which title, before, these weird sisters saluted me, and referred me to the coming on of time with "Hail, king that shalt be!"

This have I thought good to deliver thee, my dearest partner of greatness, that thou mightst not lose the dues of rejoicing by being ignorant of what greatness is promised thee. Lay it to thy heart, and farewell.

~M

Glamis thou art, and Cawdor, and shalt be what thou art promised.

Yet do I fear thy nature.
It is too full of the milk of human kindness
To catch the nearest way. Thou wouldst be great,
Art not without ambition, but without
The illness should attend it.

What thou wouldst highly,
That wouldst thou holily;
wouldst not play false,
And yet wouldst wrongly win.

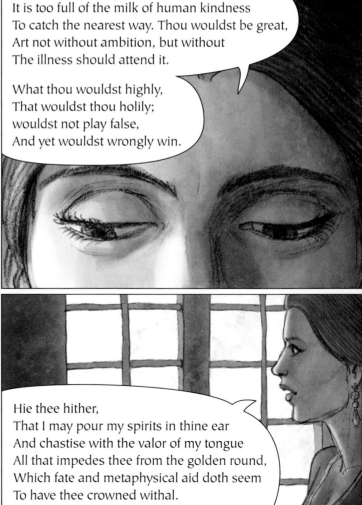

Hie thee hither,
That I may pour my spirits in thine ear
And chastise with the valor of my tongue
All that impedes thee from the golden round,
Which fate and metaphysical aid doth seem
To have thee crowned withal.

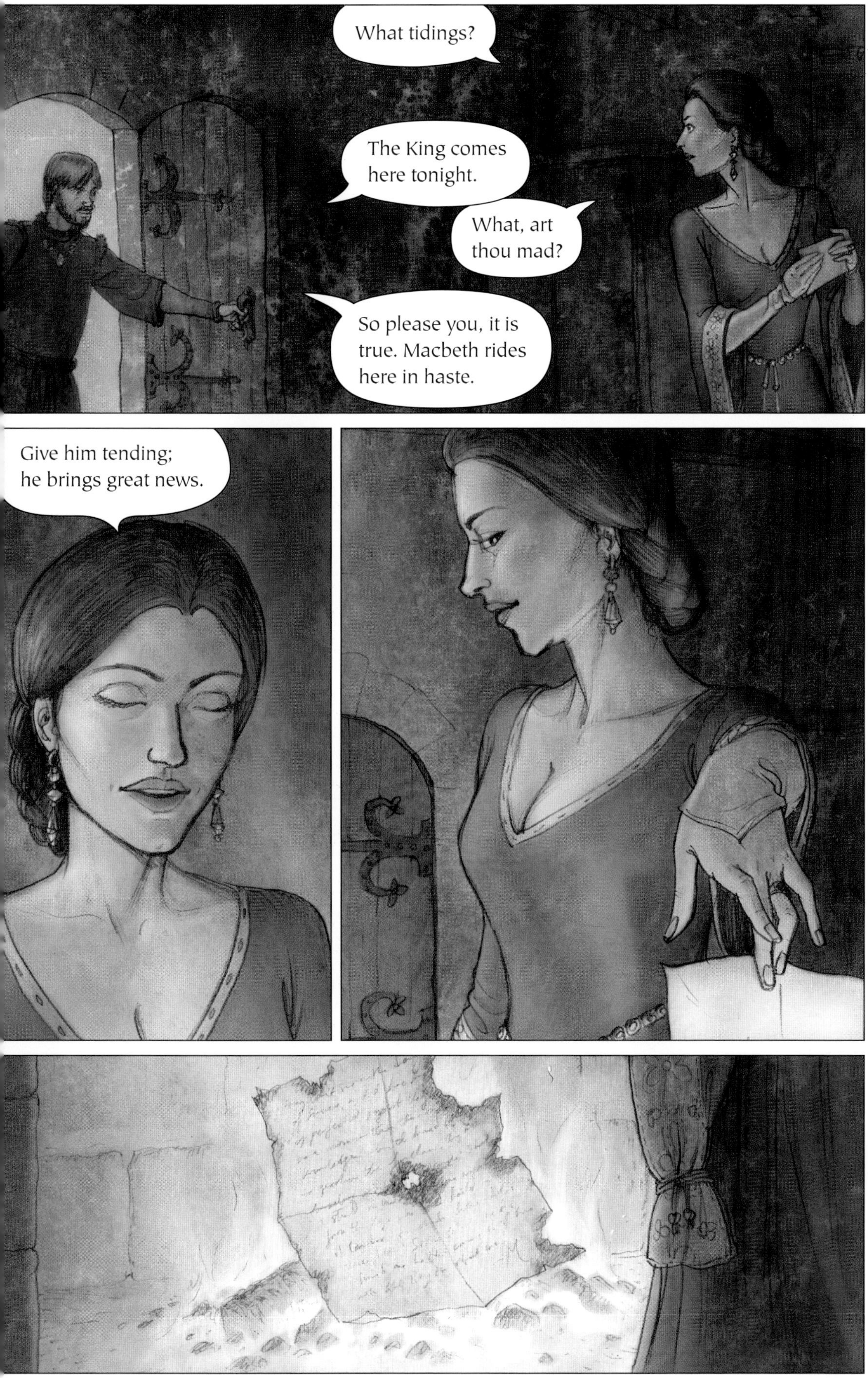
What tidings?
The King comes here tonight.
What, art thou mad?
So please you, it is true. Macbeth rides here in haste.
Give him tending; he brings great news.

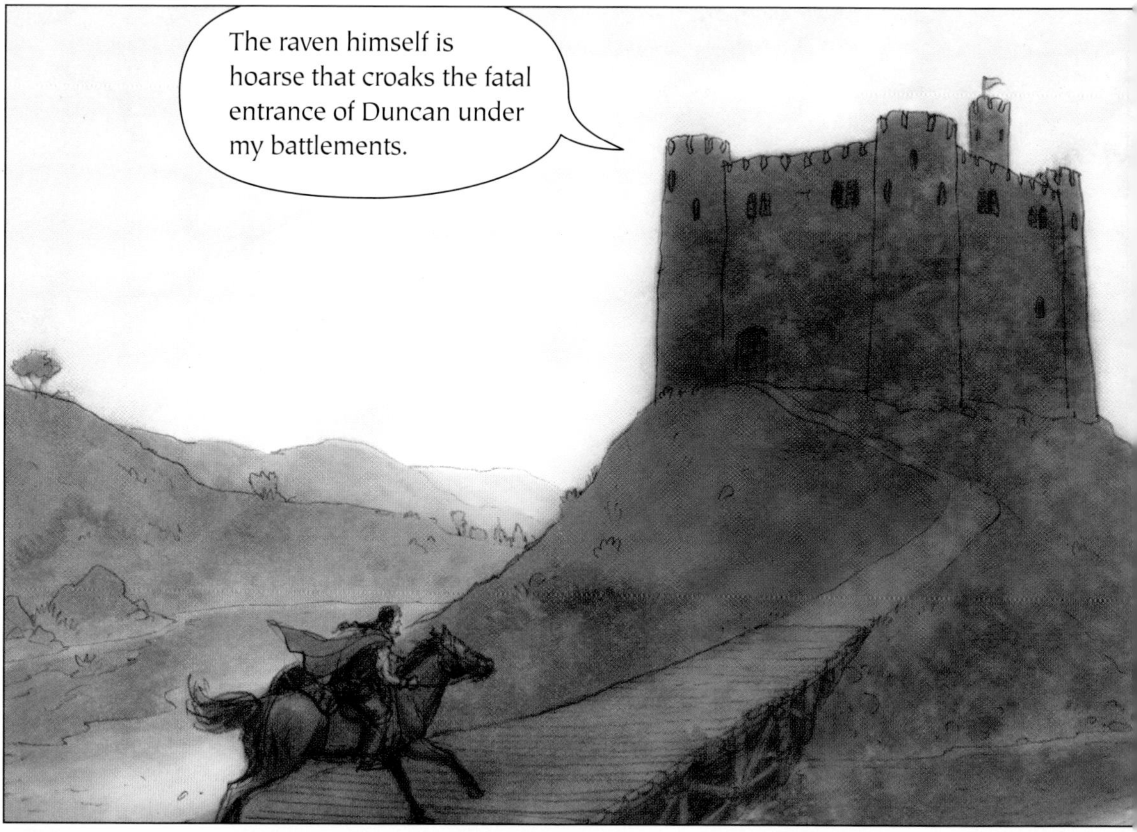
The raven himself is hoarse that croaks the fatal entrance of Duncan under my battlements.

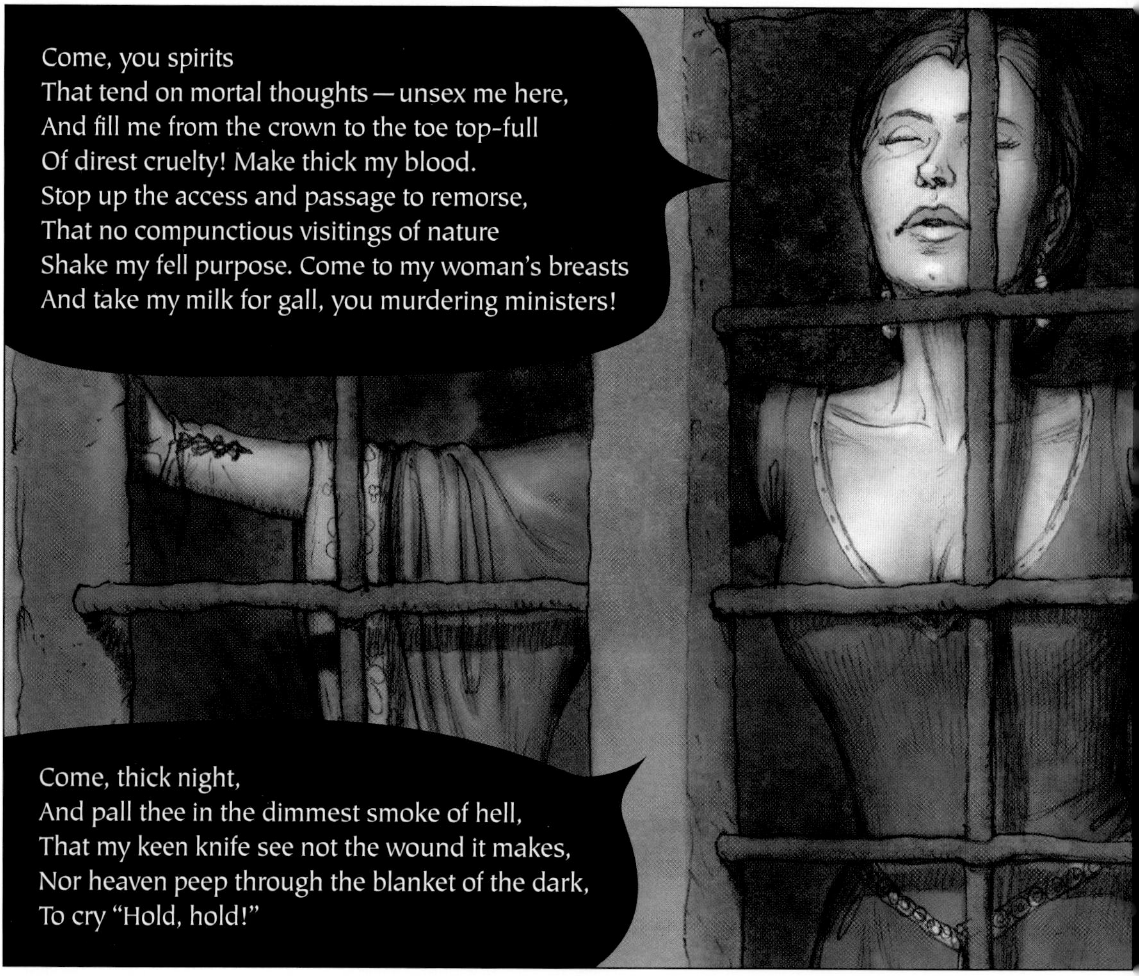
Come, you spirits
That tend on mortal thoughts — unsex me here,
And fill me from the crown to the toe top-full
Of direst cruelty! Make thick my blood.
Stop up the access and passage to remorse,
That no compunctious visitings of nature
Shake my fell purpose. Come to my woman's breasts
And take my milk for gall, you murdering ministers!
Come, thick night,
And pall thee in the dimmest smoke of hell,
That my keen knife see not the wound it makes,
Nor heaven peep through the blanket of the dark,
To cry "Hold, hold!"

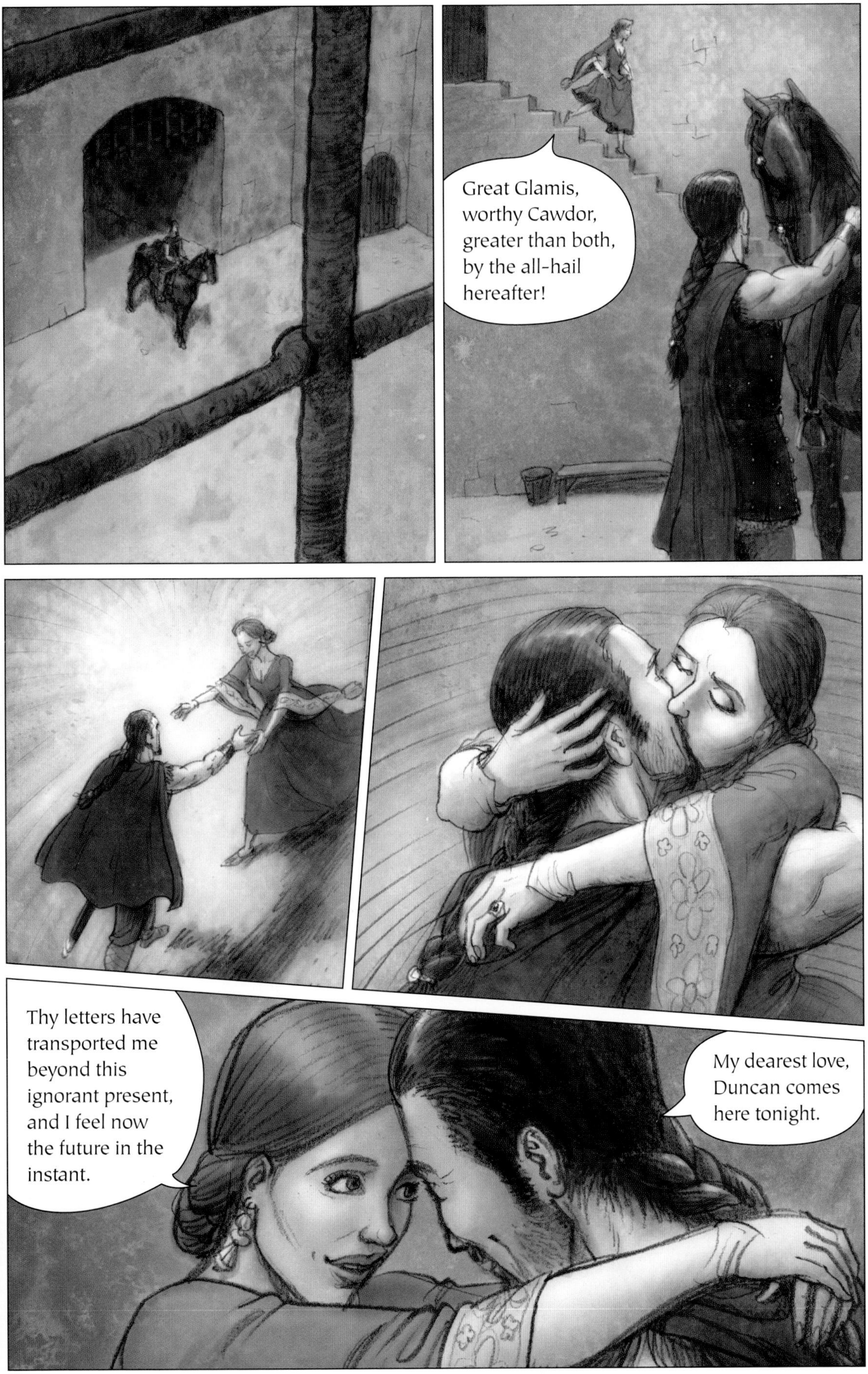
Great Glamis, worthy Cawdor, greater than both, by the all-hail hereafter!
Thy letters have transported me beyond this ignorant present, and I feel now the future in the instant.
My dearest love, Duncan comes here tonight.

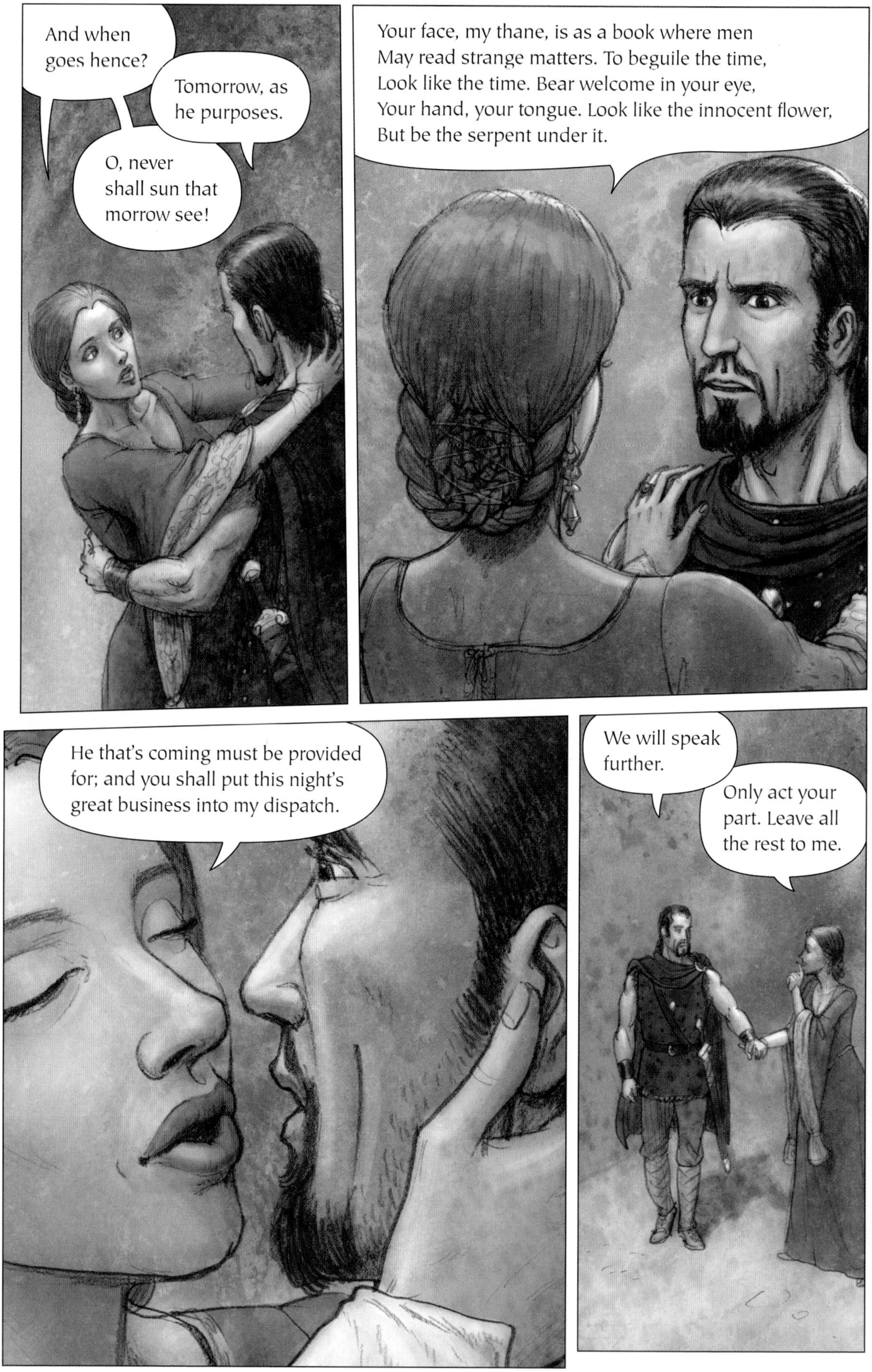

And when goes hence?
Tomorrow, as he purposes.
O, never shall sun that morrow see!
Your face, my thane, is as a book where men
May read strange matters. To beguile the time,
Look like the time. Bear welcome in your eye,
Your hand, your tongue. Look like the innocent flower,
But be the serpent under it.
He that's coming must be provided for; and you shall put this night's great business into my dispatch.
We will speak further.
Only act your part. Leave all the rest to me.

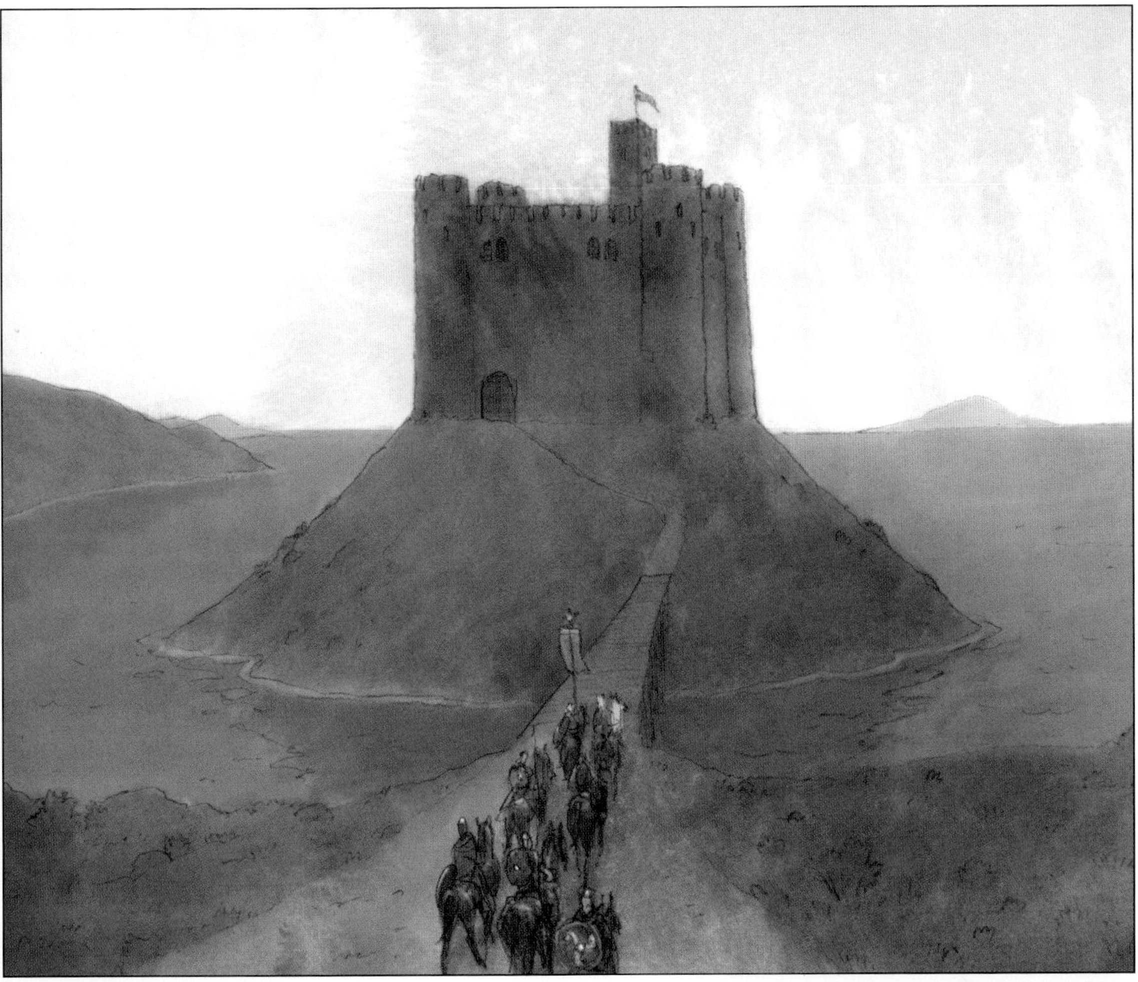

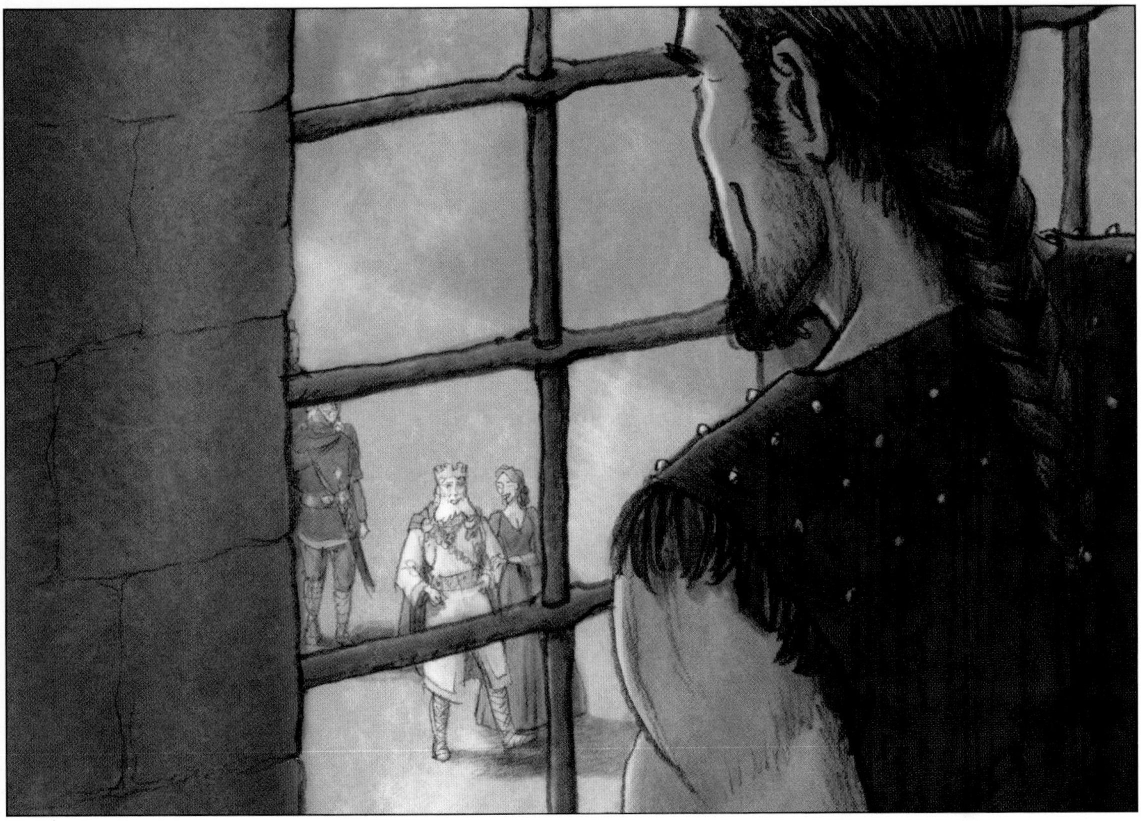

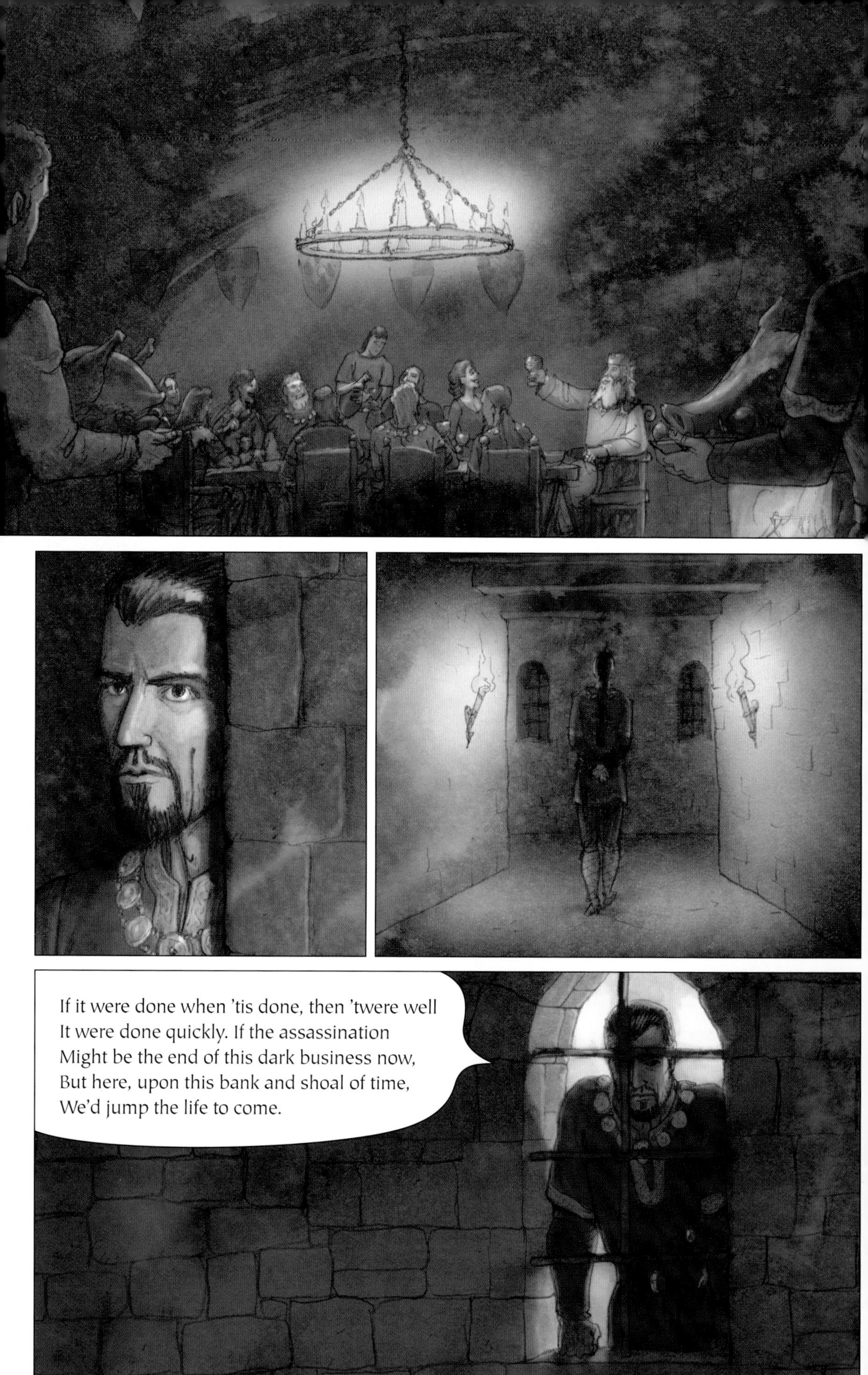
If it were done when 'tis done, then 'twere well It were done quickly. If the assassination Might be the end of this dark business now, But here, upon this bank and shoal of time, We'd jump the life to come.

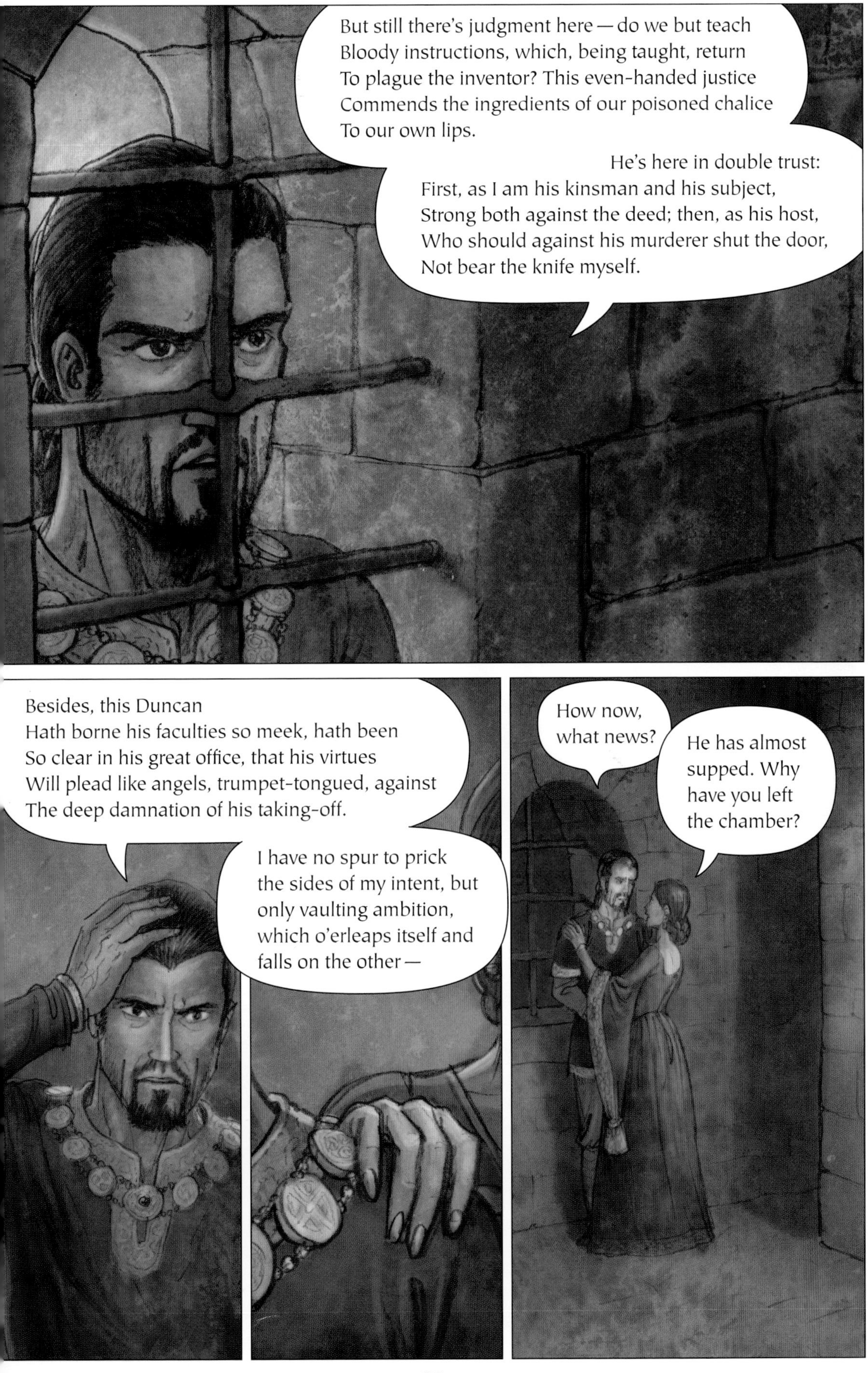
But still there's judgment here — do we but teach
Bloody instructions, which, being taught, return
To plague the inventor? This even-handed justice
Commends the ingredients of our poisoned chalice
To our own lips.
He's here in double trust:
First, as I am his kinsman and his subject,
Strong both against the deed; then, as his host,
Who should against his murderer shut the door,
Not bear the knife myself.
Besides, this Duncan
Hath borne his faculties so meek, hath been
So clear in his great office, that his virtues
Will plead like angels, trumpet-tongued, against
The deep damnation of his taking-off.
I have no spur to prick the sides of my intent, but only vaulting ambition, which o'erleaps itself and falls on the other —
How now, what news?
He has almost supped. Why have you left the chamber?

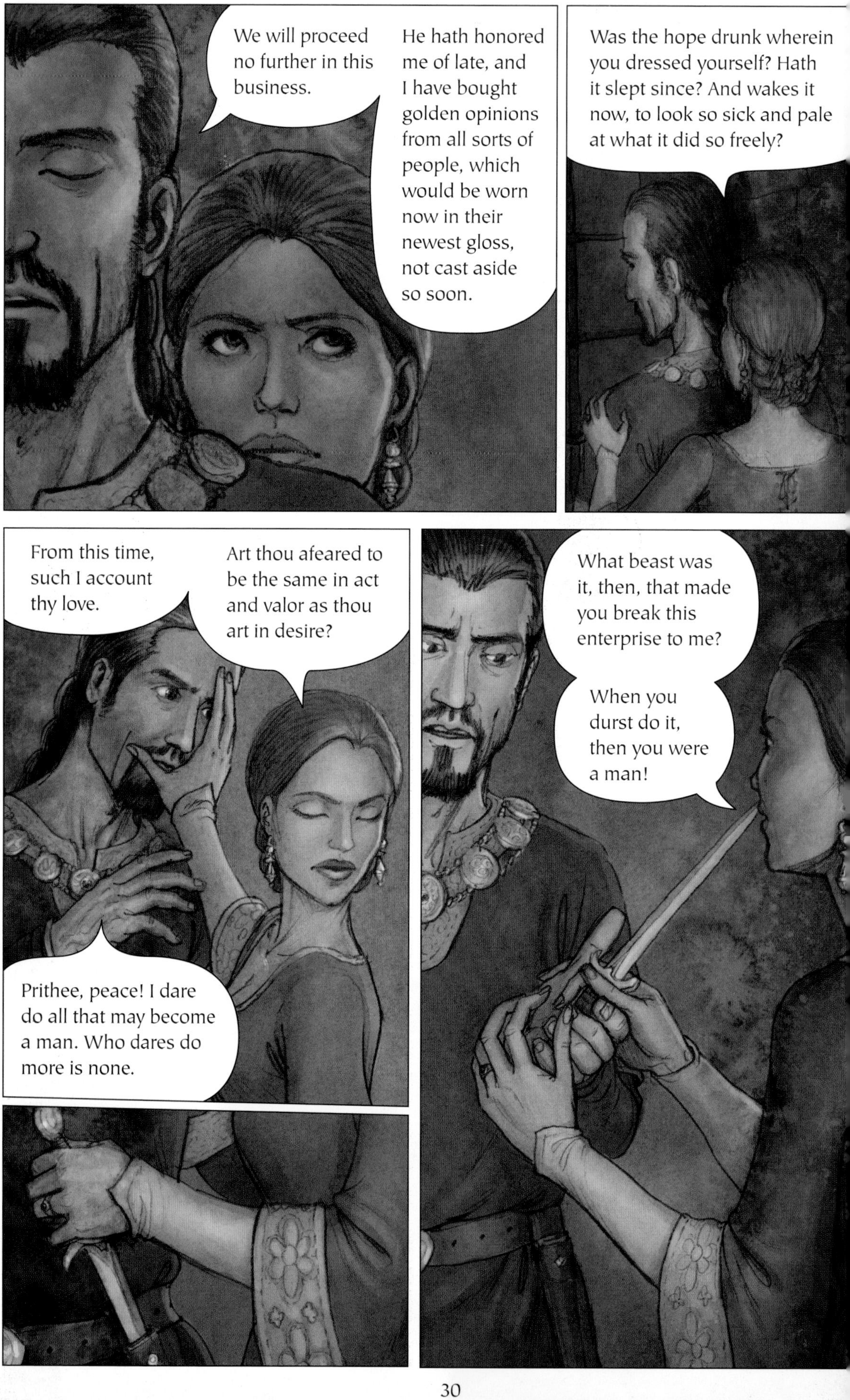
We will proceed no further in this business.
He hath honored me of late, and I have bought golden opinions from all sorts of people, which would be worn now in their newest gloss, not cast aside so soon.
Was the hope drunk wherein you dressed yourself? Hath it slept since? And wakes it now, to look so sick and pale at what it did so freely?
From this time, such I account thy love.
Art thou afeared to be the same in act and valor as thou art in desire?
Prithee, peace! I dare do all that may become a man. Who dares do more is none.
What beast was it, then, that made you break this enterprise to me?
When you durst do it, then you were a man!

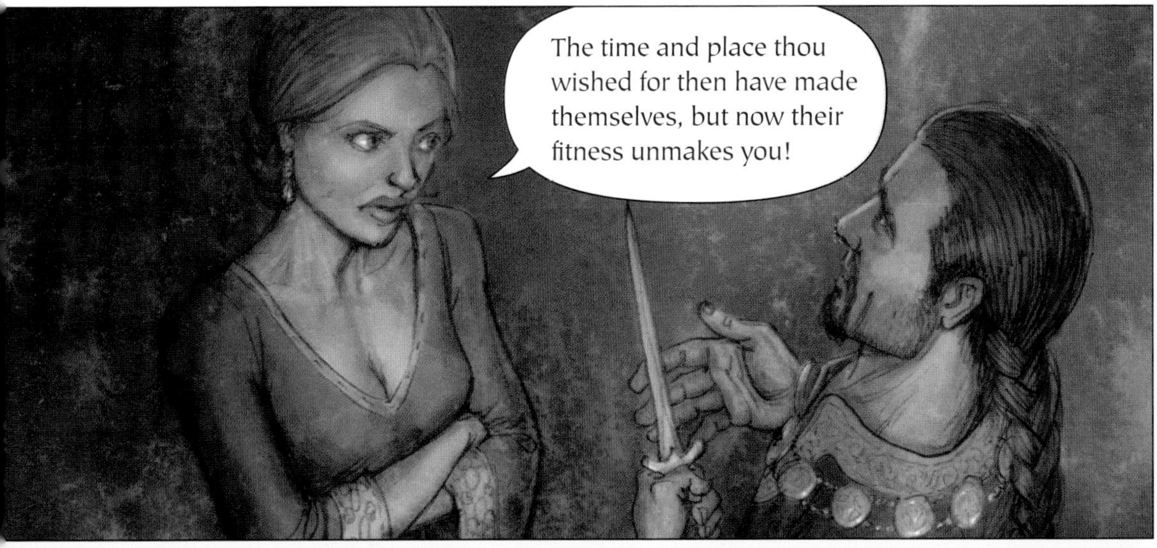
The time and place thou wished for then have made themselves, but now their fitness unmakes you!

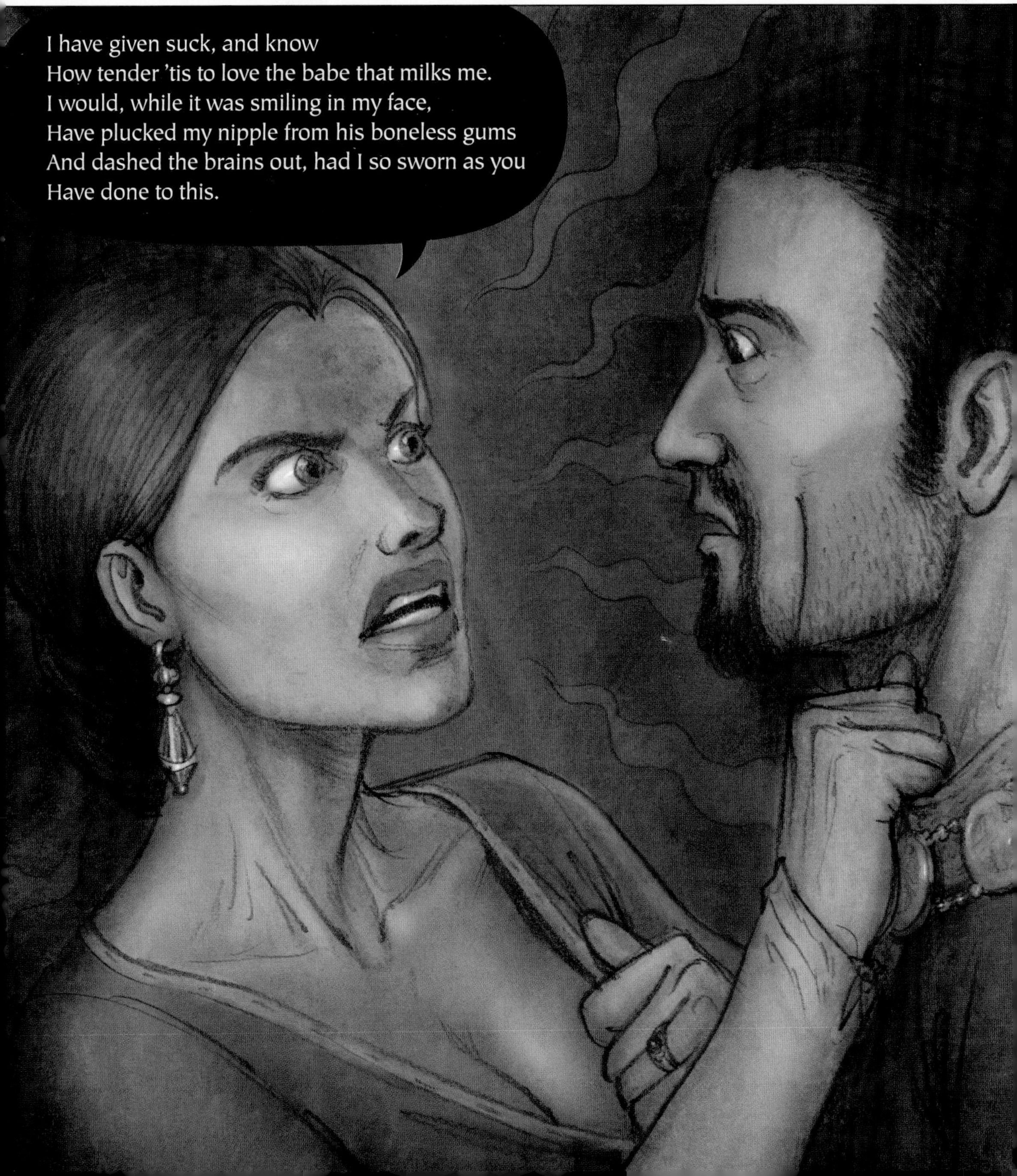
I have given suck, and know
How tender 'tis to love the babe that milks me.
I would, while it was smiling in my face,
Have plucked my nipple from his boneless gums
And dashed the brains out, had I so sworn as you
Have done to this.

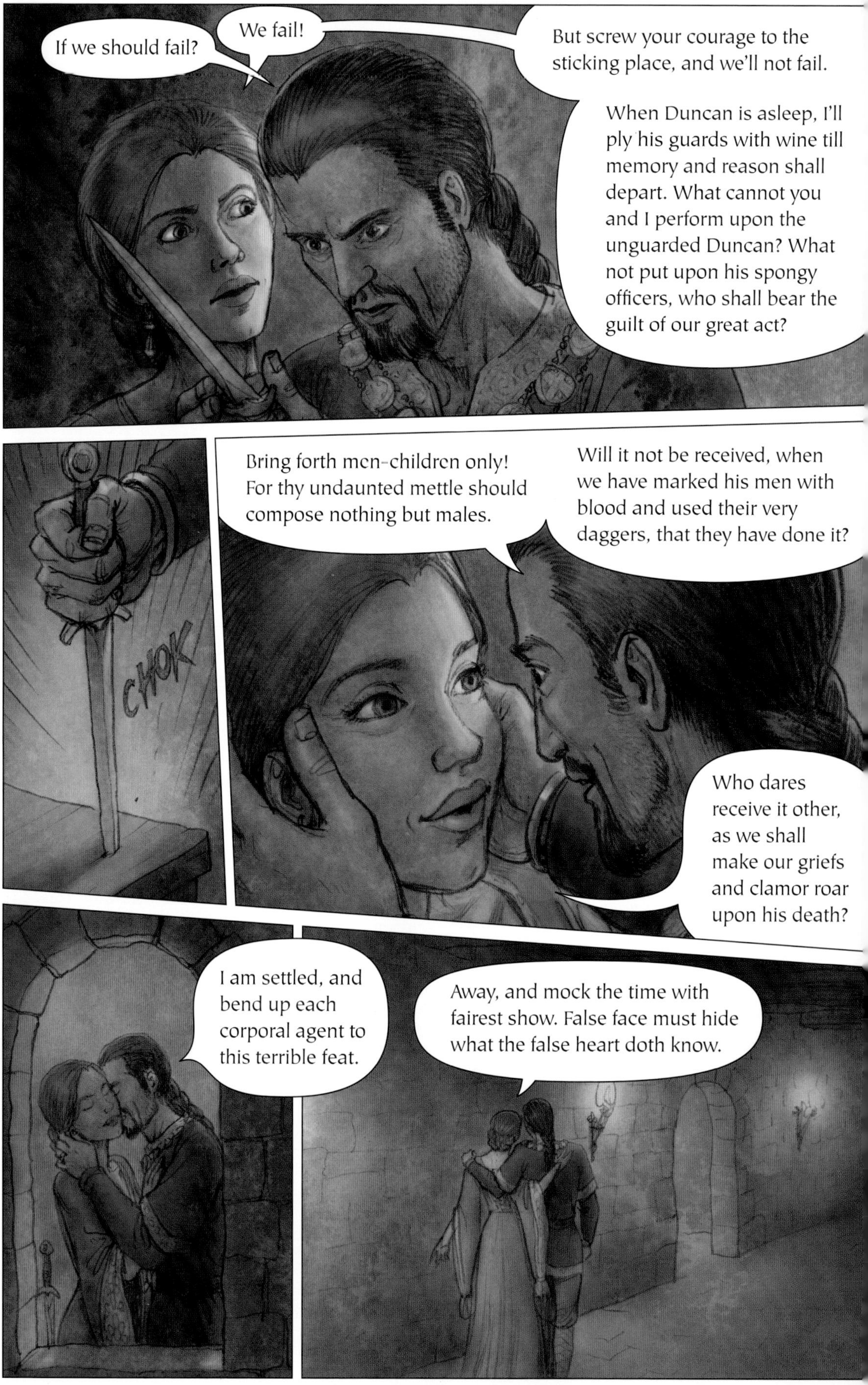
If we should fail?
We fail!
But screw your courage to the sticking place, and we'll not fail.
When Duncan is asleep, I'll ply his guards with wine till memory and reason shall depart. What cannot you and I perform upon the unguarded Duncan? What not put upon his spongy officers, who shall bear the guilt of our great act?
CHOK
Bring forth men-children only! For thy undaunted mettle should compose nothing but males.
Will it not be received, when we have marked his men with blood and used their very daggers, that they have done it?
Who dares receive it other, as we shall make our griefs and clamor roar upon his death?
I am settled, and bend up each corporal agent to this terrible feat.
Away, and mock the time with fairest show. False face must hide what the false heart doth know.

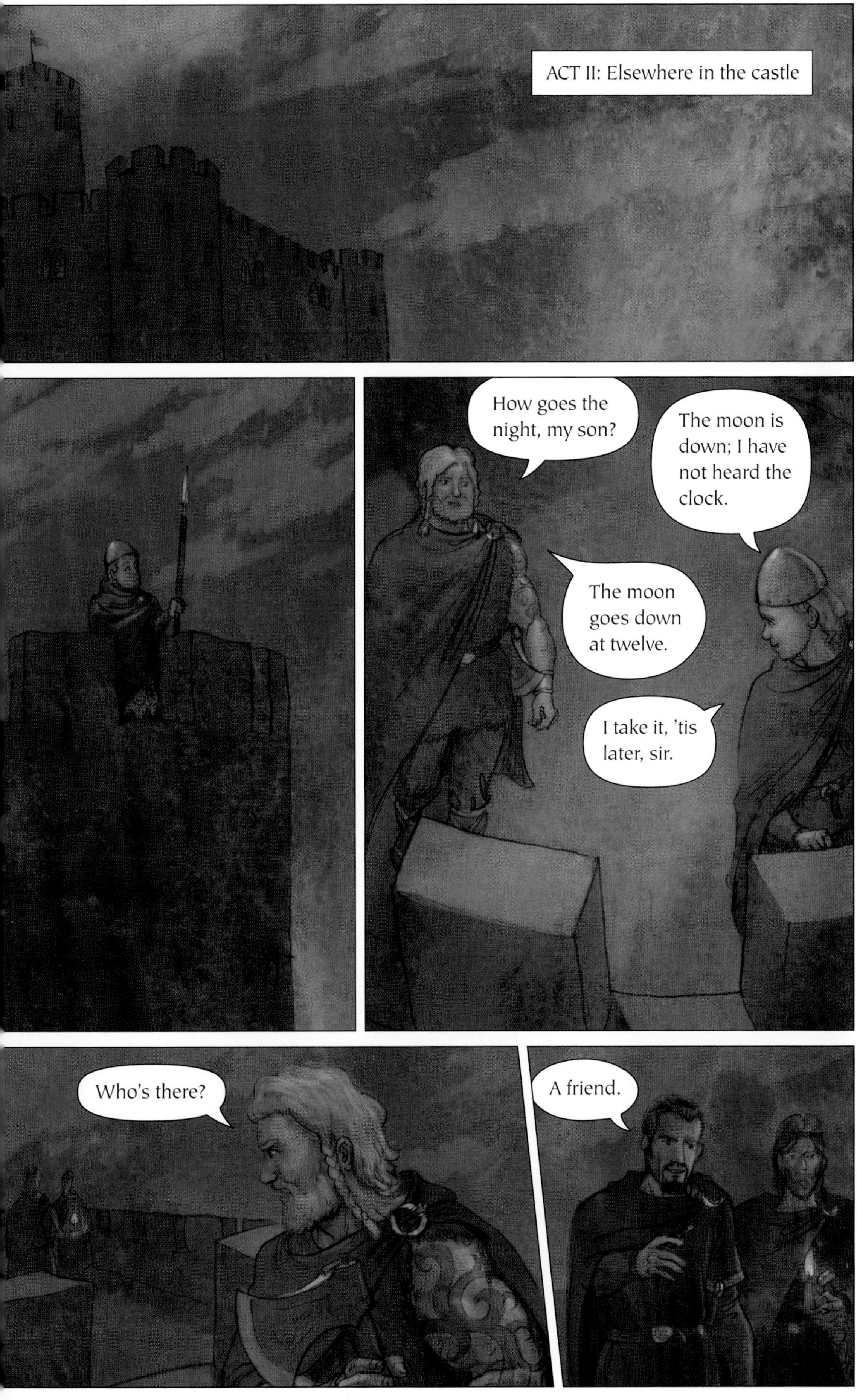
ACT II: Elsewhere in the castle
How goes the night, my son?
The moon is down; I have not heard the clock.
The moon goes down at twelve.
I take it, 'tis later, sir.
Who's there?
A friend.

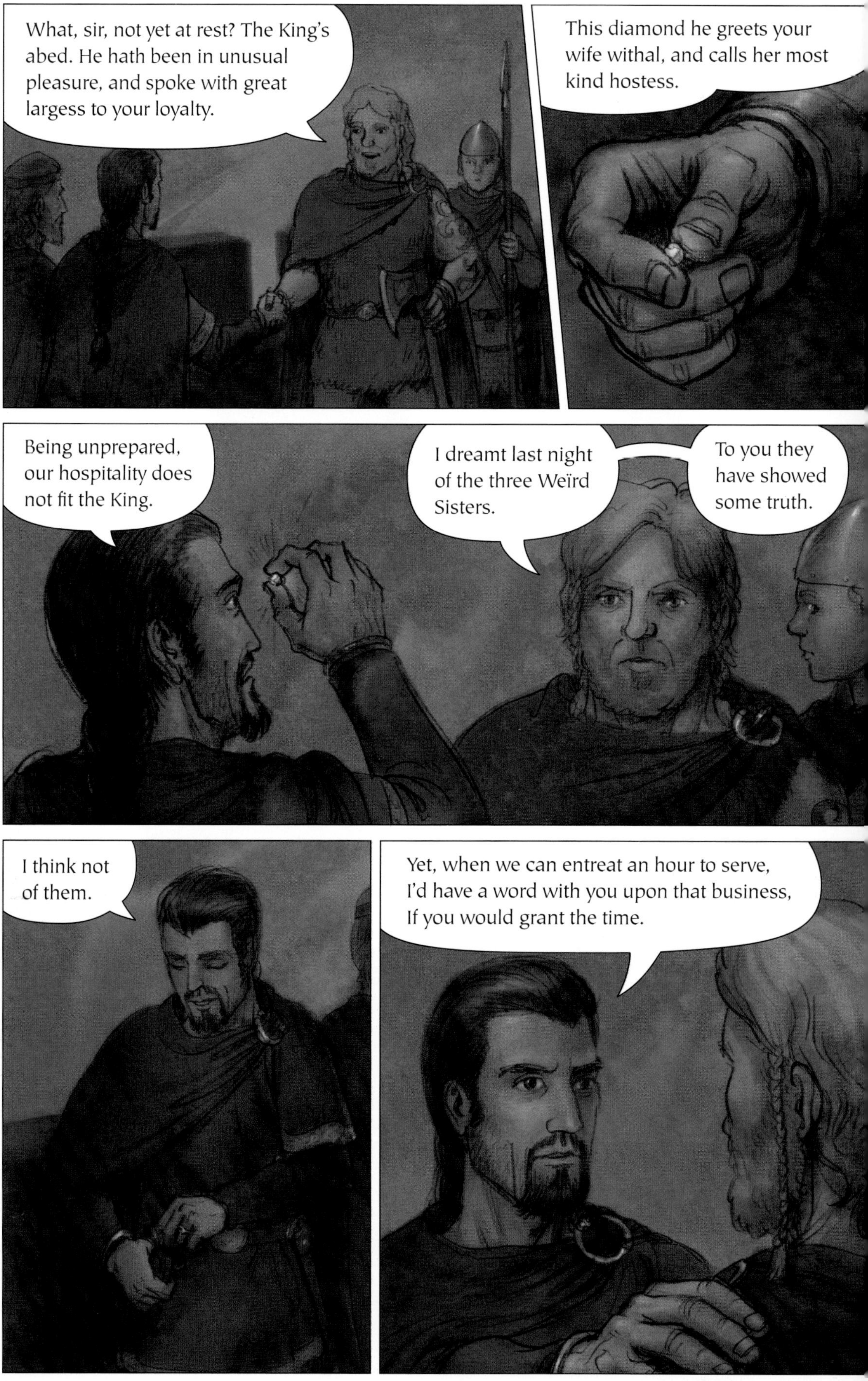
What, sir, not yet at rest? The King's abed. He hath been in unusual pleasure, and spoke with great largess to your loyalty.
This diamond he greets your wife withal, and calls her most kind hostess.
Being unprepared, our hospitality does not fit the King.
I dreamt last night of the three Weïrd Sisters.
To you they have showed some truth.
I think not of them.
Yet, when we can entreat an hour to serve,
I'd have a word with you upon that business,
If you would grant the time.

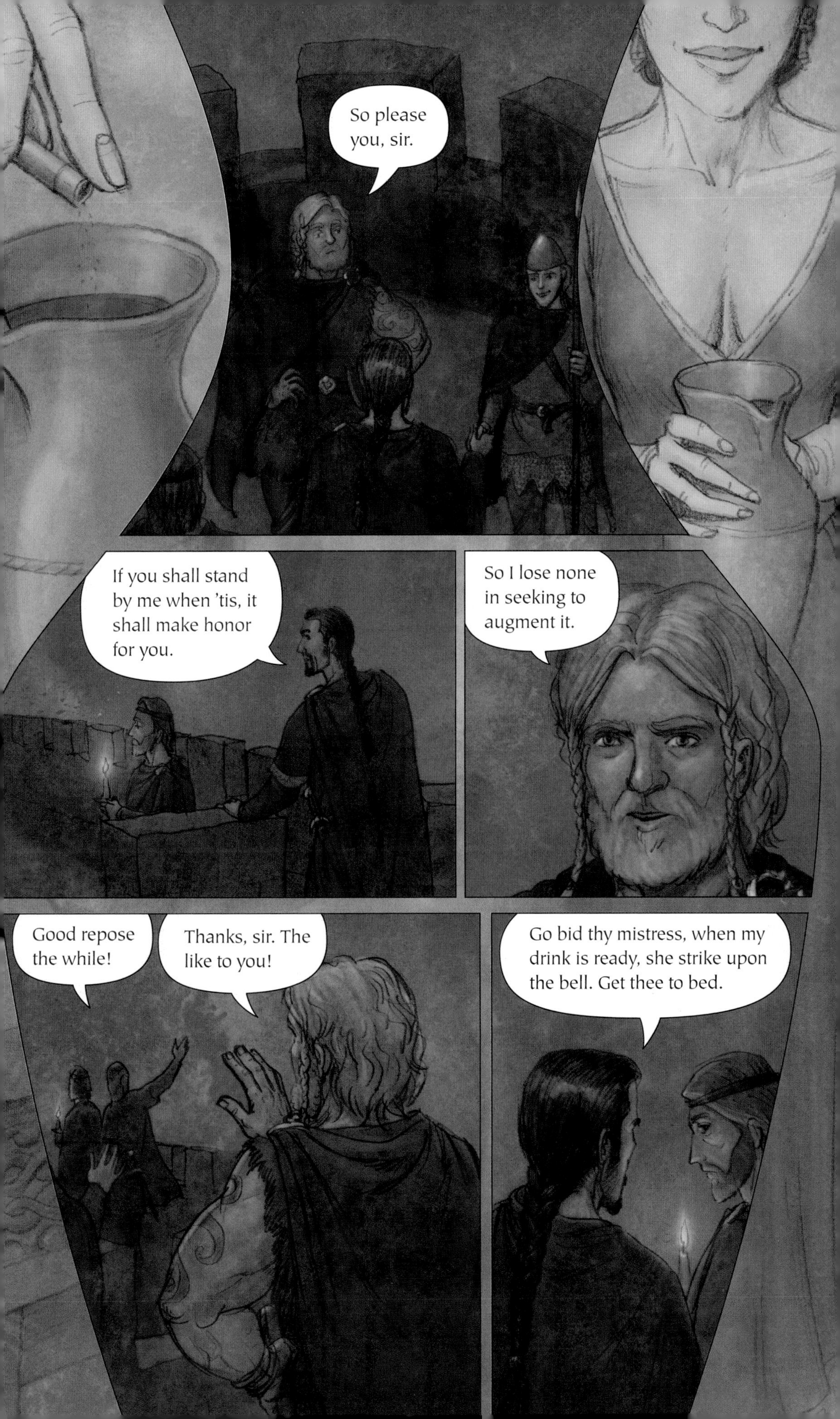
So please you, sir.
If you shall stand by me when 'tis, it shall make honor for you.
So I lose none in seeking to augment it.
Good repose the while!
Thanks, sir. The like to you!
Go bid thy mistress, when my drink is ready, she strike upon the bell. Get thee to bed.

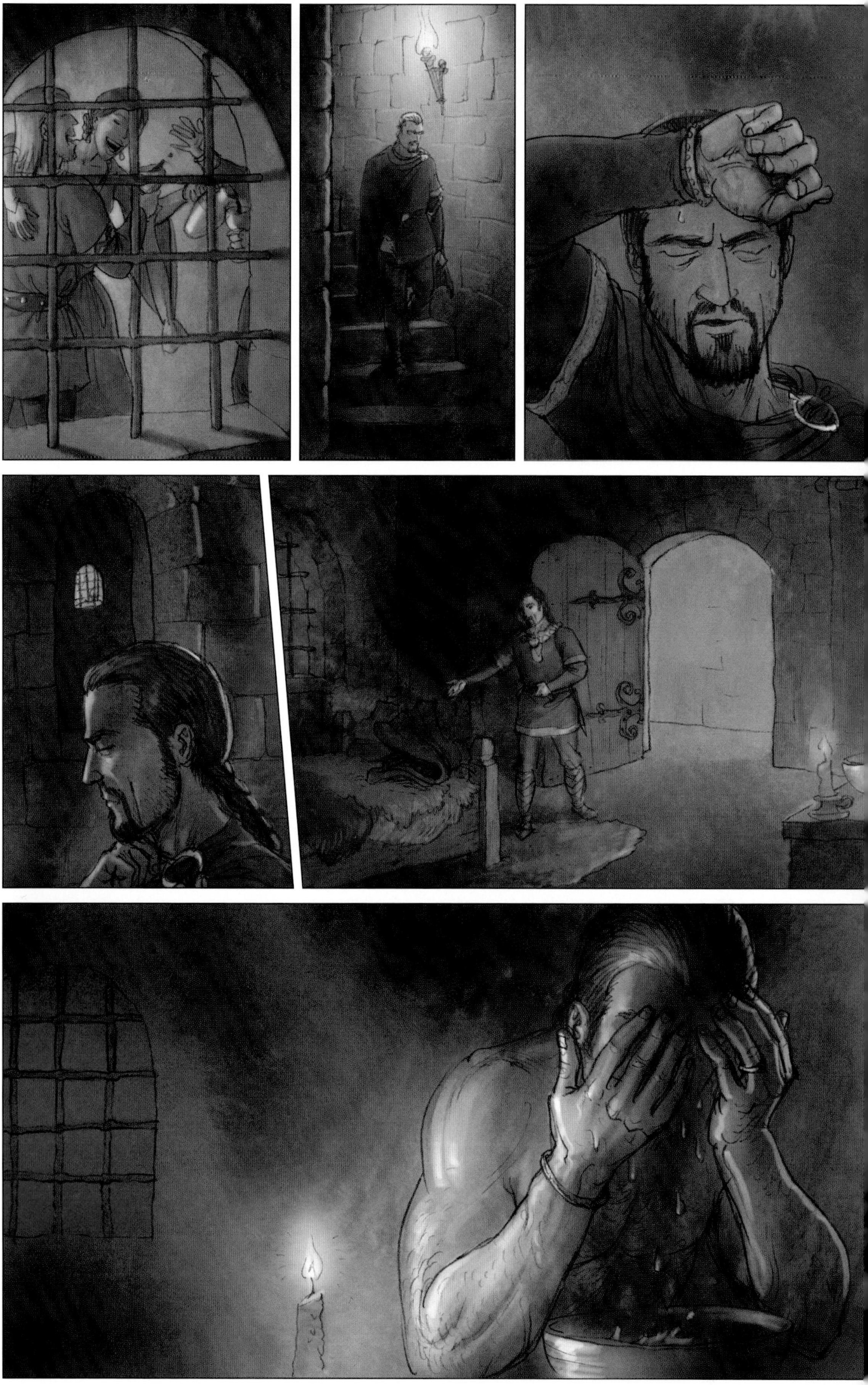

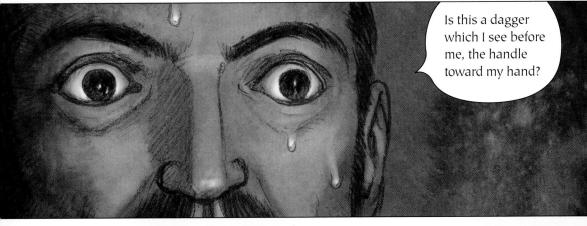

Is this a dagger which I see before me, the handle toward my hand?

Come, let me clutch thee.

I have thee not, and yet I see thee still.

Art thou not, fatal vision, sensible to feeling as to sight?

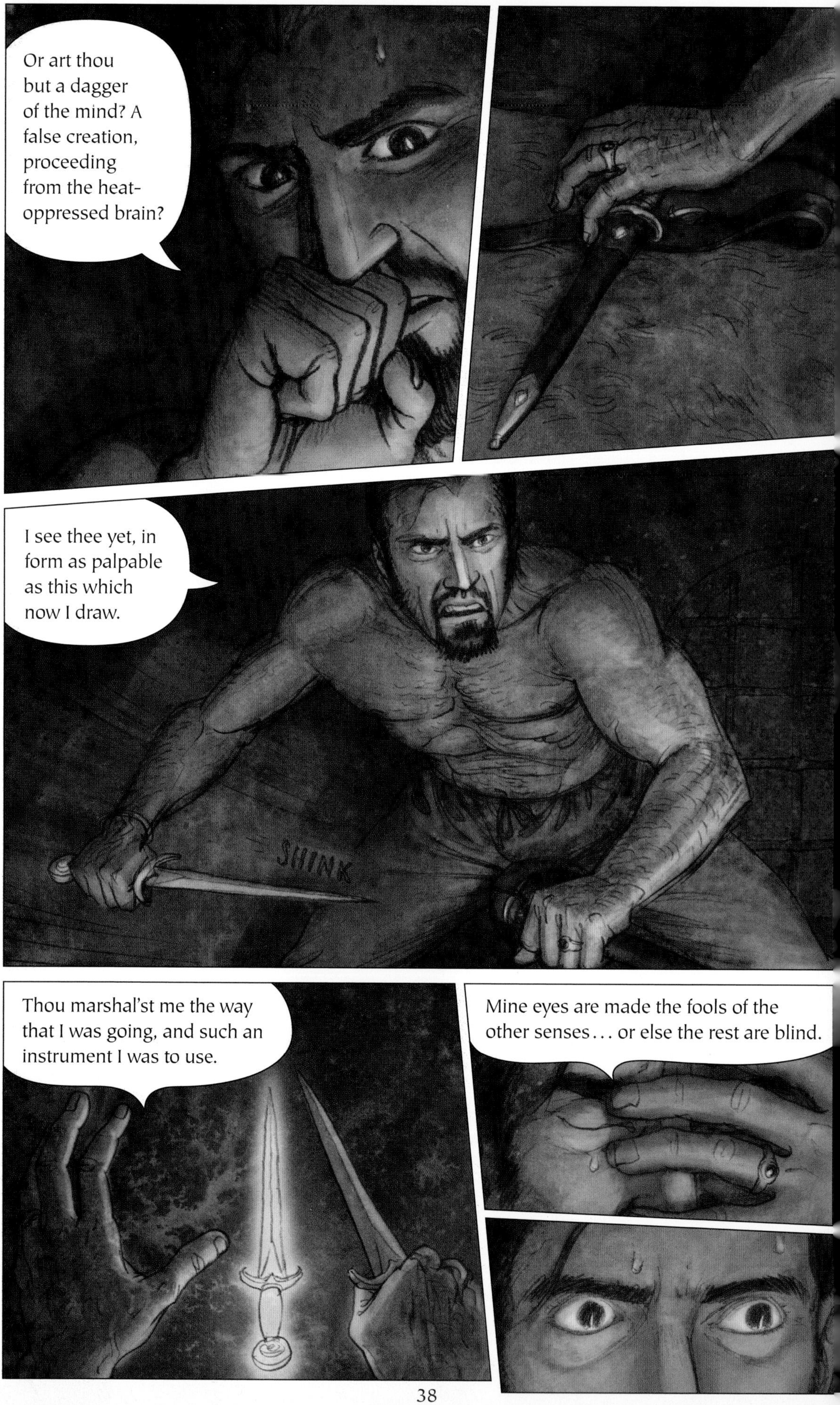
Or art thou but a dagger of the mind? A false creation, proceeding from the heat-oppressed brain?
I see thee yet, in form as palpable as this which now I draw.
SHINK
Thou marshal'st me the way that I was going, and such an instrument I was to use.
Mine eyes are made the fools of the other senses... or else the rest are blind.

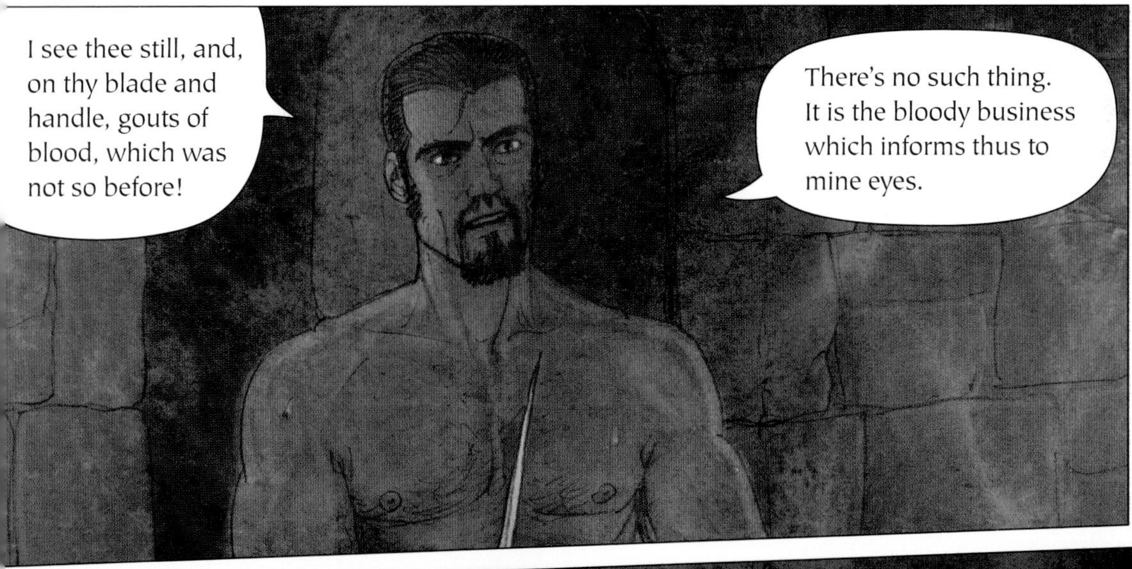
I see thee still, and, on thy blade and handle, gouts of blood, which was not so before!
There's no such thing. It is the bloody business which informs thus to mine eyes.

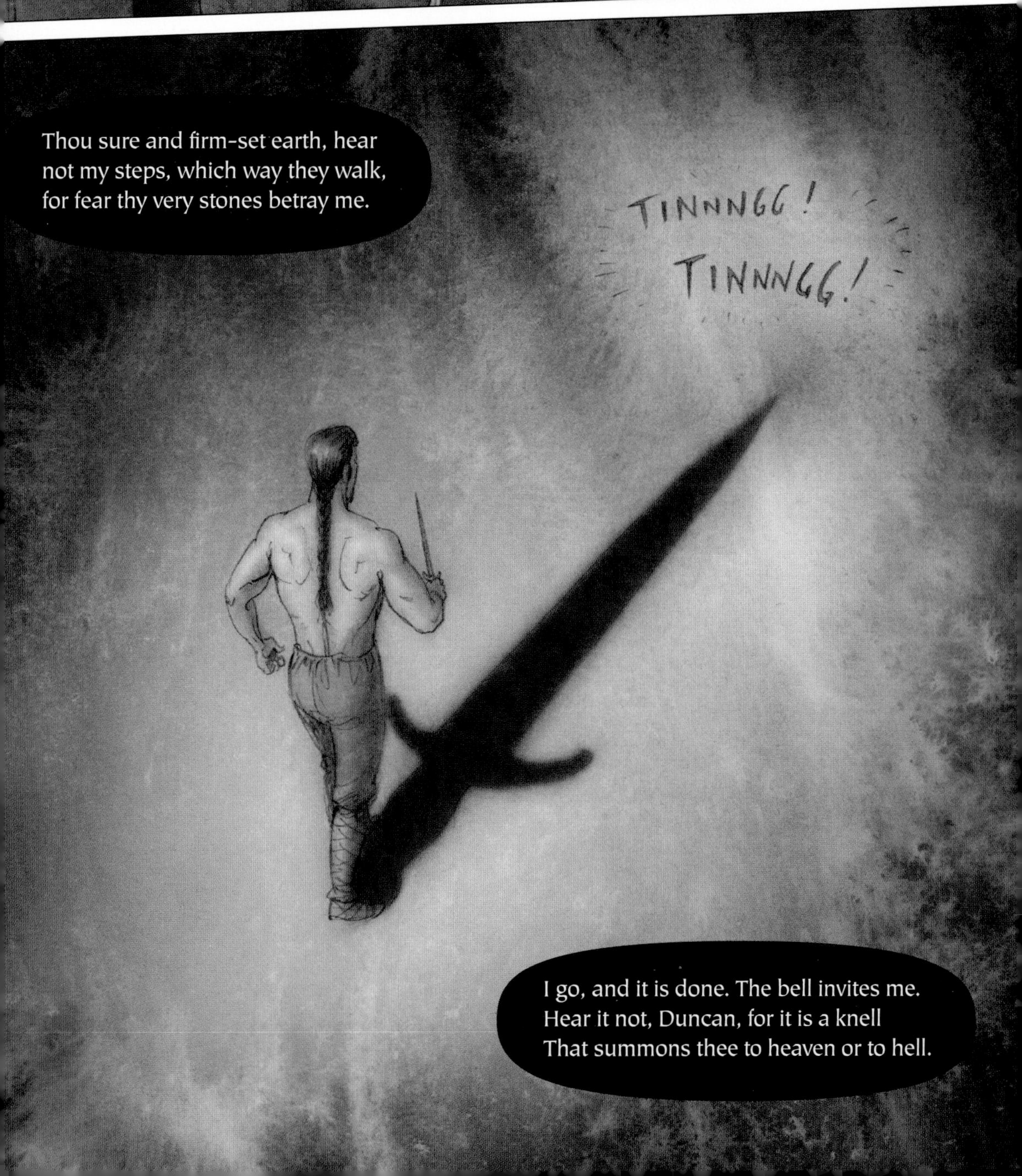
Thou sure and firm-set earth, hear not my steps, which way they walk, for fear thy very stones betray me.
TINNNGG!
TINNNGG!
I go, and it is done. The bell invites me. Hear it not, Duncan, for it is a knell That summons thee to heaven or to hell.

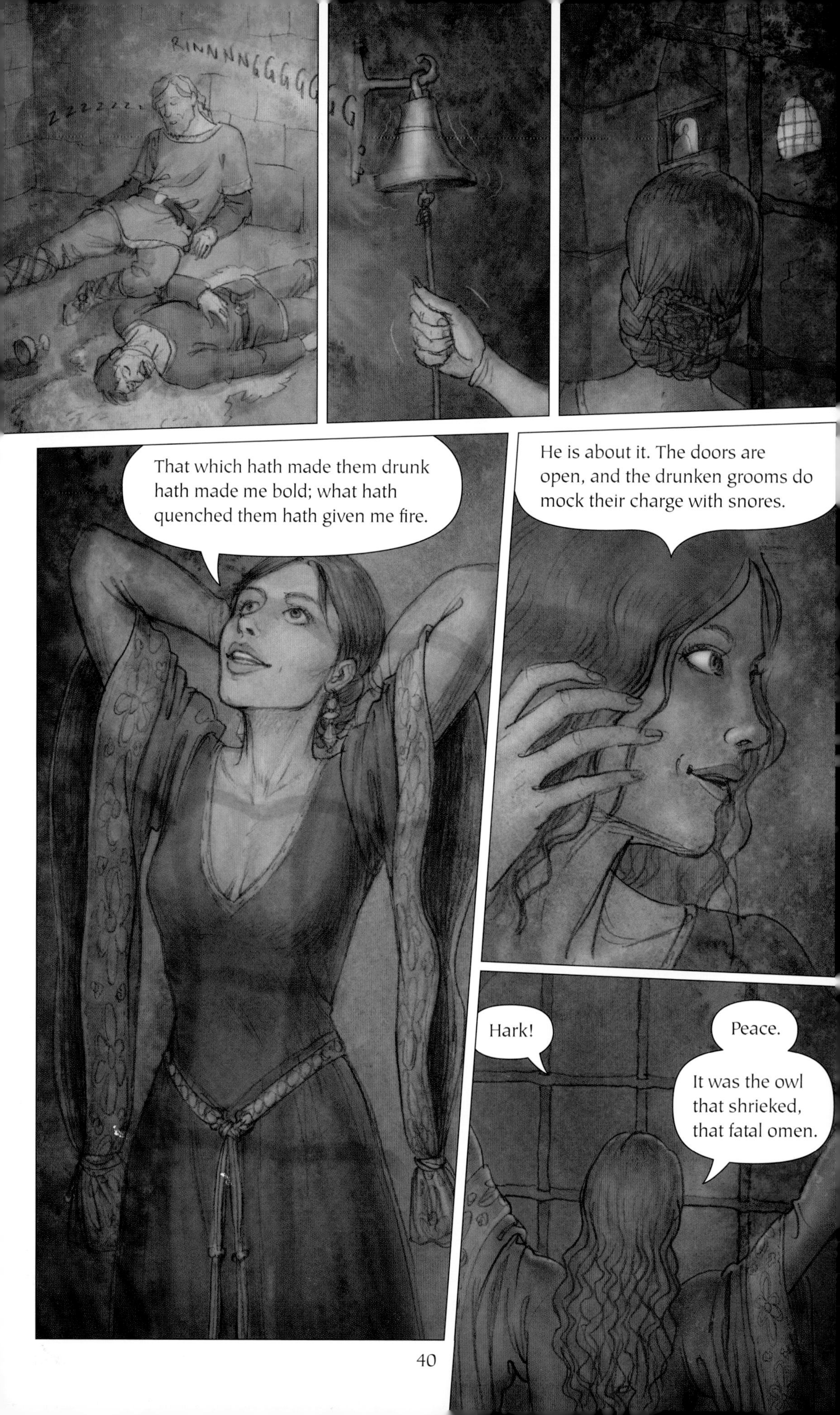
RINNNNGGGGGG
ZZZZZZ.
That which hath made them drunk hath made me bold; what hath quenched them hath given me fire.
He is about it. The doors are open, and the drunken grooms do mock their charge with snores.
Hark!
Peace.
It was the owl that shrieked, that fatal omen.

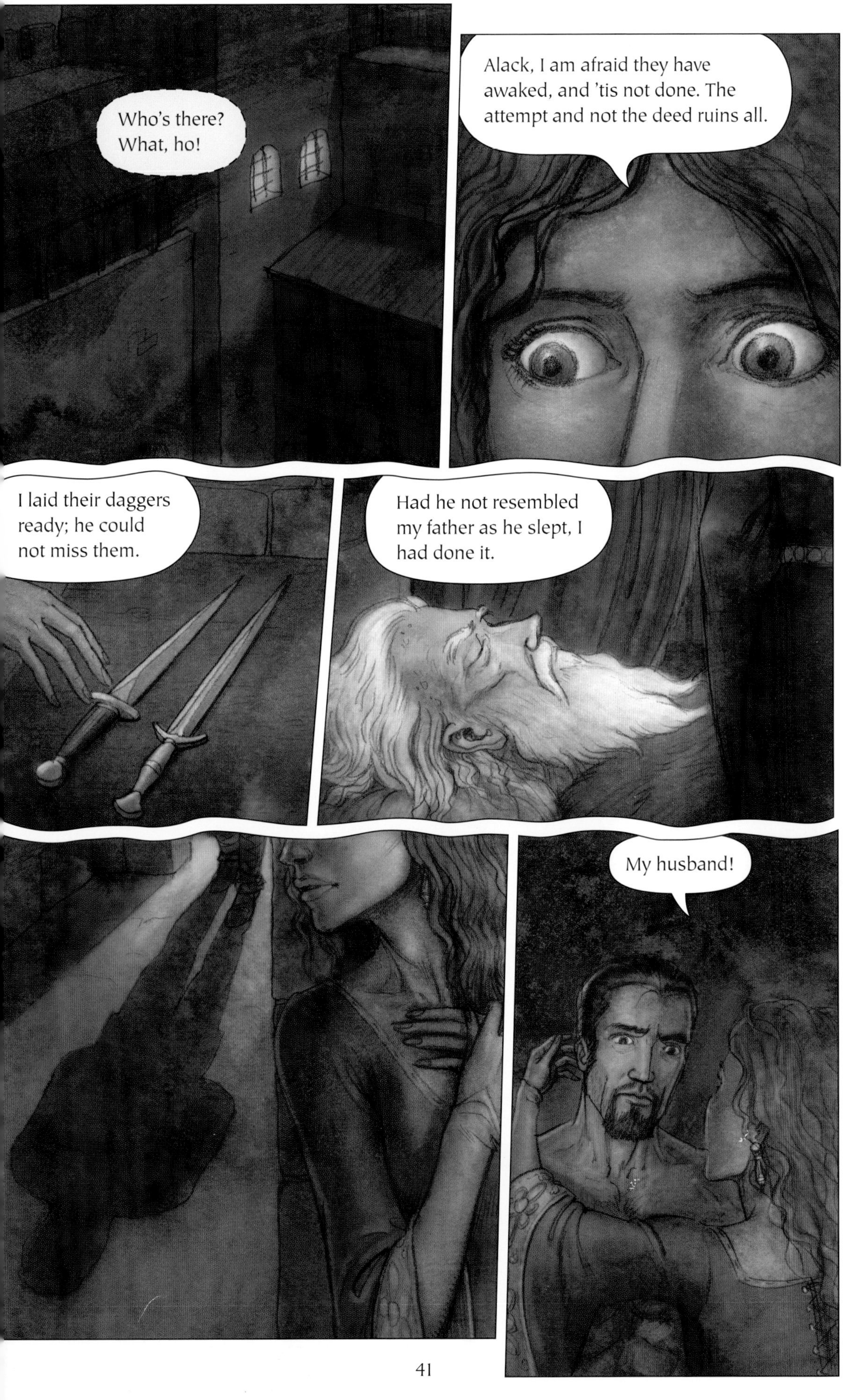
Who's there? What, ho!
Alack, I am afraid they have awaked, and 'tis not done. The attempt and not the deed ruins all.
I laid their daggers ready; he could not miss them.
Had he not resembled my father as he slept, I had done it.
My husband!

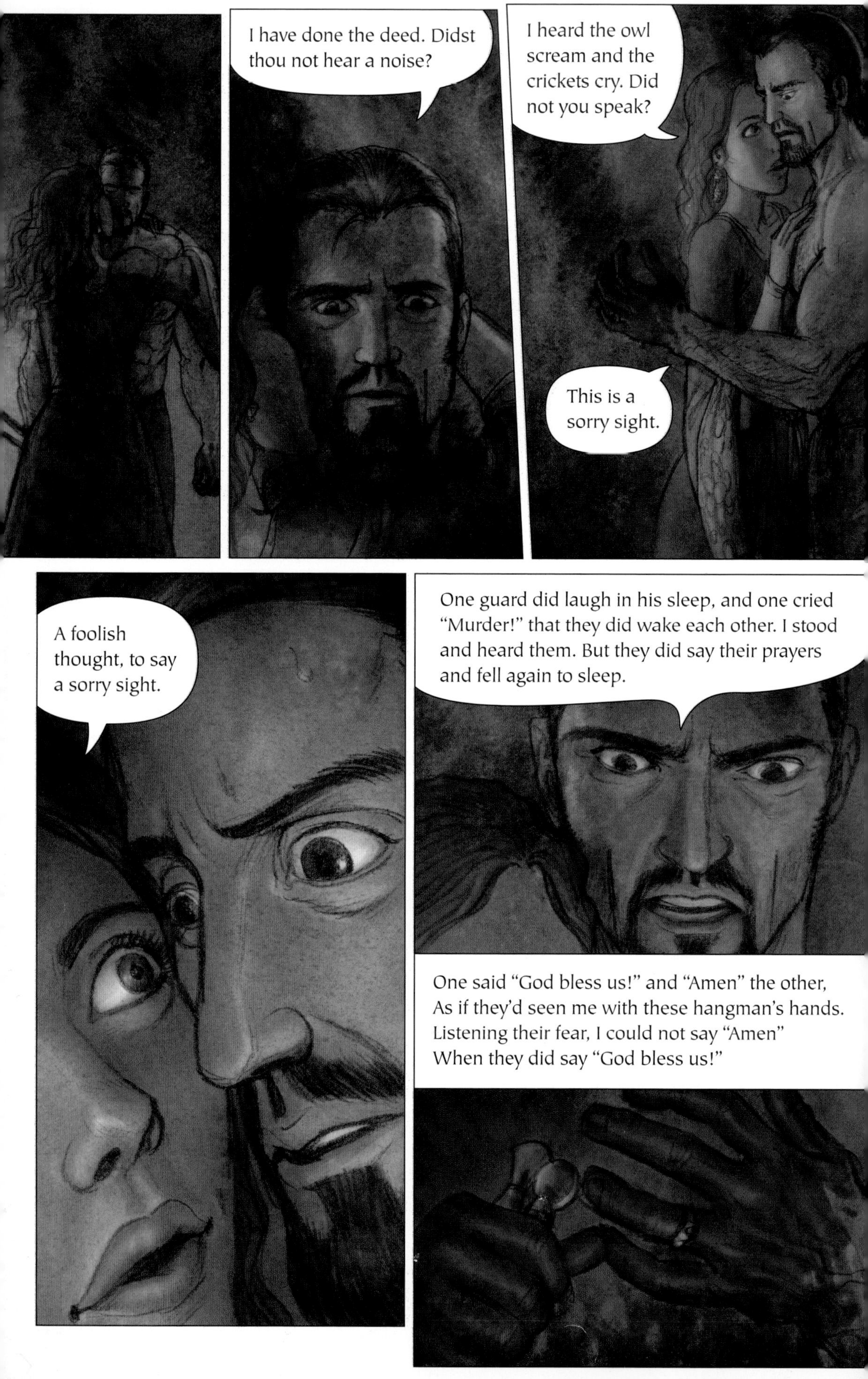
I have done the deed. Didst thou not hear a noise?
I heard the owl scream and the crickets cry. Did not you speak?
This is a sorry sight.
A foolish thought, to say a sorry sight.
One guard did laugh in his sleep, and one cried "Murder!" that they did wake each other. I stood and heard them. But they did say their prayers and fell again to sleep.
One said "God bless us!" and "Amen" the other,
As if they'd seen me with these hangman's hands.
Listening their fear, I could not say "Amen"
When they did say "God bless us!"

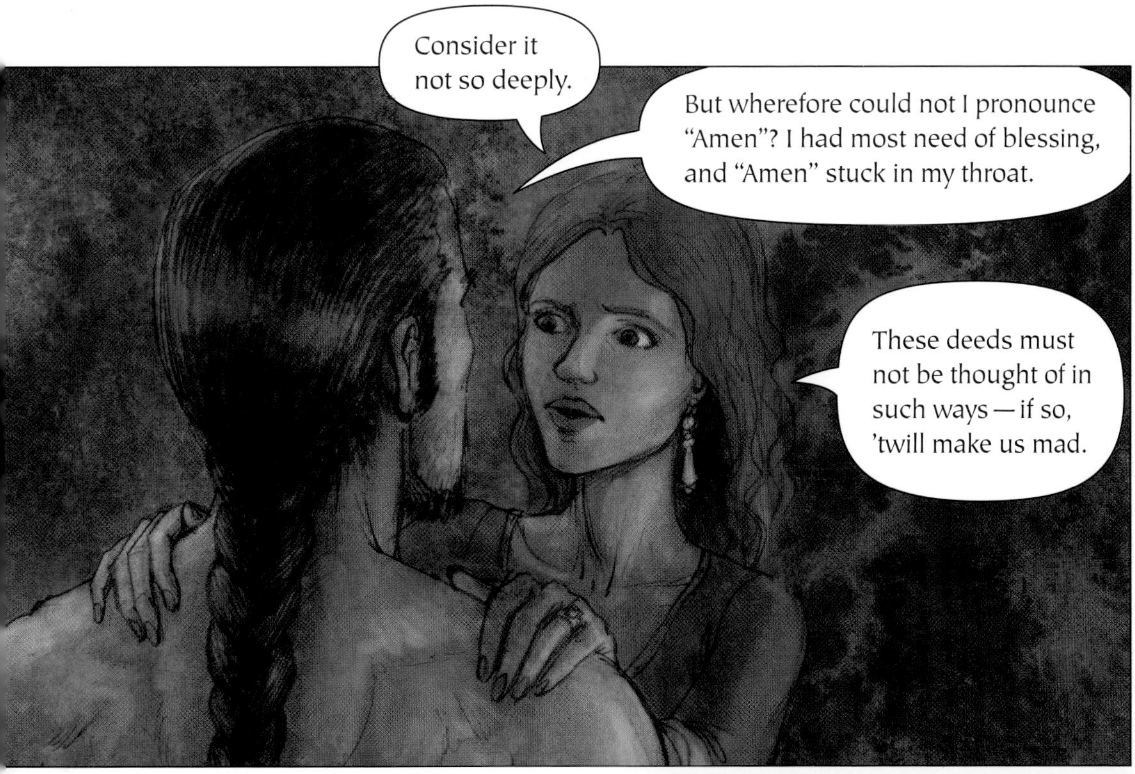
Consider it not so deeply.
But wherefore could not I pronounce "Amen"? I had most need of blessing, and "Amen" stuck in my throat.
These deeds must not be thought of in such ways — if so, 'twill make us mad.

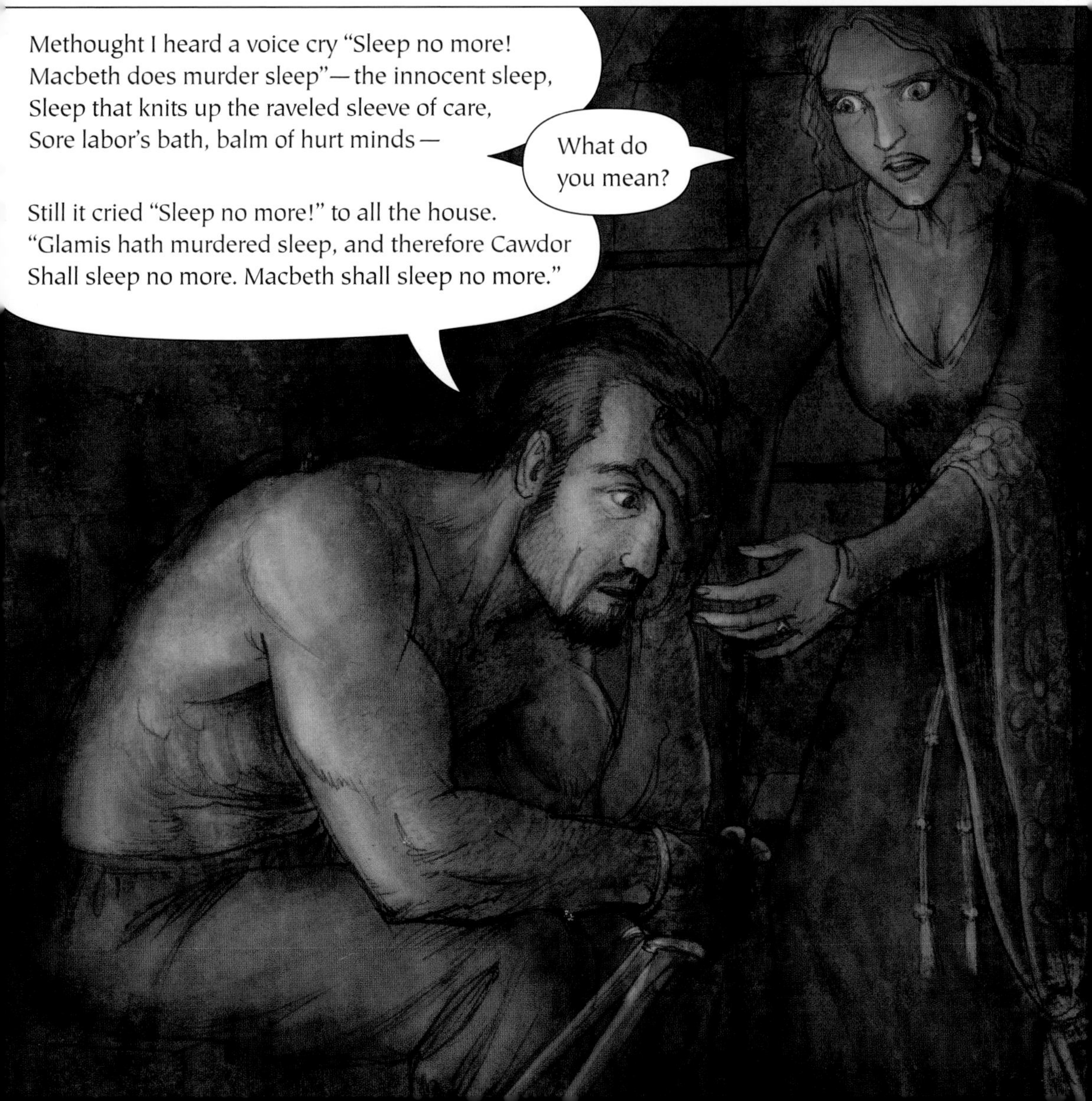
Methought I heard a voice cry "Sleep no more! Macbeth does murder sleep"— the innocent sleep, Sleep that knits up the raveled sleeve of care, Sore labor's bath, balm of hurt minds —
What do you mean?
Still it cried "Sleep no more!" to all the house. "Glamis hath murdered sleep, and therefore Cawdor Shall sleep no more. Macbeth shall sleep no more."

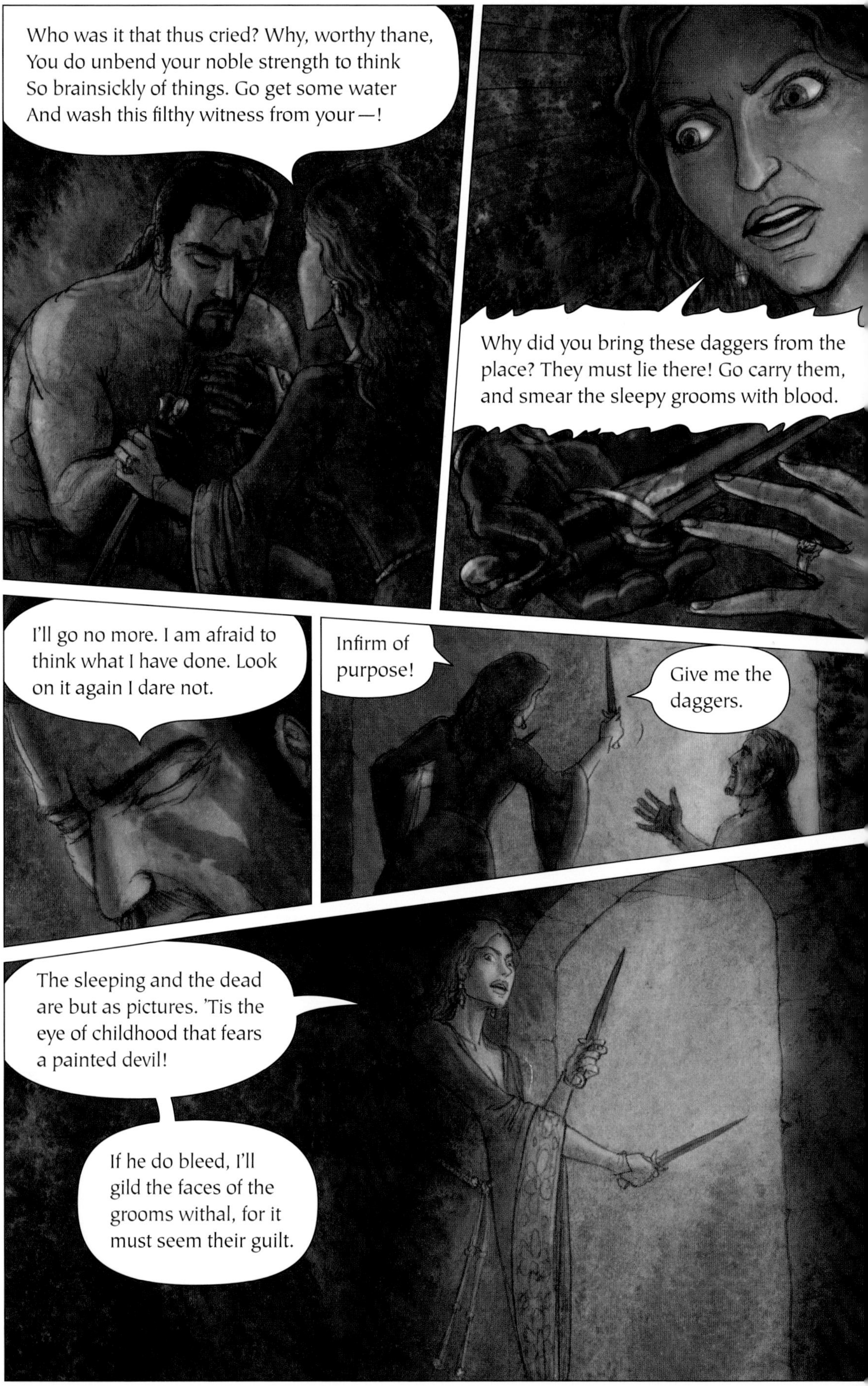
Who was it that thus cried? Why, worthy thane,
You do unbend your noble strength to think
So brainsickly of things. Go get some water
And wash this filthy witness from your—!
Why did you bring these daggers from the place? They must lie there! Go carry them, and smear the sleepy grooms with blood.
I'll go no more. I am afraid to think what I have done. Look on it again I dare not.
Infirm of purpose!
Give me the daggers.
The sleeping and the dead are but as pictures. 'Tis the eye of childhood that fears a painted devil!
If he do bleed, I'll gild the faces of the grooms withal, for it must seem their guilt.

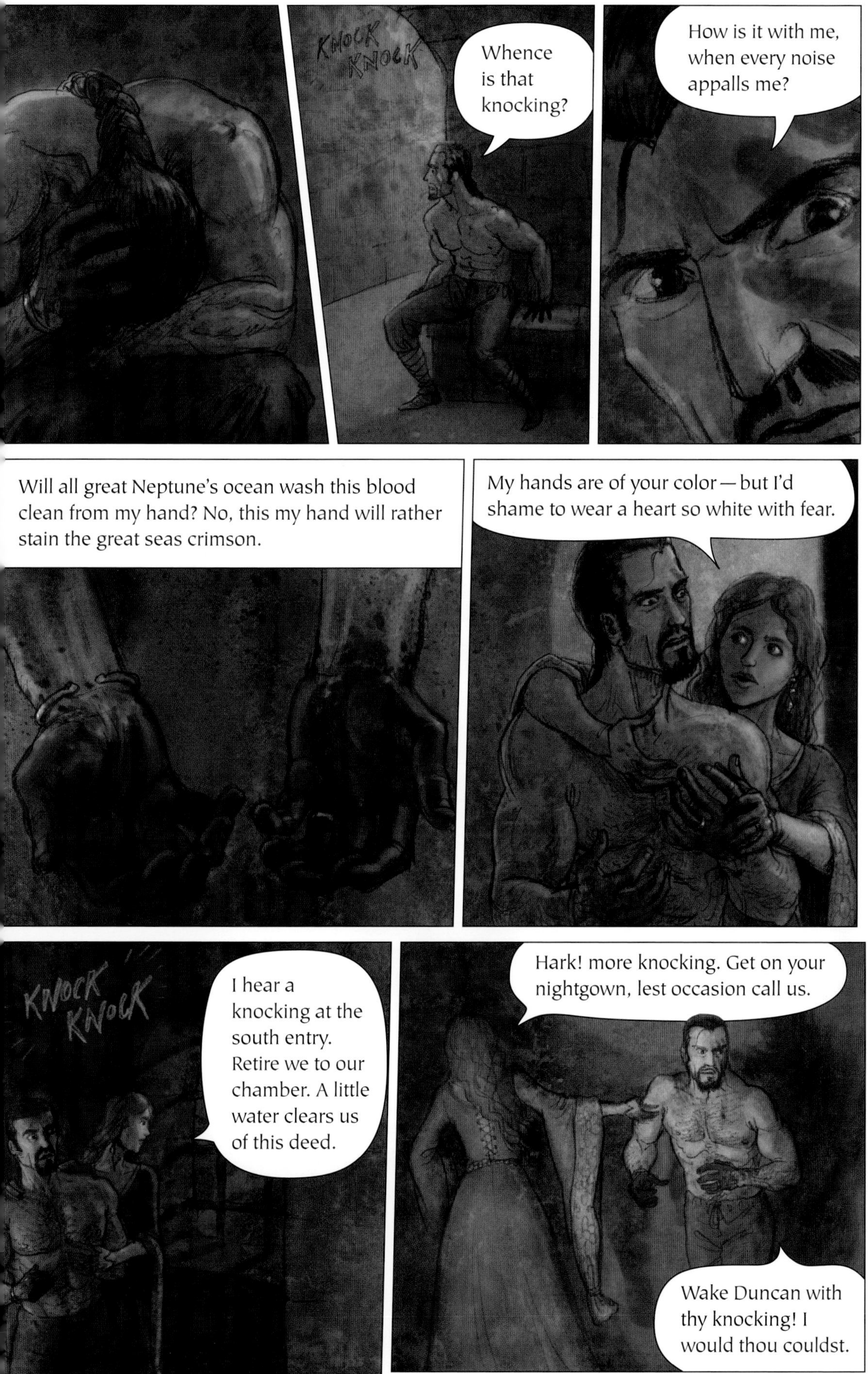
KNOCK KNOCK
Whence is that knocking?
How is it with me, when every noise appalls me?
Will all great Neptune's ocean wash this blood clean from my hand? No, this my hand will rather stain the great seas crimson.
My hands are of your color — but I'd shame to wear a heart so white with fear.
KNOCK KNOCK
I hear a knocking at the south entry. Retire we to our chamber. A little water clears us of this deed.
Hark! more knocking. Get on your nightgown, lest occasion call us.
Wake Duncan with thy knocking! I would thou couldst.

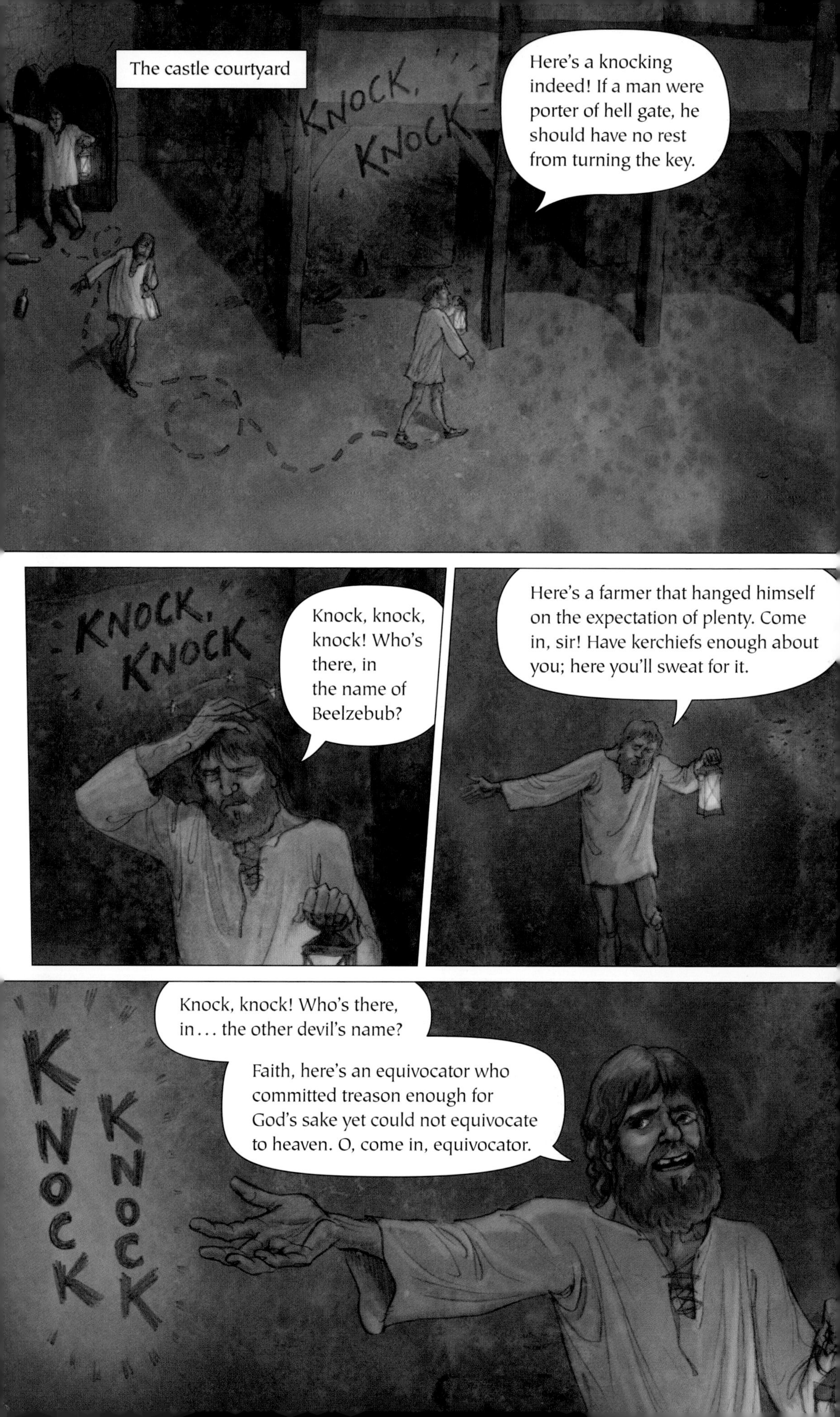
The castle courtyard
KNOCK, KNOCK
Here's a knocking indeed! If a man were porter of hell gate, he should have no rest from turning the key.
KNOCK, KNOCK
Knock, knock, knock! Who's there, in the name of Beelzebub?
Here's a farmer that hanged himself on the expectation of plenty. Come in, sir! Have kerchiefs enough about you; here you'll sweat for it.
KNOCK KNOCK
Knock, knock! Who's there, in... the other devil's name?
Faith, here's an equivocator who committed treason enough for God's sake yet could not equivocate to heaven. O, come in, equivocator.

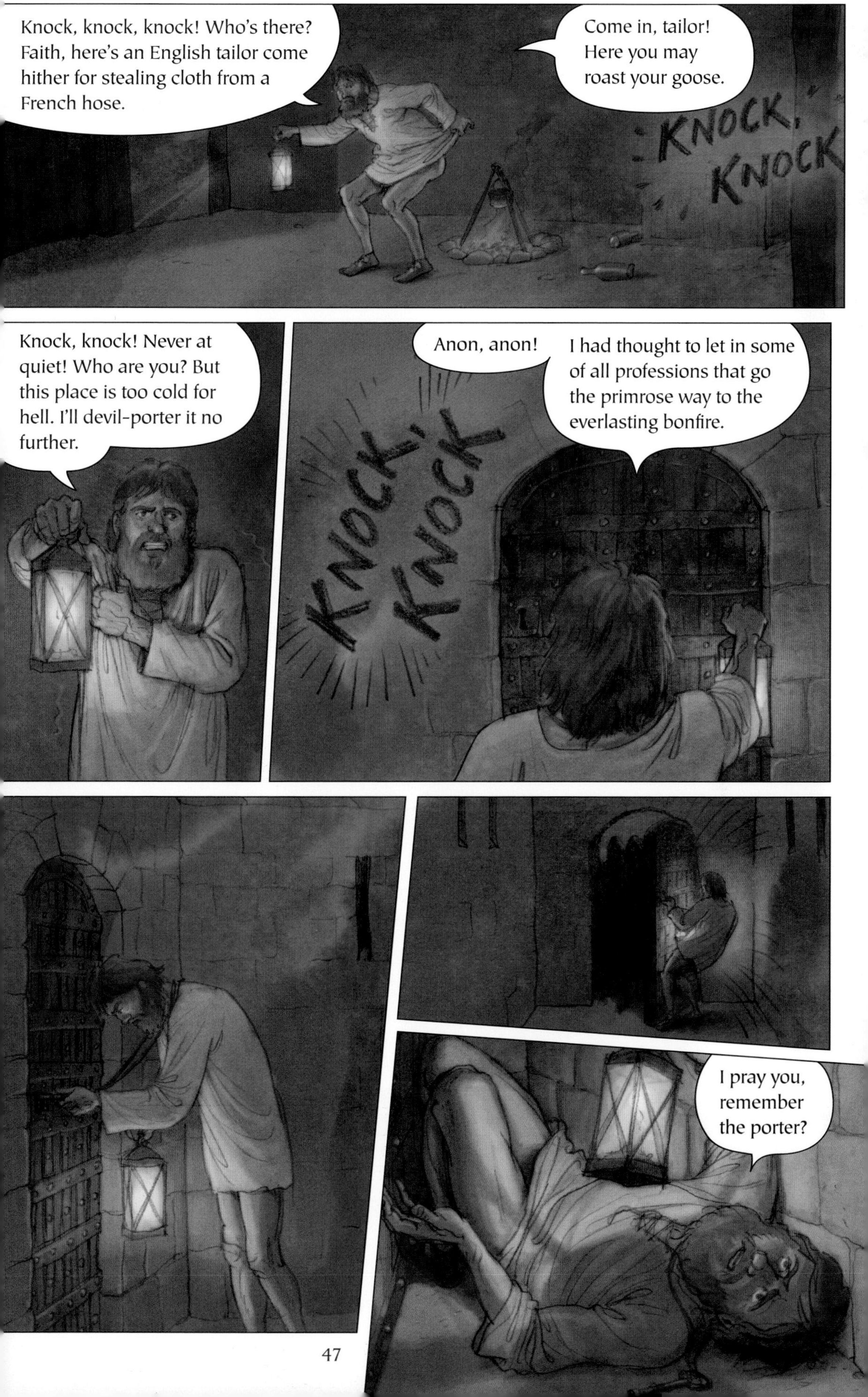
Knock, knock, knock! Who's there? Faith, here's an English tailor come hither for stealing cloth from a French hose.
Come in, tailor! Here you may roast your goose.
KNOCK, KNOCK
Knock, knock! Never at quiet! Who are you? But this place is too cold for hell. I'll devil-porter it no further.
KNOCK, KNOCK
Anon, anon!
I had thought to let in some of all professions that go the primrose way to the everlasting bonfire.
I pray you, remember the porter?

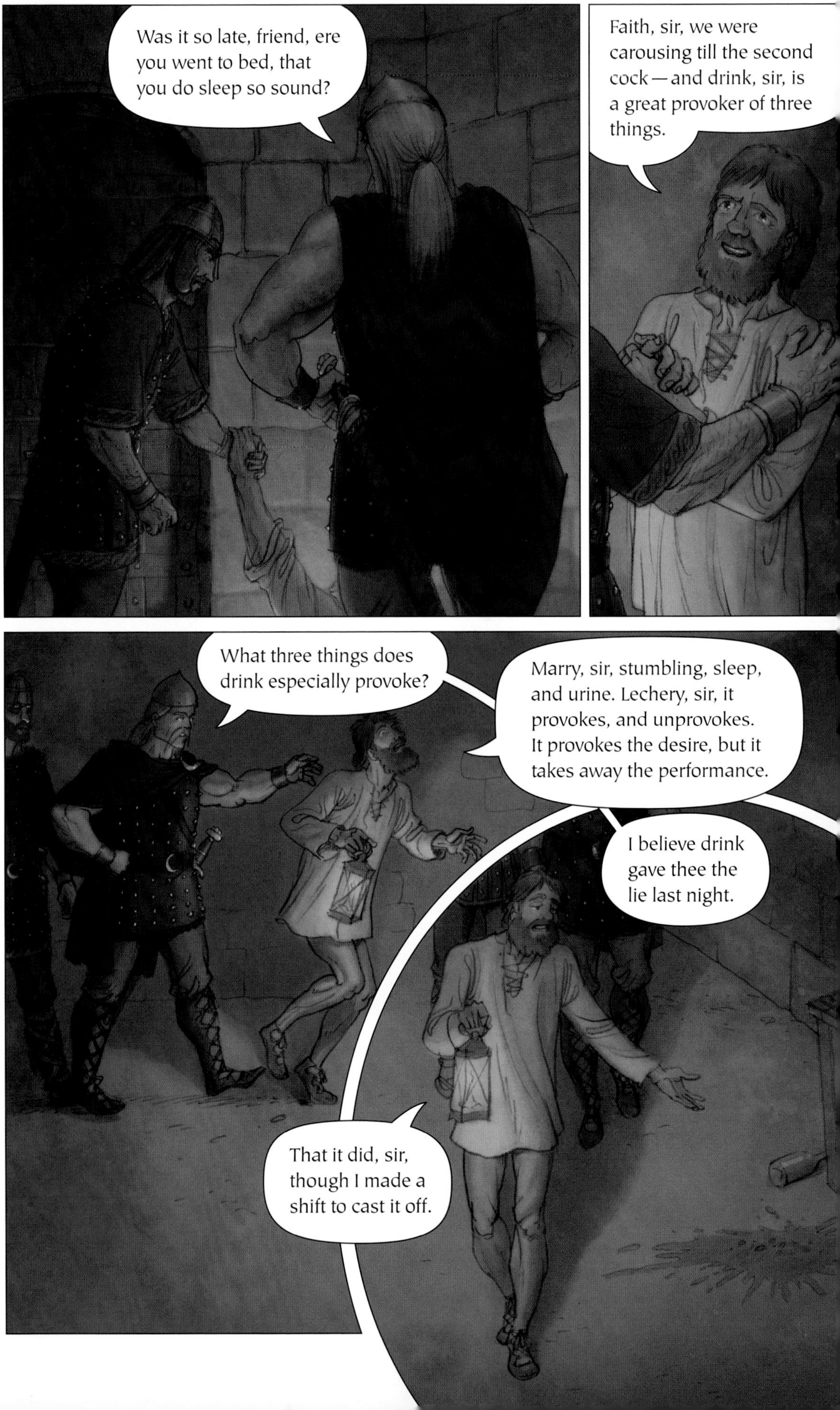
Was it so late, friend, ere you went to bed, that you do sleep so sound?
Faith, sir, we were carousing till the second cock—and drink, sir, is a great provoker of three things.
What three things does drink especially provoke?
Marry, sir, stumbling, sleep, and urine. Lechery, sir, it provokes, and unprovokes. It provokes the desire, but it takes away the performance.
I believe drink gave thee the lie last night.
That it did, sir, though I made a shift to cast it off.

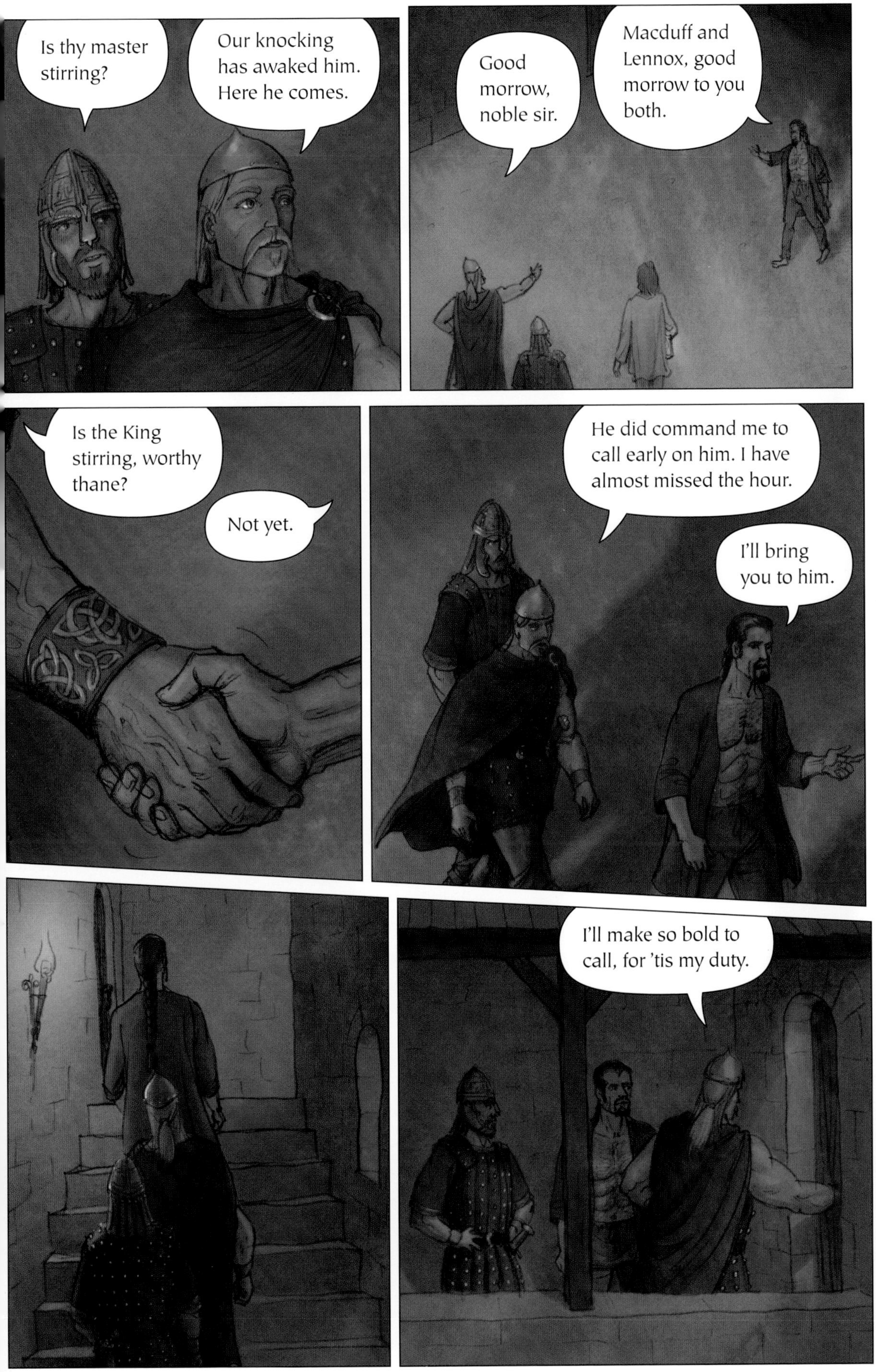

Is thy master stirring?
Our knocking has awaked him. Here he comes.
Good morrow, noble sir.
Macduff and Lennox, good morrow to you both.
Is the King stirring, worthy thane?
Not yet.
He did command me to call early on him. I have almost missed the hour.
I'll bring you to him.
I'll make so bold to call, for 'tis my duty.

Goes the King hence today?

He does. He did appoint so.

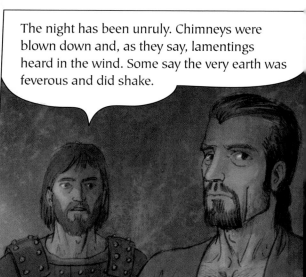

The night has been unruly. Chimneys were blown down and, as they say, lamentings heard in the wind. Some say the very earth was feverous and did shake.

'Twas a rough night.

My young remembrance cannot parallel an equal to it.

O horror, horror, horror! Tongue nor heart cannot conceive nor name thee!

What's the matter?

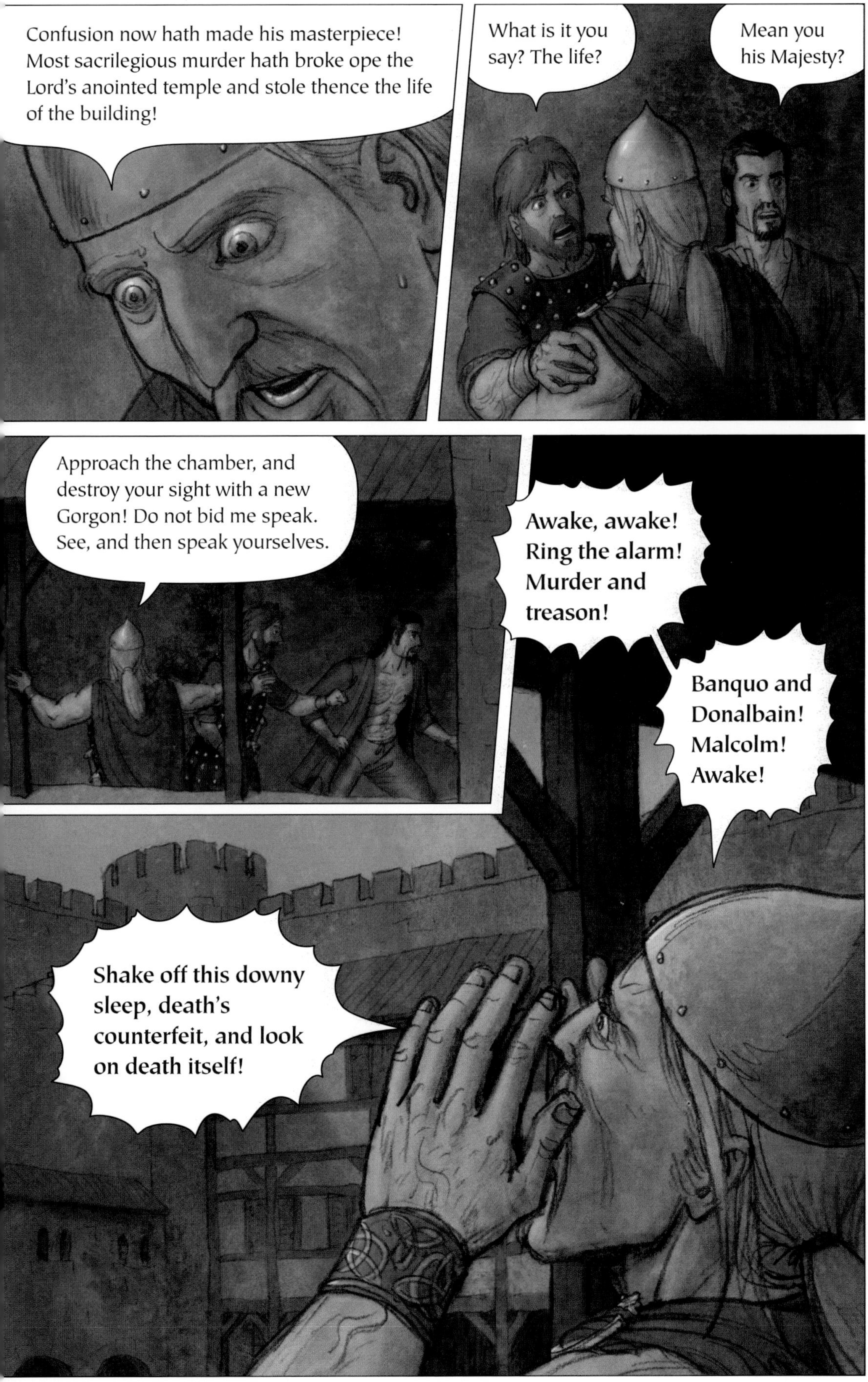
Confusion now hath made his masterpiece! Most sacrilegious murder hath broke ope the Lord's anointed temple and stole thence the life of the building!
What is it you say? The life?
Mean you his Majesty?
Approach the chamber, and destroy your sight with a new Gorgon! Do not bid me speak. See, and then speak yourselves.
Awake, awake! Ring the alarm! Murder and treason!
Banquo and Donalbain! Malcolm! Awake!
Shake off this downy sleep, death's counterfeit, and look on death itself!

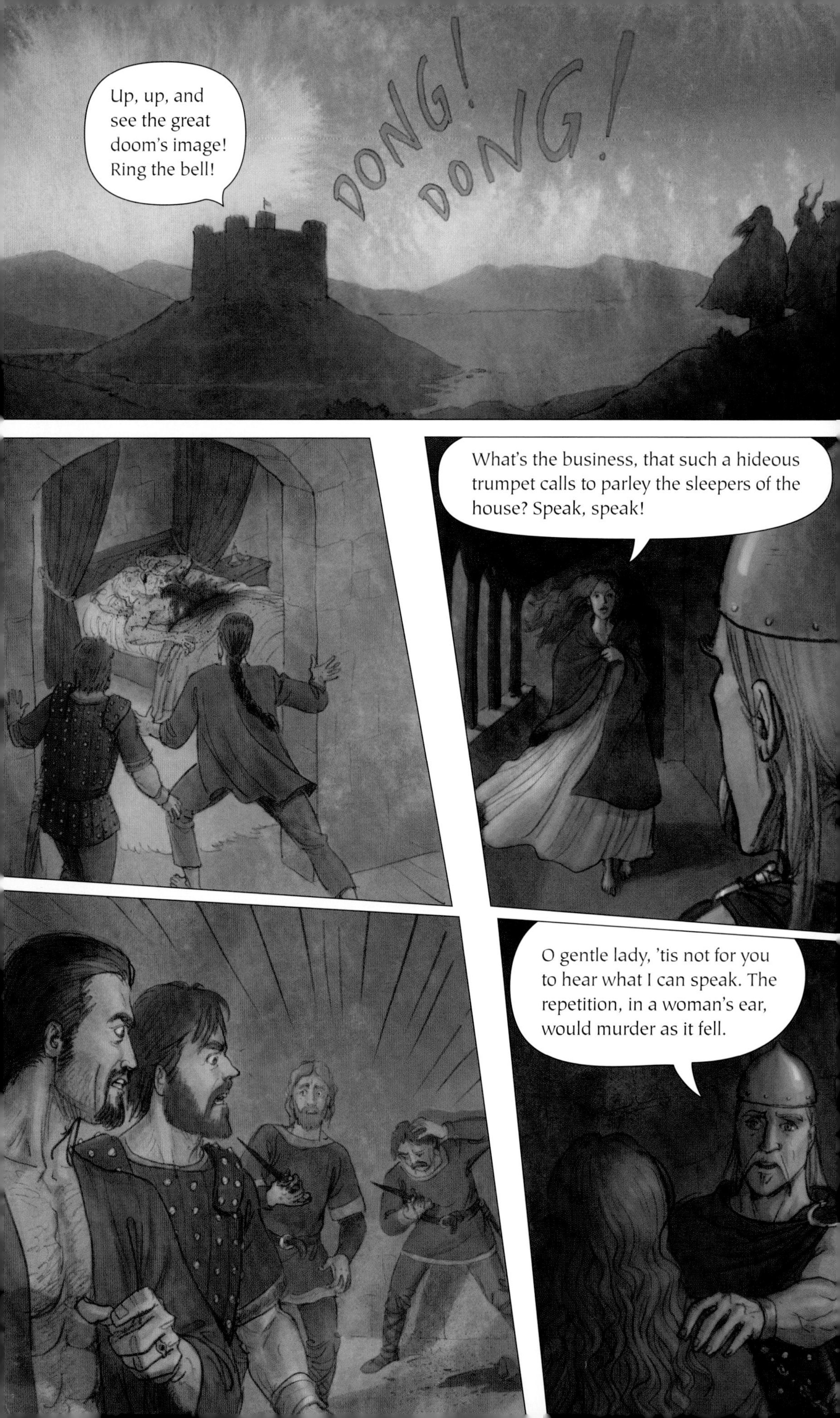
Up, up, and see the great doom's image! Ring the bell!
DONG! DONG!
What's the business, that such a hideous trumpet calls to parley the sleepers of the house? Speak, speak!
O gentle lady, 'tis not for you to hear what I can speak. The repetition, in a woman's ear, would murder as it fell.

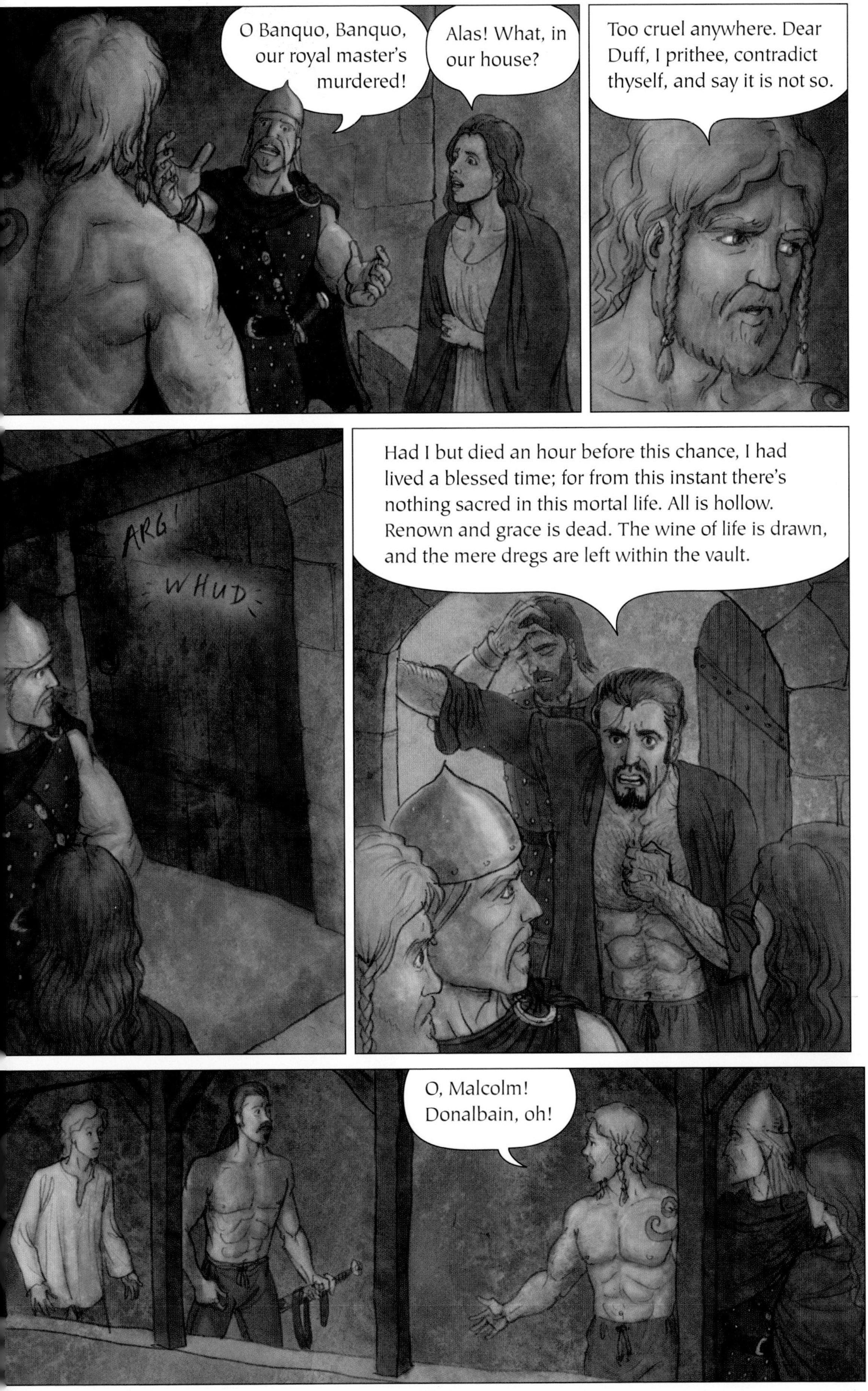
O Banquo, Banquo, our royal master's murdered!
Alas! What, in our house?
Too cruel anywhere. Dear Duff, I prithee, contradict thyself, and say it is not so.
ARG!
WHUD
Had I but died an hour before this chance, I had lived a blessed time; for from this instant there's nothing sacred in this mortal life. All is hollow. Renown and grace is dead. The wine of life is drawn, and the mere dregs are left within the vault.
O, Malcolm! Donalbain, oh!

What is amiss?

You are, and do not know it.

The spring, the head, the fountain of your blood is stopped; the very source of it is stopped.

Your royal father's murdered.

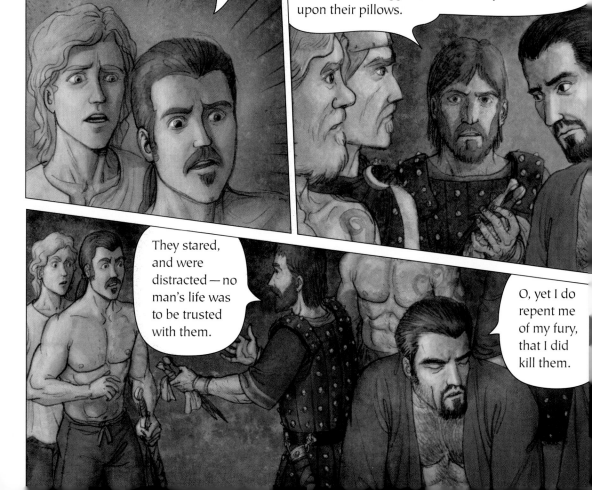

By whom?

Those of his chamber, as it seemed, had done it. Their hands and faces were all badged with blood. So were their daggers, which unwiped we found upon their pillows.

They stared, and were distracted — no man's life was to be trusted with them.

O, yet I do repent me of my fury, that I did kill them.

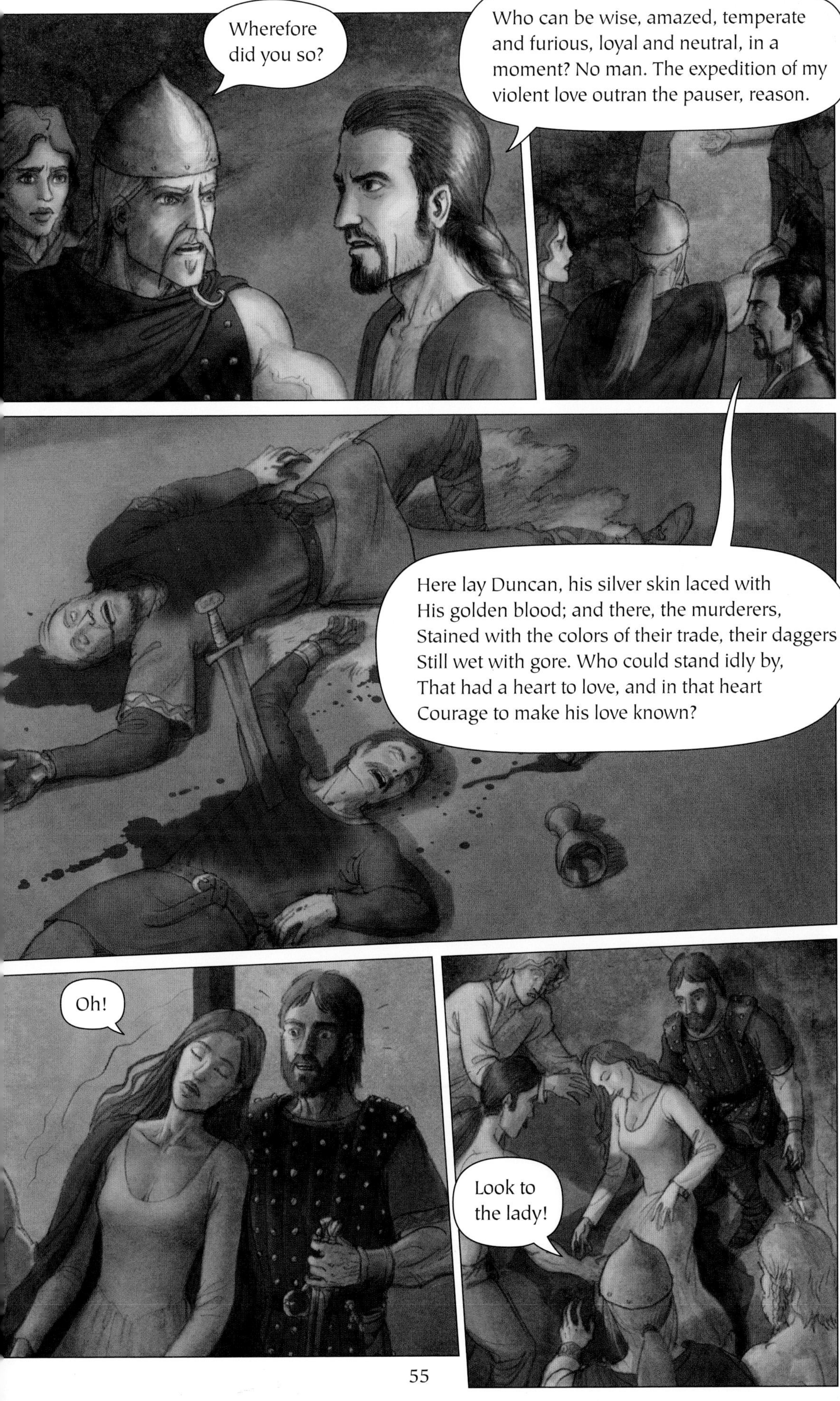
Wherefore did you so?
Who can be wise, amazed, temperate and furious, loyal and neutral, in a moment? No man. The expedition of my violent love outran the pauser, reason.
Here lay Duncan, his silver skin laced with His golden blood; and there, the murderers, Stained with the colors of their trade, their daggers Still wet with gore. Who could stand idly by, That had a heart to love, and in that heart Courage to make his love known?
Oh!
Look to the lady!

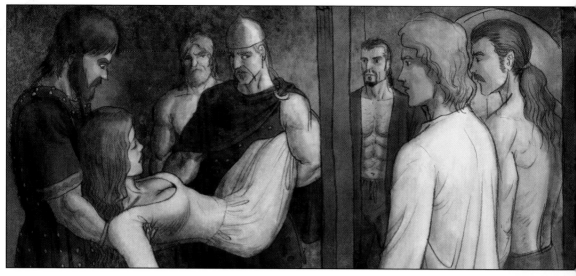

Why do we hold our tongues?

What should be spoken here, where danger pens us in? Let's away. Our tears are not yet brewed.

Look to the lady. And when we have retired and dressed, then let us meet, and question this most bloody piece of work, to know it further.

Fears and scruples shake us.

Nor our strong sorrow ready yet to act.

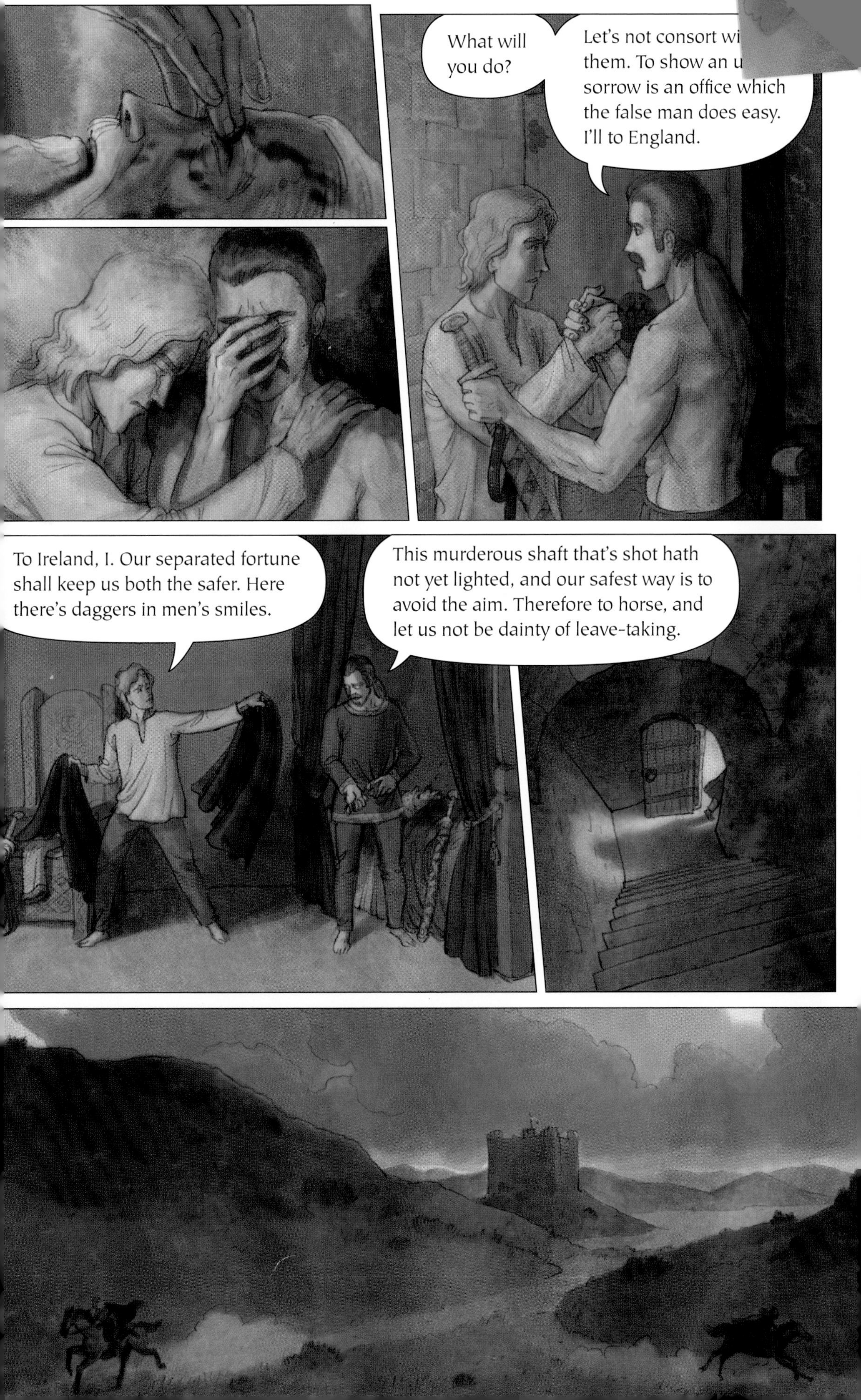
What will you do?
Let's not consort wi
them. To show an u
sorrow is an office which
the false man does easy.
I'll to England.
To Ireland, I. Our separated fortune shall keep us both the safer. Here there's daggers in men's smiles.
This murderous shaft that's shot hath not yet lighted, and our safest way is to avoid the aim. Therefore to horse, and let us not be dainty of leave-taking.

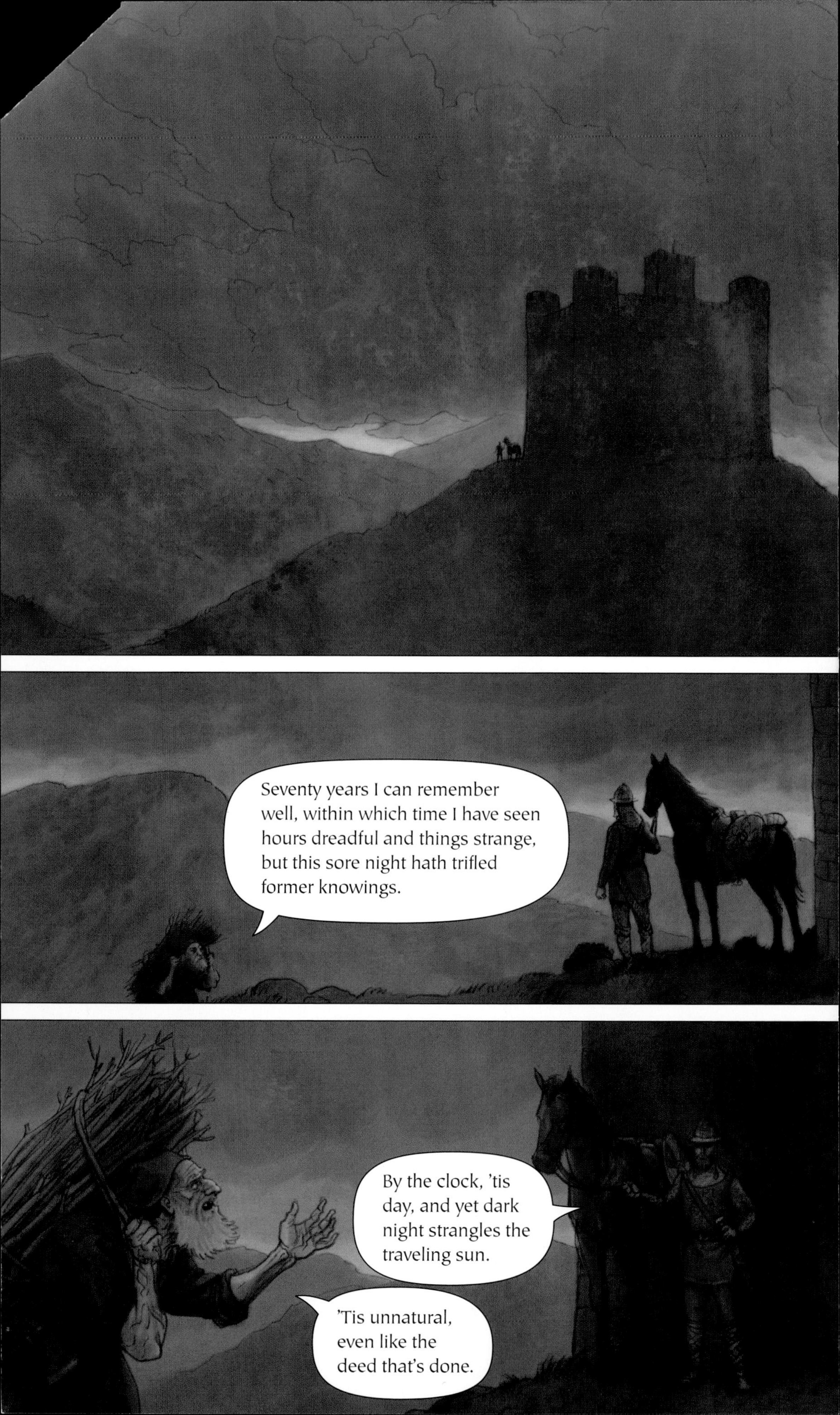
Seventy years I can remember well, within which time I have seen hours dreadful and things strange, but this sore night hath trifled former knowings.
By the clock, ’tis day, and yet dark night strangles the traveling sun.
’Tis unnatural, even like the deed that’s done.

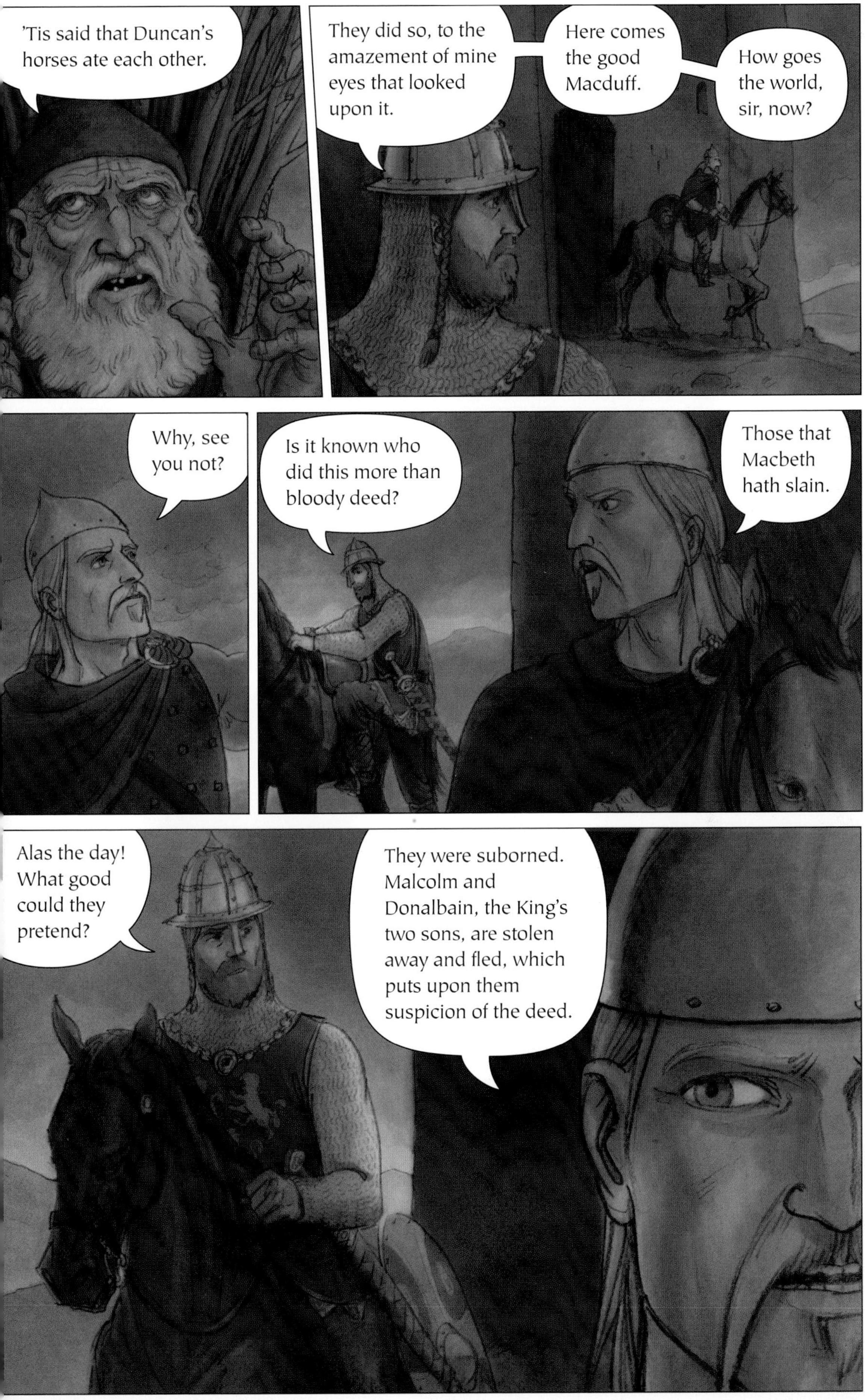
'Tis said that Duncan's horses ate each other.
They did so, to the amazement of mine eyes that looked upon it.
Here comes the good Macduff.
How goes the world, sir, now?
Why, see you not?
Is it known who did this more than bloody deed?
Those that Macbeth hath slain.
Alas the day! What good could they pretend?
They were suborned. Malcolm and Donalbain, the King's two sons, are stolen away and fled, which puts upon them suspicion of the deed.

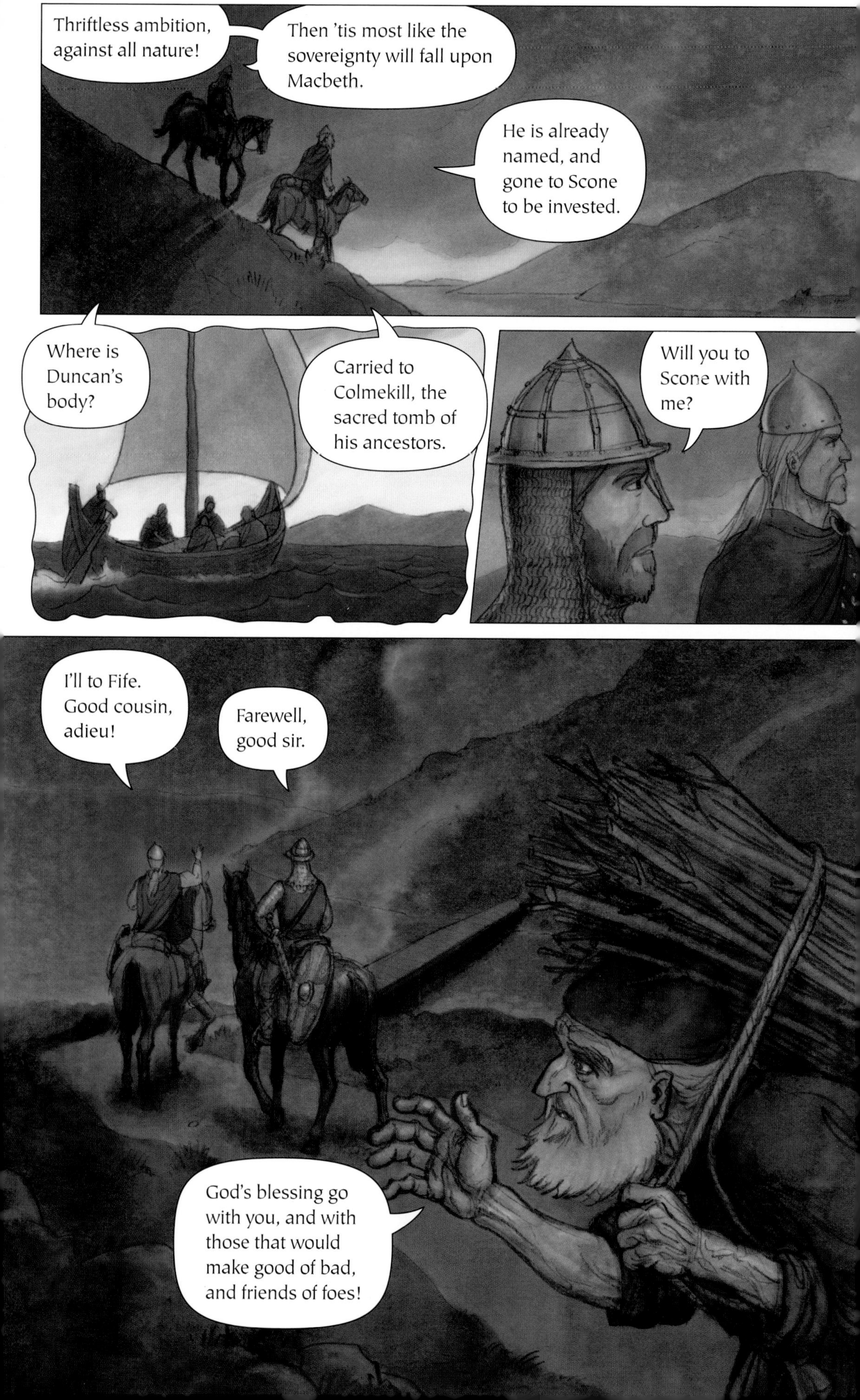
Thriftless ambition, against all nature!
Then 'tis most like the sovereignty will fall upon Macbeth.
He is already named, and gone to Scone to be invested.
Where is Duncan's body?
Carried to Colmekill, the sacred tomb of his ancestors.
Will you to Scone with me?
I'll to Fife. Good cousin, adieu!
Farewell, good sir.
God's blessing go with you, and with those that would make good of bad, and friends of foes!

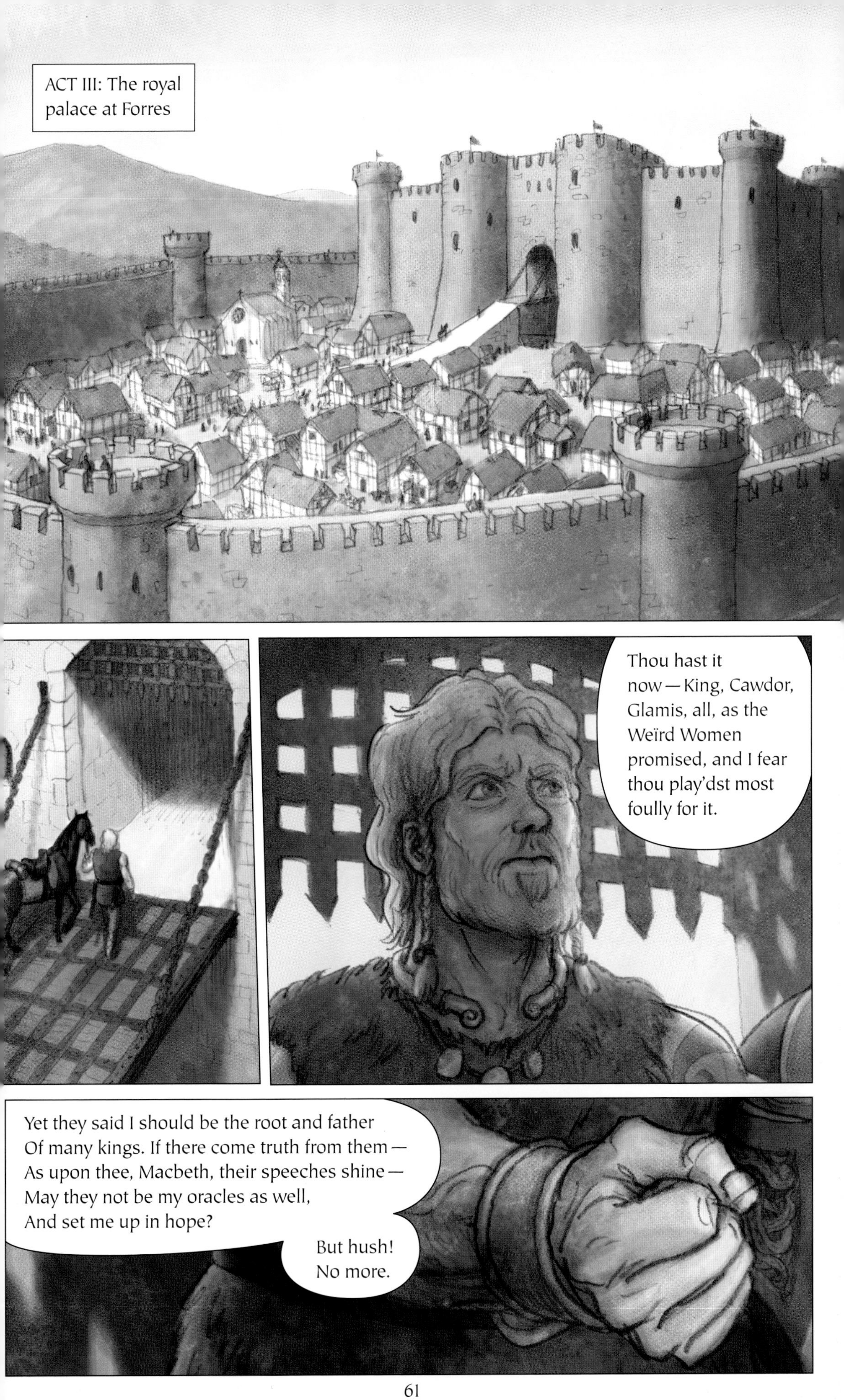
ACT III: The royal palace at Forres
Thou hast it now — King, Cawdor, Glamis, all, as the Weïrd Women promised, and I fear thou play'dst most foully for it.
Yet they said I should be the root and father
Of many kings. If there come truth from them —
As upon thee, Macbeth, their speeches shine —
May they not be my oracles as well,
And set me up in hope?
But hush! No more.

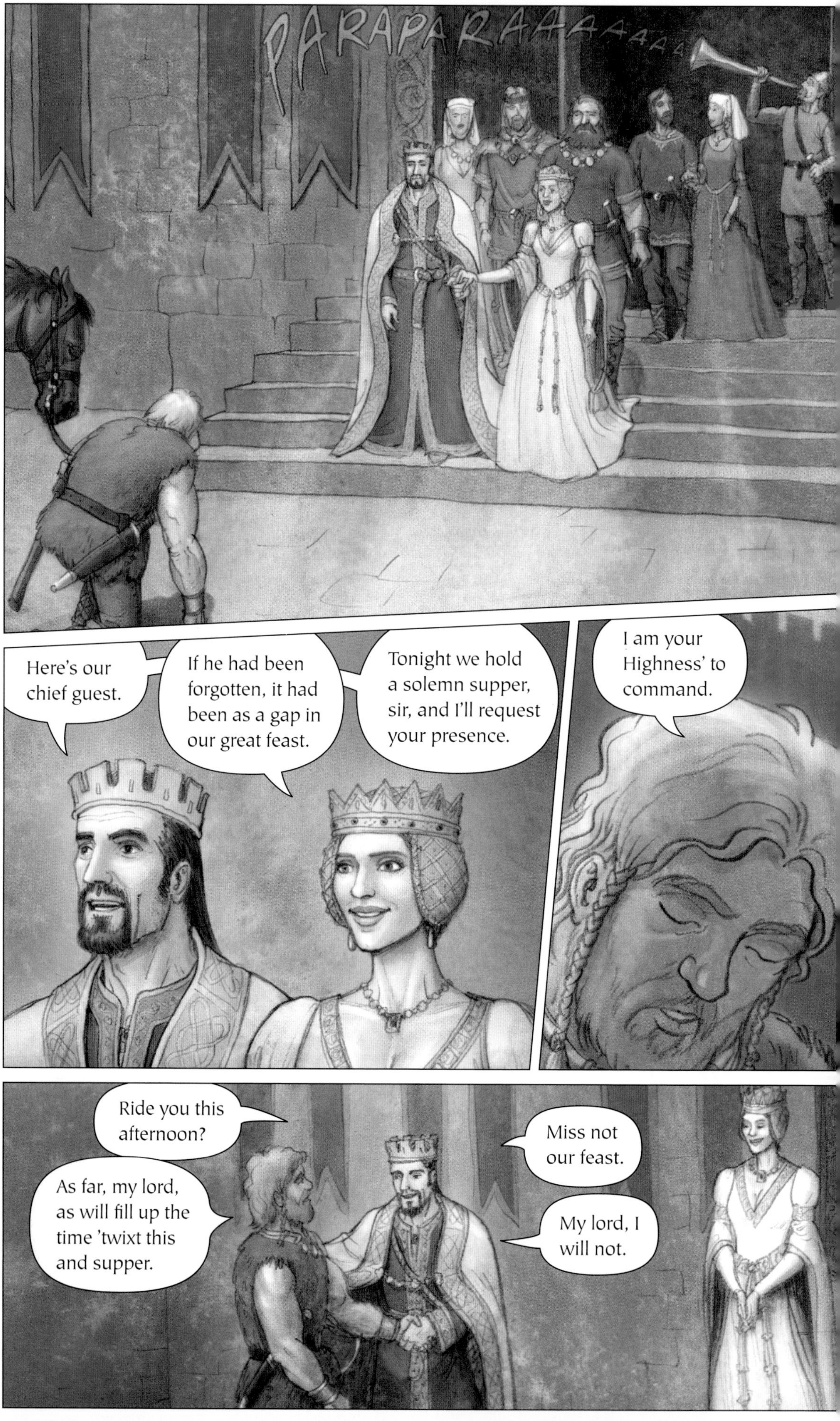
PARAPARAAAAAAA
Here's our chief guest.
If he had been forgotten, it had been as a gap in our great feast.
Tonight we hold a solemn supper, sir, and I'll request your presence.
I am your Highness' to command.
Ride you this afternoon?
As far, my lord, as will fill up the time 'twixt this and supper.
Miss not our feast.
My lord, I will not.

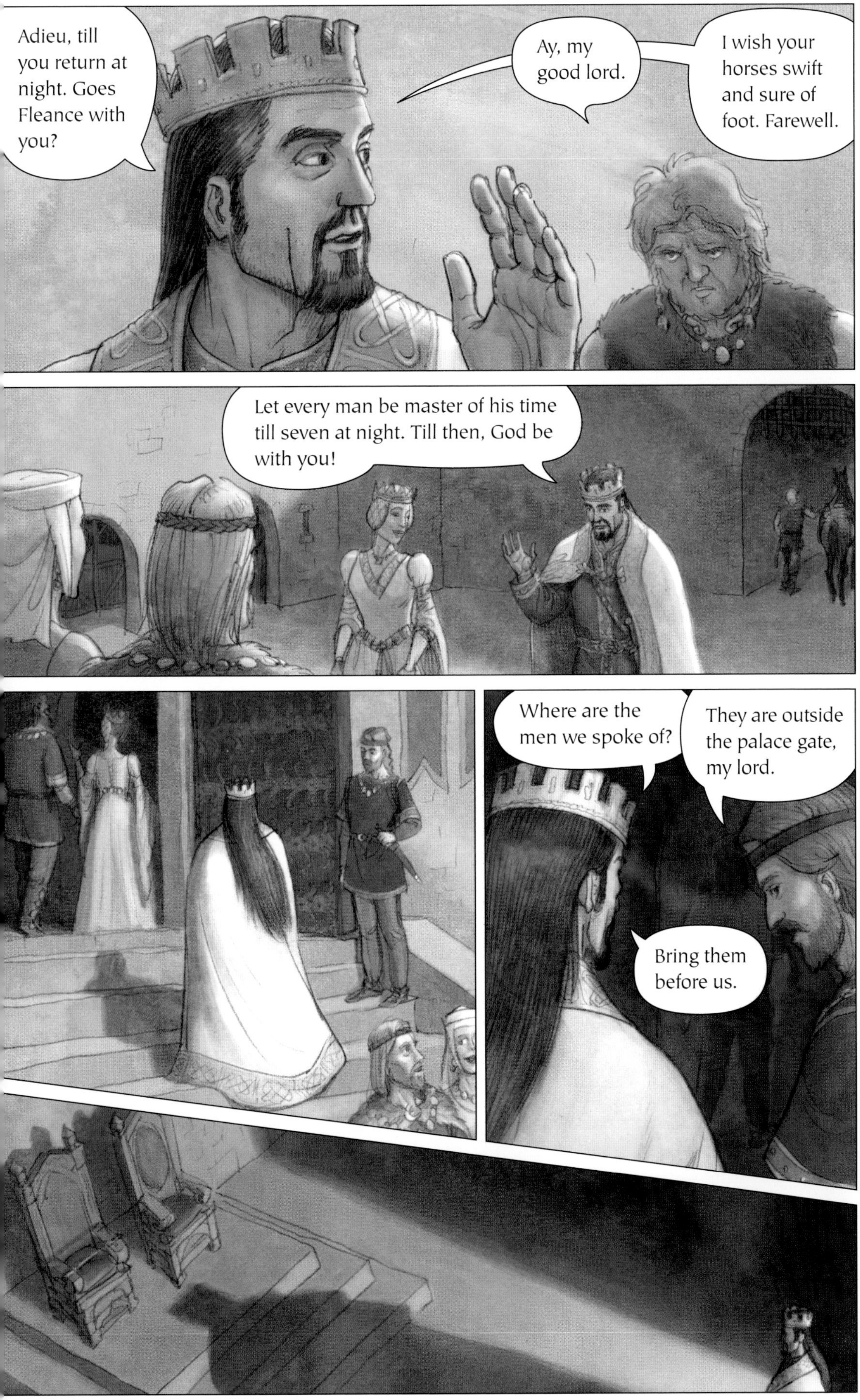
Adieu, till you return at night. Goes Fleance with you?
Ay, my good lord.
I wish your horses swift and sure of foot. Farewell.
Let every man be master of his time till seven at night. Till then, God be with you!
Where are the men we spoke of?
They are outside the palace gate, my lord.
Bring them before us.

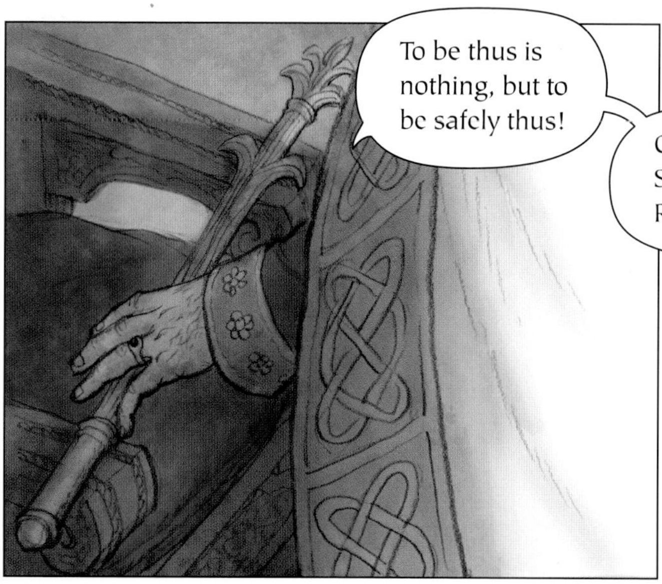
To be thus is nothing, but to be safely thus!
Our fears in Banquo
Stick deep, and in his royalty of nature
Reigns that which would be feared.

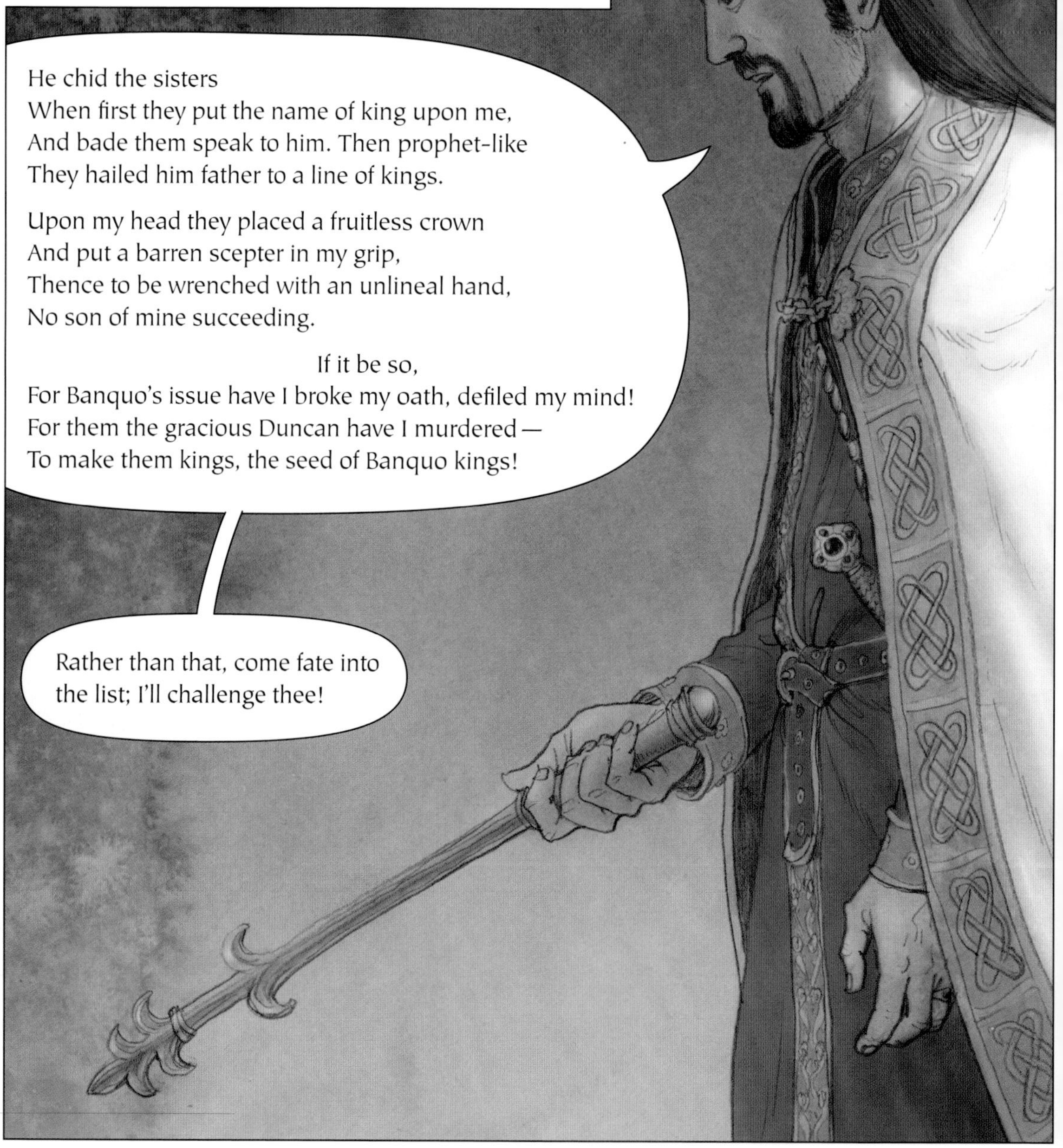
He chid the sisters
When first they put the name of king upon me,
And bade them speak to him. Then prophet-like
They hailed him father to a line of kings.
Upon my head they placed a fruitless crown
And put a barren scepter in my grip,
Thence to be wrenched with an unlineal hand,
No son of mine succeeding.
If it be so,
For Banquo's issue have I broke my oath, defiled my mind!
For them the gracious Duncan have I murdered—
To make them kings, the seed of Banquo kings!
Rather than that, come fate into the list; I'll challenge thee!

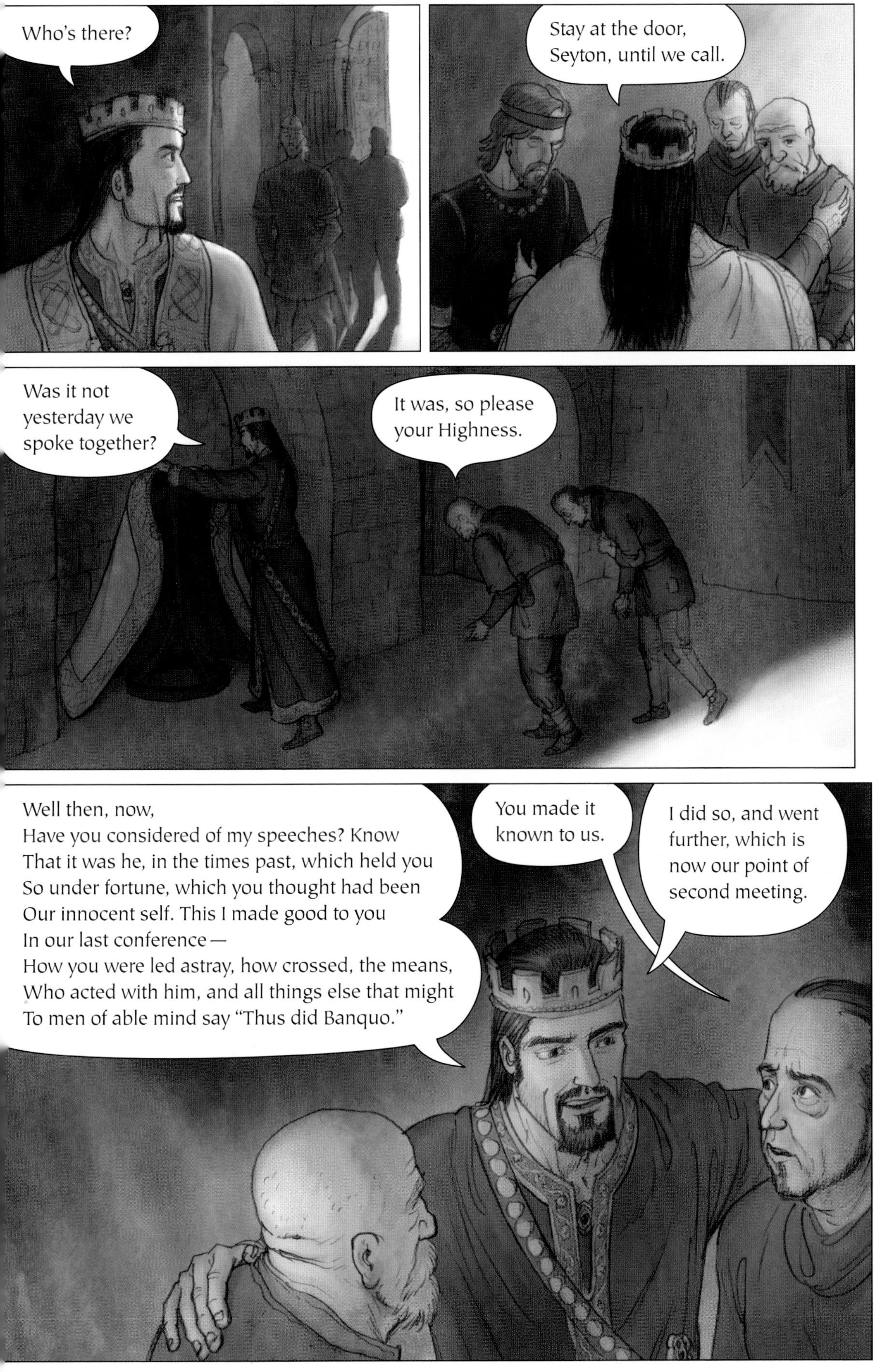

Who's there?
Stay at the door, Seyton, until we call.
Was it not yesterday we spoke together?
It was, so please your Highness.
Well then, now,
Have you considered of my speeches? Know
That it was he, in the times past, which held you
So under fortune, which you thought had been
Our innocent self. This I made good to you
In our last conference—
How you were led astray, how crossed, the means,
Who acted with him, and all things else that might
To men of able mind say "Thus did Banquo."
You made it known to us.
I did so, and went further, which is now our point of second meeting.

Is patience so predominant in your nature
That you can let this go? Are you so gospeled
To pray for this good man and for his issue,
Whose heavy hand hath bowed you to the grave
And beggared yours forever?

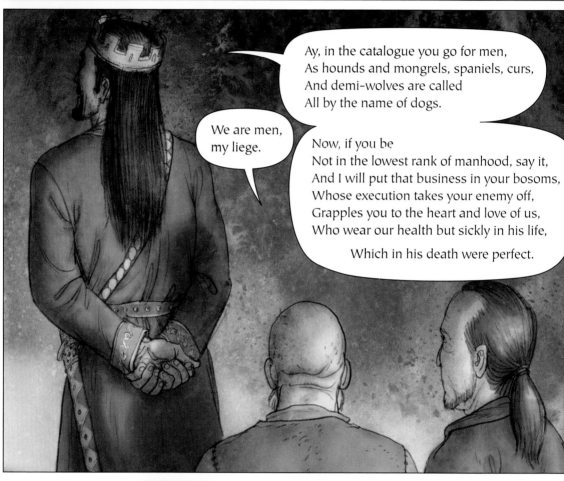

Ay, in the catalogue you go for men,
As hounds and mongrels, spaniels, curs,
And demi-wolves are called
All by the name of dogs.

We are men, my liege.

Now, if you be
Not in the lowest rank of manhood, say it,
And I will put that business in your bosoms,
Whose execution takes your enemy off,
Grapples you to the heart and love of us,
Who wear our health but sickly in his life,

Which in his death were perfect.

I am one, my liege, whom the vile blows and buffets of the world have so incensed that I am reckless what I do to spite the world.

And I another.

66

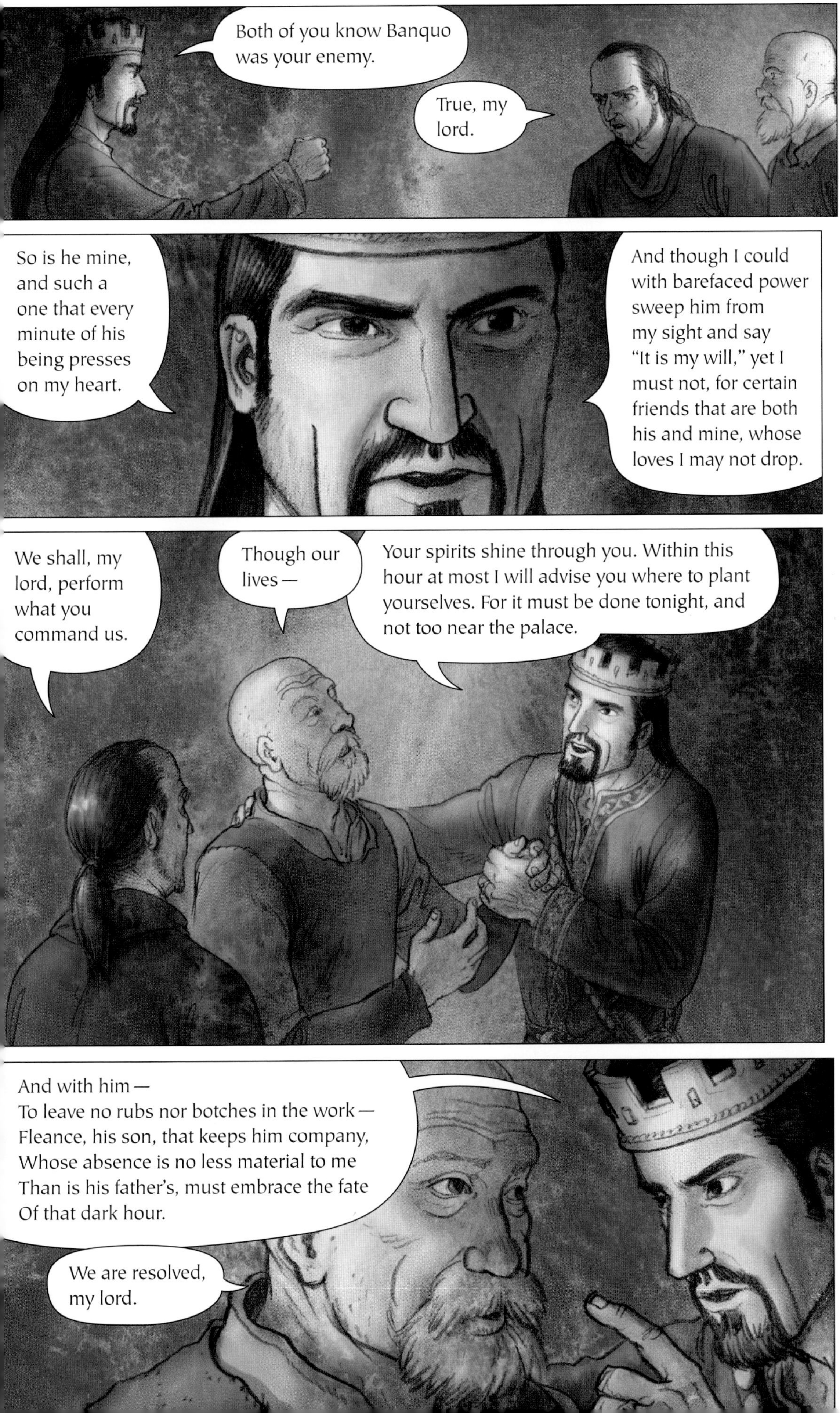
Both of you know Banquo was your enemy.
True, my lord.
So is he mine, and such a one that every minute of his being presses on my heart.
And though I could with barefaced power sweep him from my sight and say "It is my will," yet I must not, for certain friends that are both his and mine, whose loves I may not drop.
We shall, my lord, perform what you command us.
Though our lives —
Your spirits shine through you. Within this hour at most I will advise you where to plant yourselves. For it must be done tonight, and not too near the palace.
And with him —
To leave no rubs nor botches in the work —
Fleance, his son, that keeps him company,
Whose absence is no less material to me
Than is his father's, must embrace the fate
Of that dark hour.
We are resolved, my lord.

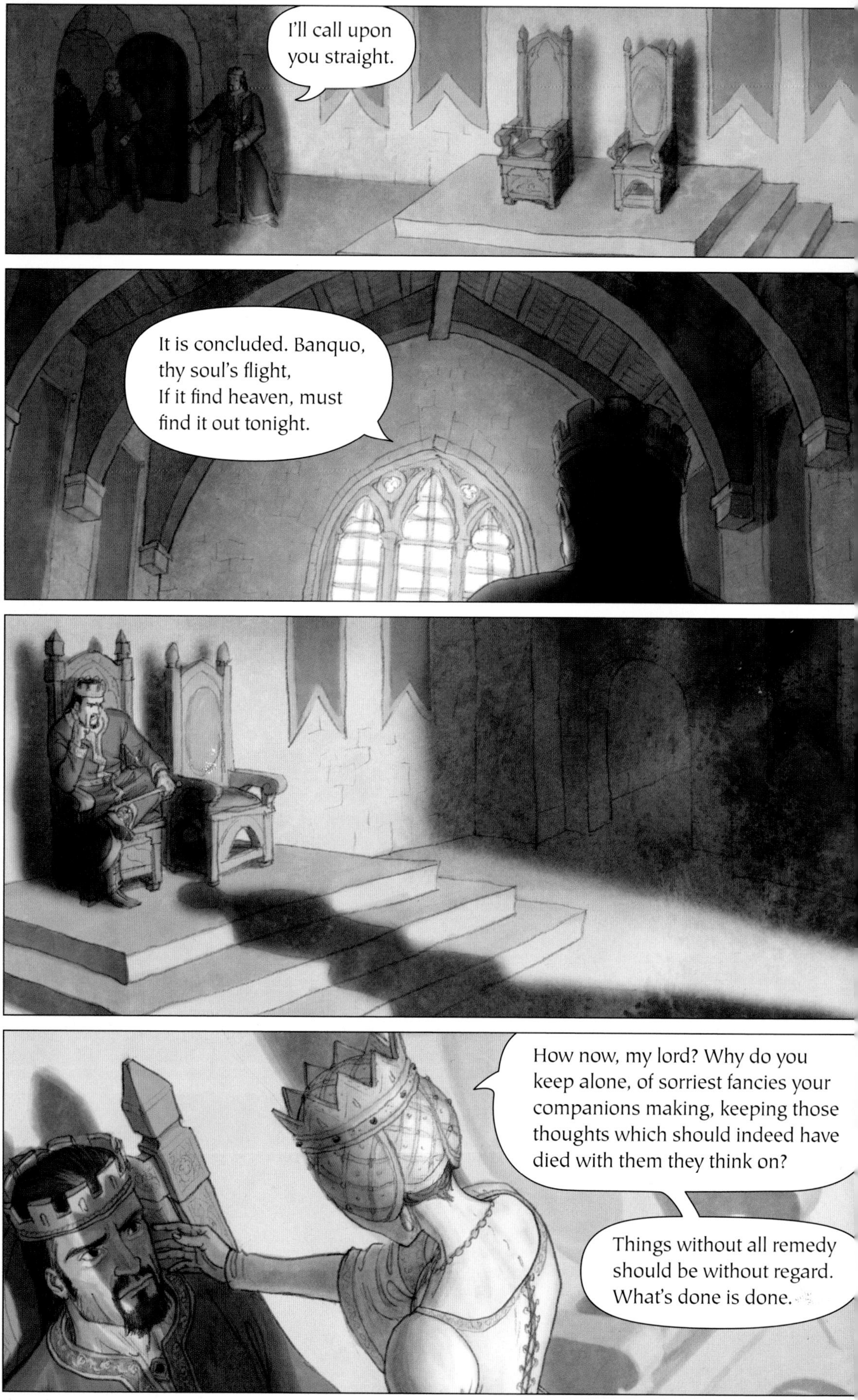

I'll call upon you straight.
It is concluded. Banquo, thy soul's flight, If it find heaven, must find it out tonight.
How now, my lord? Why do you keep alone, of sorriest fancies your companions making, keeping those thoughts which should indeed have died with them they think on?
Things without all remedy should be without regard. What's done is done.

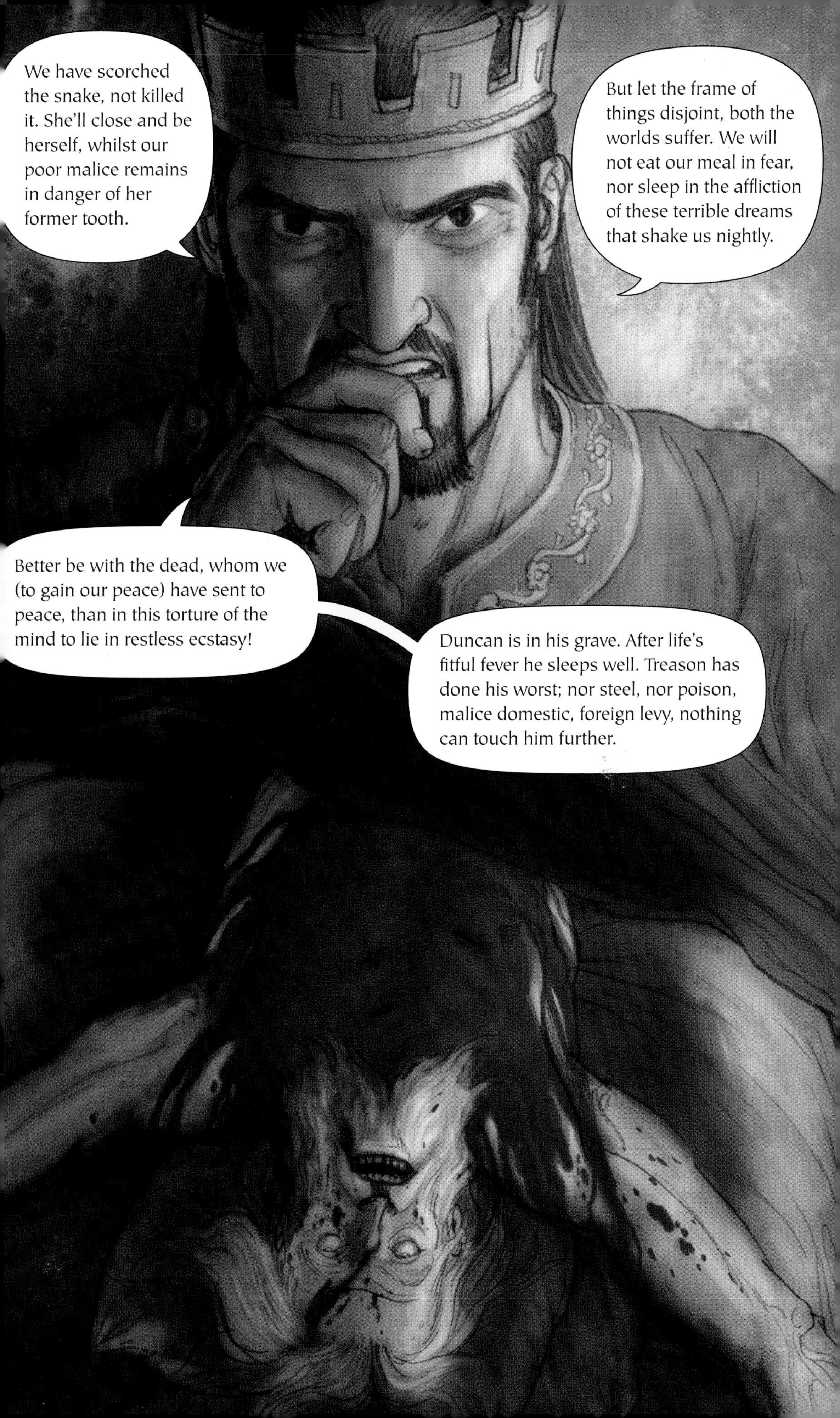
We have scorched the snake, not killed it. She'll close and be herself, whilst our poor malice remains in danger of her former tooth.
But let the frame of things disjoint, both the worlds suffer. We will not eat our meal in fear, nor sleep in the affliction of these terrible dreams that shake us nightly.
Better be with the dead, whom we (to gain our peace) have sent to peace, than in this torture of the mind to lie in restless ecstasy!
Duncan is in his grave. After life's fitful fever he sleeps well. Treason has done his worst; nor steel, nor poison, malice domestic, foreign levy, nothing can touch him further.

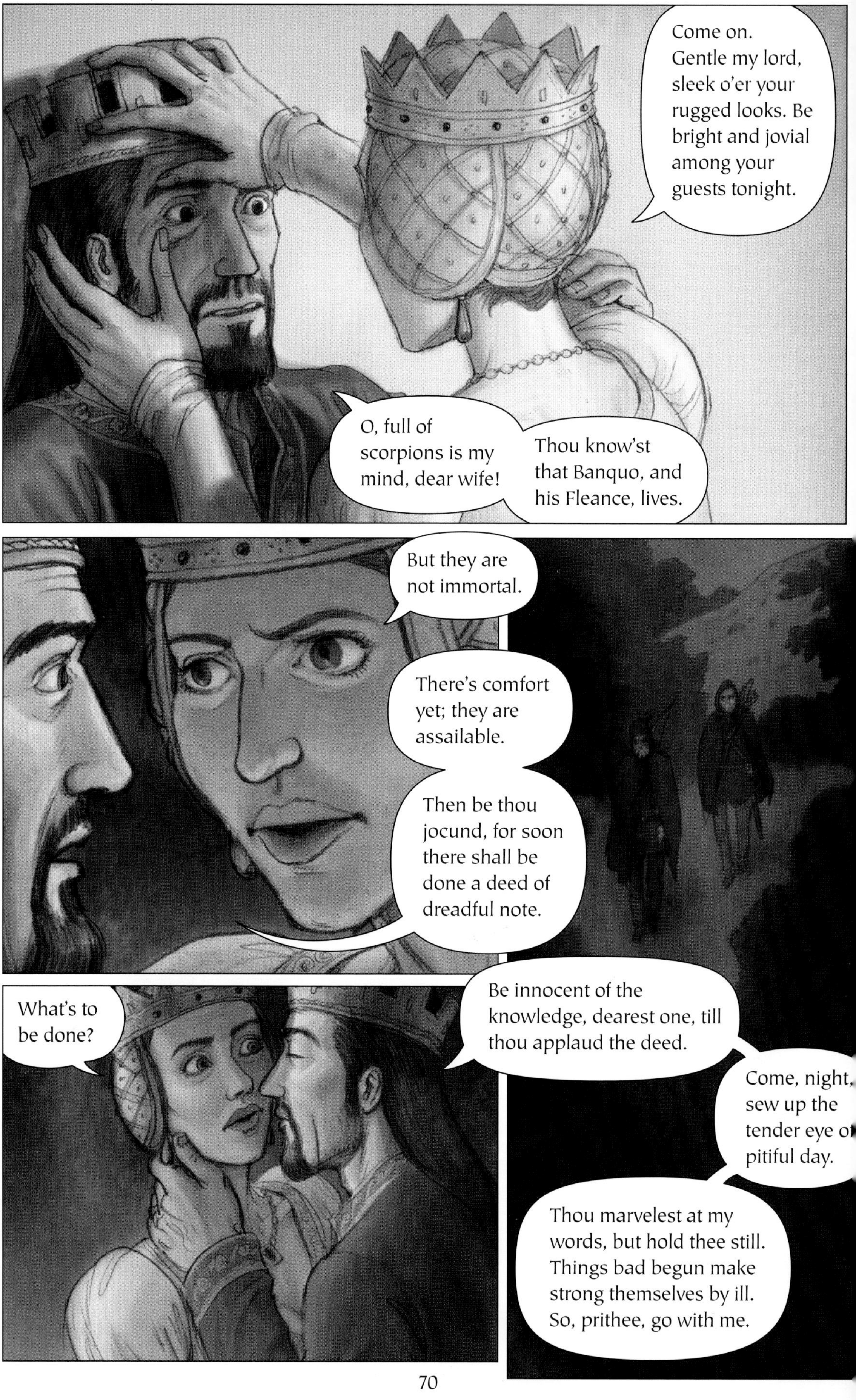
Come on. Gentle my lord, sleek o'er your rugged looks. Be bright and jovial among your guests tonight.
O, full of scorpions is my mind, dear wife!
Thou know'st that Banquo, and his Fleance, lives.
But they are not immortal.
There's comfort yet; they are assailable.
Then be thou jocund, for soon there shall be done a deed of dreadful note.
What's to be done?
Be innocent of the knowledge, dearest one, till thou applaud the deed.
Come, night, sew up the tender eye of pitiful day.
Thou marvelest at my words, but hold thee still. Things bad begun make strong themselves by ill. So, prithee, go with me.

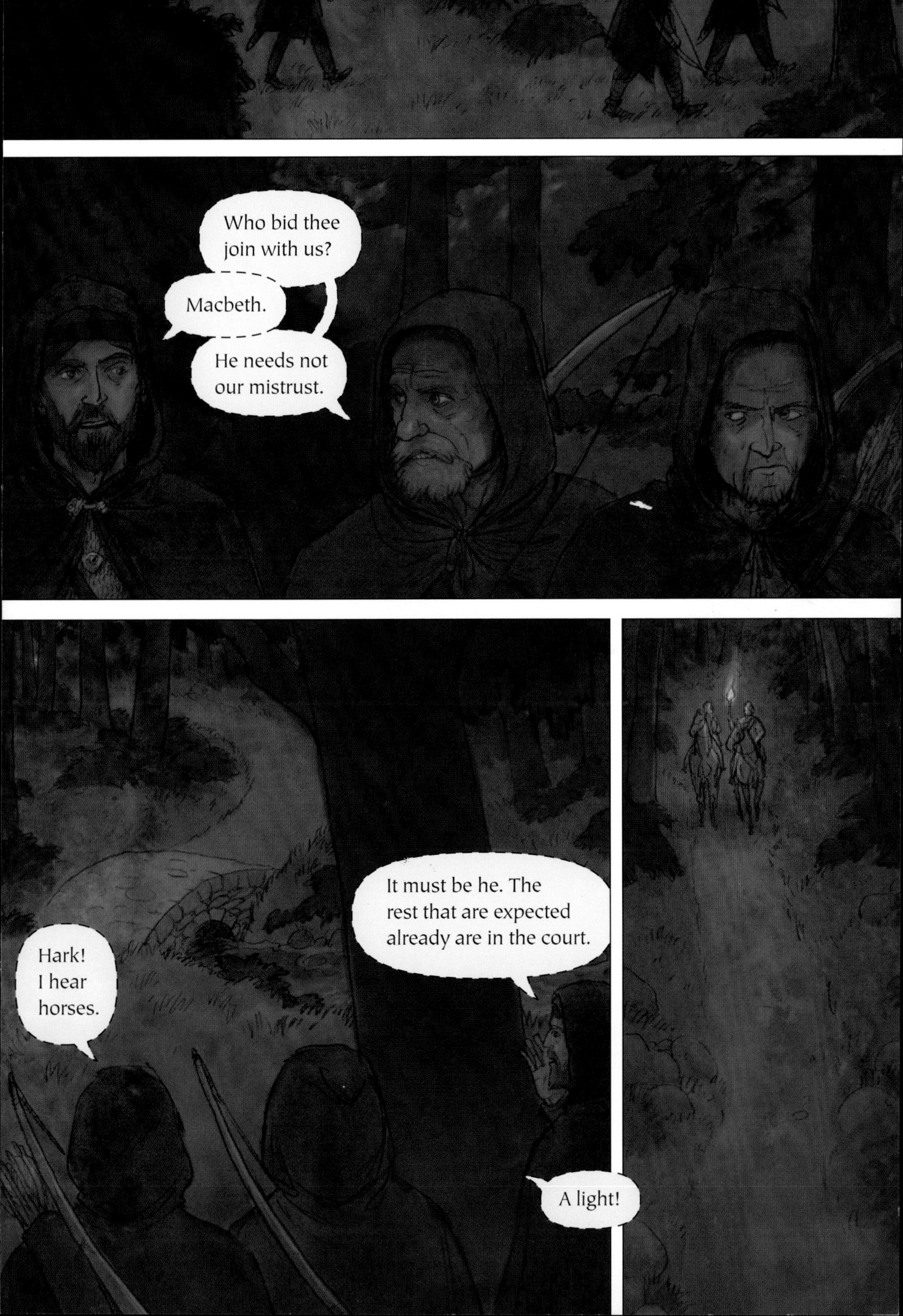
Who bid thee join with us?
Macbeth.
He needs not our mistrust.
Hark! I hear horses.
It must be he. The rest that are expected already are in the court.
A light!

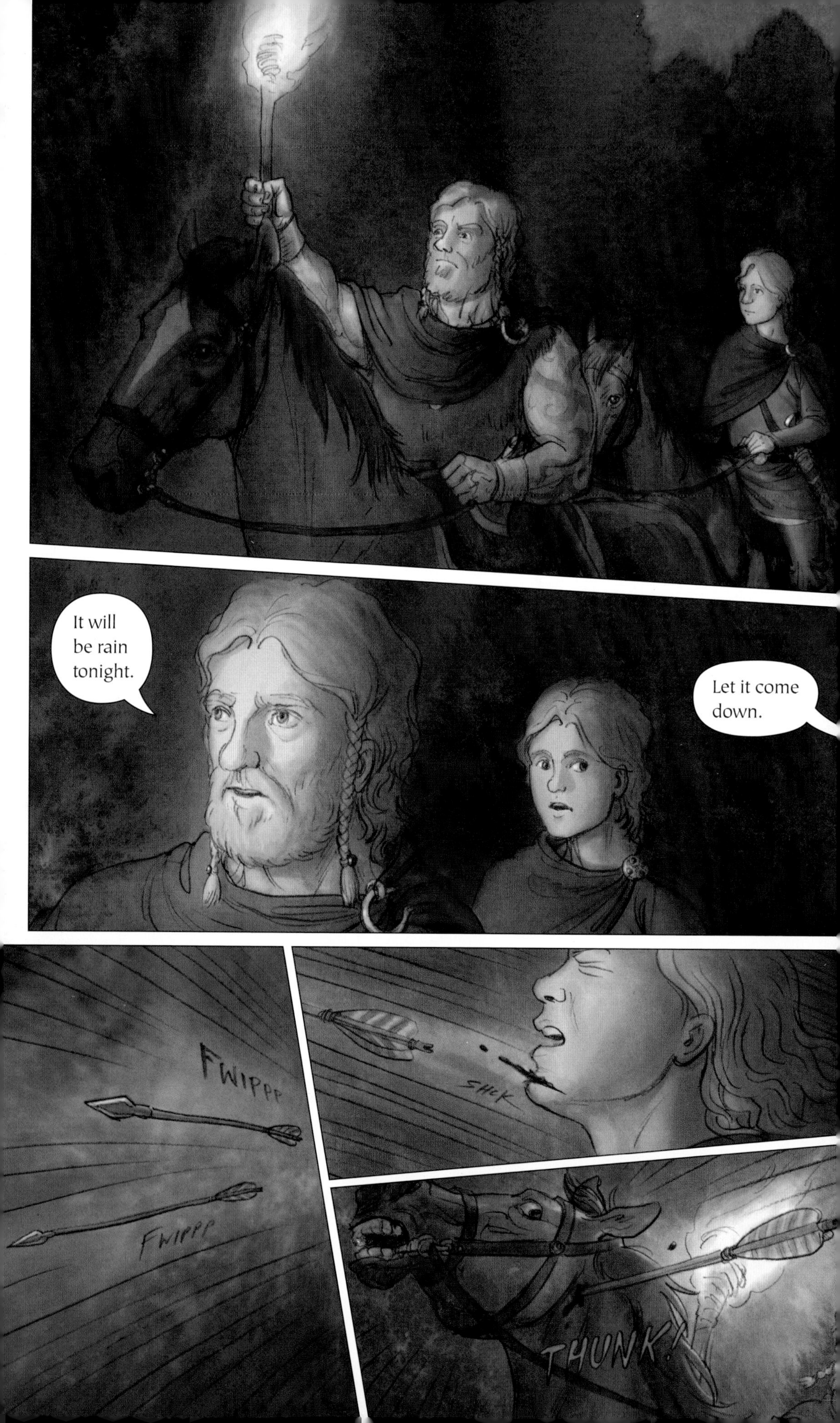
It will be rain tonight.
Let it come down.
FWIPPP
FWIPPP
SHUK
THUNK!

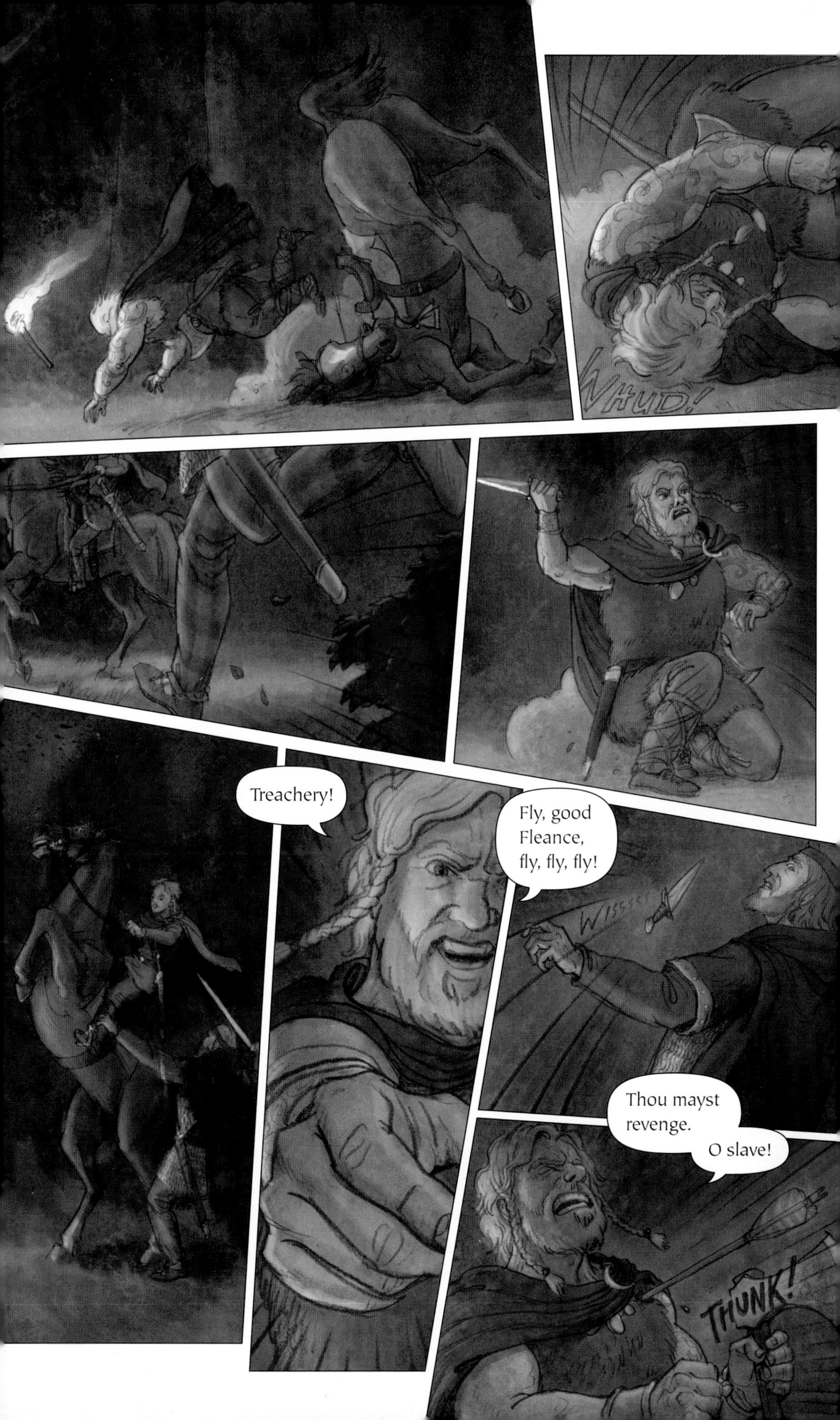
WHUD!
Treachery!
Fly, good Fleance, fly, fly, fly!
Thou mayst revenge.
O slave!
THUNK!

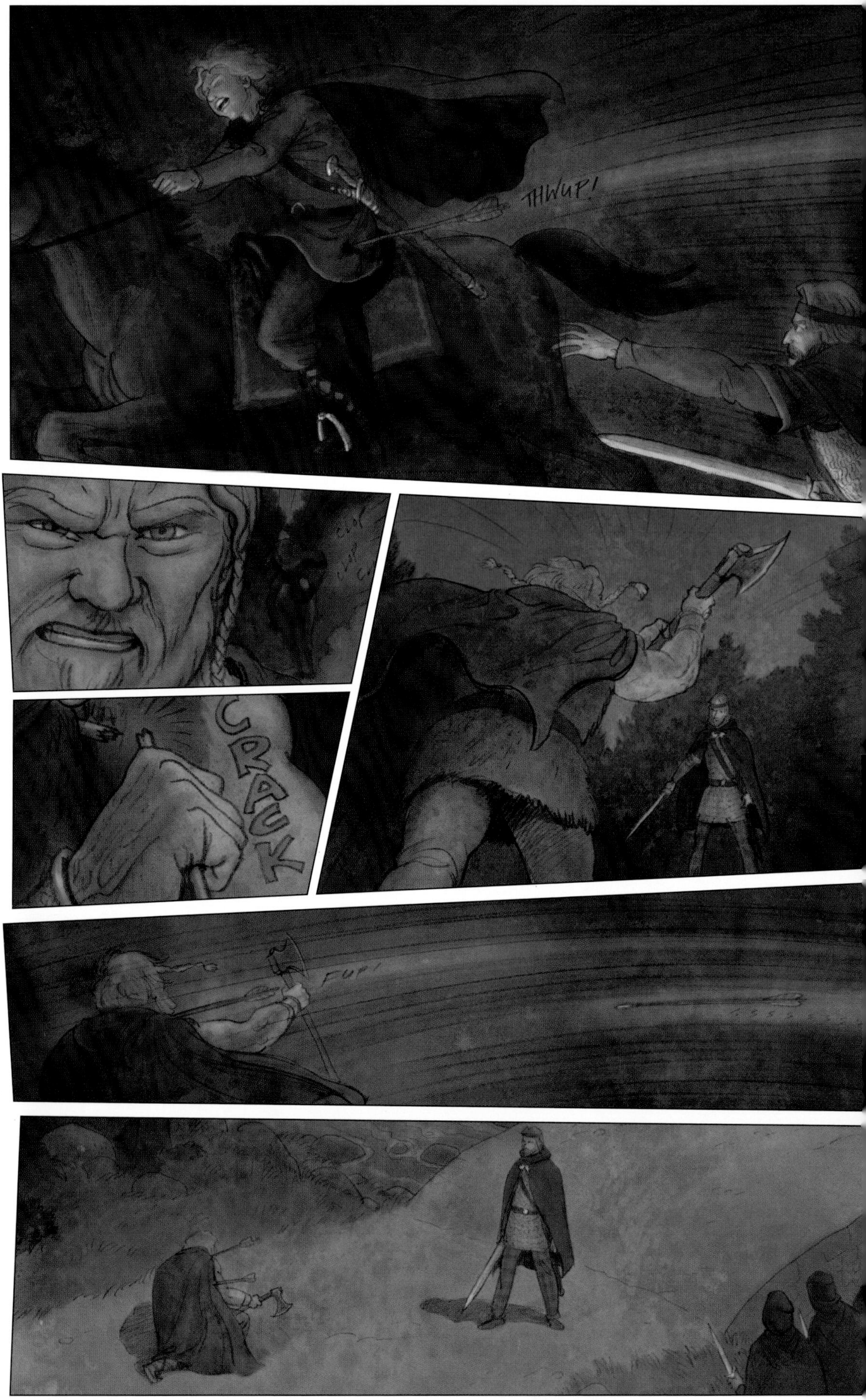
THWUP!
CRACK
FUP!

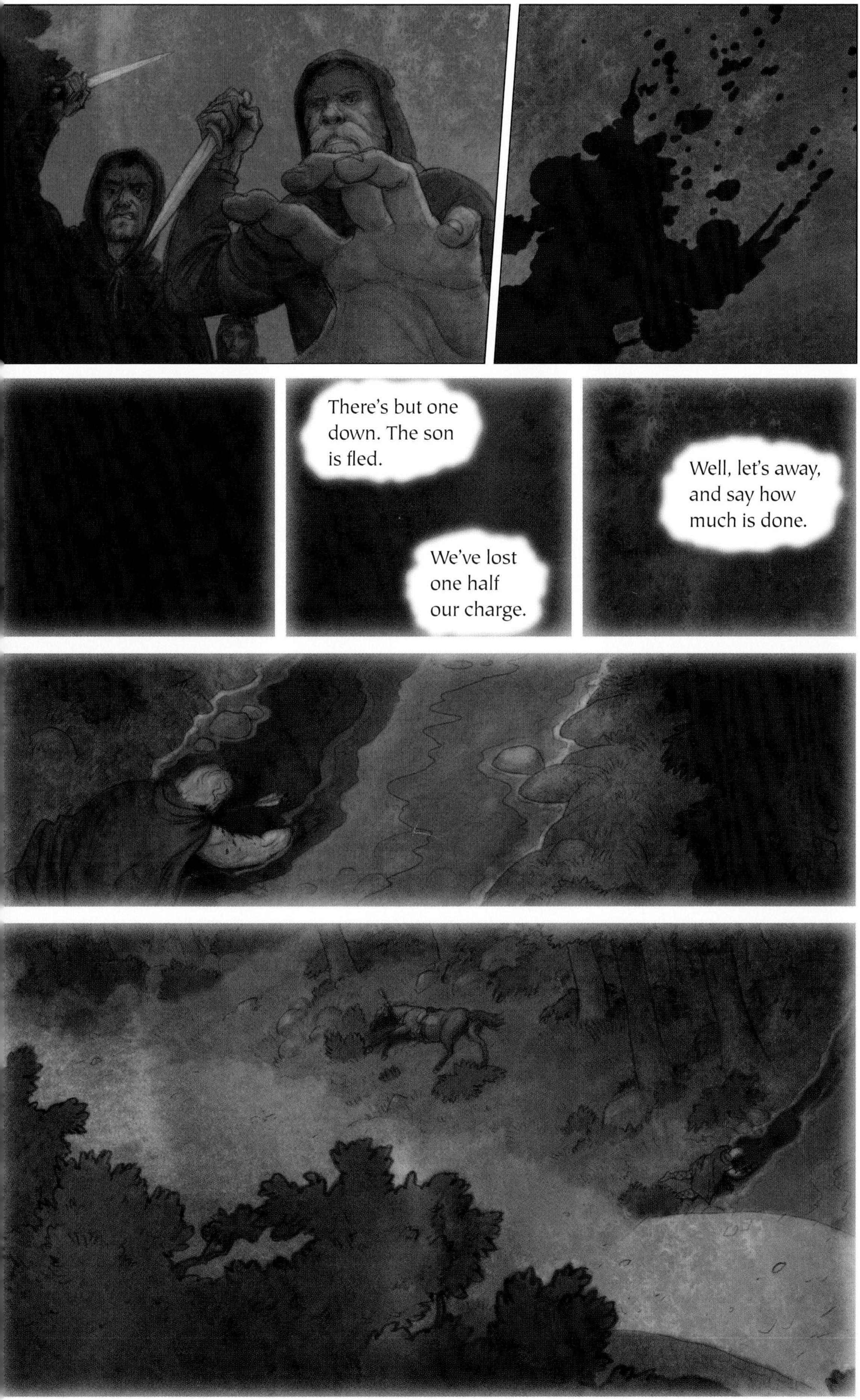
There's but one down. The son is fled.
We've lost one half our charge.
Well, let's away, and say how much is done.

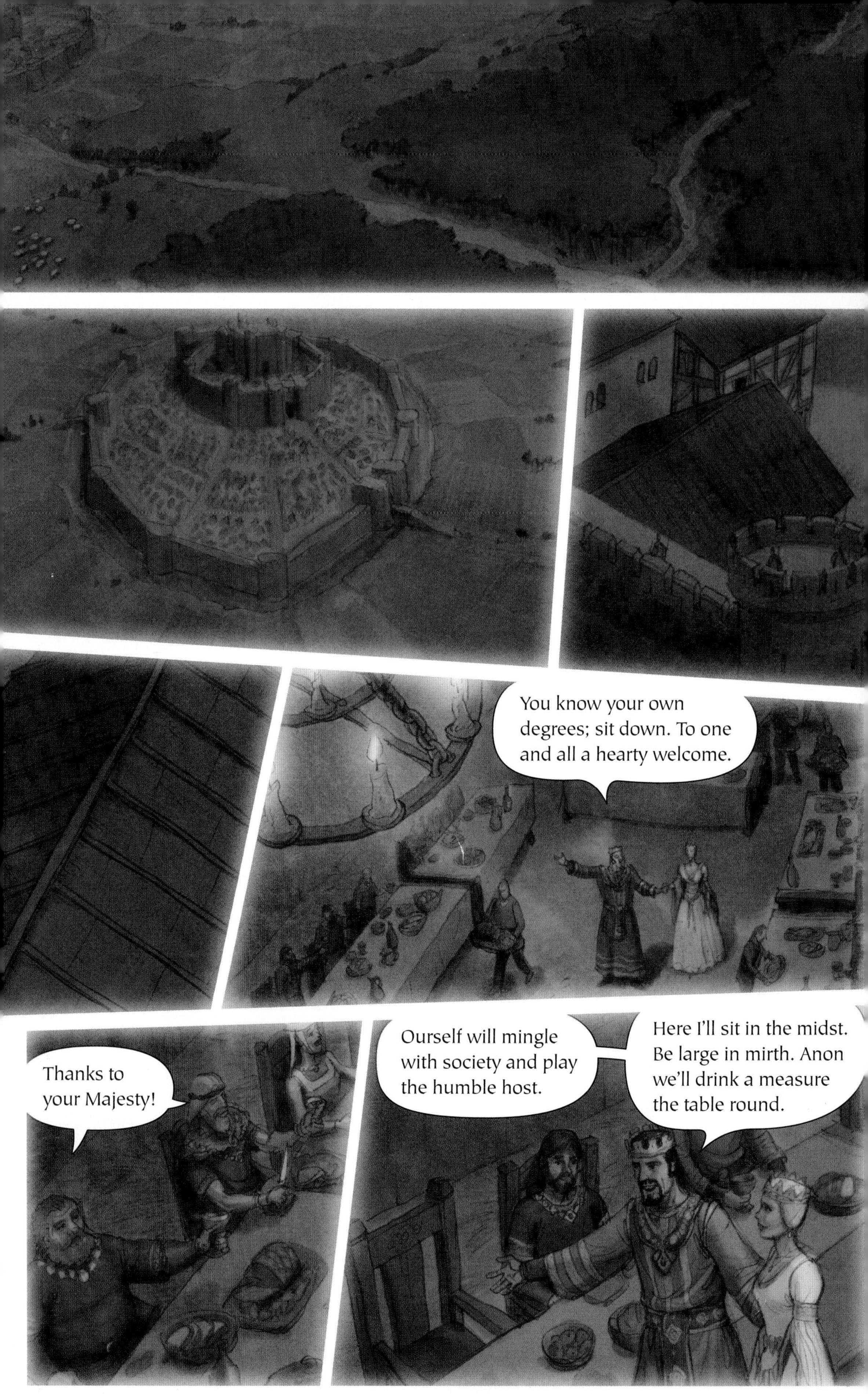
You know your own degrees; sit down. To one and all a hearty welcome.
Thanks to your Majesty!
Ourself will mingle with society and play the humble host.
Here I'll sit in the midst. Be large in mirth. Anon we'll drink a measure the table round.

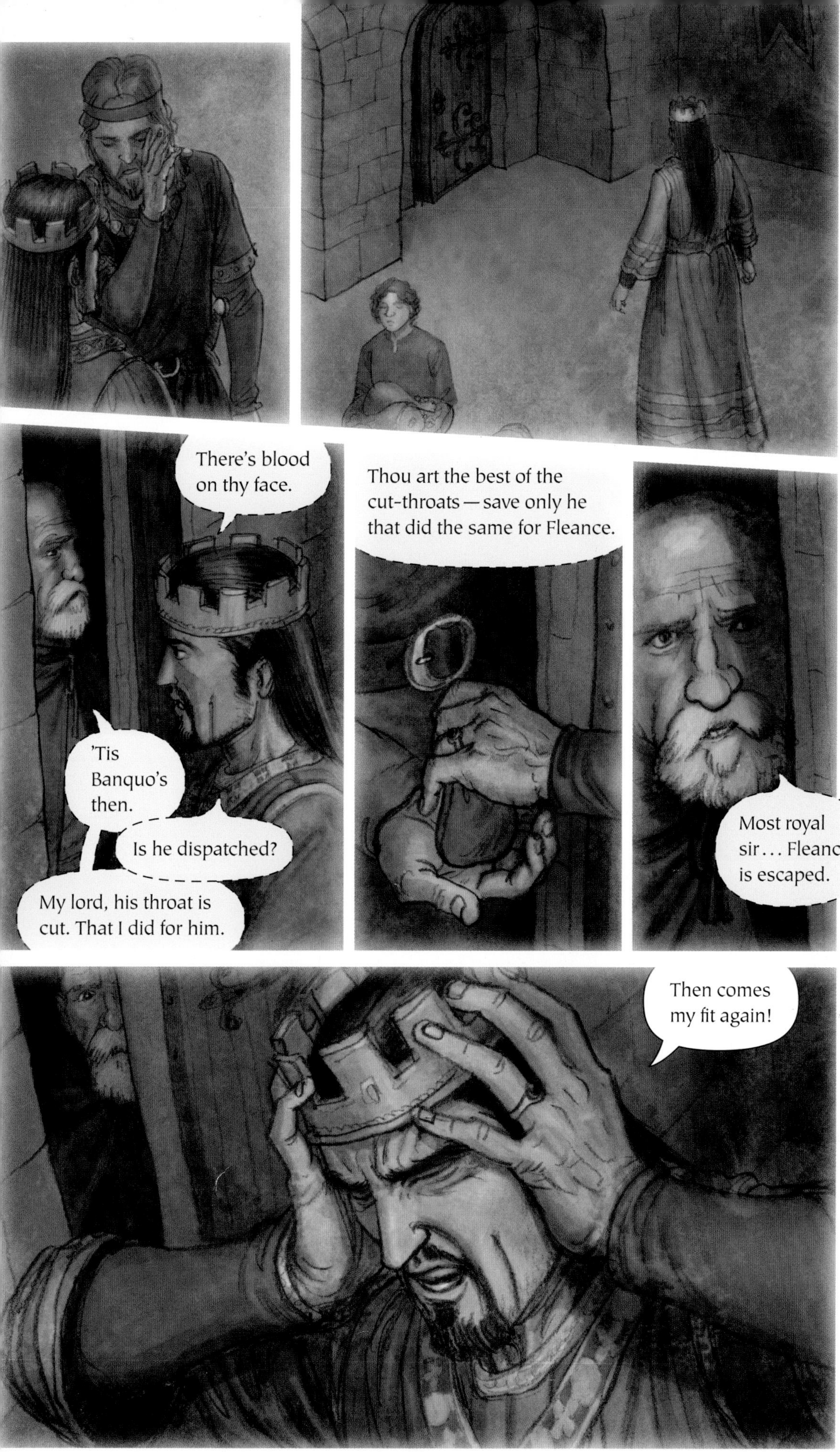
There's blood on thy face.
'Tis Banquo's then.
Is he dispatched?
My lord, his throat is cut. That I did for him.
Thou art the best of the cut-throats — save only he that did the same for Fleance.
Most royal sir . . . Fleance is escaped.
Then comes my fit again!

I had else been perfect, Whole as the marble, solid as the rock, as vast and carefree as the open sky. But now I am cabined, cribbed, confined, bound in by teeming doubts and fears!

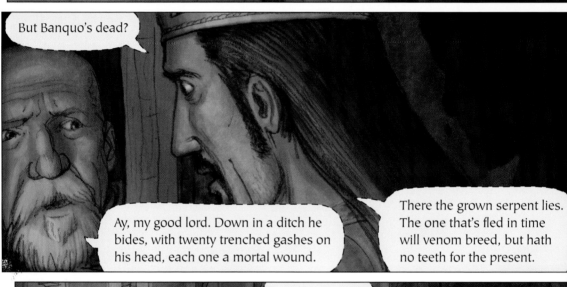

But Banquo's dead?

Ay, my good lord. Down in a ditch he bides, with twenty trenched gashes on his head, each one a mortal wound.

There the grown serpent lies. The one that's fled in time will venom breed, but hath no teeth for the present.

Get thee gone. Tomorrow we'll speak again.

My royal lord, you do not give good cheer. The sauce to meat is ceremony; dinner is bare without it.

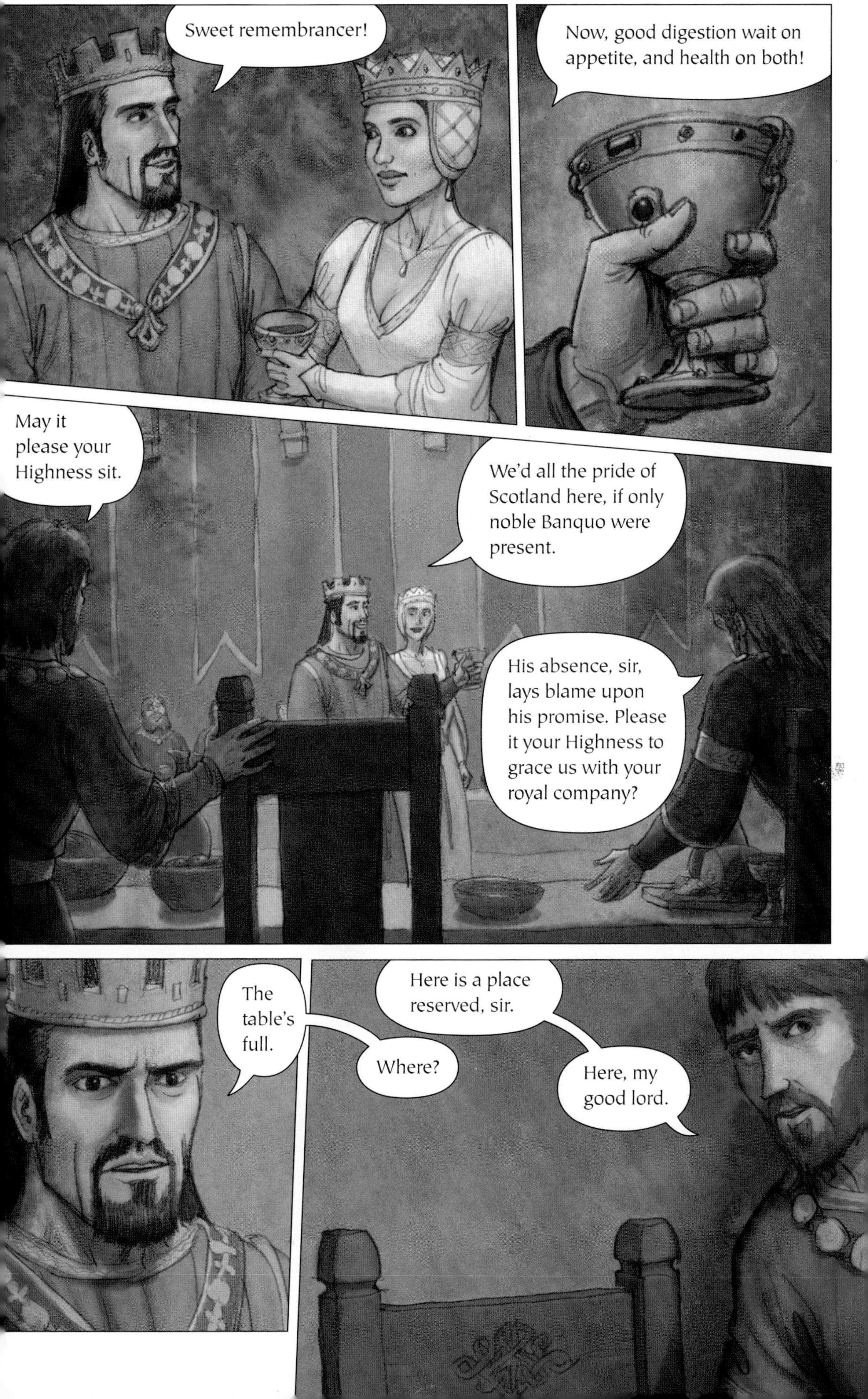
Sweet remembrancer!
Now, good digestion wait on appetite, and health on both!
May it please your Highness sit.
We'd all the pride of Scotland here, if only noble Banquo were present.
His absence, sir, lays blame upon his promise. Please it your Highness to grace us with your royal company?
The table's full.
Here is a place reserved, sir.
Where?
Here, my good lord.

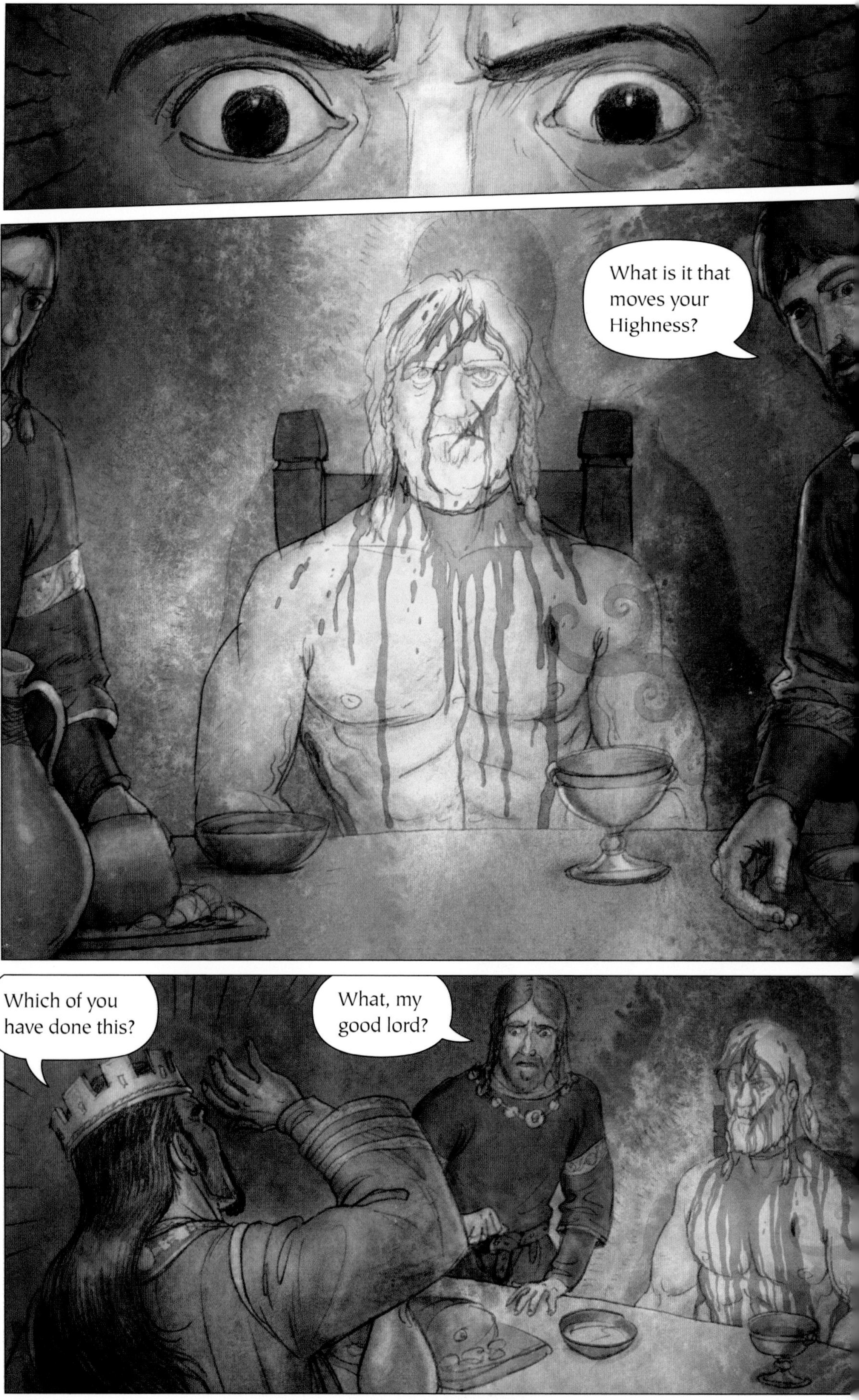
What is it that moves your Highness?
Which of you have done this?
What, my good lord?

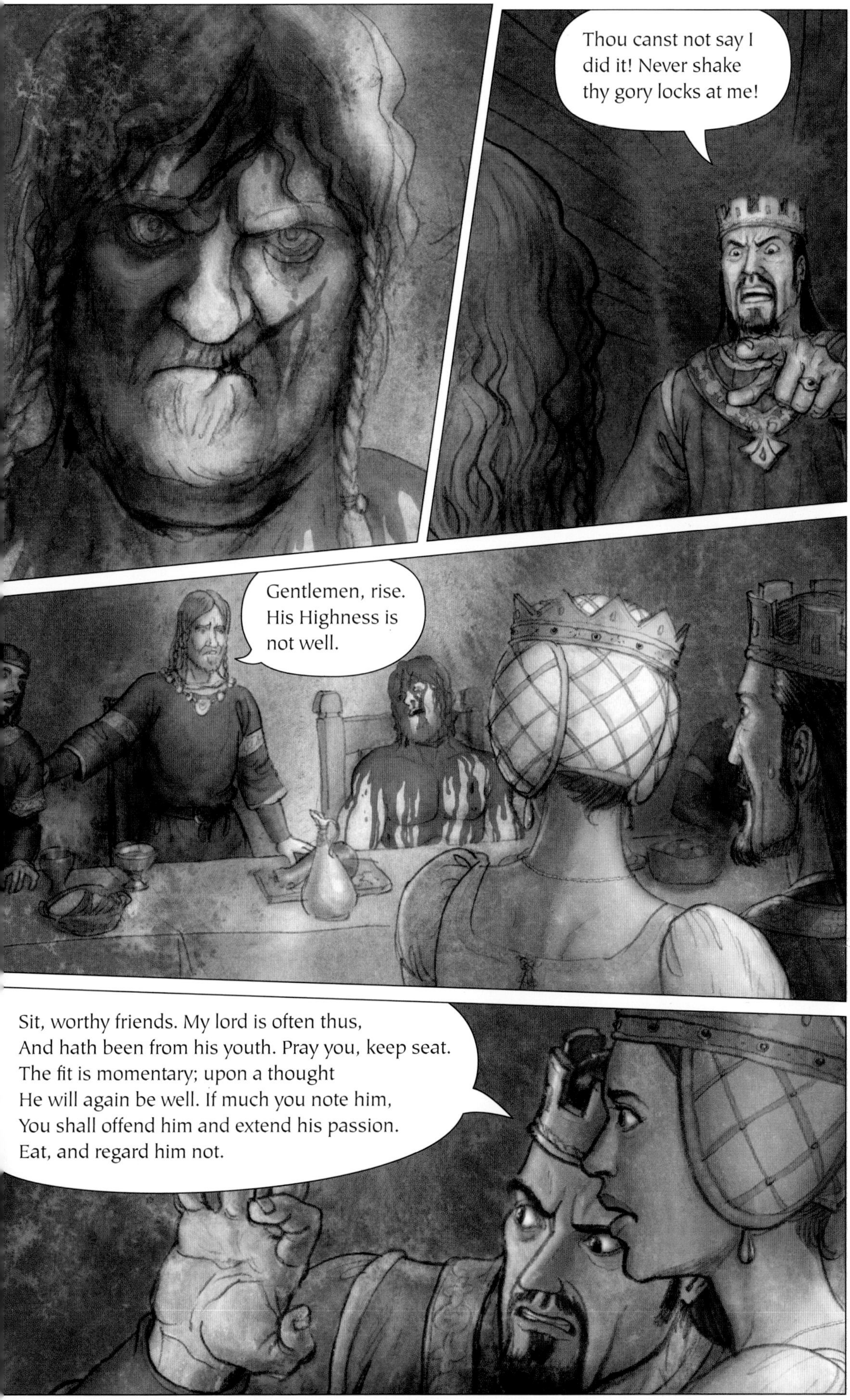
Thou canst not say I did it! Never shake thy gory locks at me!
Gentlemen, rise. His Highness is not well.
Sit, worthy friends. My lord is often thus,
And hath been from his youth. Pray you, keep seat.
The fit is momentary; upon a thought
He will again be well. If much you note him,
You shall offend him and extend his passion.
Eat, and regard him not.

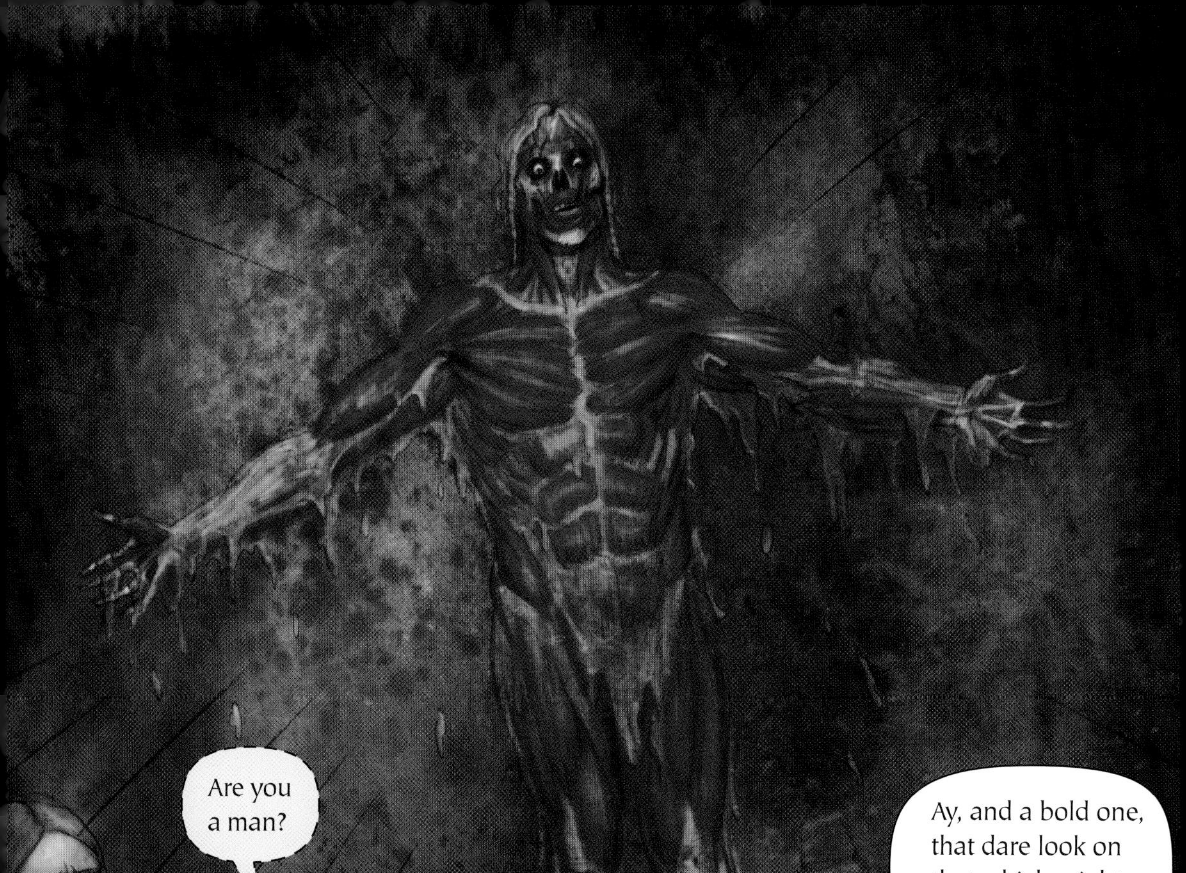
Are you a man?
Ay, and a bold one, that dare look on that which might appall the devil!

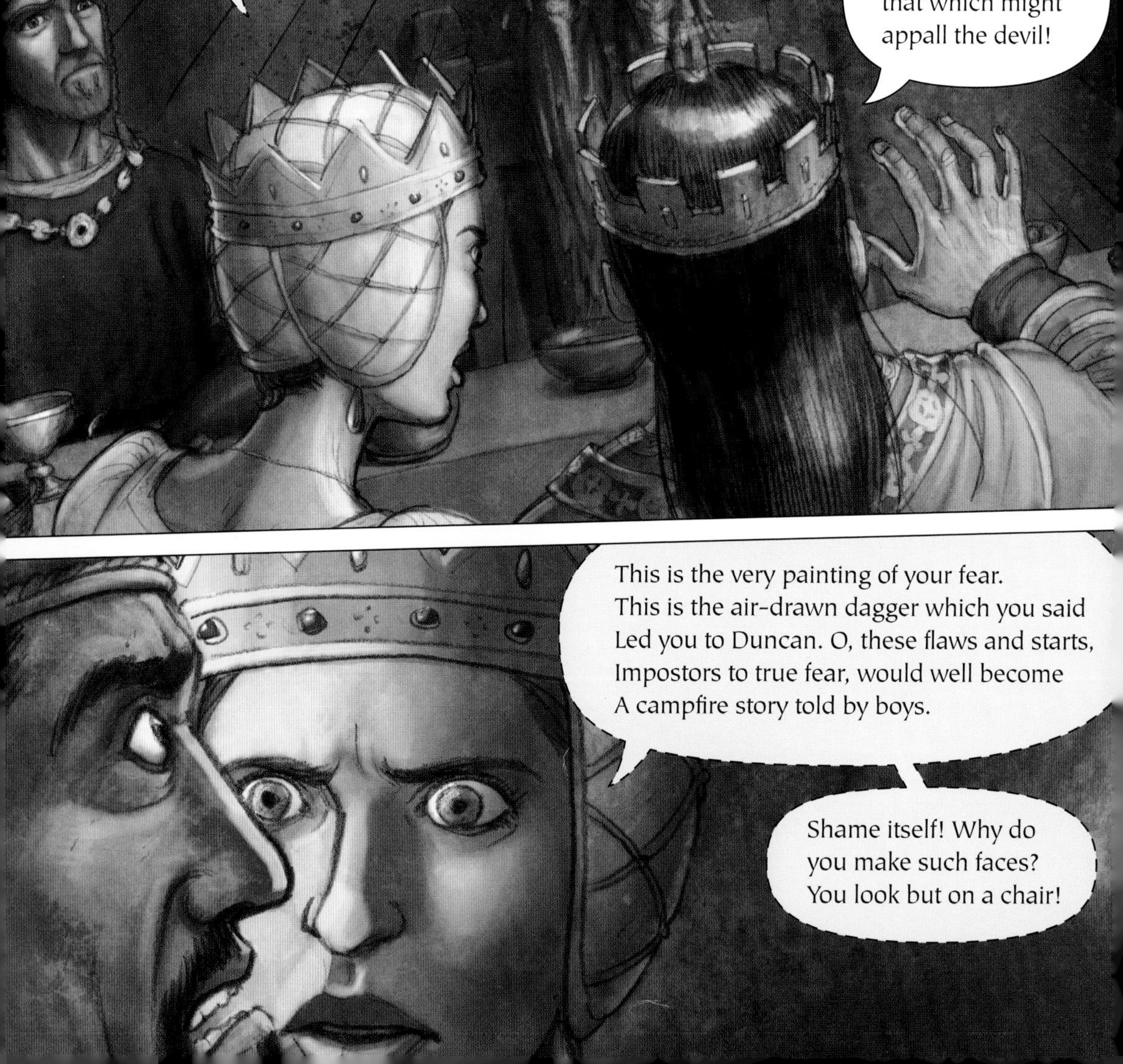
This is the very painting of your fear. This is the air-drawn dagger which you said Led you to Duncan. O, these flaws and starts, Impostors to true fear, would well become A campfire story told by boys.
Shame itself! Why do you make such faces? You look but on a chair!

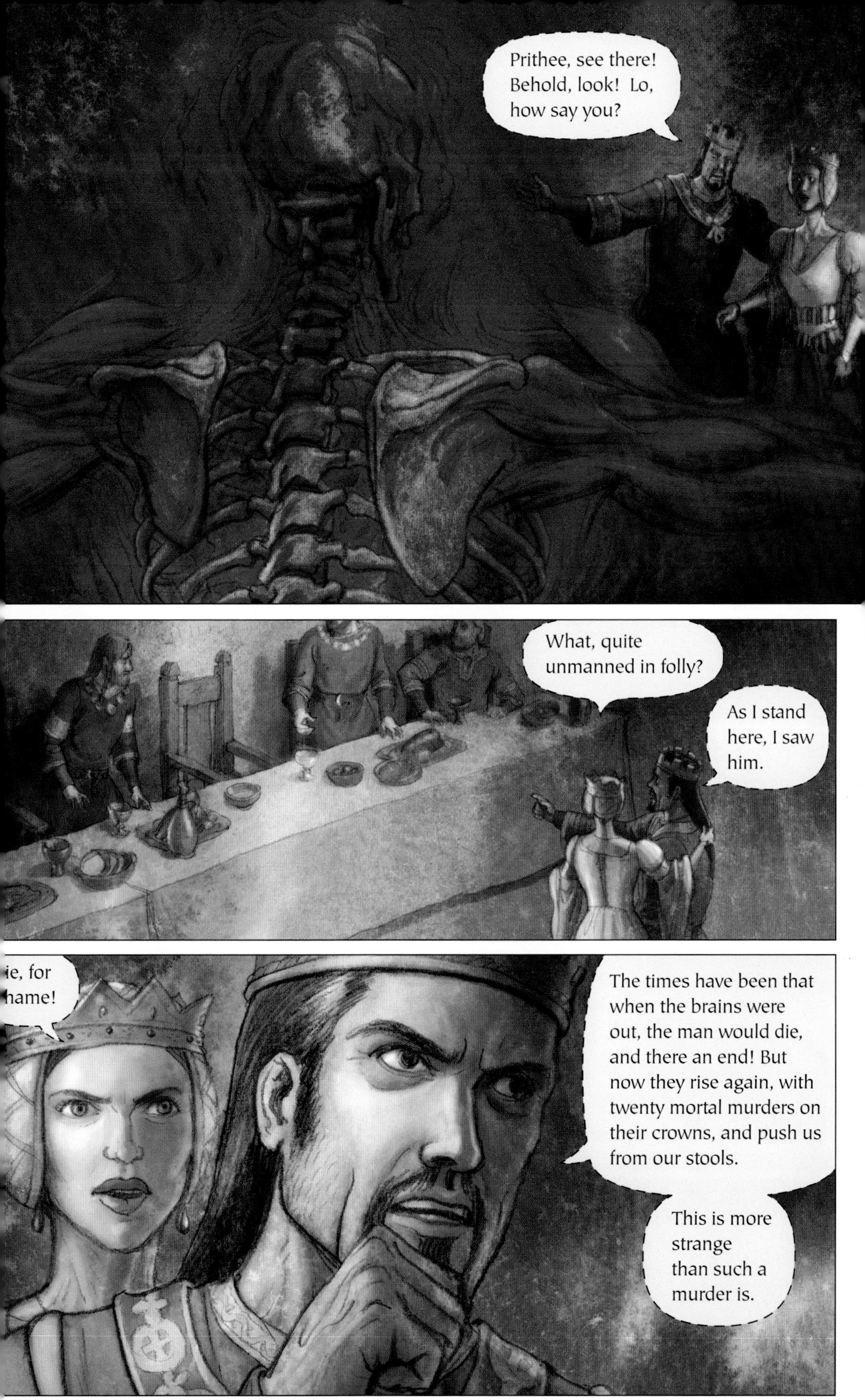
Prithee, see there! Behold, look! Lo, how say you?
What, quite unmanned in folly?
As I stand here, I saw him.
ie, for hame!
The times have been that when the brains were out, the man would die, and there an end! But now they rise again, with twenty mortal murders on their crowns, and push us from our stools.
This is more strange than such a murder is.

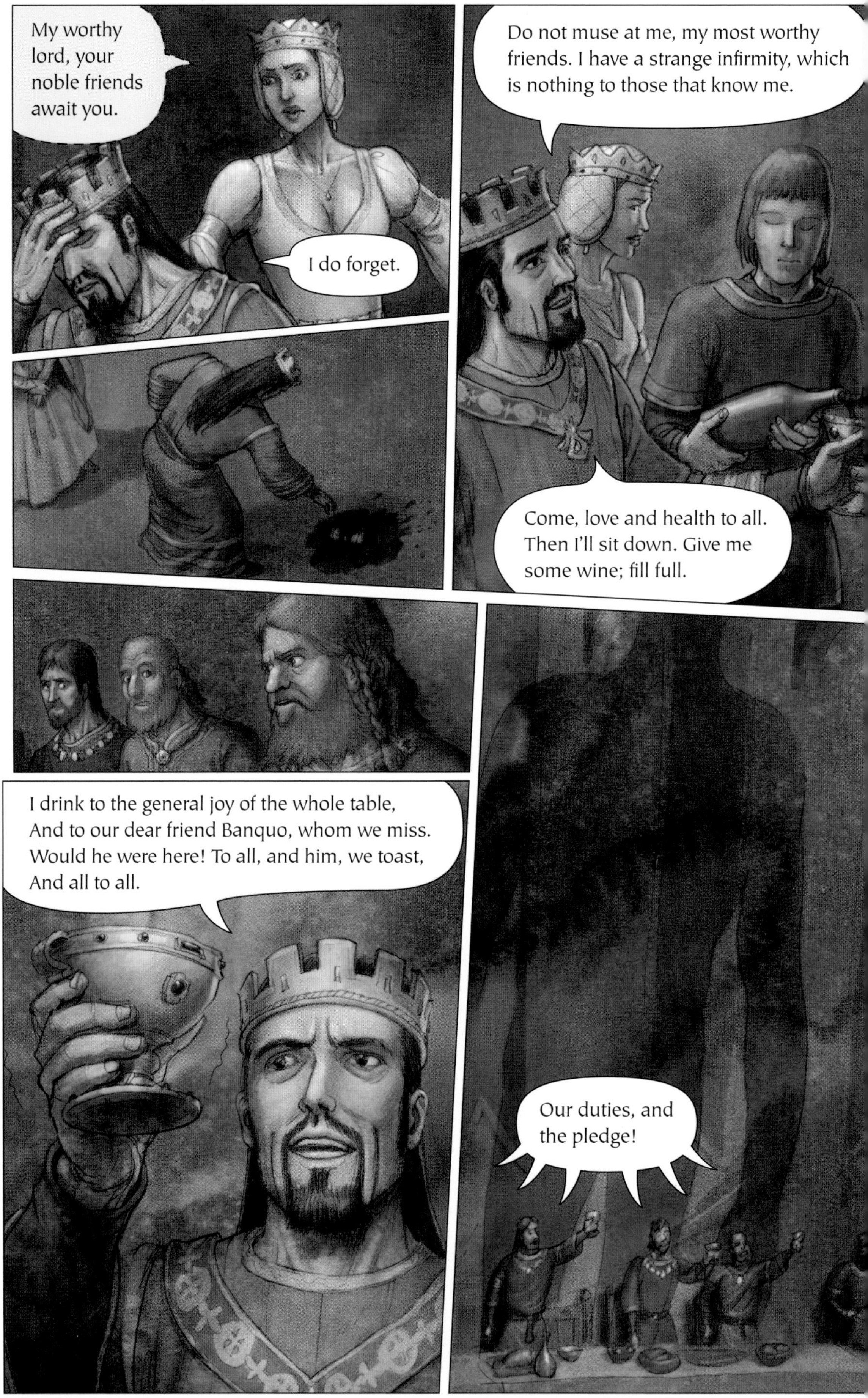
My worthy lord, your noble friends await you.
I do forget.
Do not muse at me, my most worthy friends. I have a strange infirmity, which is nothing to those that know me.
Come, love and health to all. Then I'll sit down. Give me some wine; fill full.
I drink to the general joy of the whole table,
And to our dear friend Banquo, whom we miss.
Would he were here! To all, and him, we toast,
And all to all.
Our duties, and the pledge!

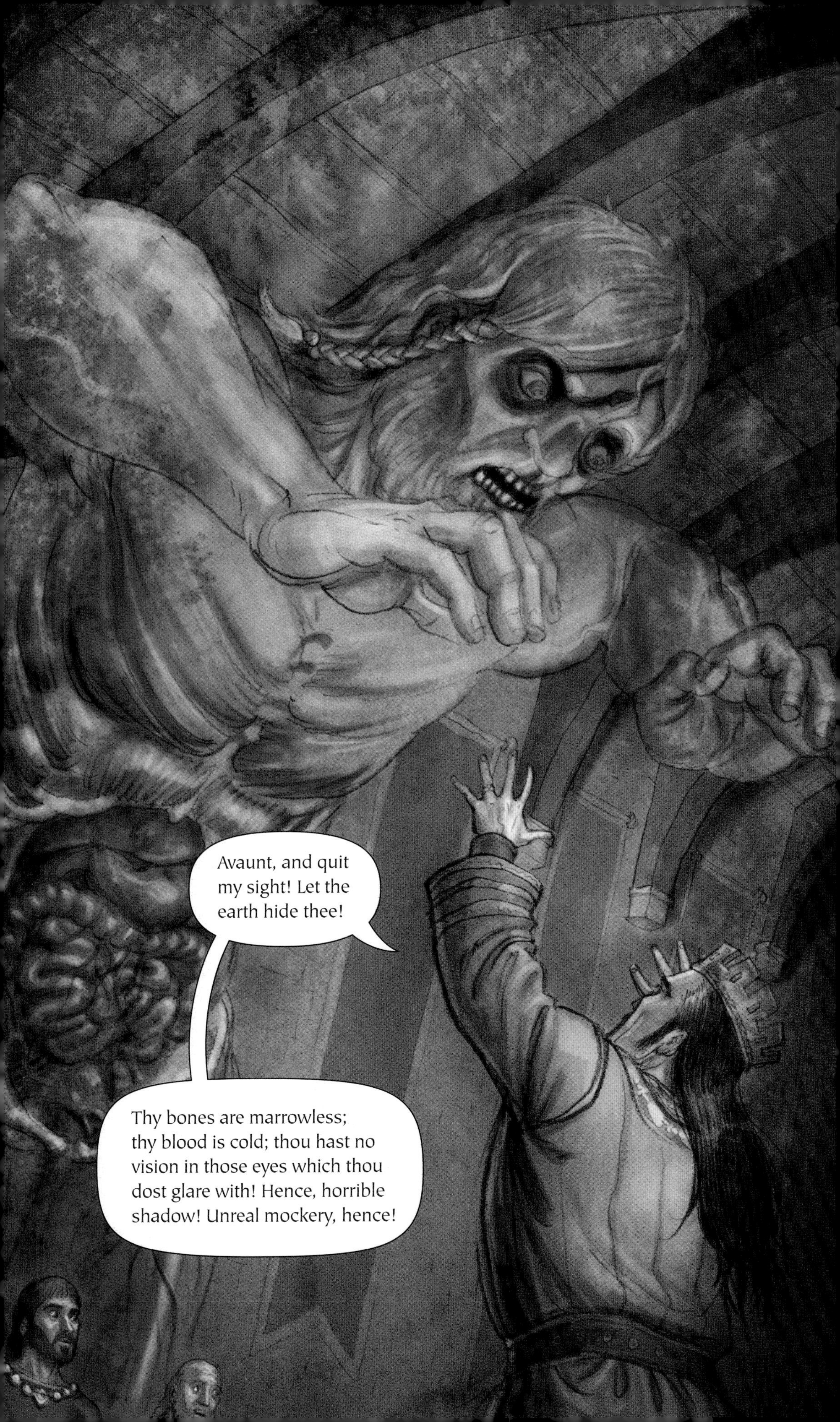
Avaunt, and quit my sight! Let the earth hide thee!
Thy bones are marrowless; thy blood is cold; thou hast no vision in those eyes which thou dost glare with! Hence, horrible shadow! Unreal mockery, hence!

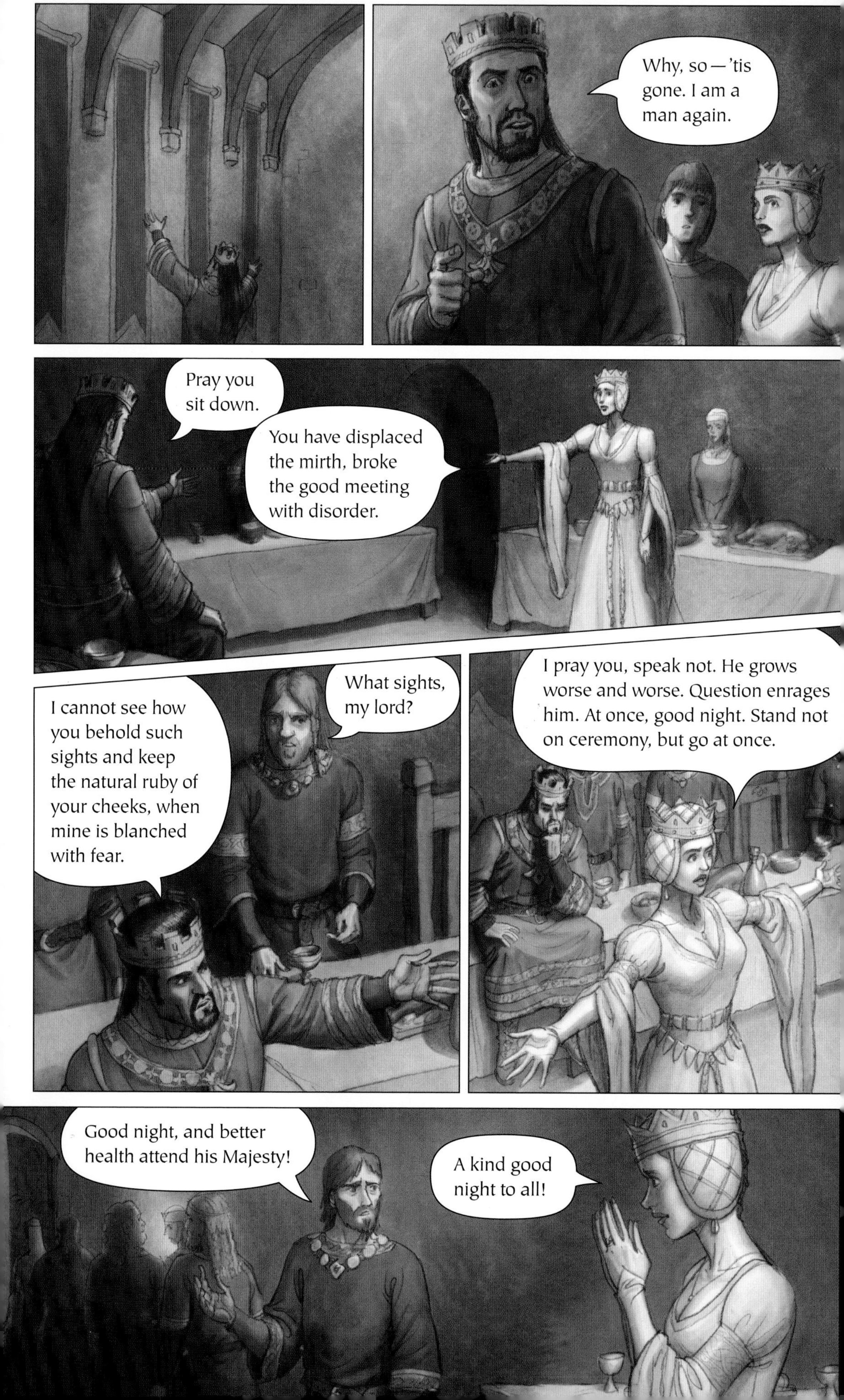
Why, so — 'tis gone. I am a man again.
Pray you sit down.
You have displaced the mirth, broke the good meeting with disorder.
I cannot see how you behold such sights and keep the natural ruby of your cheeks, when mine is blanched with fear.
What sights, my lord?
I pray you, speak not. He grows worse and worse. Question enrages him. At once, good night. Stand not on ceremony, but go at once.
Good night, and better health attend his Majesty!
A kind good night to all!

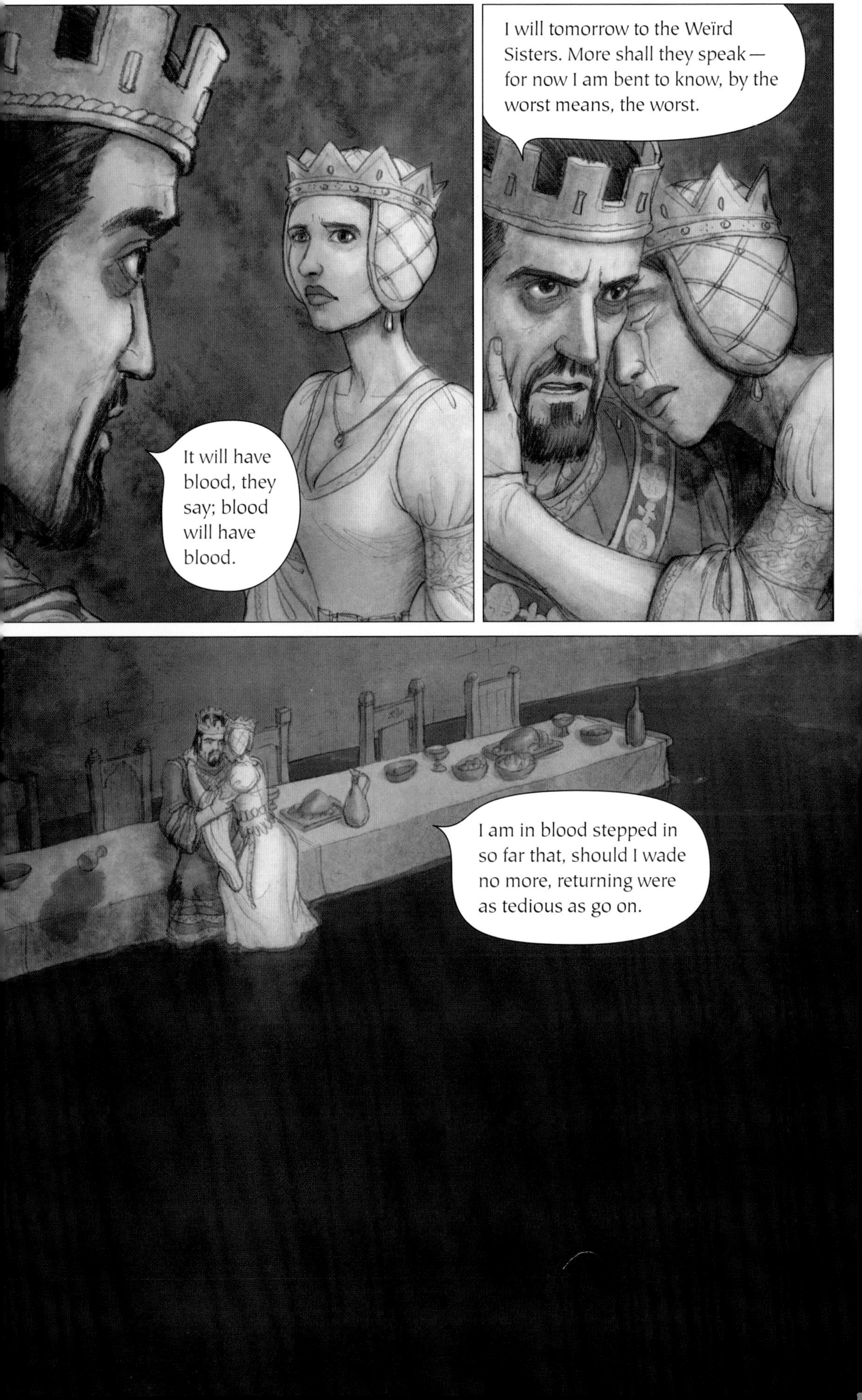
It will have blood, they say; blood will have blood.
I will tomorrow to the Weïrd Sisters. More shall they speak — for now I am bent to know, by the worst means, the worst.
I am in blood stepped in so far that, should I wade no more, returning were as tedious as go on.

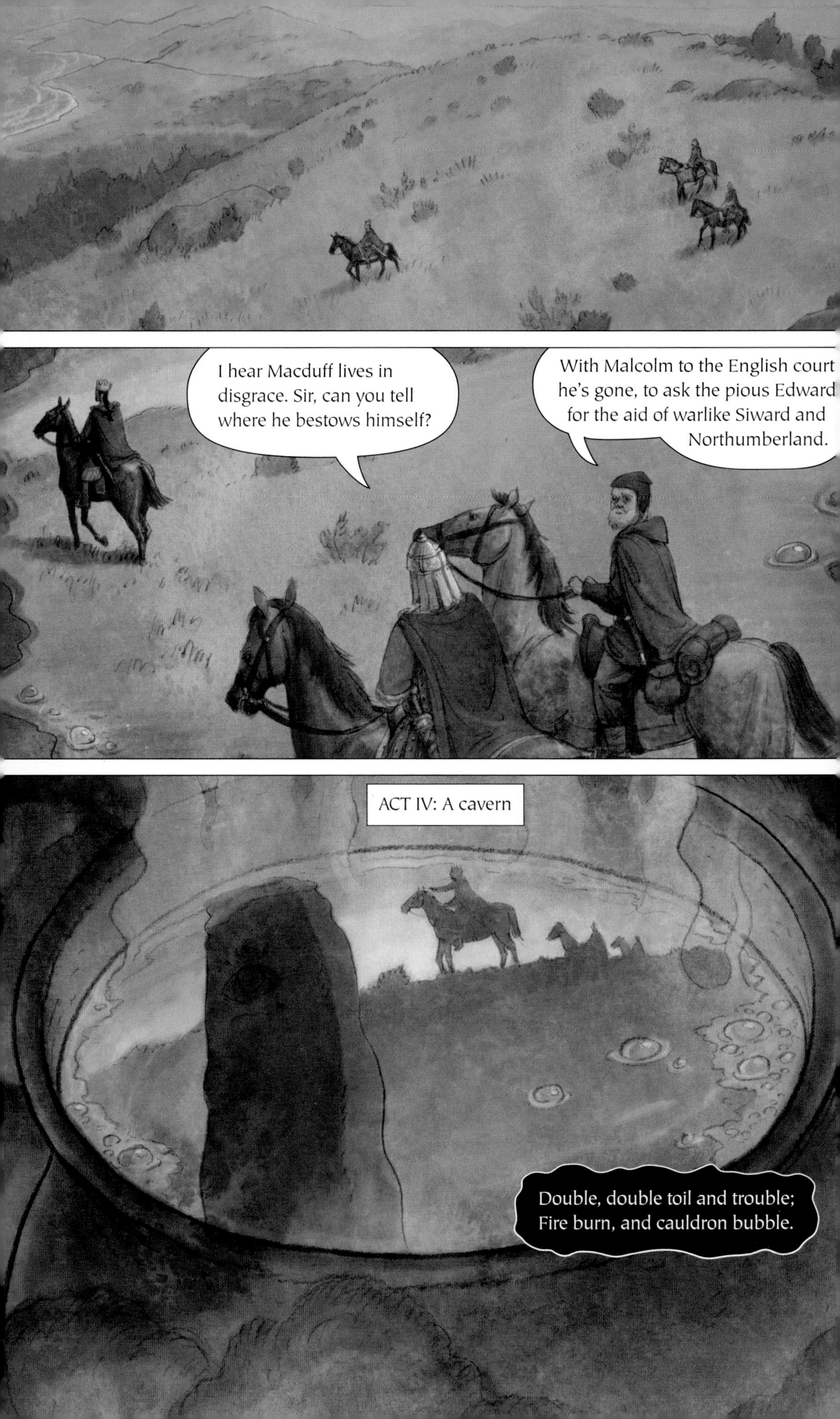
I hear Macduff lives in disgrace. Sir, can you tell where he bestows himself?
With Malcolm to the English court he's gone, to ask the pious Edward for the aid of warlike Siward and Northumberland.
ACT IV: A cavern
Double, double toil and trouble; Fire burn, and cauldron bubble.

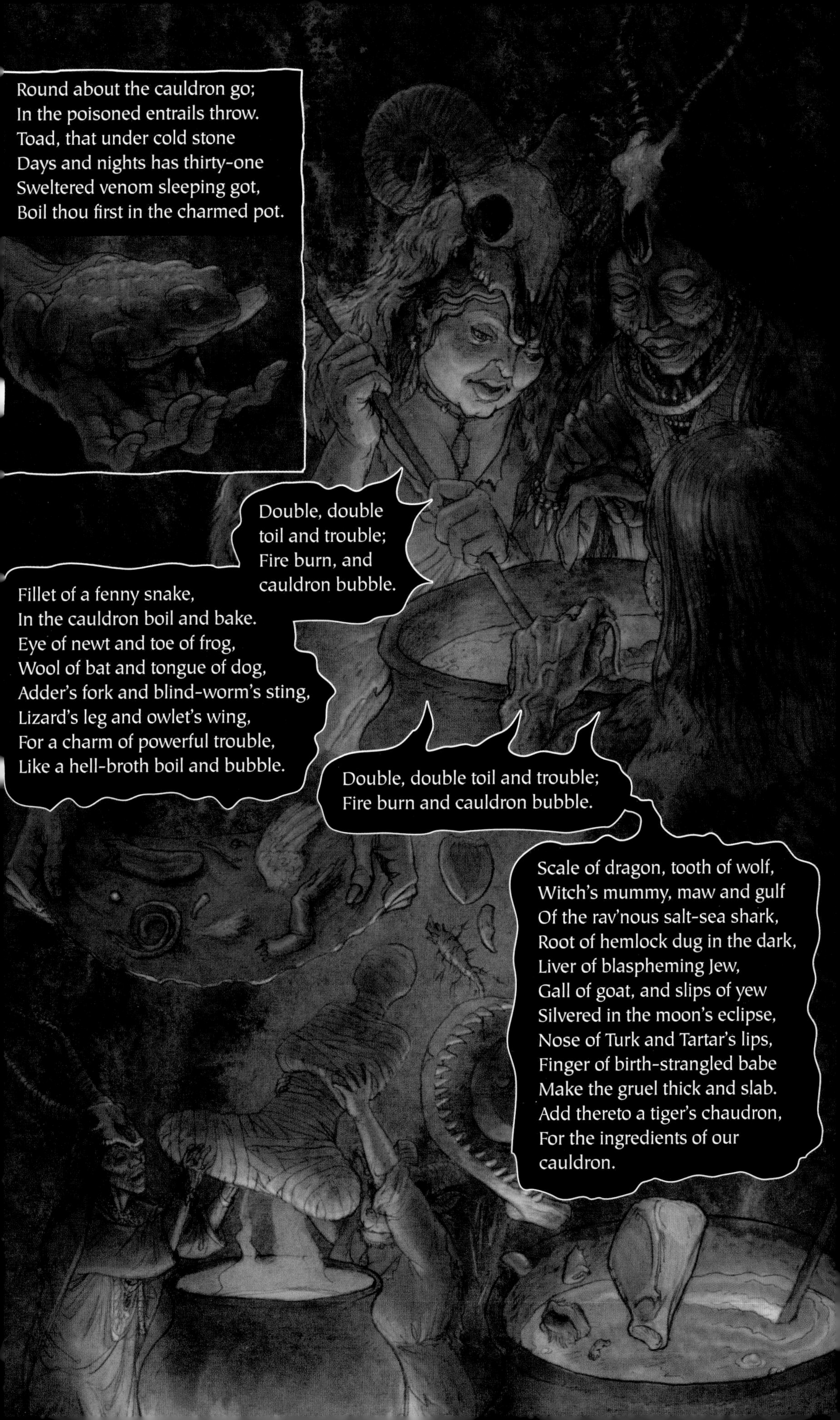
Round about the cauldron go;
In the poisoned entrails throw.
Toad, that under cold stone
Days and nights has thirty-one
Sweltered venom sleeping got,
Boil thou first in the charmed pot.
Double, double toil and trouble; Fire burn, and cauldron bubble.
Fillet of a fenny snake,
In the cauldron boil and bake.
Eye of newt and toe of frog,
Wool of bat and tongue of dog,
Adder's fork and blind-worm's sting,
Lizard's leg and owlet's wing,
For a charm of powerful trouble,
Like a hell-broth boil and bubble.
Double, double toil and trouble;
Fire burn and cauldron bubble.
Scale of dragon, tooth of wolf,
Witch's mummy, maw and gulf
Of the rav'nous salt-sea shark,
Root of hemlock dug in the dark,
Liver of blaspheming Jew,
Gall of goat, and slips of yew
Silvered in the moon's eclipse,
Nose of Turk and Tartar's lips,
Finger of birth-strangled babe
Make the gruel thick and slab.
Add thereto a tiger's chaudron,
For the ingredients of our
cauldron.

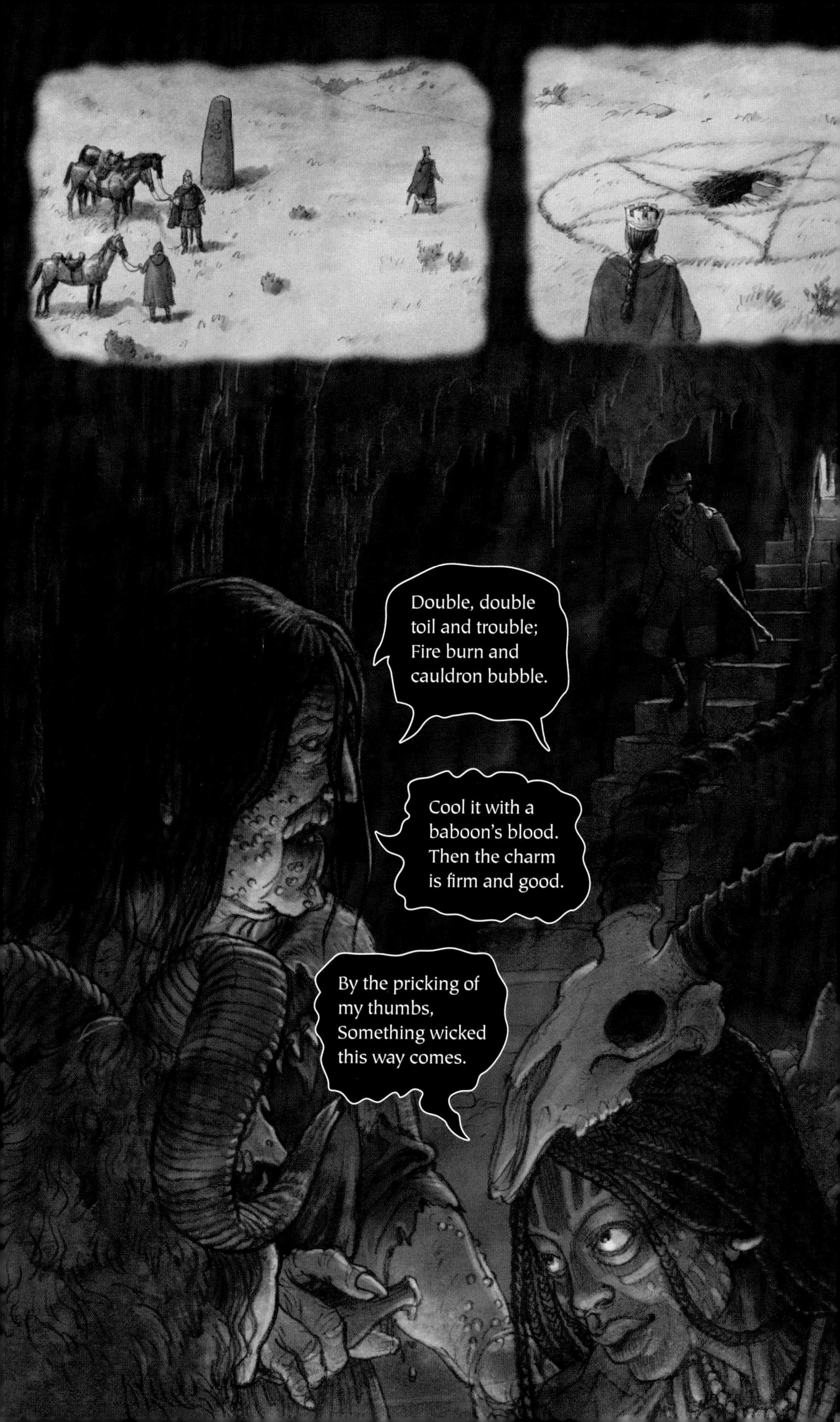
Double, double toil and trouble; Fire burn and cauldron bubble.
Cool it with a baboon's blood. Then the charm is firm and good.
By the pricking of my thumbs, Something wicked this way comes.

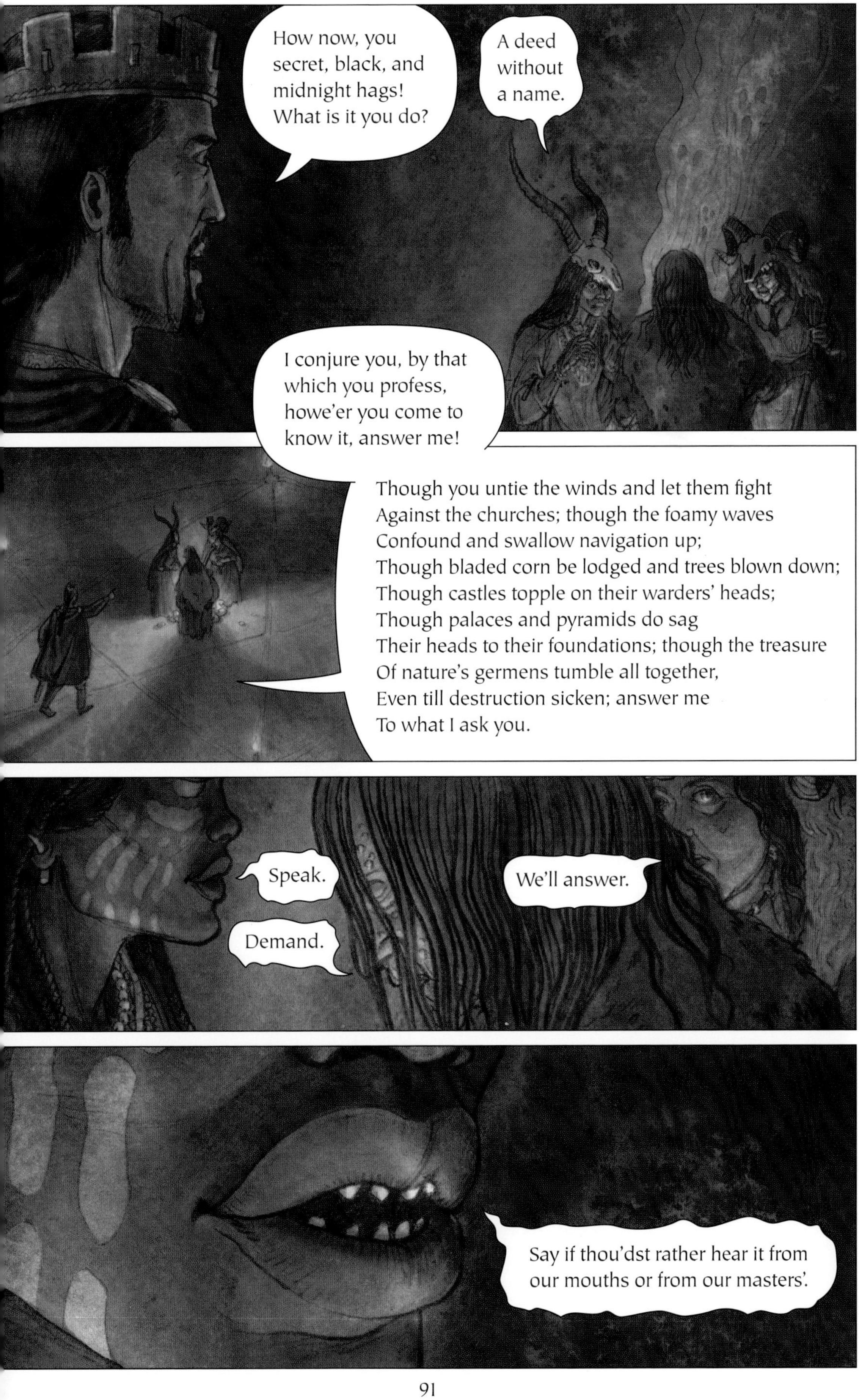
How now, you secret, black, and midnight hags! What is it you do?
A deed without a name.
I conjure you, by that which you profess, howe'er you come to know it, answer me!
Though you untie the winds and let them fight
Against the churches; though the foamy waves
Confound and swallow navigation up;
Though bladed corn be lodged and trees blown down;
Though castles topple on their warders' heads;
Though palaces and pyramids do sag
Their heads to their foundations; though the treasure
Of nature's germens tumble all together,
Even till destruction sicken; answer me
To what I ask you.
Speak.
Demand.
We'll answer.
Say if thou'dst rather hear it from our mouths or from our masters'.

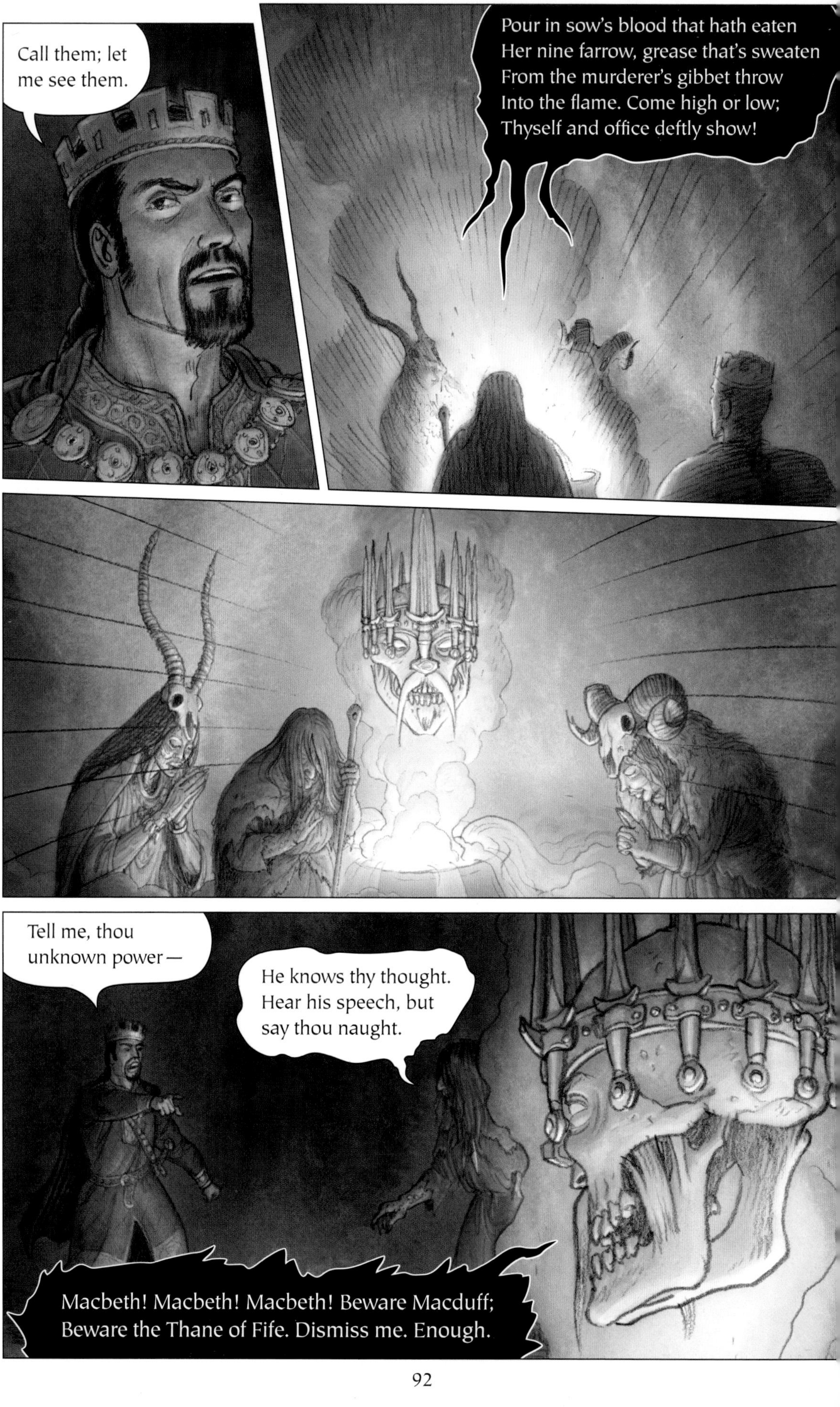

Call them; let me see them.
Pour in sow's blood that hath eaten Her nine farrow, grease that's sweaten From the murderer's gibbet throw Into the flame. Come high or low; Thyself and office deftly show!
Tell me, thou unknown power—
He knows thy thought. Hear his speech, but say thou naught.
Macbeth! Macbeth! Macbeth! Beware Macduff; Beware the Thane of Fife. Dismiss me. Enough.

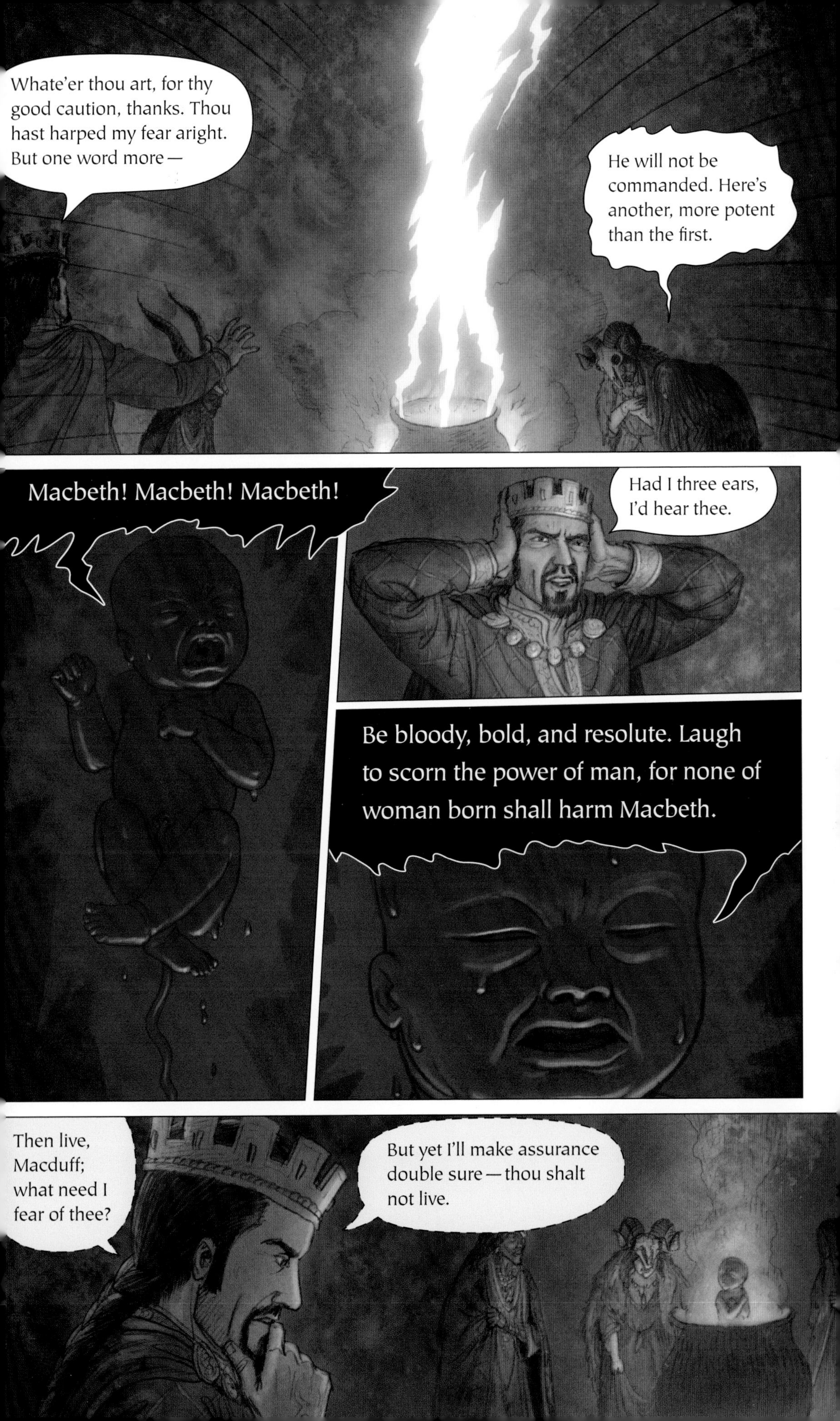
Whate'er thou art, for thy good caution, thanks. Thou hast harped my fear aright. But one word more —
He will not be commanded. Here's another, more potent than the first.
Macbeth! Macbeth! Macbeth!
Had I three ears, I'd hear thee.
Be bloody, bold, and resolute. Laugh to scorn the power of man, for none of woman born shall harm Macbeth.
Then live, Macduff; what need I fear of thee?
But yet I'll make assurance double sure — thou shalt not live.

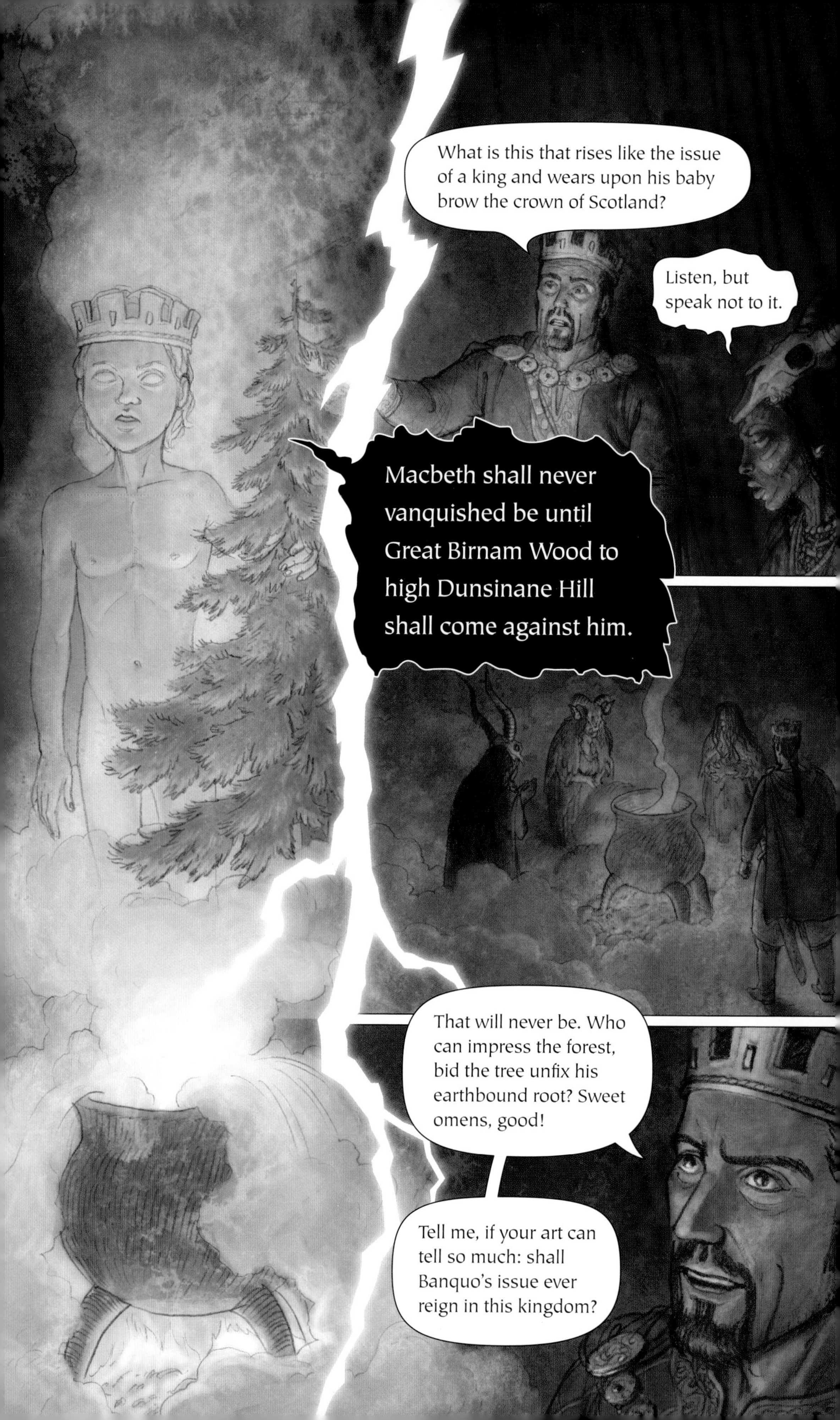
What is this that rises like the issue of a king and wears upon his baby brow the crown of Scotland?
Listen, but speak not to it.
Macbeth shall never vanquished be until Great Birnam Wood to high Dunsinane Hill shall come against him.
That will never be. Who can impress the forest, bid the tree unfix his earthbound root? Sweet omens, good!
Tell me, if your art can tell so much: shall Banquo's issue ever reign in this kingdom?

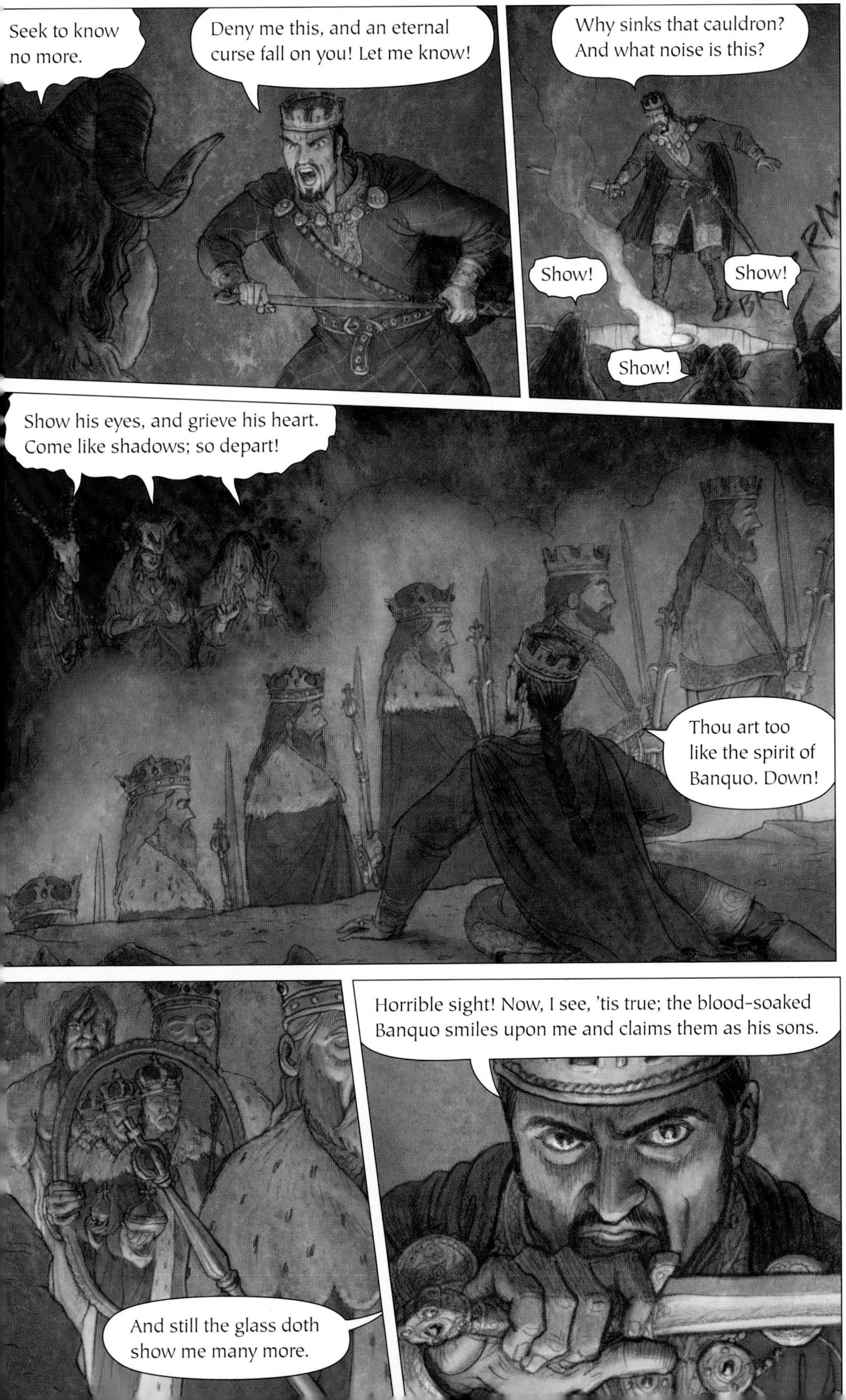
Seek to know no more.
Deny me this, and an eternal curse fall on you! Let me know!
Why sinks that cauldron? And what noise is this?
Show!
Show!
Show!
Show his eyes, and grieve his heart. Come like shadows; so depart!
Thou art too like the spirit of Banquo. Down!
And still the glass doth show me many more.
Horrible sight! Now, I see, 'tis true; the blood-soaked Banquo smiles upon me and claims them as his sons.

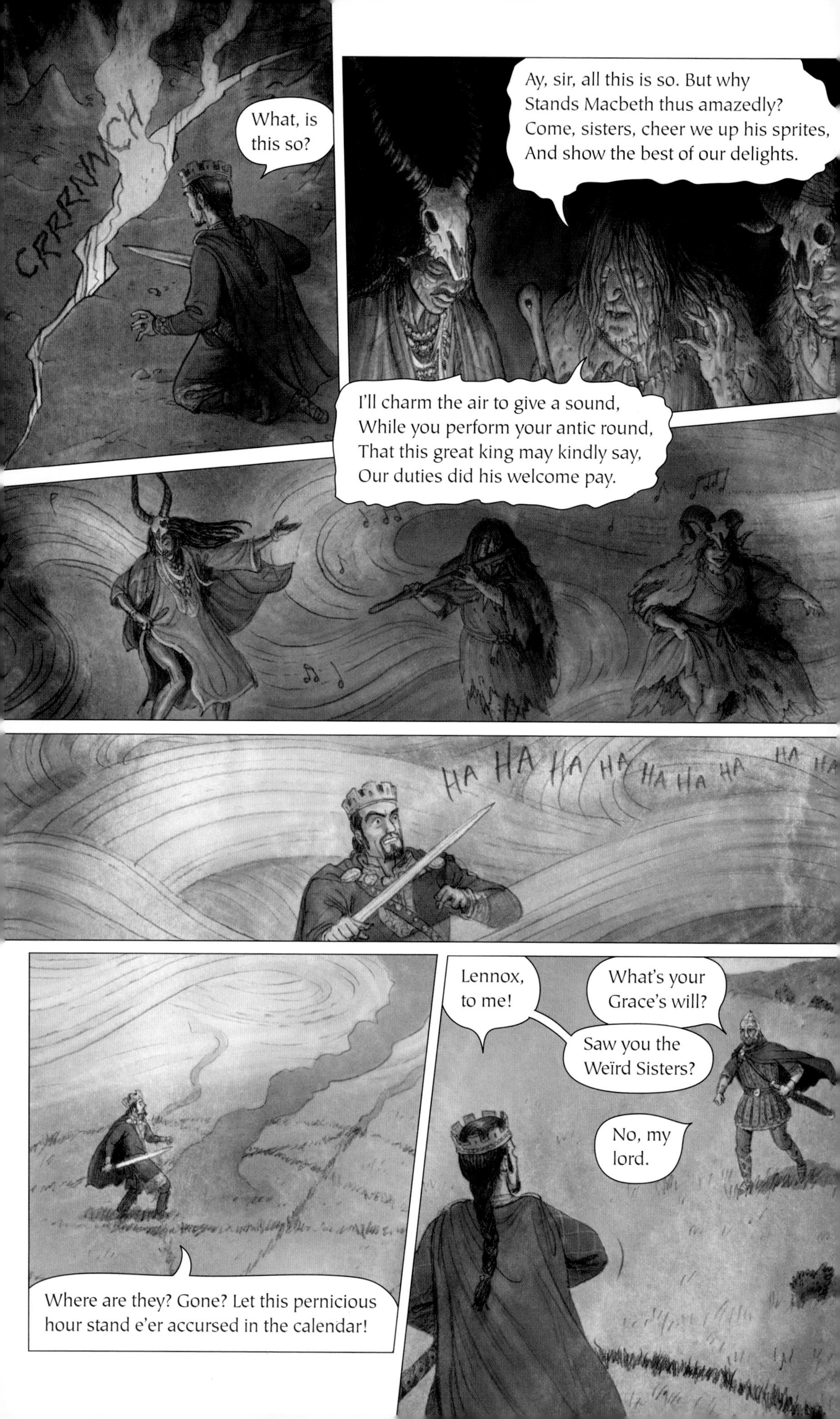
CRRRNNCH
What, is this so?
Ay, sir, all this is so. But why
Stands Macbeth thus amazedly?
Come, sisters, cheer we up his sprites,
And show the best of our delights.
I'll charm the air to give a sound,
While you perform your antic round,
That this great king may kindly say,
Our duties did his welcome pay.
HA HA HA HA HA HA HA HA HA
Where are they? Gone? Let this pernicious hour stand e'er accursed in the calendar!
Lennox, to me!
What's your Grace's will?
Saw you the Weïrd Sisters?
No, my lord.

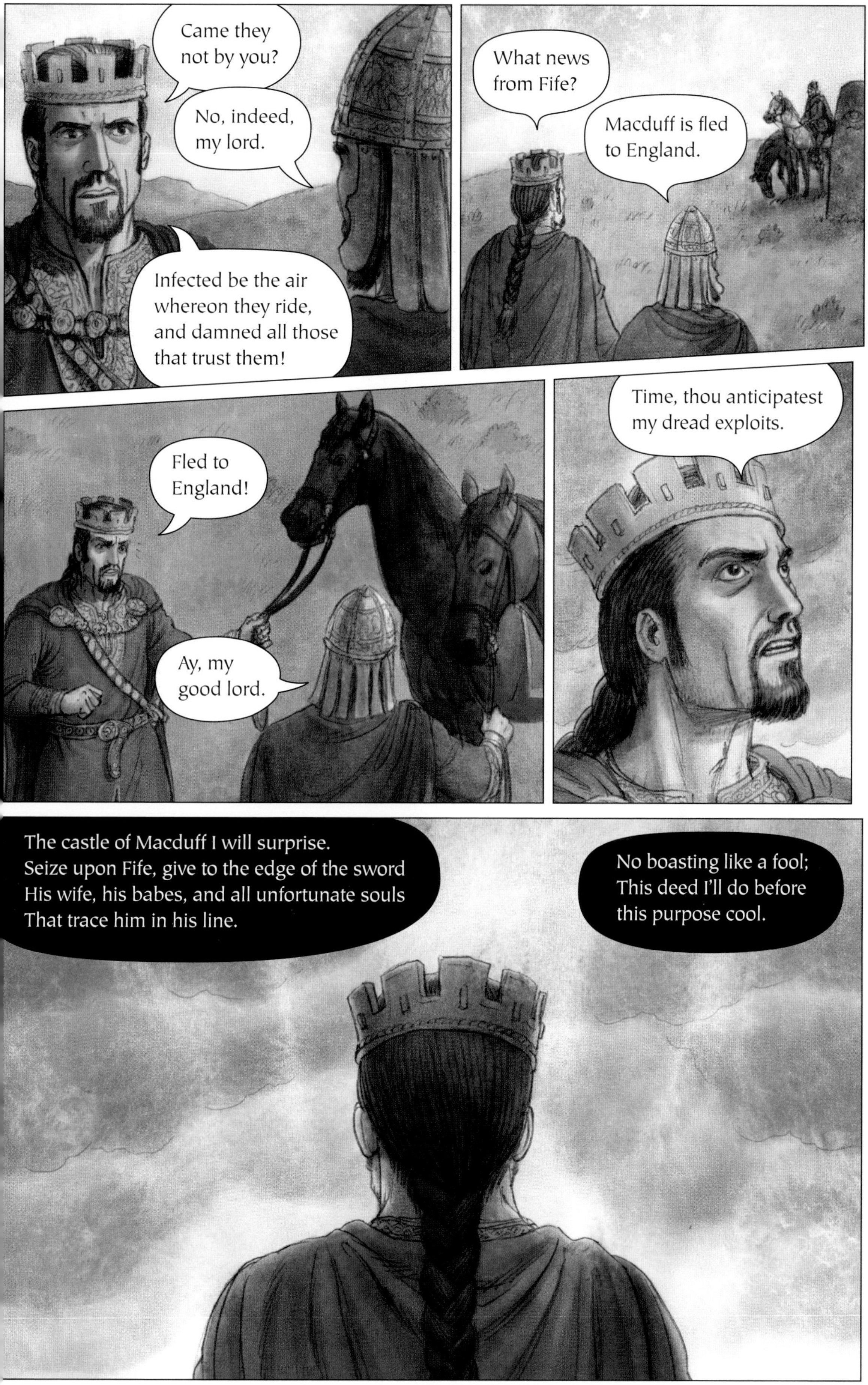
Came they not by you?
No, indeed, my lord.
Infected be the air whereon they ride, and damned all those that trust them!
What news from Fife?
Macduff is fled to England.
Fled to England!
Ay, my good lord.
Time, thou anticipatest my dread exploits.
The castle of Macduff I will surprise. Seize upon Fife, give to the edge of the sword His wife, his babes, and all unfortunate souls That trace him in his line.
No boasting like a fool; This deed I'll do before this purpose cool.

Fife. Macduff's castle.

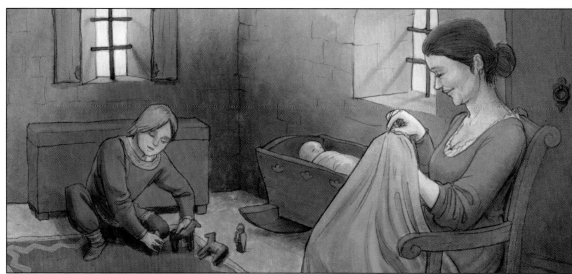

Bless you, fair dame! I am not to you known,
Though in your interest I have come.
Grave danger does approach you swiftly.
If you will take a homely man's advice,
Be not found here. Hence with your little ones!

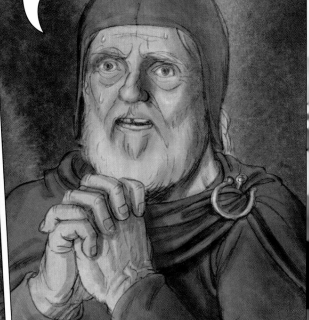

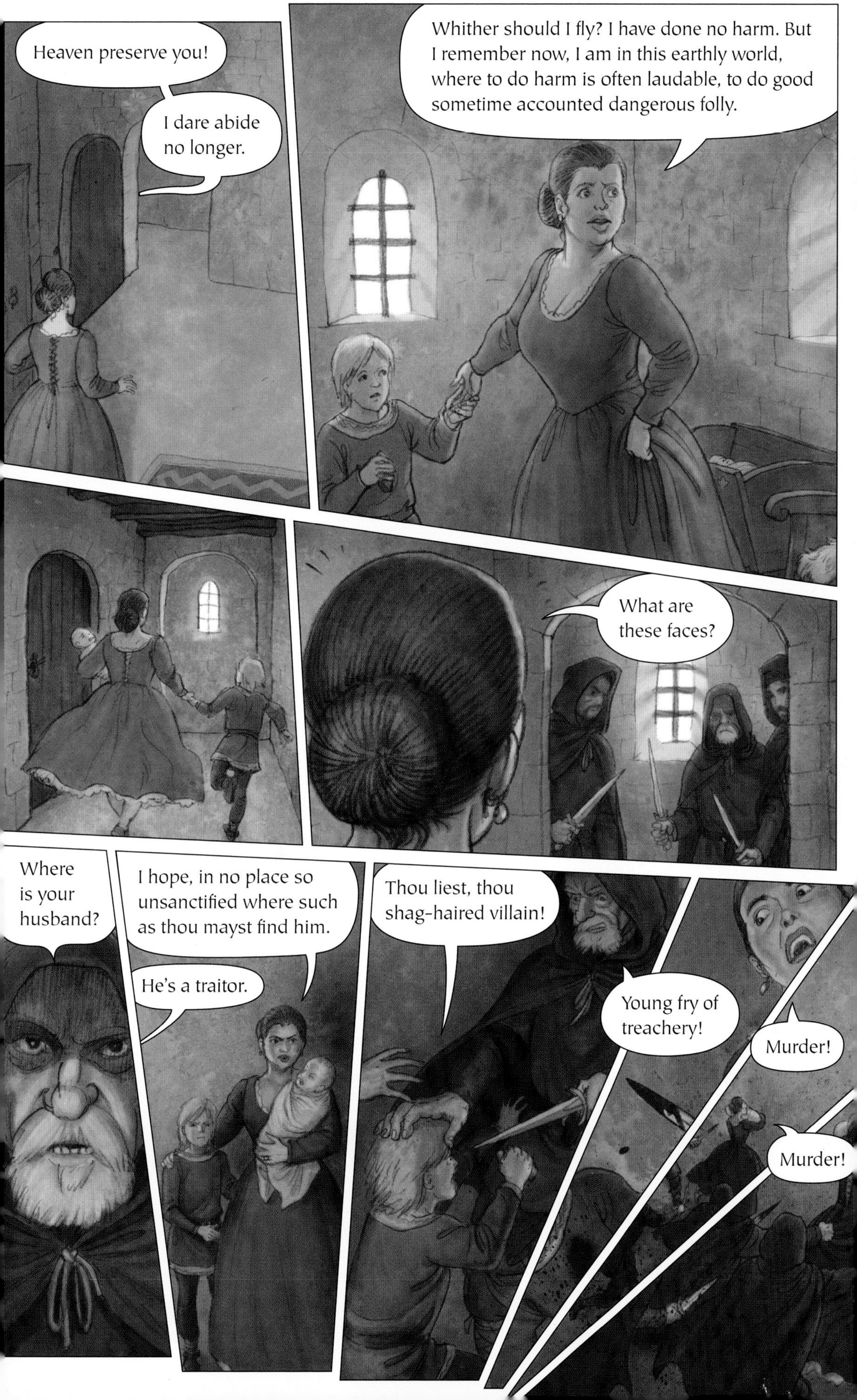
Heaven preserve you!
I dare abide no longer.
Whither should I fly? I have done no harm. But I remember now, I am in this earthly world, where to do harm is often laudable, to do good sometime accounted dangerous folly.
What are these faces?
Where is your husband?
I hope, in no place so unsanctified where such as thou mayst find him.
He's a traitor.
Thou liest, thou shag-haired villain!
Young fry of treachery!
Murder!
Murder!

England. The King's palace.

All?

Merciful heaven!

My children too?

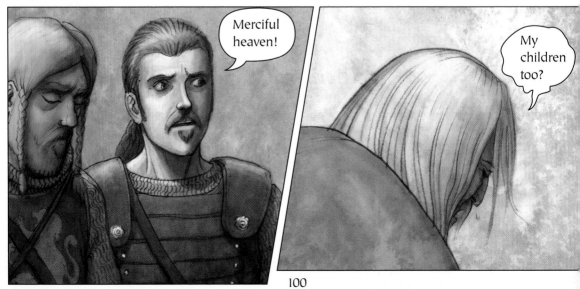

100

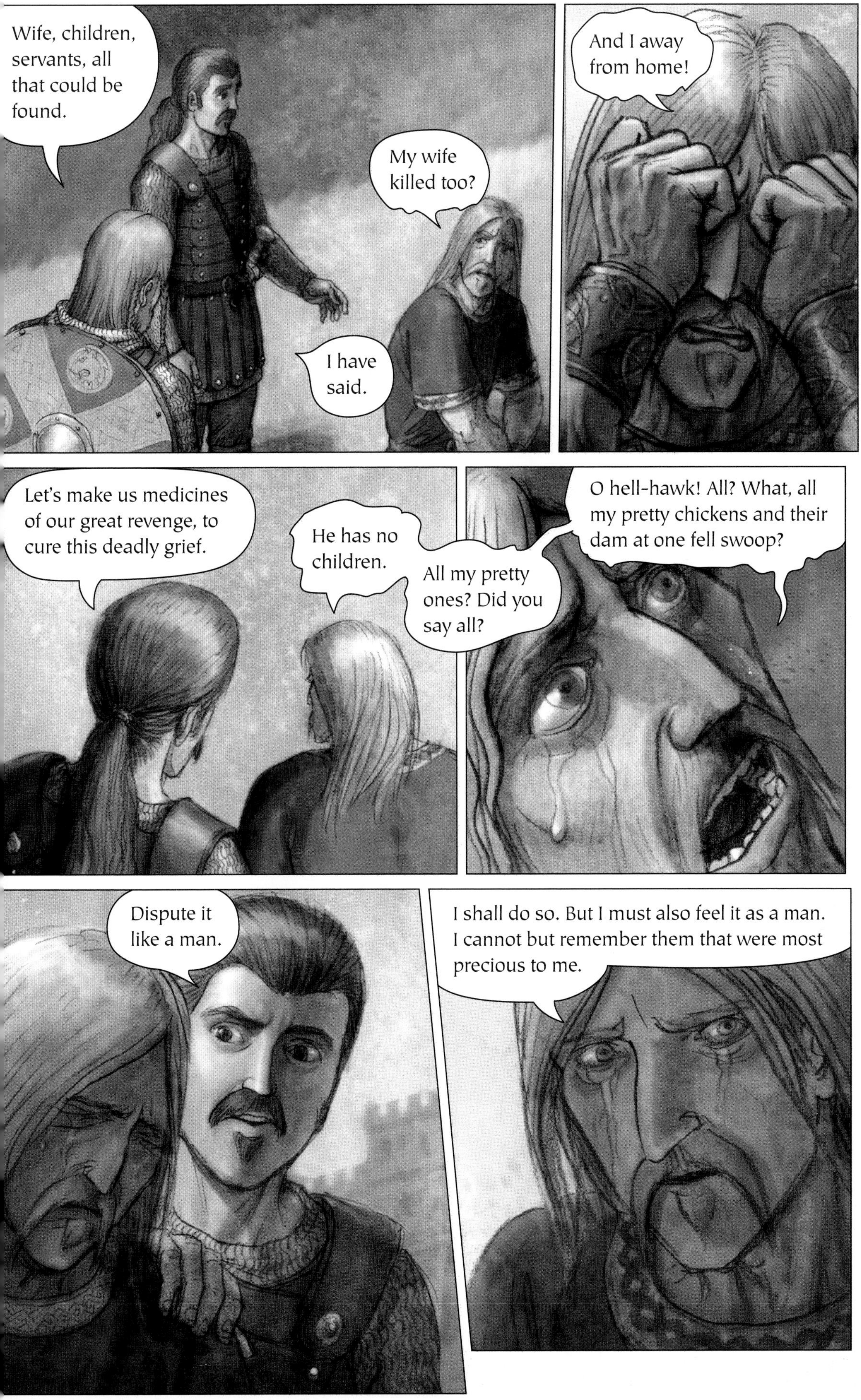
Wife, children, servants, all that could be found.
My wife killed too?
I have said.
And I away from home!
Let's make us medicines of our great revenge, to cure this deadly grief.
He has no children.
All my pretty ones? Did you say all?
O hell-hawk! All? What, all my pretty chickens and their dam at one fell swoop?
Dispute it like a man.
I shall do so. But I must also feel it as a man. I cannot but remember them that were most precious to me.

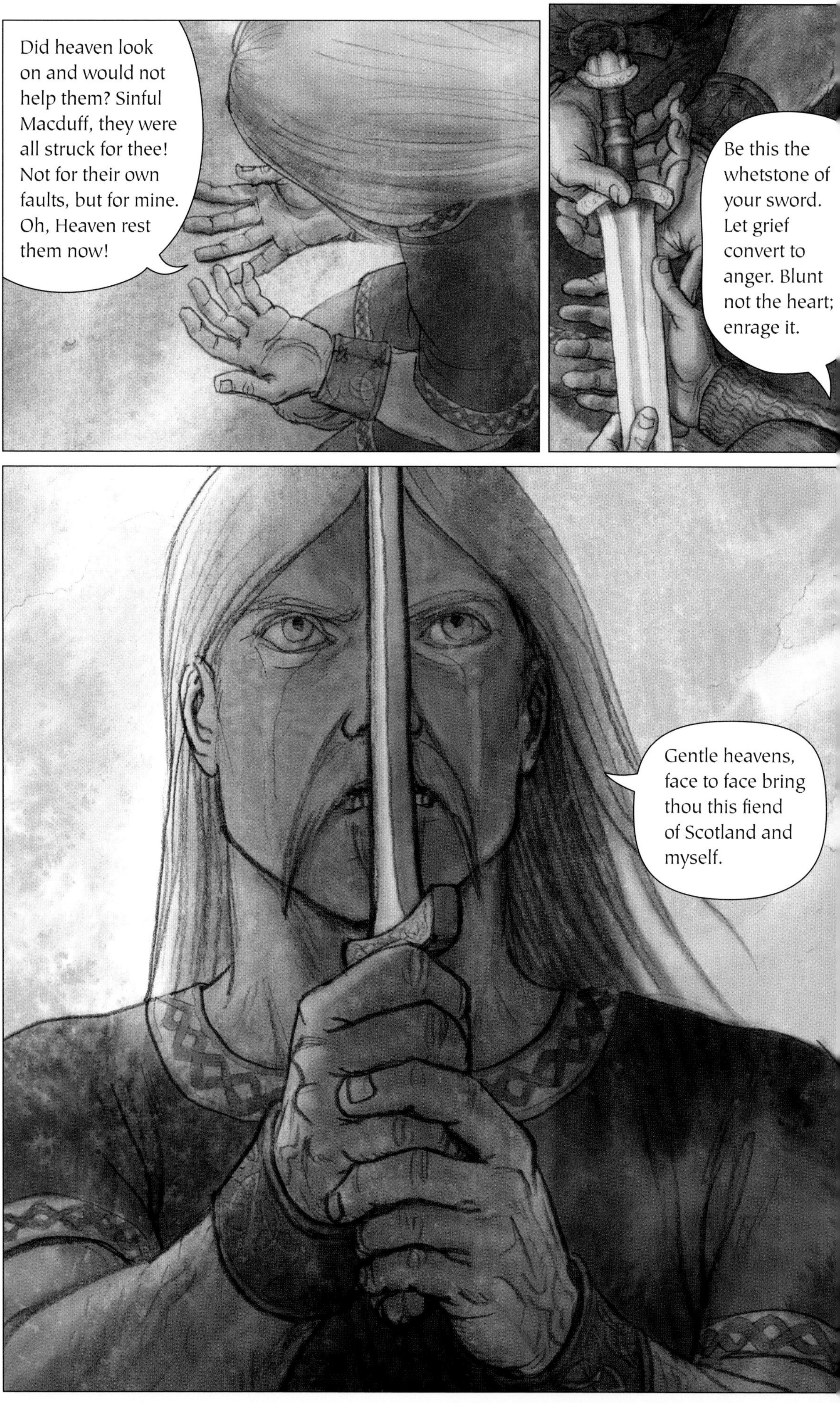
Did heaven look on and would not help them? Sinful Macduff, they were all struck for thee! Not for their own faults, but for mine. Oh, Heaven rest them now!
Be this the whetstone of your sword. Let grief convert to anger. Blunt not the heart; enrage it.
Gentle heavens, face to face bring thou this fiend of Scotland and myself.

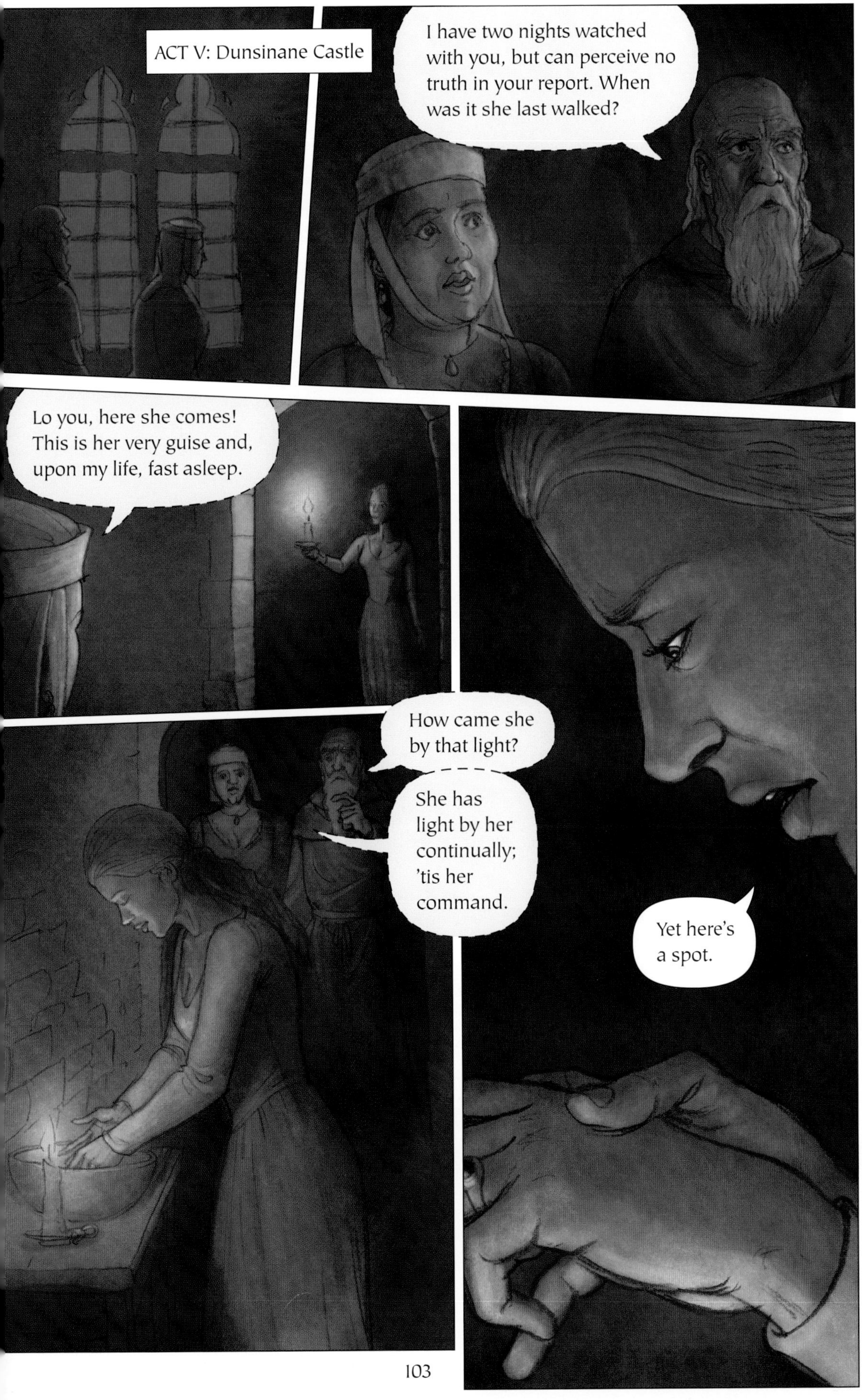
ACT V: Dunsinane Castle
I have two nights watched with you, but can perceive no truth in your report. When was it she last walked?
Lo you, here she comes! This is her very guise and, upon my life, fast asleep.
How came she by that light?
She has light by her continually; 'tis her command.
Yet here's a spot.

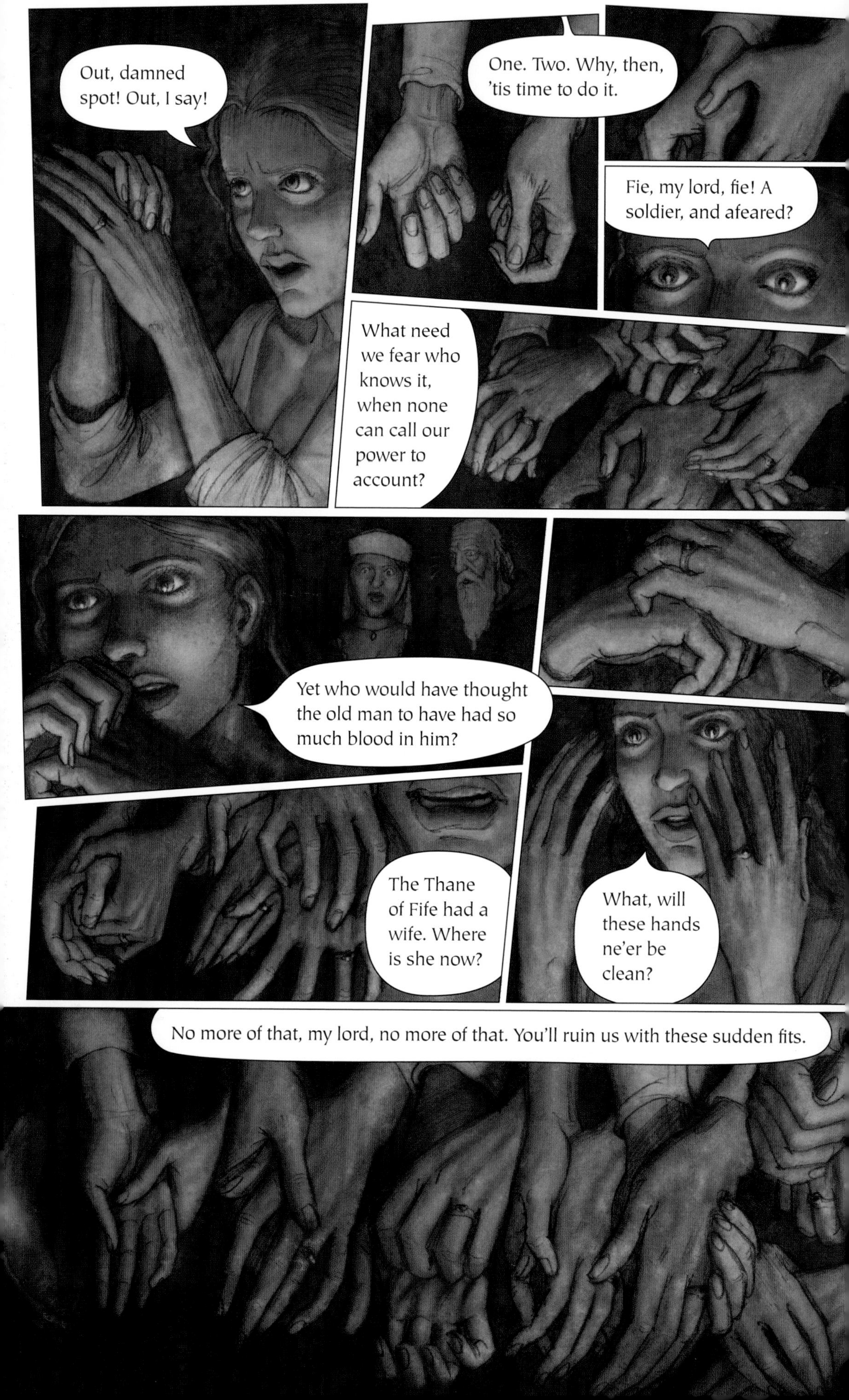
Out, damned spot! Out, I say!
One. Two. Why, then, 'tis time to do it.
Fie, my lord, fie! A soldier, and afeared?
What need we fear who knows it, when none can call our power to account?
Yet who would have thought the old man to have had so much blood in him?
The Thane of Fife had a wife. Where is she now?
What, will these hands ne'er be clean?
No more of that, my lord, no more of that. You'll ruin us with these sudden fits.

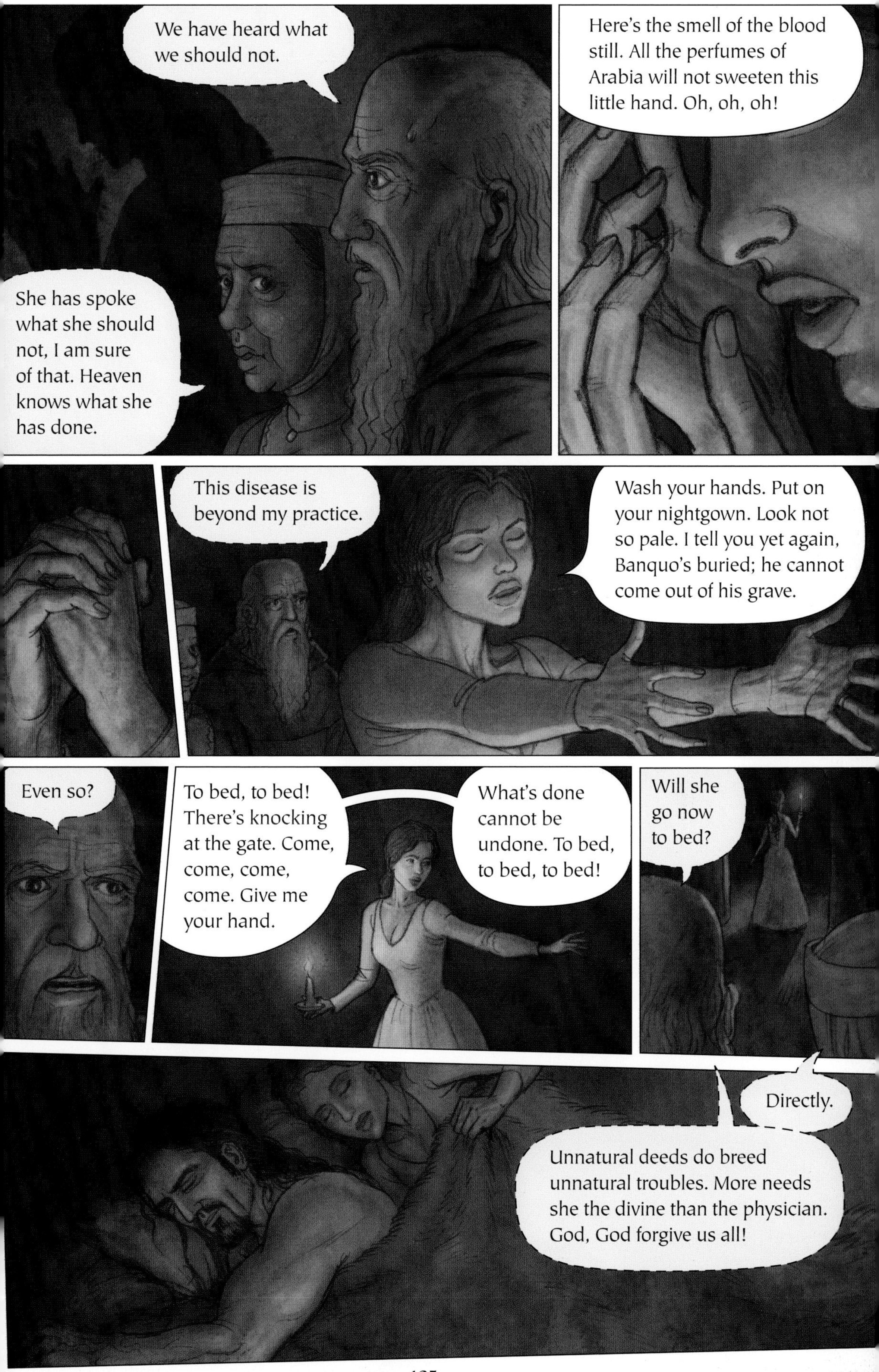
We have heard what we should not.
She has spoke what she should not, I am sure of that. Heaven knows what she has done.
Here's the smell of the blood still. All the perfumes of Arabia will not sweeten this little hand. Oh, oh, oh!
This disease is beyond my practice.
Wash your hands. Put on your nightgown. Look not so pale. I tell you yet again, Banquo's buried; he cannot come out of his grave.
Even so?
To bed, to bed! There's knocking at the gate. Come, come, come, come. Give me your hand.
What's done cannot be undone. To bed, to bed, to bed!
Will she go now to bed?
Directly.
Unnatural deeds do breed unnatural troubles. More needs she the divine than the physician. God, God forgive us all!

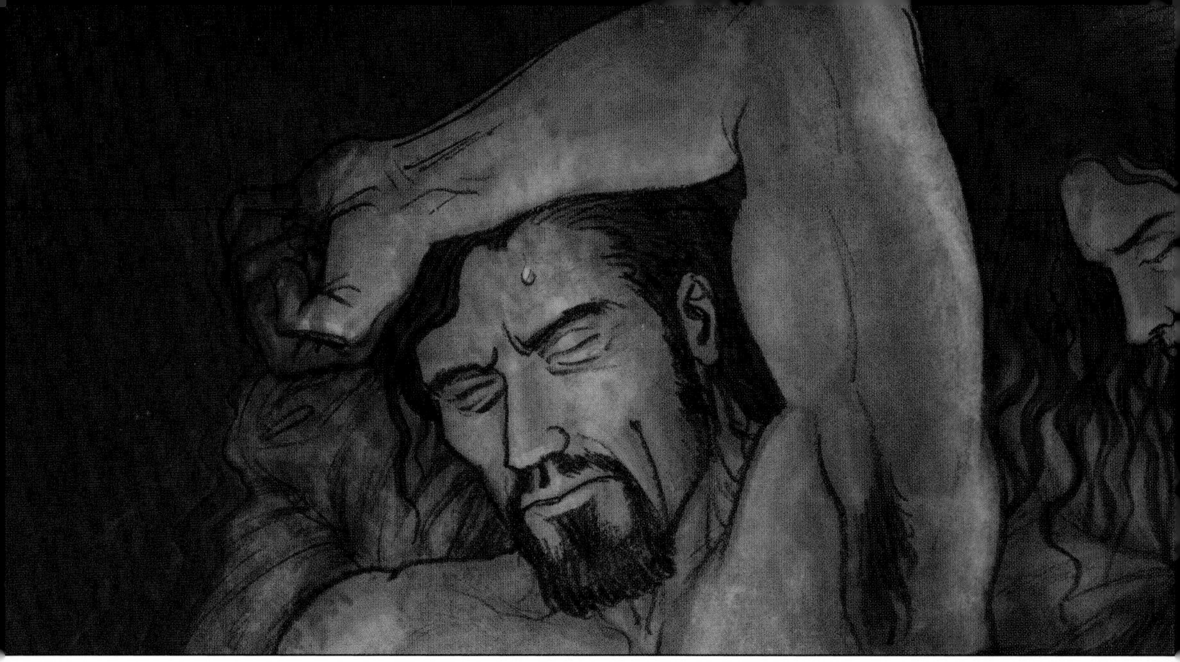

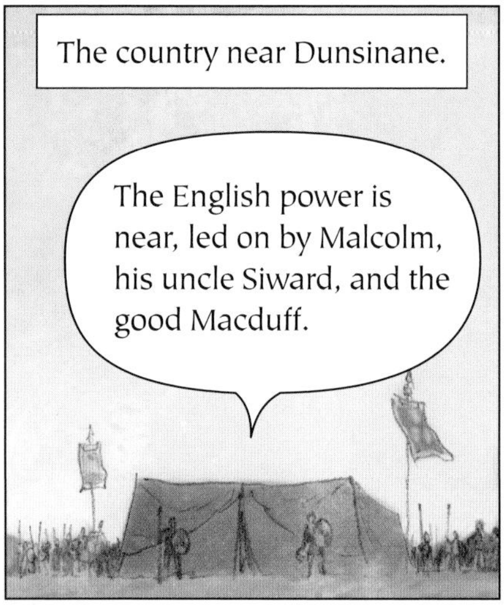
The country near Dunsinane.
The English power is near, led on by Malcolm, his uncle Siward, and the good Macduff.

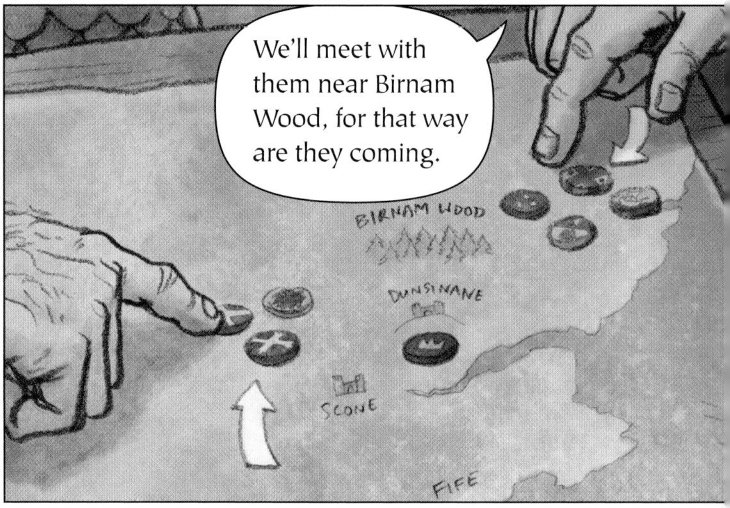
We'll meet with them near Birnam Wood, for that way are they coming.
BIRNAM WOOD
DUNSINANE
SCONE
FIFE

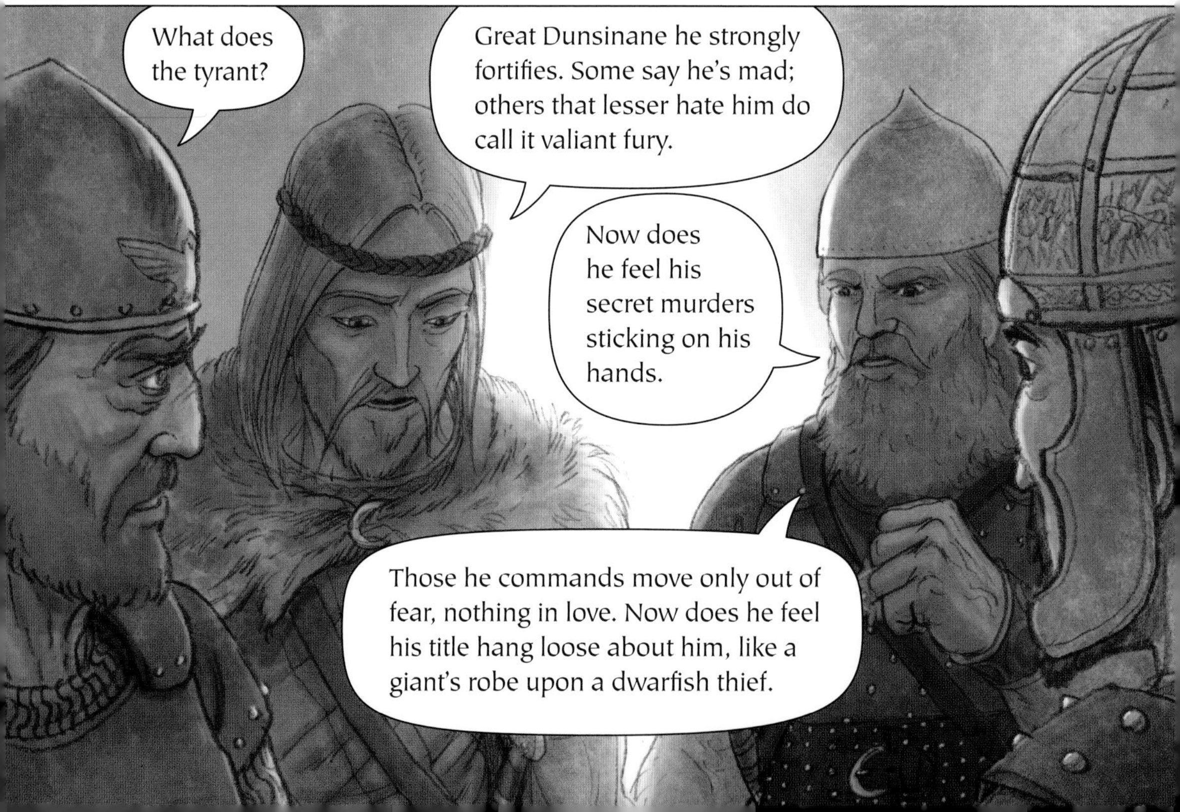
What does the tyrant?
Great Dunsinane he strongly fortifies. Some say he's mad; others that lesser hate him do call it valiant fury.
Now does he feel his secret murders sticking on his hands.
Those he commands move only out of fear, nothing in love. Now does he feel his title hang loose about him, like a giant's robe upon a dwarfish thief.

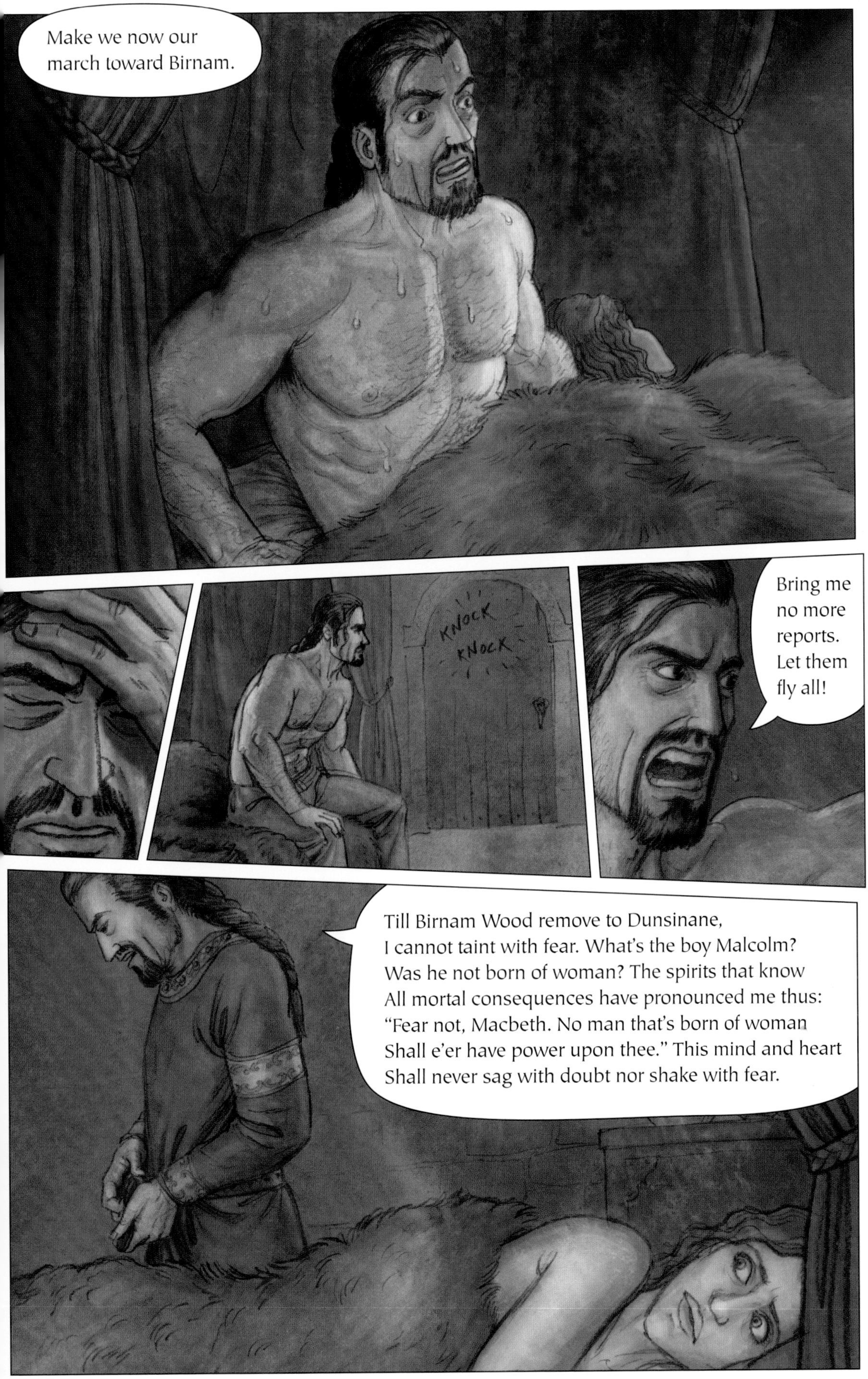
Make we now our march toward Birnam.
KNOCK KNOCK
Bring me no more reports. Let them fly all!
Till Birnam Wood remove to Dunsinane,
I cannot taint with fear. What's the boy Malcolm?
Was he not born of woman? The spirits that know
All mortal consequences have pronounced me thus:
"Fear not, Macbeth. No man that's born of woman
Shall e'er have power upon thee." This mind and heart
Shall never sag with doubt nor shake with fear.

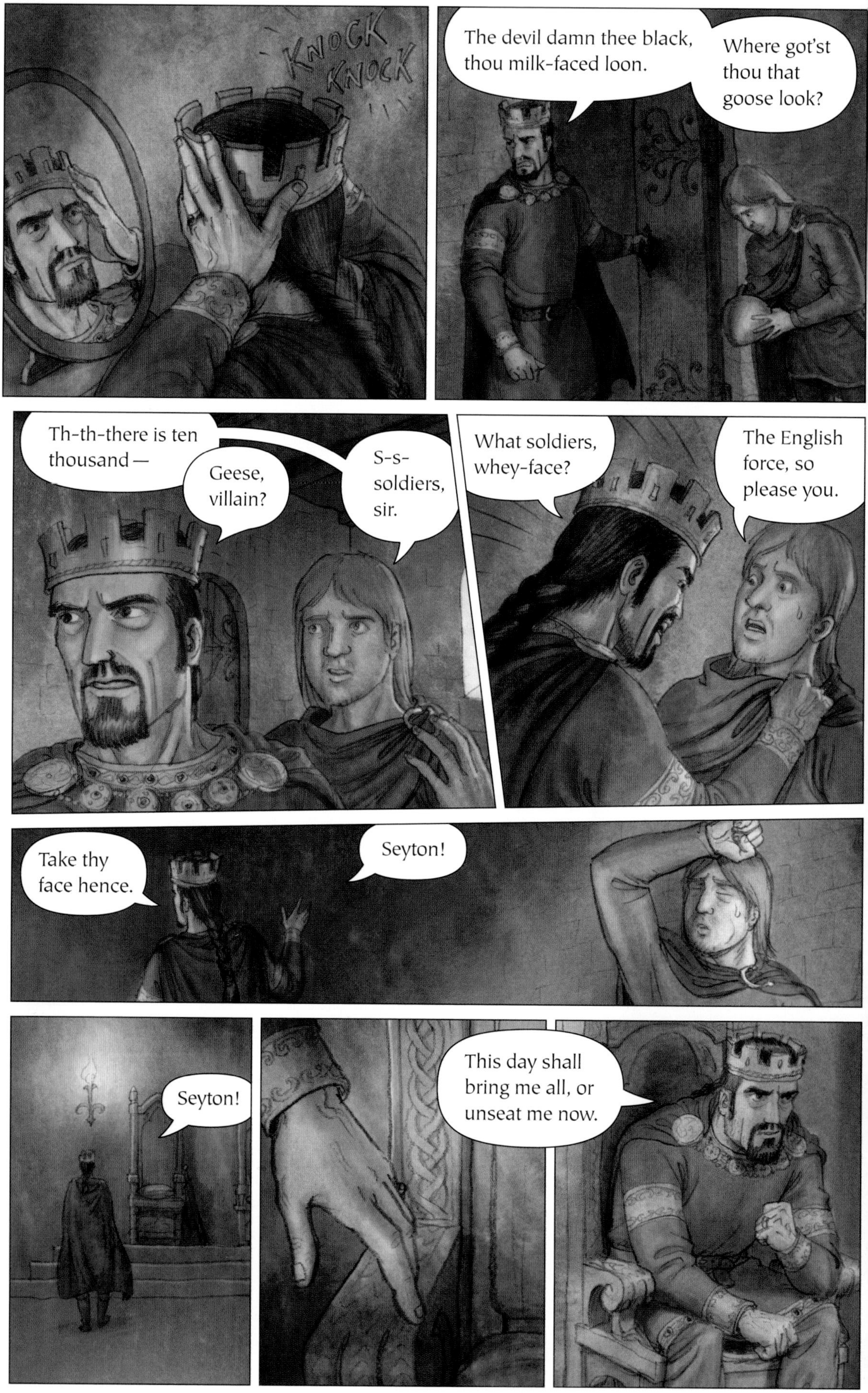
KNOCK KNOCK
The devil damn thee black, thou milk-faced loon.
Where got'st thou that goose look?
Th-th-there is ten thousand —
Geese, villain?
S-s-soldiers, sir.
What soldiers, whey-face?
The English force, so please you.
Take thy face hence.
Seyton!
Seyton!
This day shall bring me all, or unseat me now.

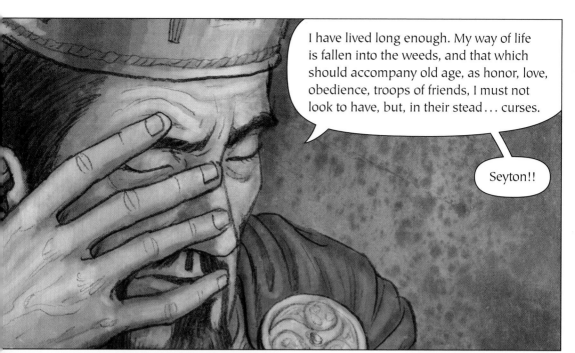

I have lived long enough. My way of life is fallen into the weeds, and that which should accompany old age, as honor, love, obedience, troops of friends, I must not look to have, but, in their stead... curses.

Seyton!!

What is your gracious pleasure?

What news more?

All is confirmed, my lord, which was reported.

I'll fight till from my bones my flesh be hacked.

Give me my armor.

'Tis not needed yet.

I'll put it on.

Send out more horses. Scour the country round. Hang those that talk of fear. Give me mine armor.

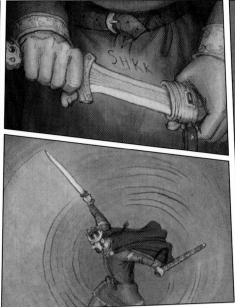

How does your patient, doctor?

Not so sick, my lord, as she is troubled with ... fancies, that keep her from her rest.

Cure her of that.

Canst thou not minister to a mind diseased,
Pluck from the memory a rooted sorrow,
Raze out the written troubles of the brain,
And with some sweet oblivious antidote
Cleanse the stuffed bosom of that perilous stuff
Which weighs upon the heart?

Therein the patient Must minister to himself.

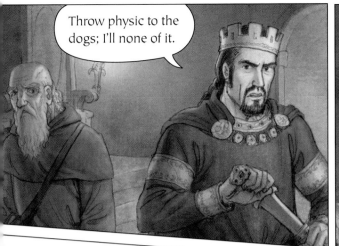

Throw physic to the dogs; I'll none of it.

Come, put mine armor on. Give me my staff. Be quick.

If thou couldst, doctor, take
The pulses of my land, find her disease,
And purge it to a sound and pristine health,
I would applaud thee to the very echo,
That should applaud again.

Ay, my good lord.

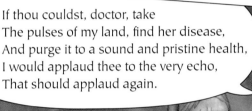

I know what should be purged.

I will not be afraid of death and bane till Birnam forest come to Dunsinane.

Were I from Dunsinane away and clear, profit again should hardly draw me here.

111

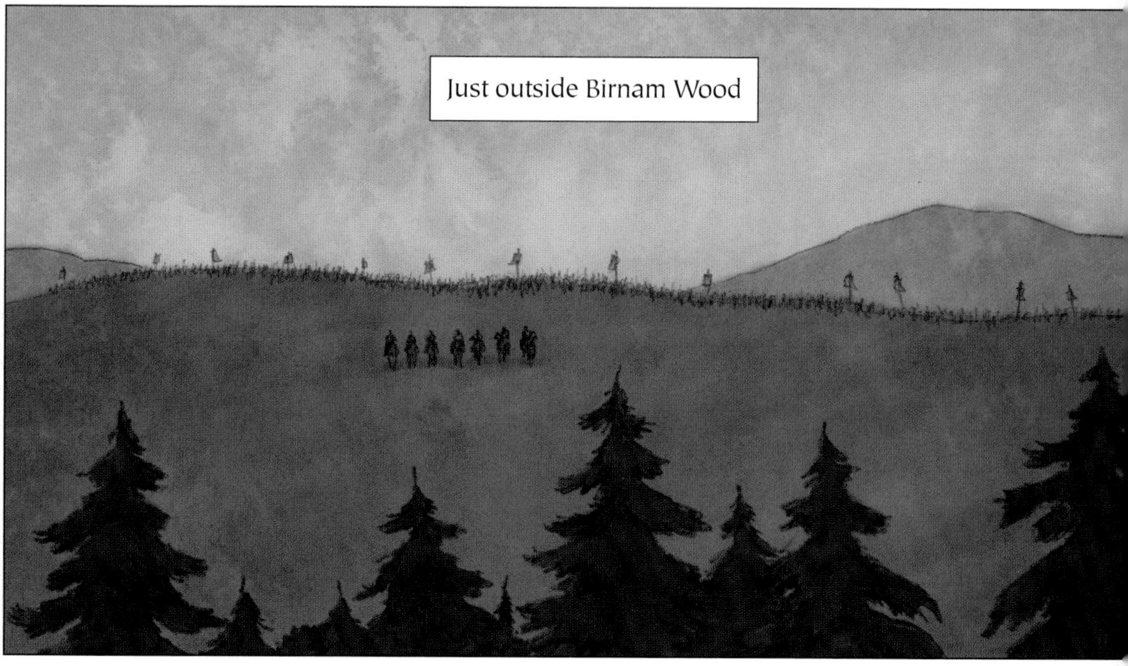
Just outside Birnam Wood

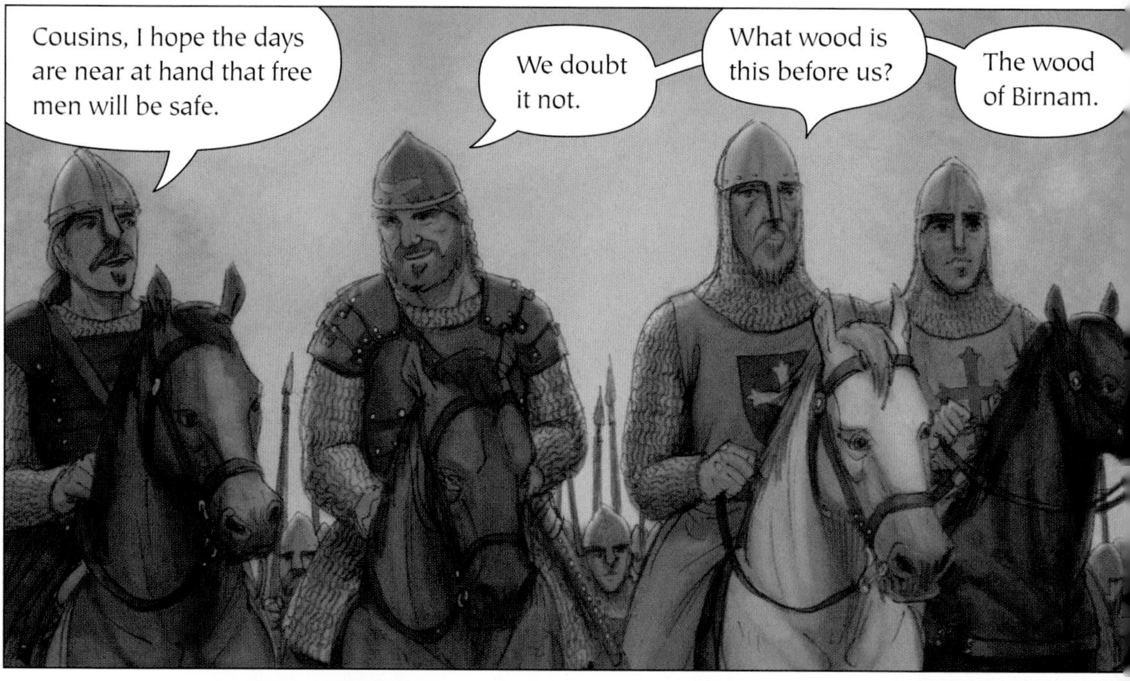
Cousins, I hope the days are near at hand that free men will be safe.
We doubt it not.
What wood is this before us?
The wood of Birnam.

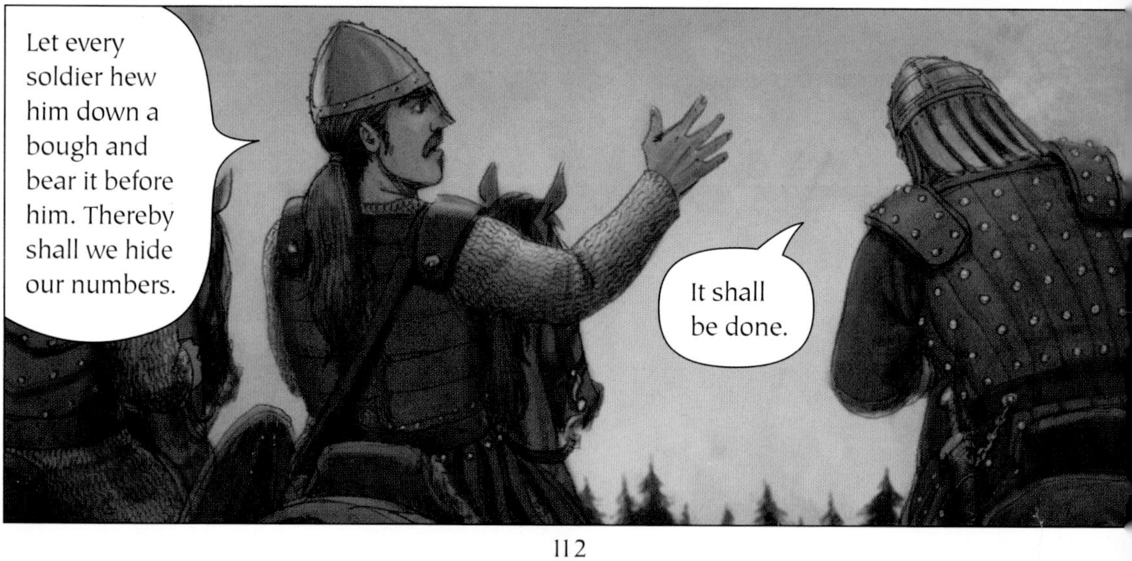
Let every soldier hew him down a bough and bear it before him. Thereby shall we hide our numbers.
It shall be done.

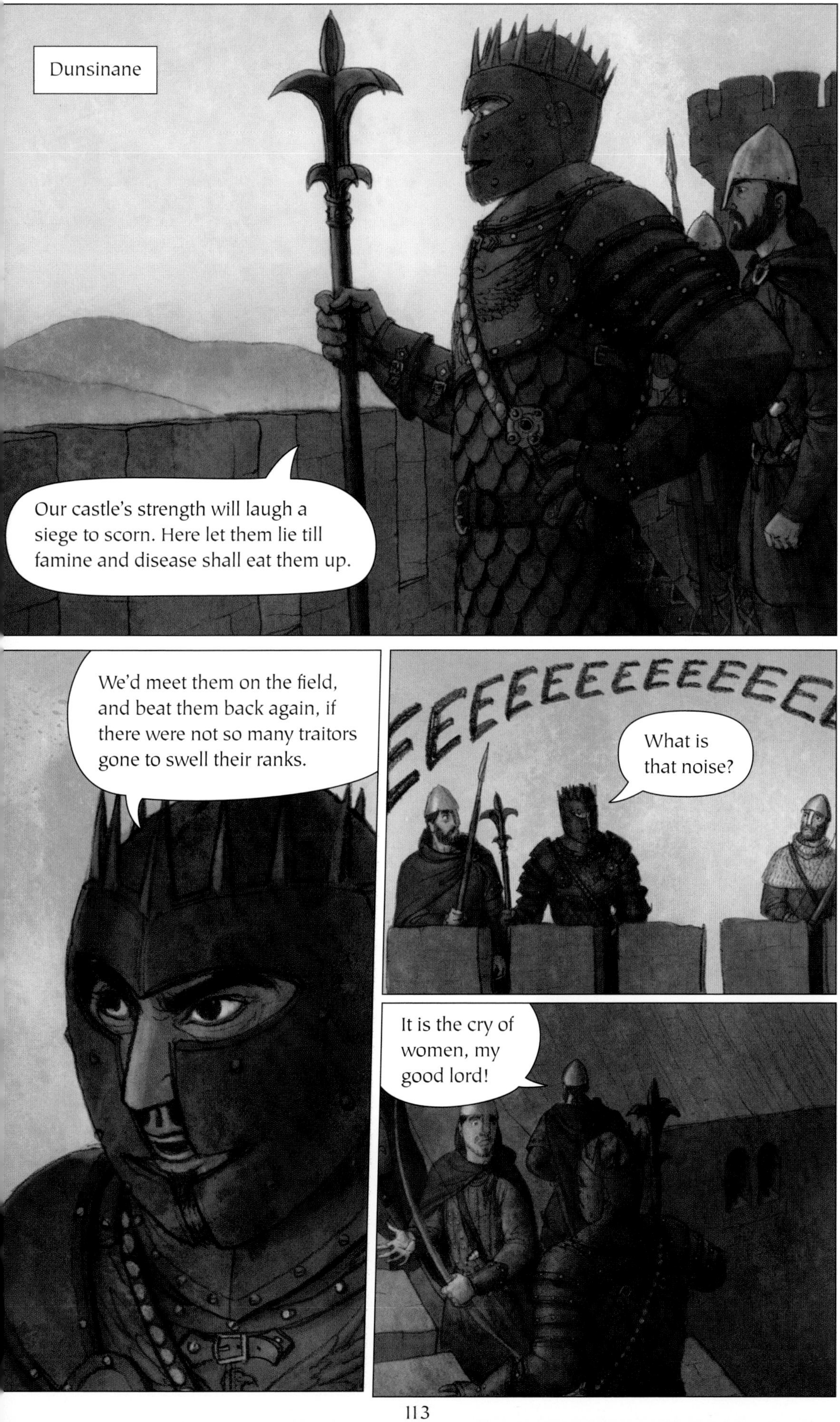
Dunsinane
Our castle's strength will laugh a siege to scorn. Here let them lie till famine and disease shall eat them up.
We'd meet them on the field, and beat them back again, if there were not so many traitors gone to swell their ranks.
EEEEEEEEEEEEE
What is that noise?
It is the cry of women, my good lord!

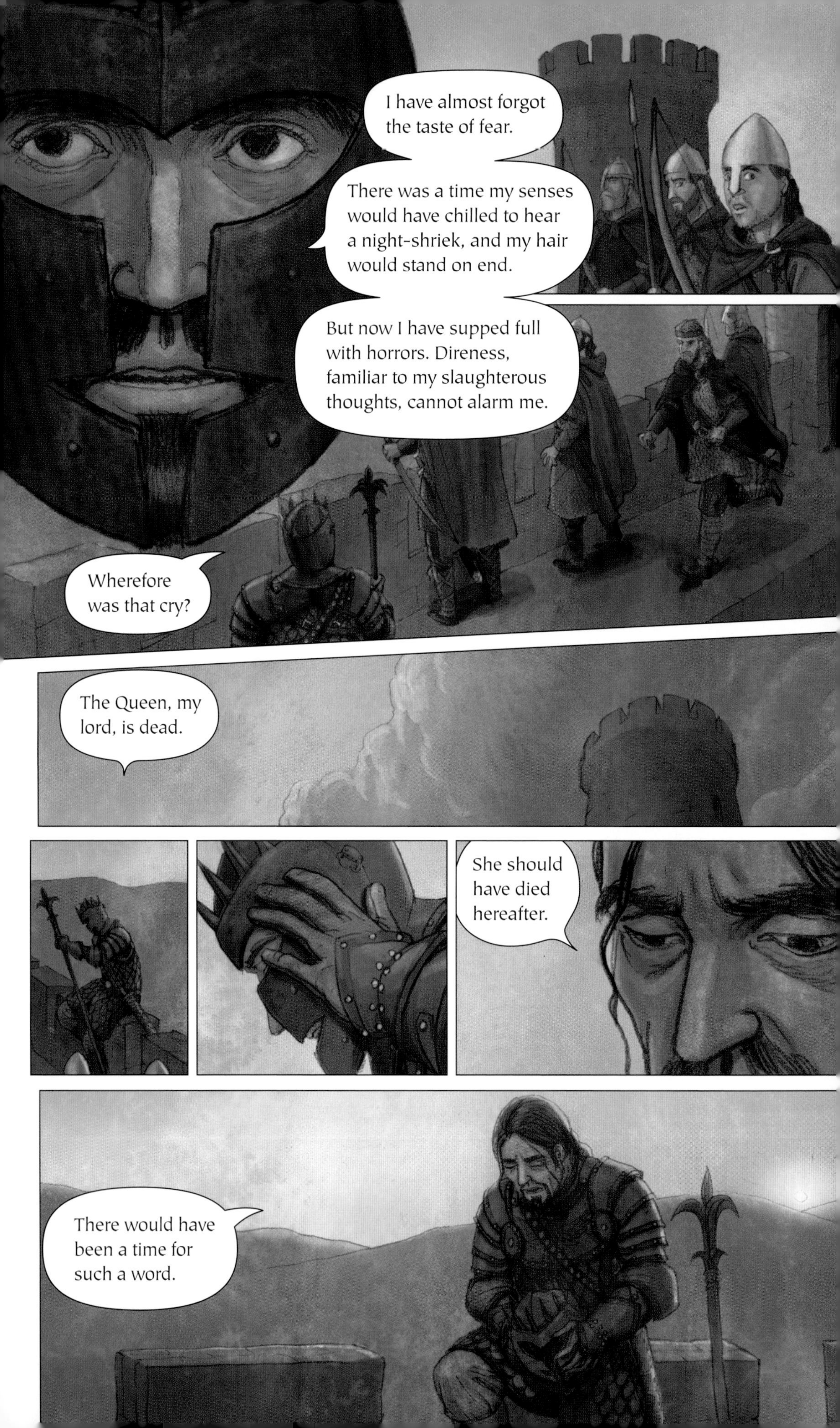
I have almost forgot the taste of fear.
There was a time my senses would have chilled to hear a night-shriek, and my hair would stand on end.
But now I have supped full with horrors. Direness, familiar to my slaughterous thoughts, cannot alarm me.
Wherefore was that cry?
The Queen, my lord, is dead.
She should have died hereafter.
There would have been a time for such a word.

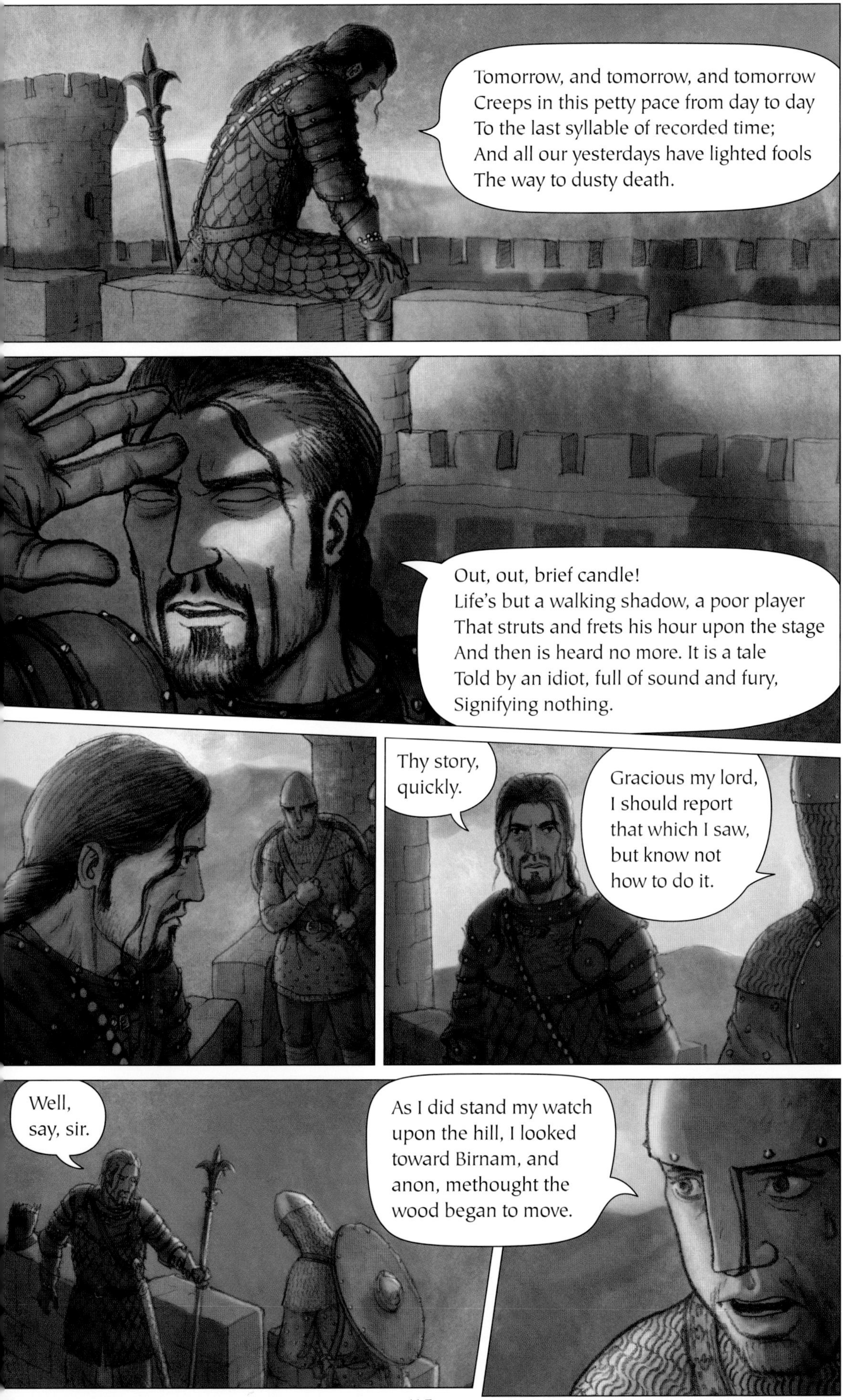
Tomorrow, and tomorrow, and tomorrow Creeps in this petty pace from day to day To the last syllable of recorded time; And all our yesterdays have lighted fools The way to dusty death.
Out, out, brief candle! Life's but a walking shadow, a poor player That struts and frets his hour upon the stage And then is heard no more. It is a tale Told by an idiot, full of sound and fury, Signifying nothing.
Thy story, quickly.
Gracious my lord, I should report that which I saw, but know not how to do it.
Well, say, sir.
As I did stand my watch upon the hill, I looked toward Birnam, and anon, methought the wood began to move.

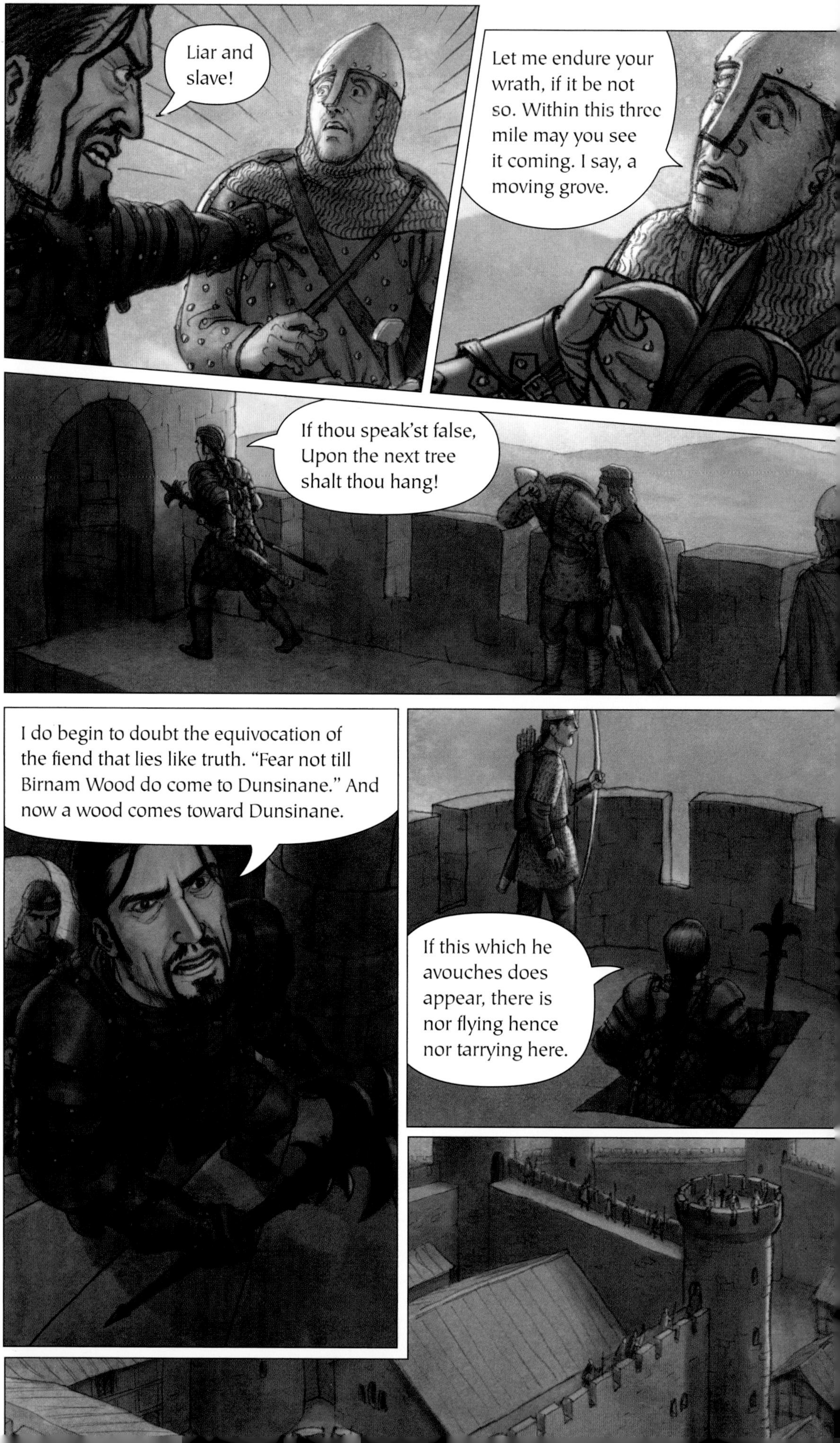
Liar and slave!
Let me endure your wrath, if it be not so. Within this three mile may you see it coming. I say, a moving grove.
If thou speak'st false, Upon the next tree shalt thou hang!
I do begin to doubt the equivocation of the fiend that lies like truth. "Fear not till Birnam Wood do come to Dunsinane." And now a wood comes toward Dunsinane.
If this which he avouches does appear, there is nor flying hence nor tarrying here.

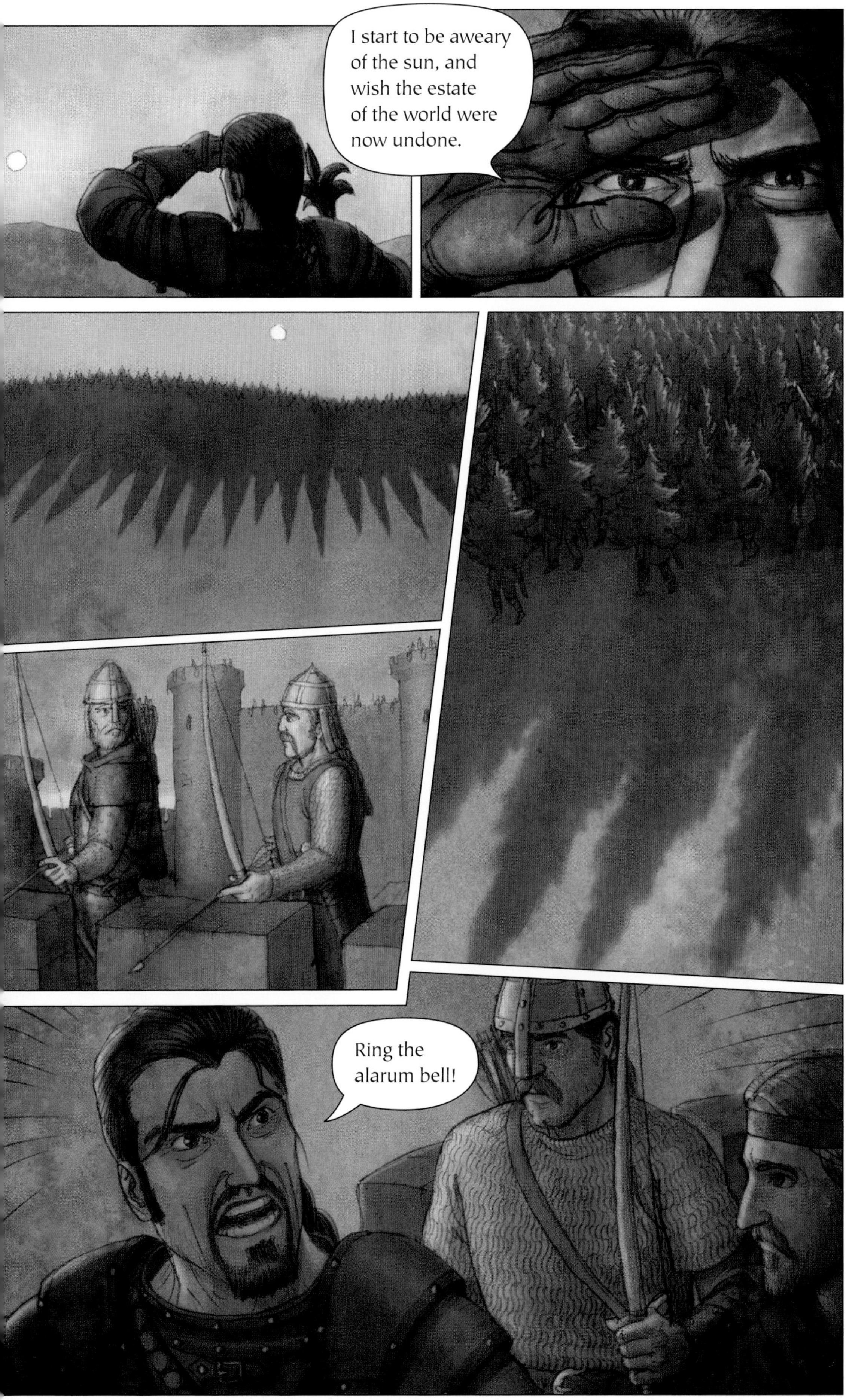
I start to be aweary of the sun, and wish the estate of the world were now undone.
Ring the alarum bell!

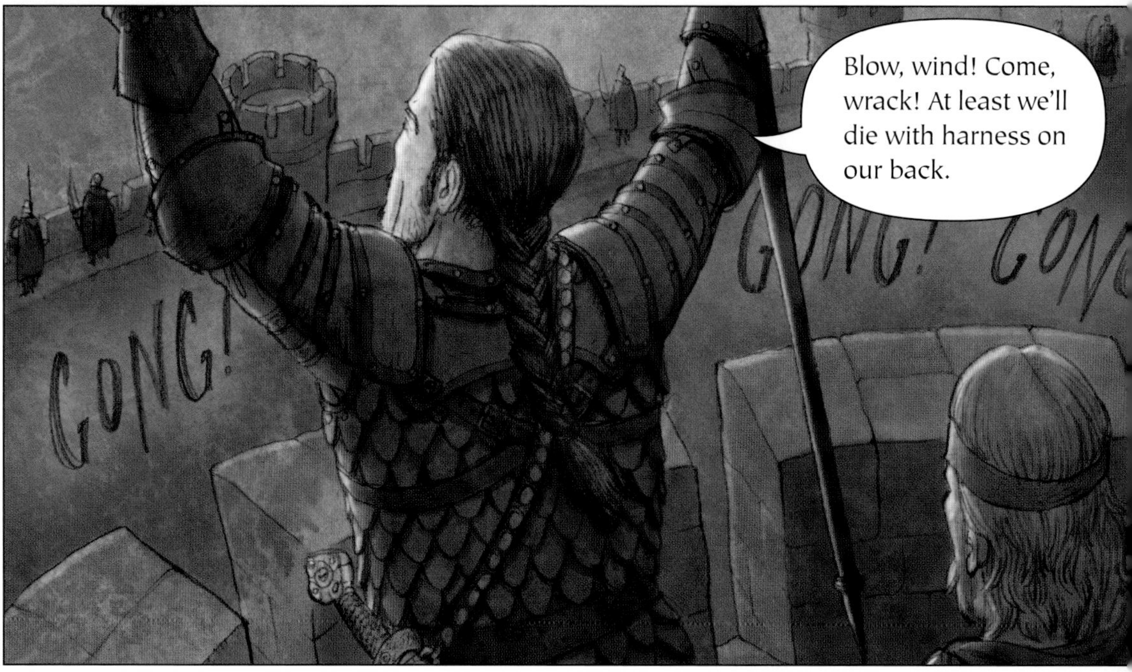
Blow, wind! Come, wrack! At least we'll die with harness on our back.
GONG!
GONG!

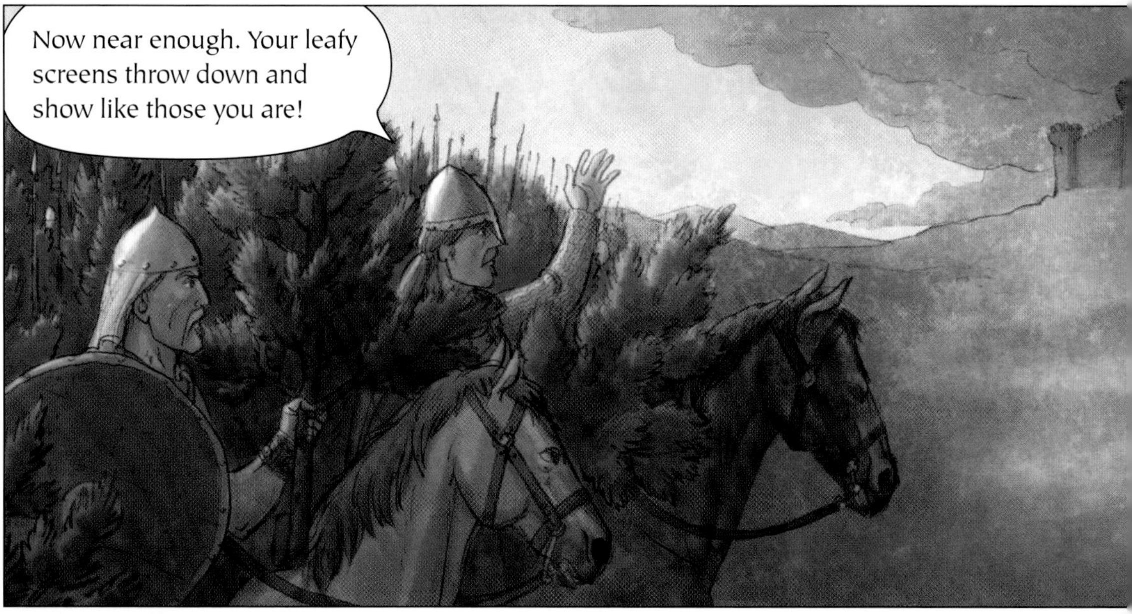
Now near enough. Your leafy screens throw down and show like those you are!

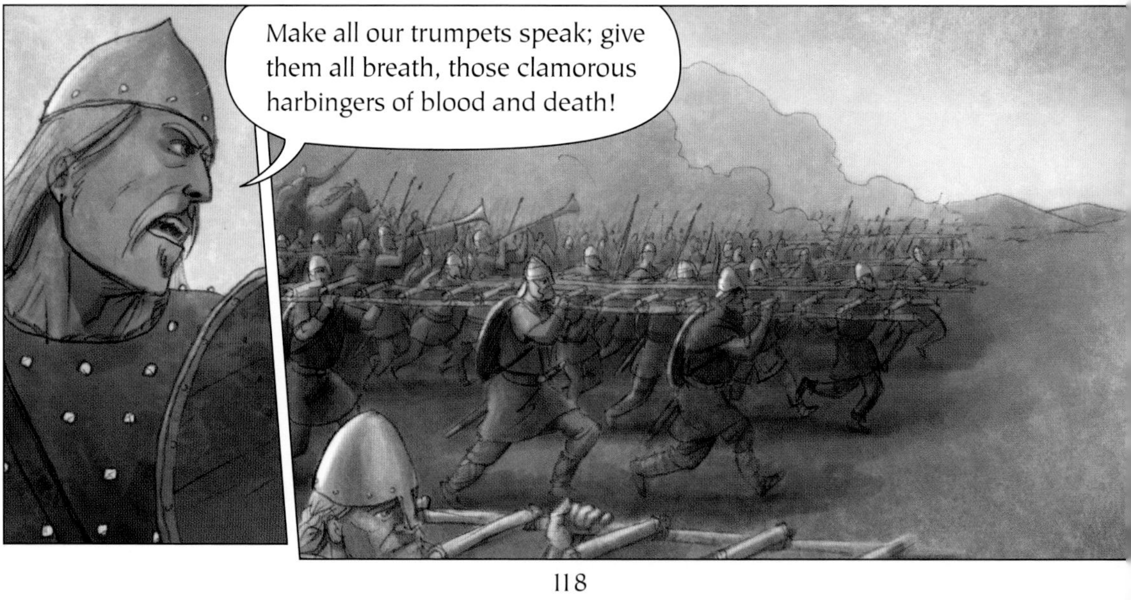
Make all our trumpets speak; give them all breath, those clamorous harbingers of blood and death!

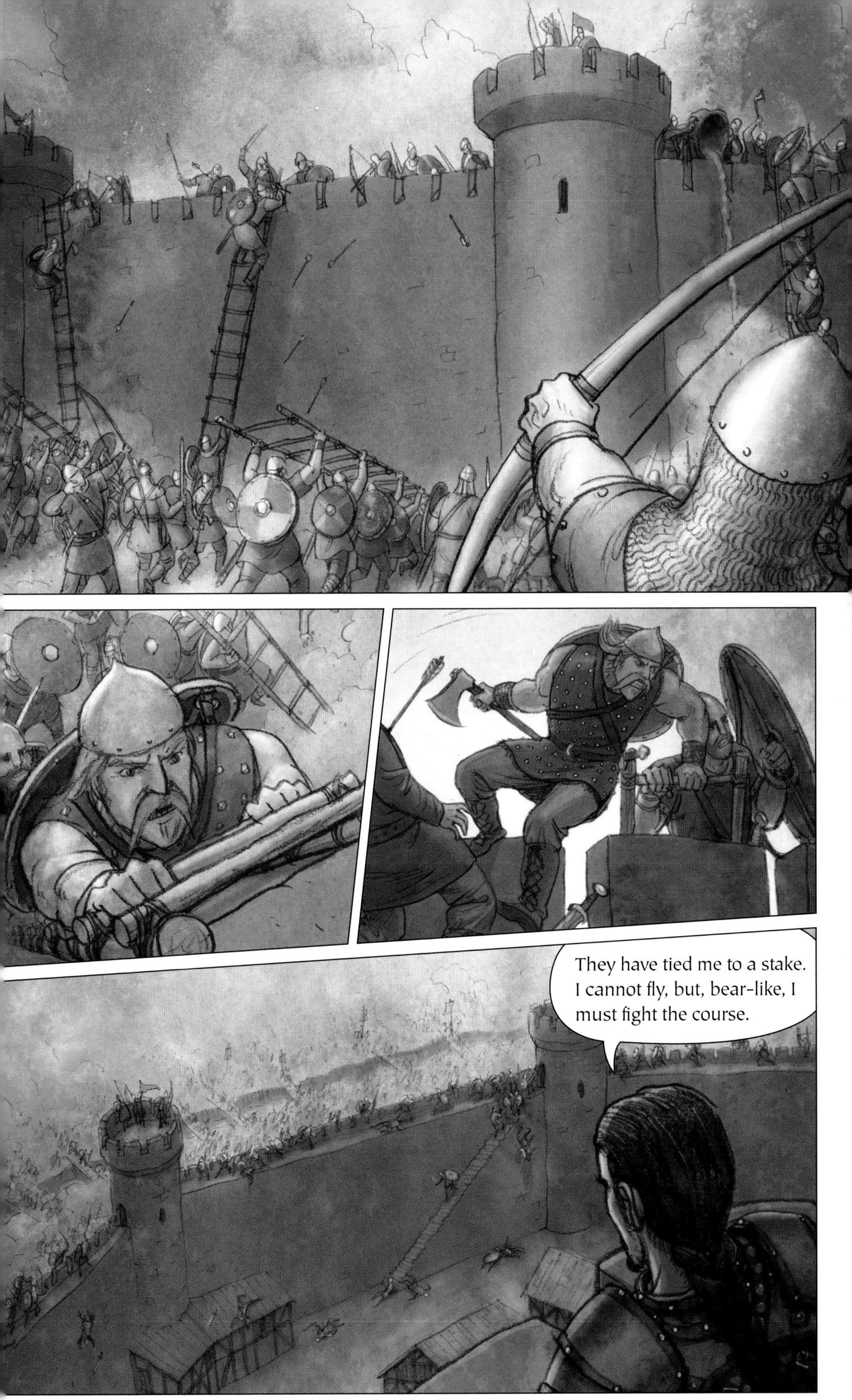
They have tied me to a stake. I cannot fly, but, bear-like, I must fight the course.

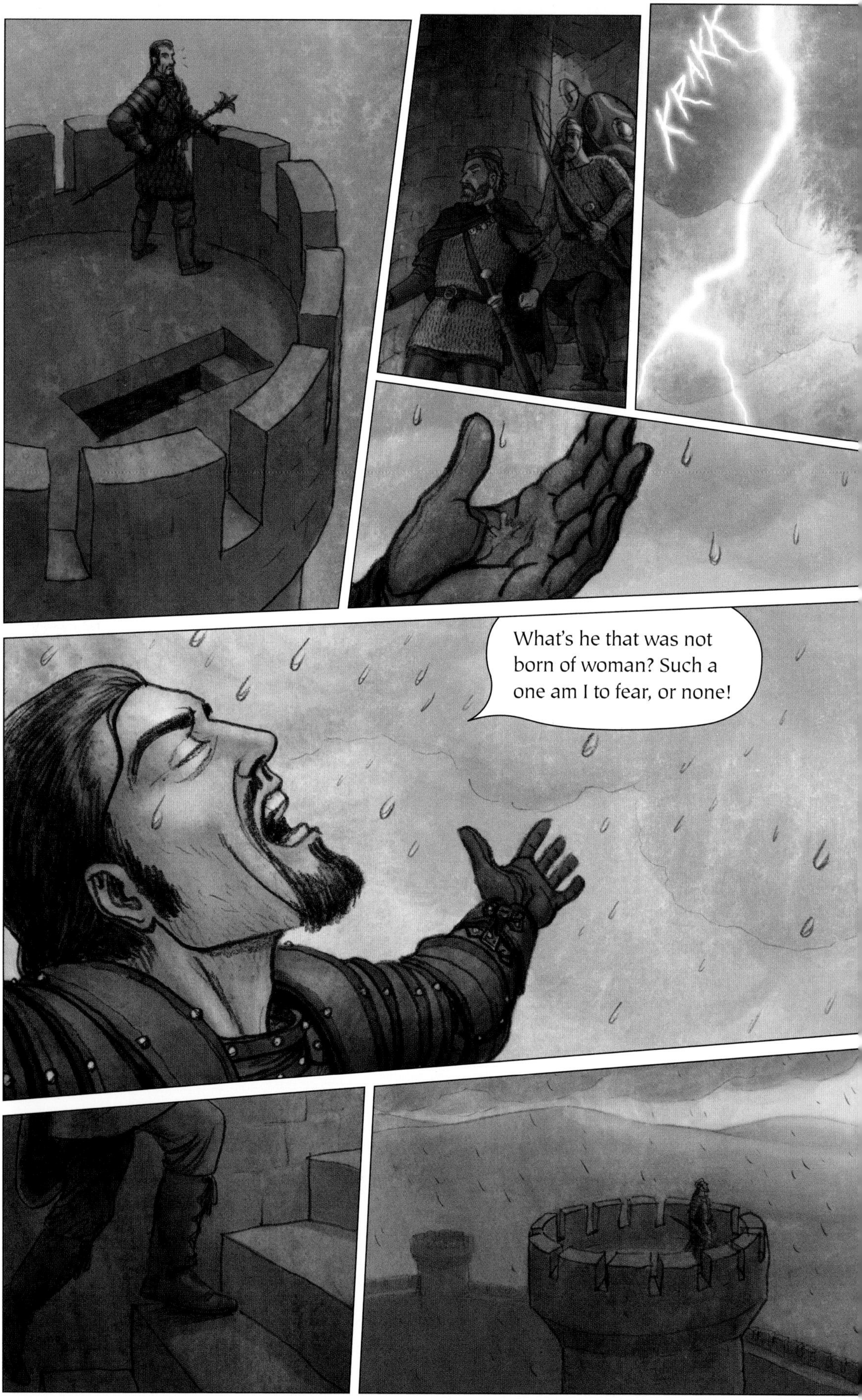
KRAKK
What's he that was not born of woman? Such a one am I to fear, or none!

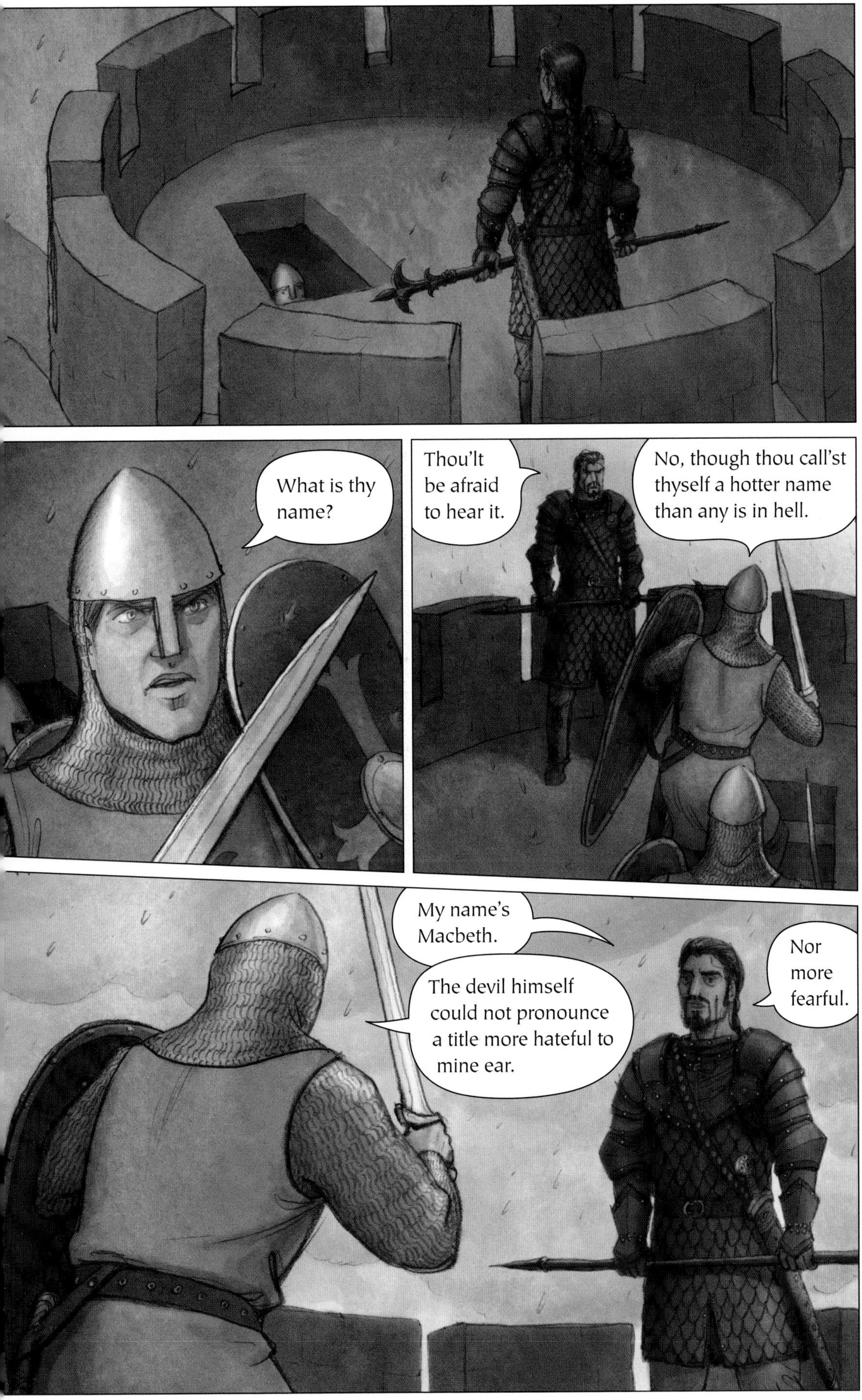
What is thy name?
Thou'lt be afraid to hear it.
No, though thou call'st thyself a hotter name than any is in hell.
My name's Macbeth.
The devil himself could not pronounce a title more hateful to mine ear.
Nor more fearful.

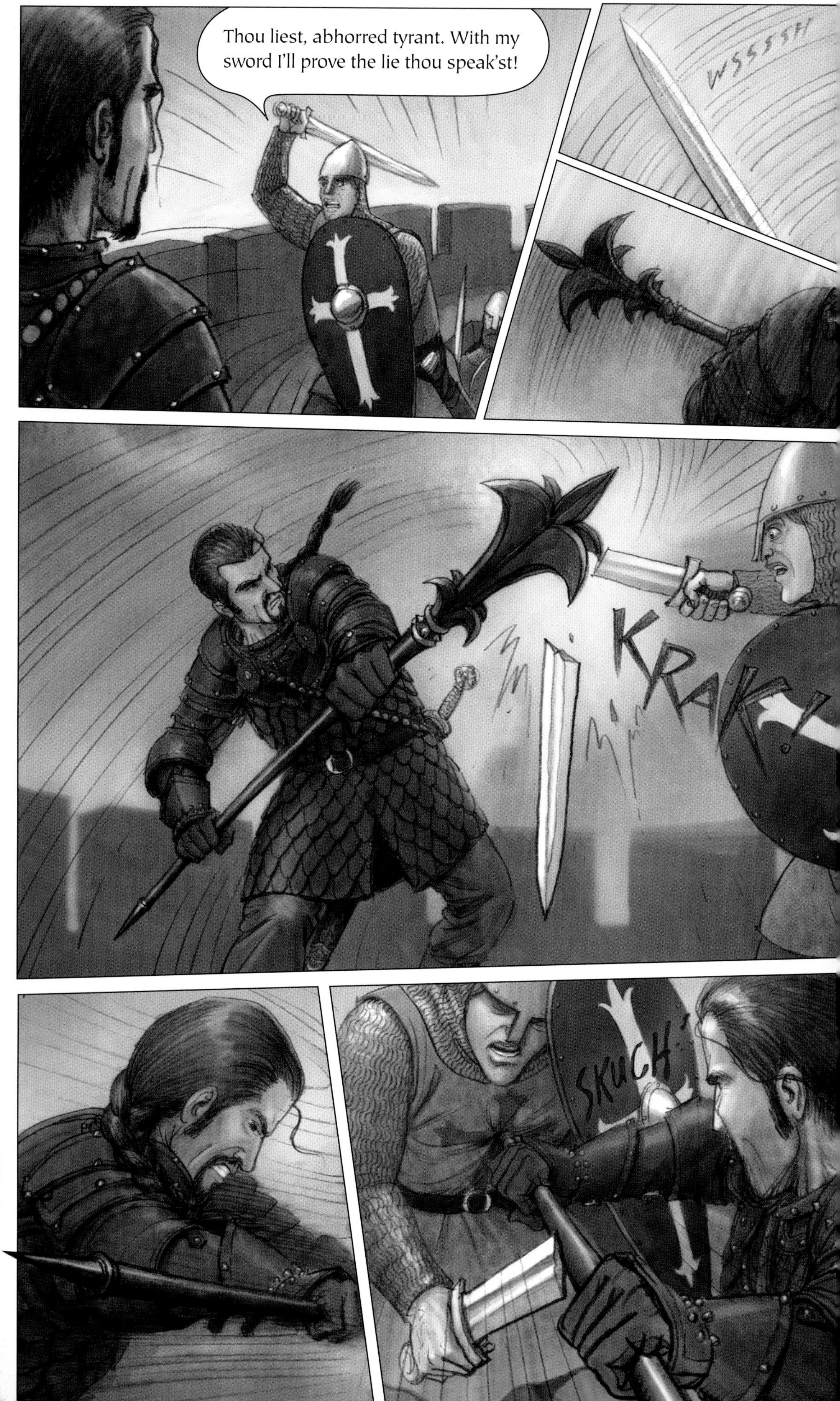
Thou liest, abhorred tyrant. With my sword I'll prove the lie thou speak'st!
WSSSSH
KRAK!
SKUCH!

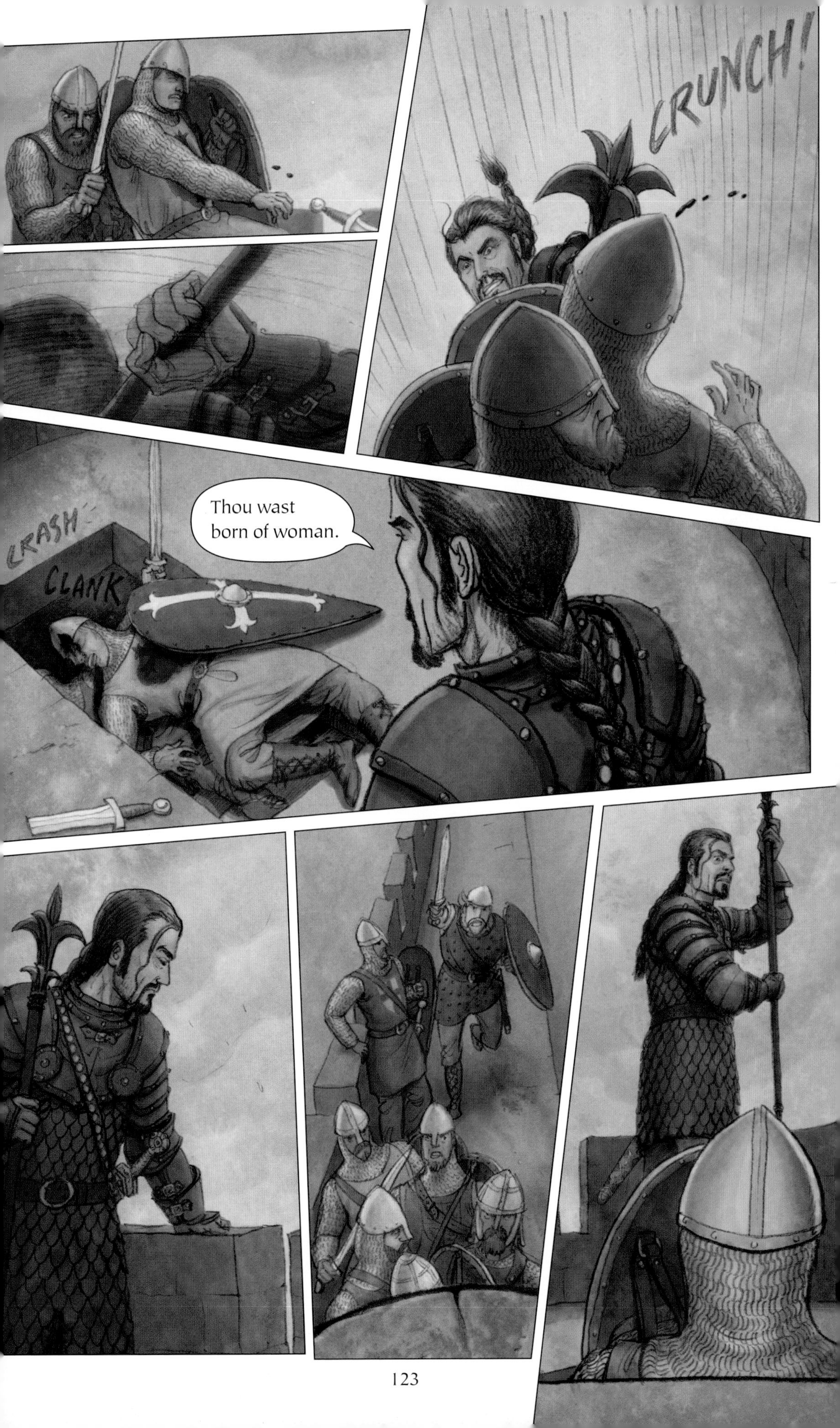
CRUNCH!
CRASH
CLANK
Thou wast born of woman.

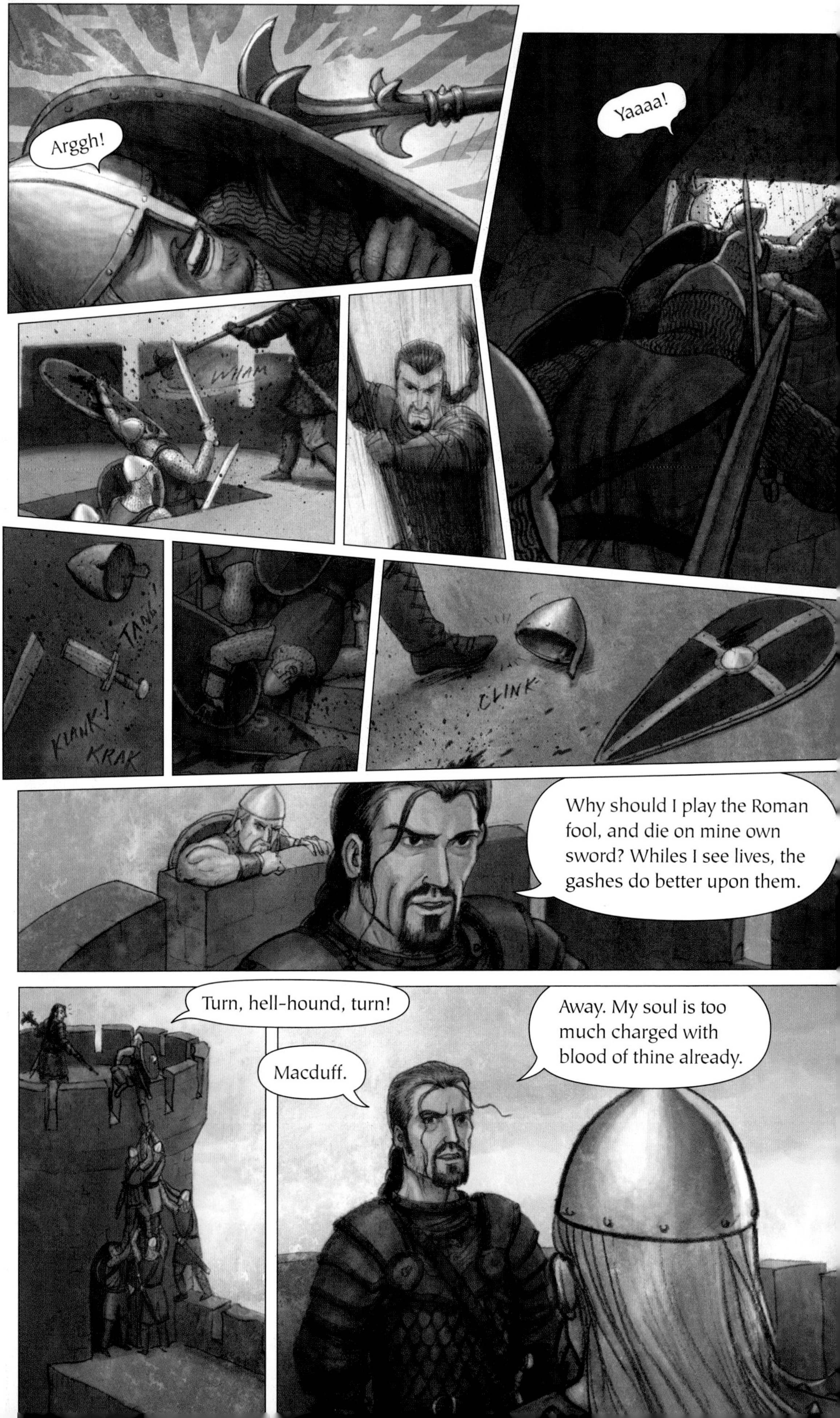
Arggh!
Yaaaa!
WHAM
TANG!
KLANK!
KRAK
CLINK
Why should I play the Roman fool, and die on mine own sword? Whiles I see lives, the gashes do better upon them.
Turn, hell-hound, turn!
Macduff.
Away. My soul is too much charged with blood of thine already.

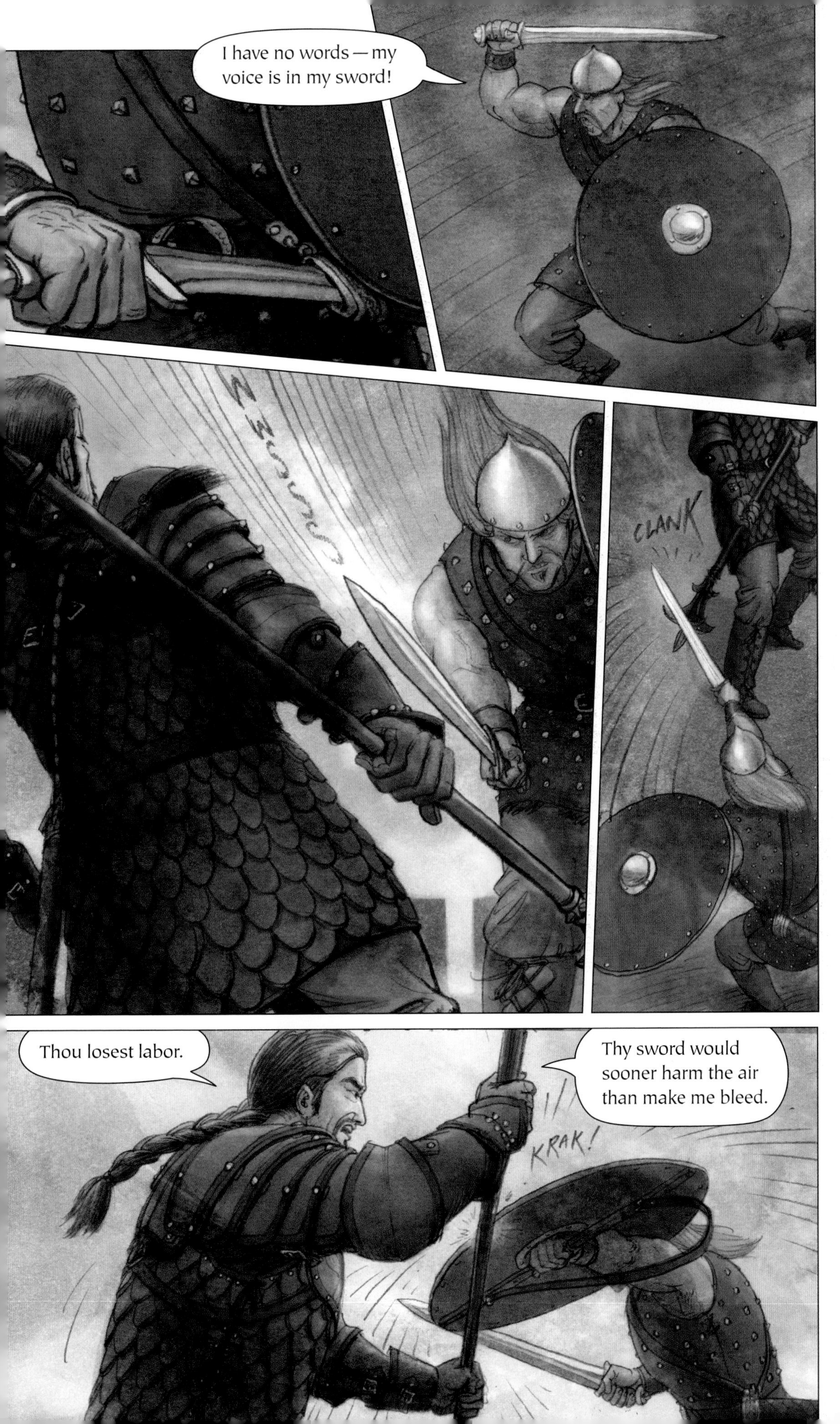
I have no words — my voice is in my sword!
CLANK
Thou losest labor.
Thy sword would sooner harm the air than make me bleed.
KRAK!

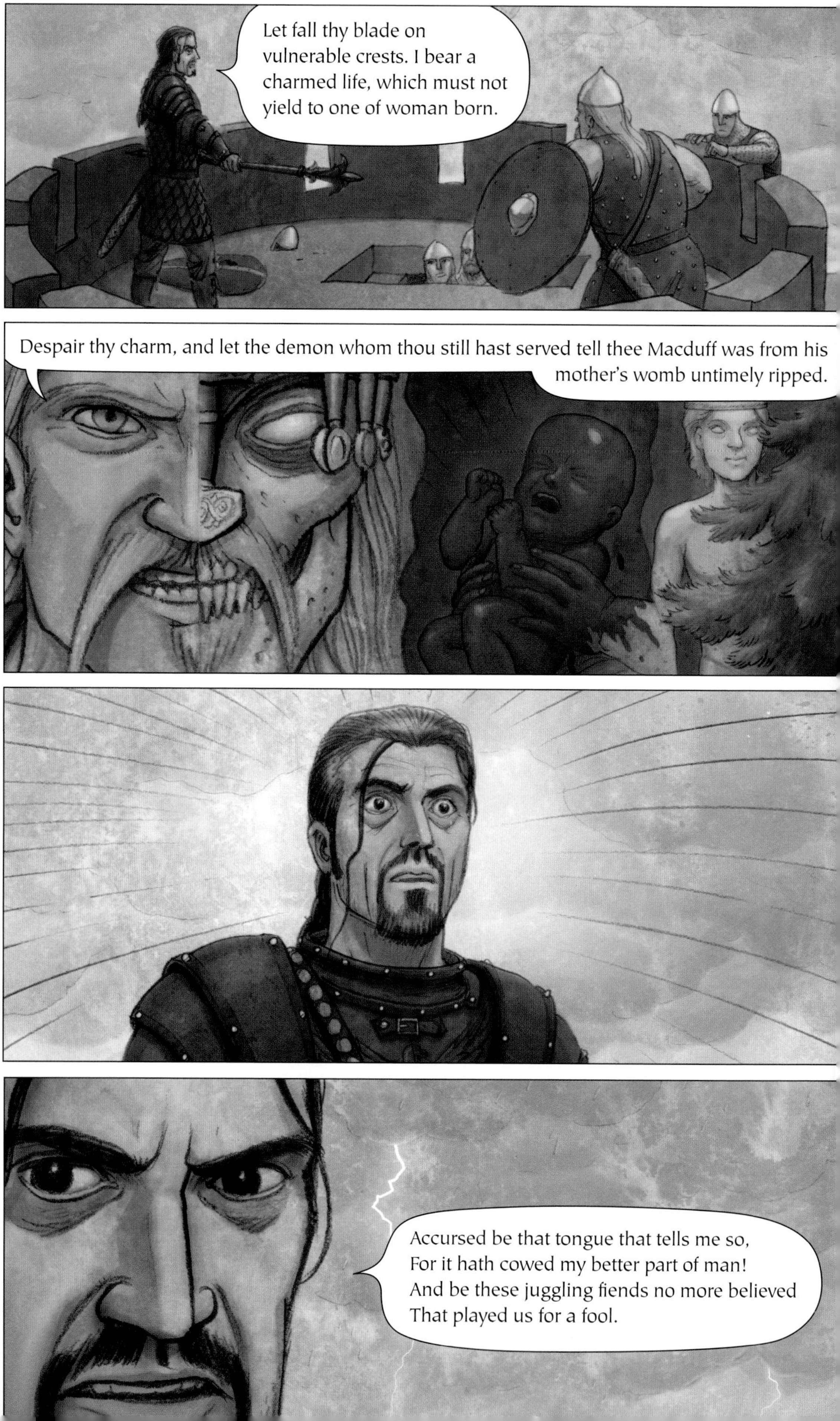
Let fall thy blade on vulnerable crests. I bear a charmed life, which must not yield to one of woman born.
Despair thy charm, and let the demon whom thou still hast served tell thee Macduff was from his mother's womb untimely ripped.
Accursed be that tongue that tells me so,
For it hath cowed my better part of man!
And be these juggling fiends no more believed
That played us for a fool.

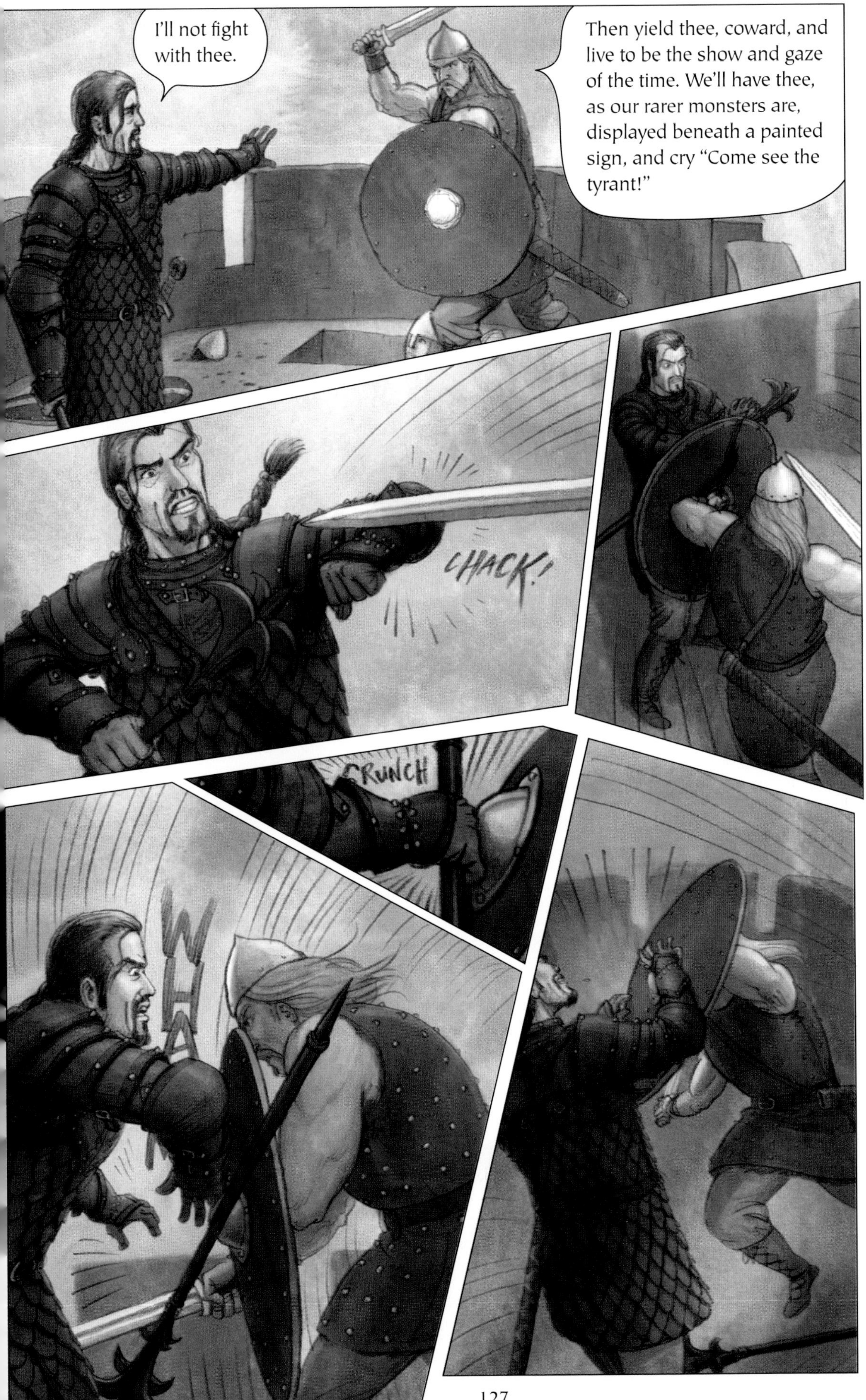
I'll not fight with thee.
Then yield thee, coward, and live to be the show and gaze of the time. We'll have thee, as our rarer monsters are, displayed beneath a painted sign, and cry "Come see the tyrant!"
CHACK!
CRUNCH

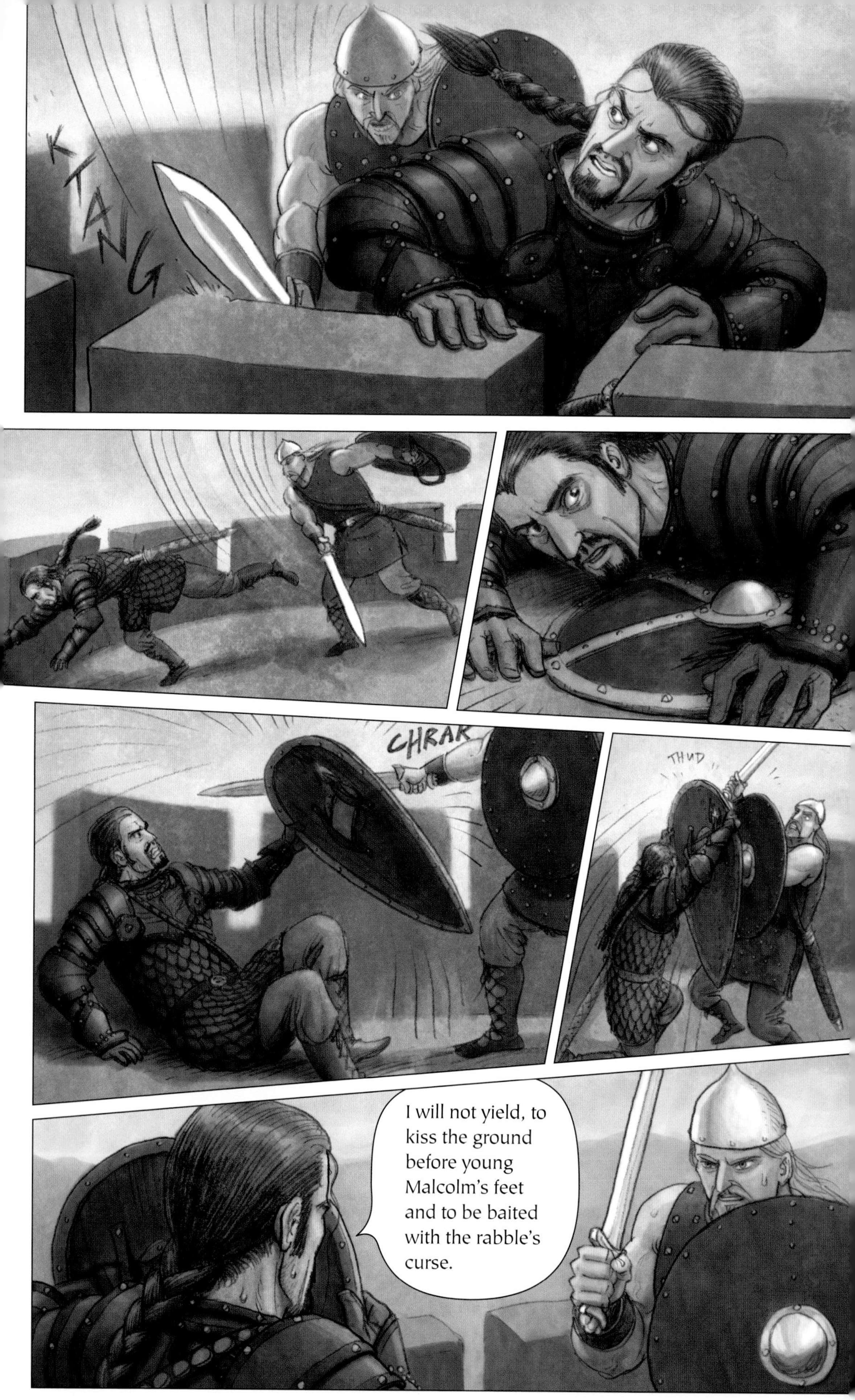
KTANG
CHRAK
THUD
I will not yield, to kiss the ground before young Malcolm's feet and to be baited with the rabble's curse.

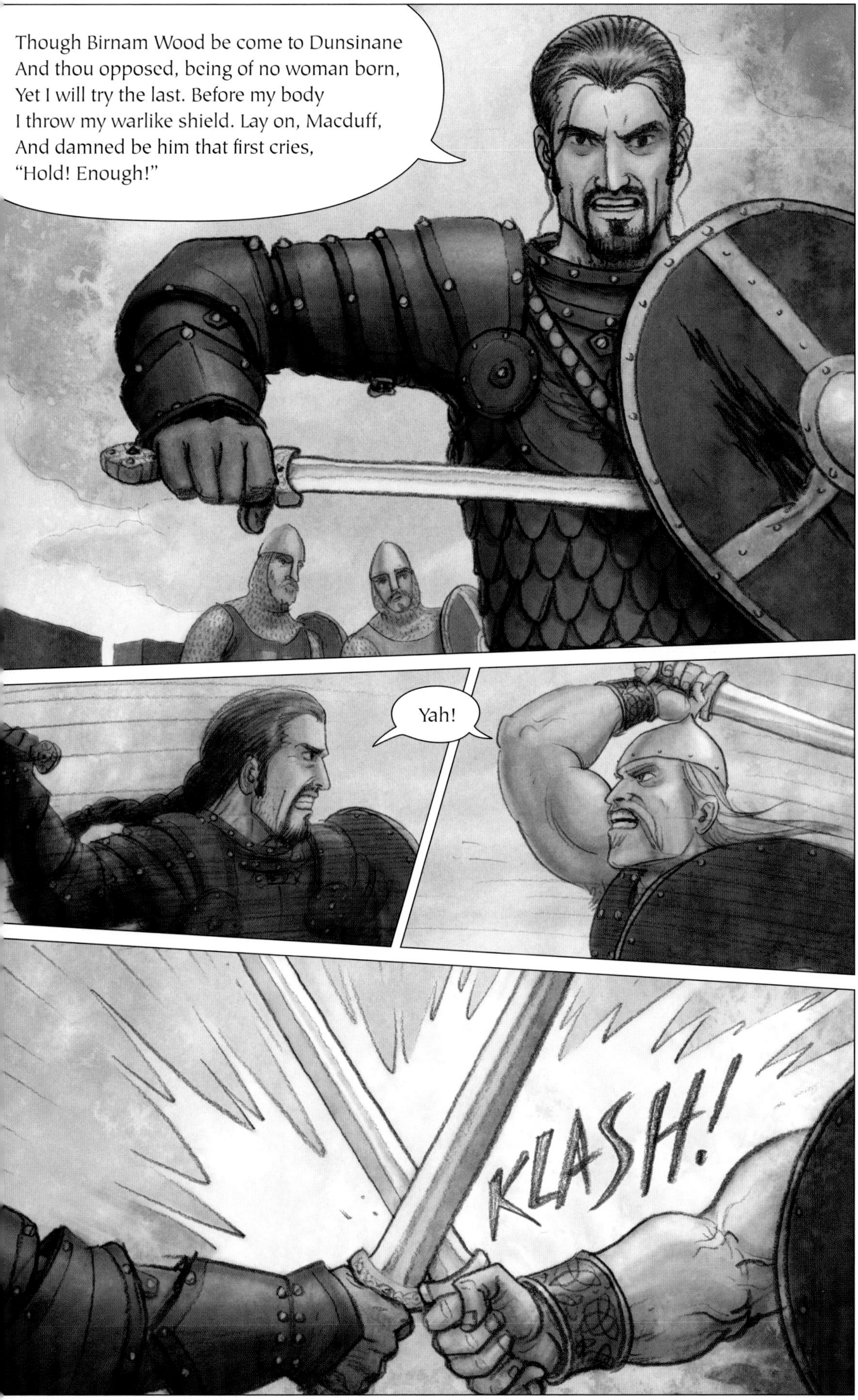
Though Birnam Wood be come to Dunsinane
And thou opposed, being of no woman born,
Yet I will try the last. Before my body
I throw my warlike shield. Lay on, Macduff,
And damned be him that first cries,
"Hold! Enough!"
Yah!
KLASH!

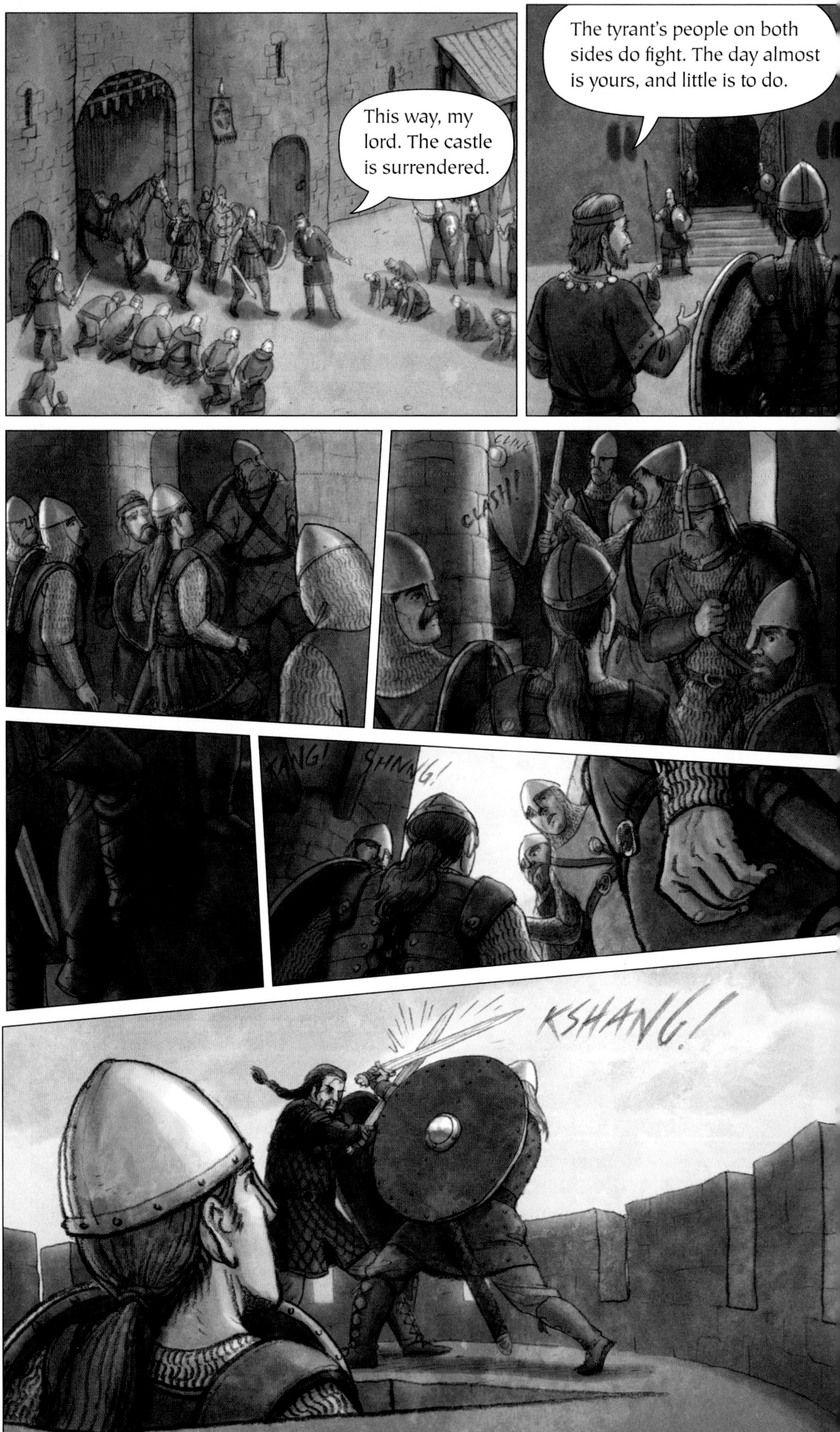
This way, my lord. The castle is surrendered.
The tyrant's people on both sides do fight. The day almost is yours, and little is to do.
CLINK
CLASH!
XANG!
SHNNG!
KSHANG!

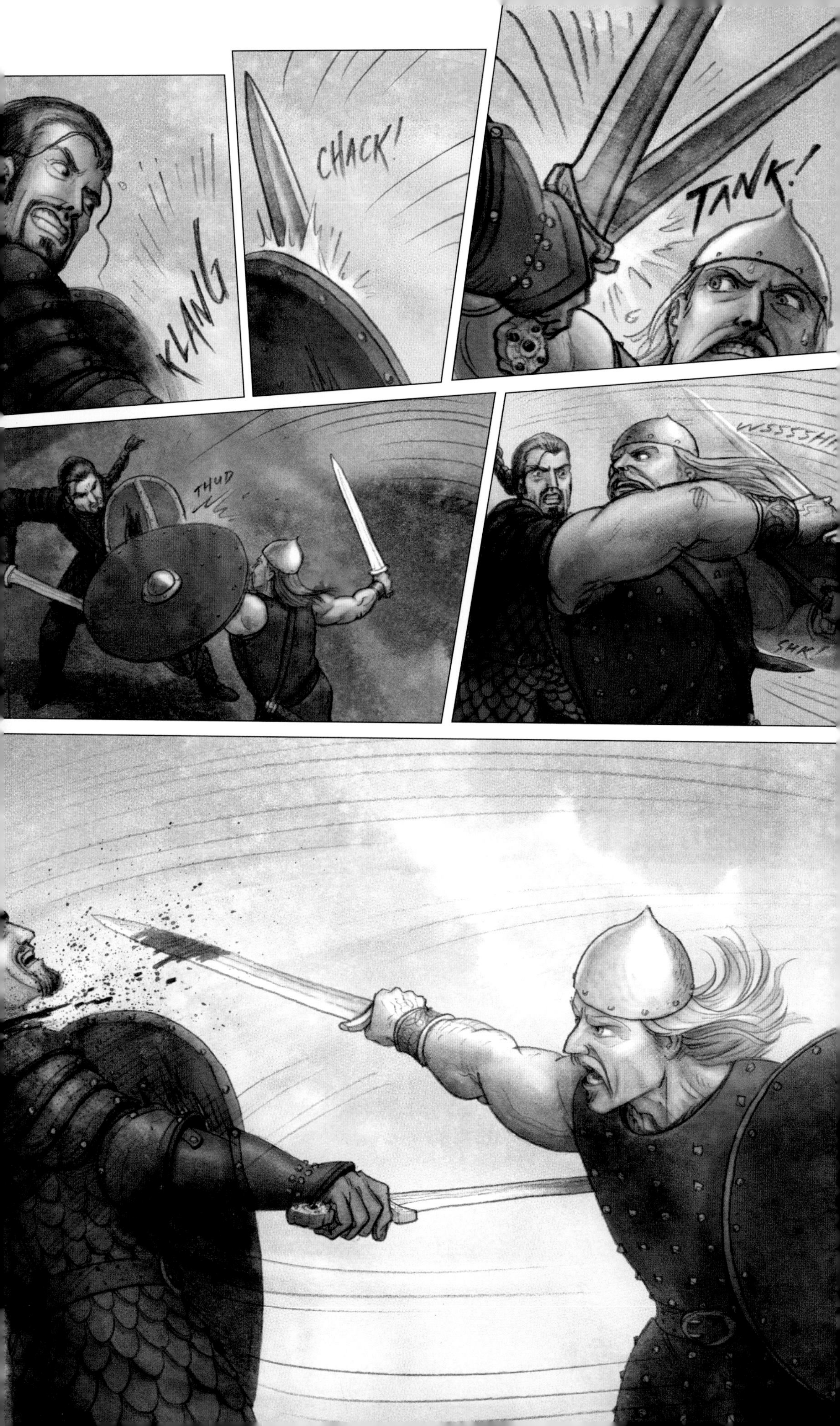
KLANG
CHACK!
TANK!
THUD
WSSSSH
SHK!

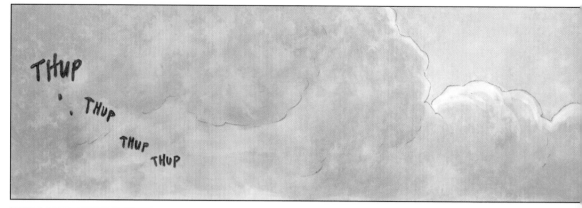

THUP

THUP

THUP

THUP

RSSM

Hail, King! For so thou art.

Behold, where stands the usurper's cursed head.

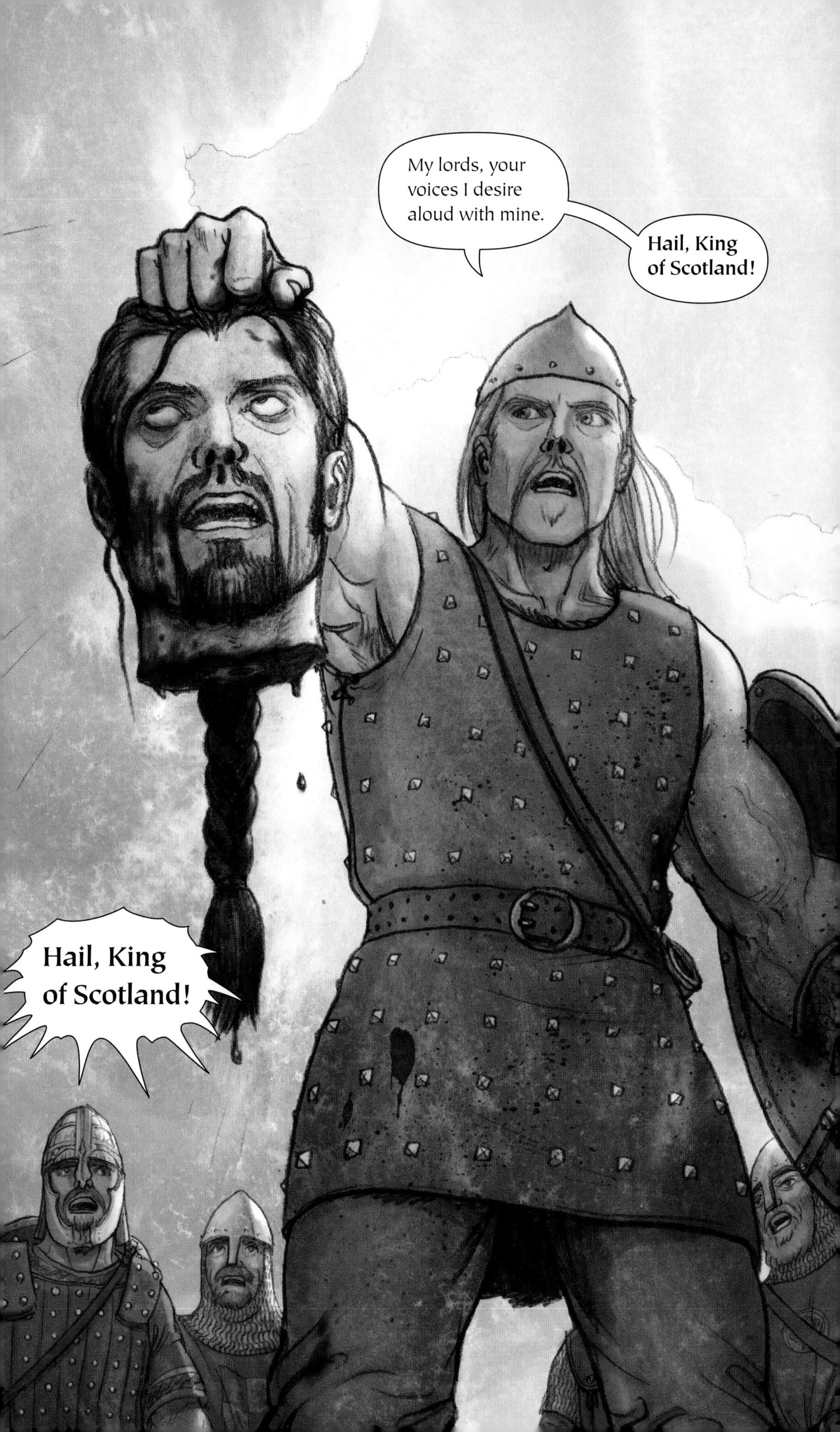
My lords, your voices I desire aloud with mine.
Hail, King of Scotland!
Hail, King of Scotland!

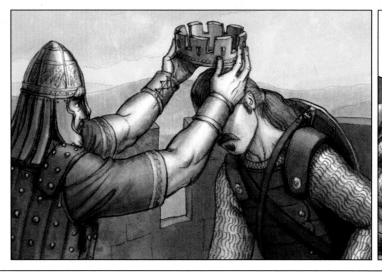

We shall be swift to recompense your loves, and make us even with you.

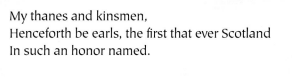

My thanes and kinsmen,
Henceforth be earls, the first that ever Scotland
In such an honor named.

We'll call our friends
Home from abroad that fled the tyranny
Of this dead butcher and his fiend-like queen,
Who, as 'tis thought, by self and violent hands
Took off her life.

This, and what needful else that calls upon us, by the grace of Grace, we will perform in measure, time and place.

Hail!

Hail!

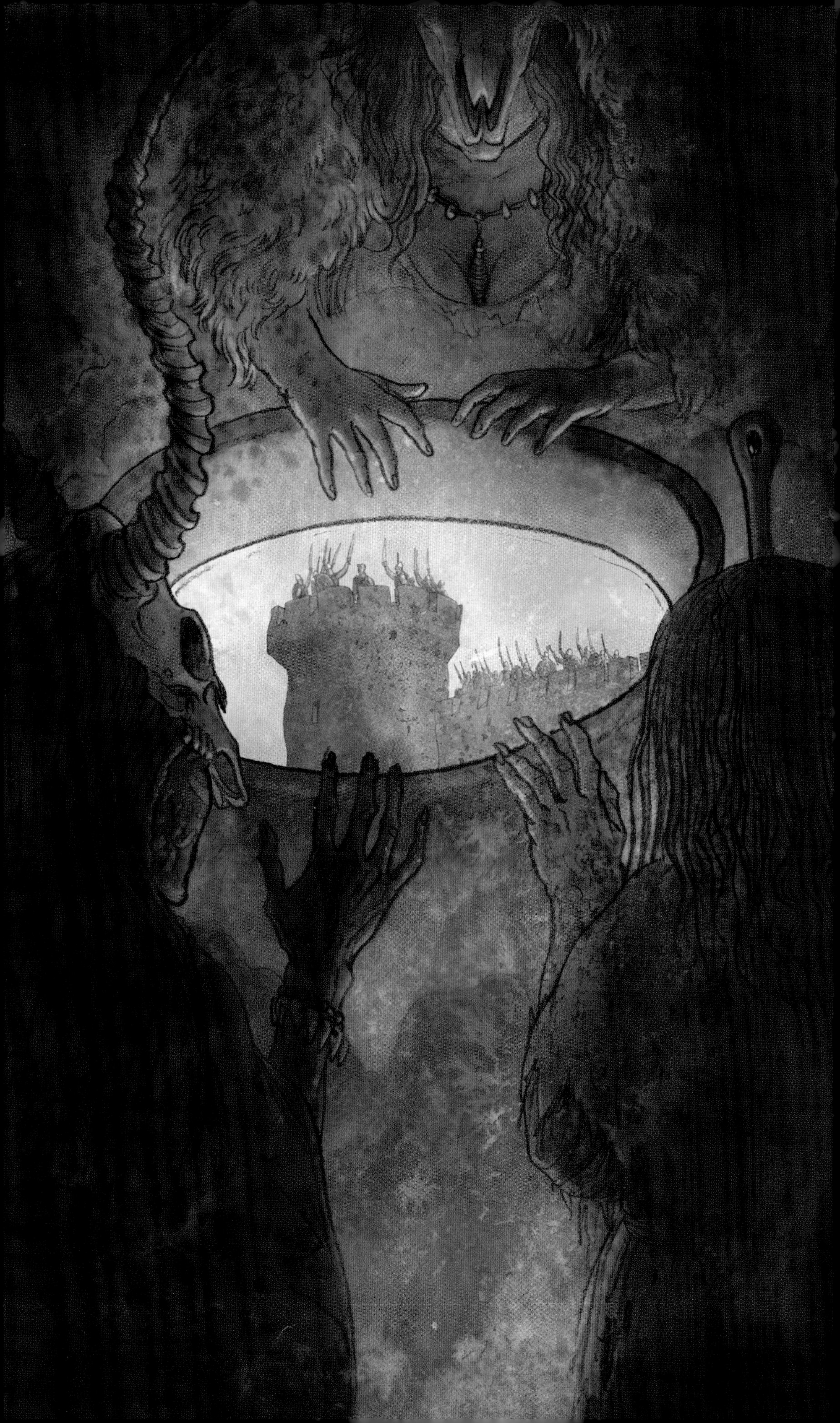

Historical Notes with Concept Sketches

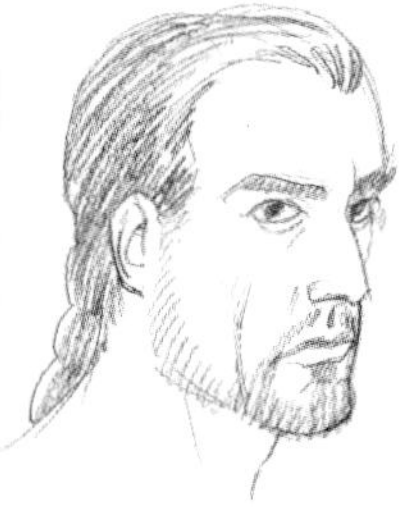

Macbeth was an actual historical king of Scotland (Mac Bethad mac Findlaích) who reigned from 1040 to 1057. His story was recounted in Raphael Holinshed's *Chronicles of England, Scotland, and Ireland,* which was probably Shakespeare's main source for this play. Historical scholarship was pretty weak at the time, so the accuracy of Holinshed's account is dubious, and in any case Shakespeare did not stick to it, instead exercising plenty of creative and dramatic license. According to Holinshed, the real Macbeth plotted *with* Banquo to kill Duncan, reigned peacefully for seventeen years, and was killed by Malcolm rather than Macduff. Macbeth was succeeded briefly by his stepson Lulach (missing from the play), who was then also killed by Malcolm. Malcolm became king in 1058 and reigned until 1093, when he was succeeded by his brother Donald Bain (Donalbain, or "Donald the fair"), who lost and regained his crown several times in a tumultuous reign. According to Holinshed, Banquo's son Fleance fled to Wales, and Fleance's son later returned to Scotland and became the royal steward. His descendants became the Stuart line of kings, eventually leading to King James I—who succeeded Elizabeth I and was probably Shakespeare's patron at the time he wrote *Macbeth.* Again, that's according to Holinshed. More recent scholars have made a pretty solid case that Banquo and Fleance are actually fictional characters.

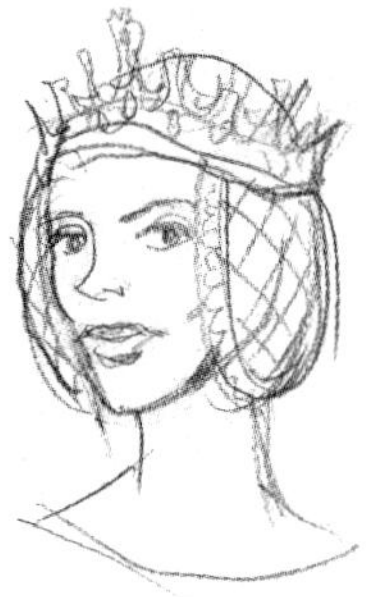

Despite these historical inaccuracies, we can be fairly certain that Macbeth was a real person who lived at a specific time, so I felt I should keep him in 11th-century Scotland and depict the setting in a more or less historically accurate fashion. We don't have much archaeological evidence to pinpoint differences between the dress or habits of the 10th, 11th, and 12th centuries, or in Scotland versus Scandinavia. But it's generally agreed that most of the Scottish stereotypes we know today—kilts, claymores, bagpipes, the tartan patterns we call plaid, and so on—didn't arrive until the 14th century (though there were some primitive tartan patterns used at least as far back as the eighth century BCE).

Most surprising to me was the fact that castles were not introduced into the British Isles until the Norman invasion of 1066—nine years after the historical Macbeth died. So when Shakespeare repeatedly set scenes in "so-and-so's castle," he may have been unaware of the history, using the word very loosely, or (most likely) imagining a rather later period of Scottish history. This is probably also an example of how little regard was given to historical accuracy in the Elizabethan theatre. Generally there was little or no attempt made to get the period right; it was simply a matter of dressing the actors in cast-off court clothes appropriate to their character's rank.

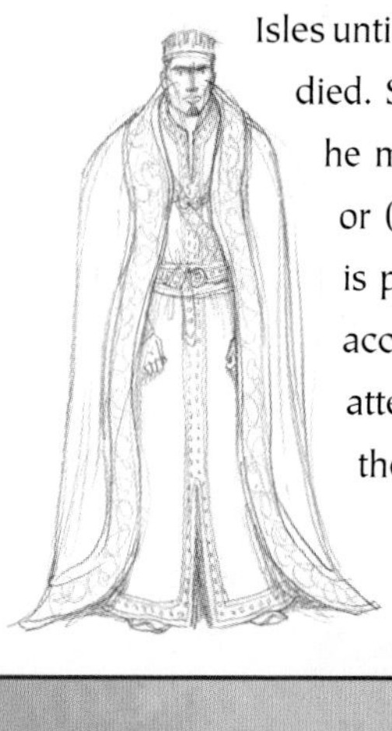

After weighing the various options, I decided that the best visual compromise, to respect both Shakespeare's text and the historical events, was to draw the setting of my adaptation as roughly 12th century.

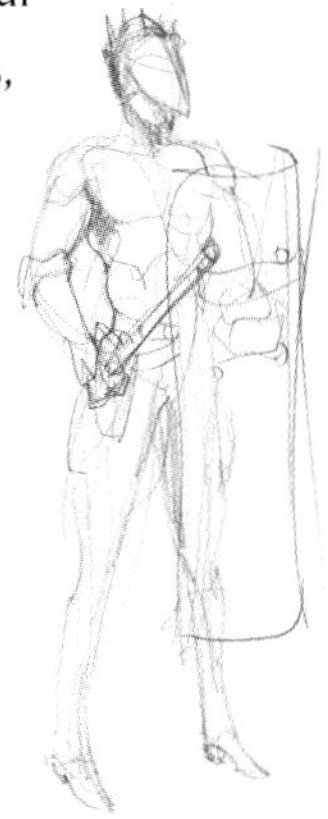

Notes on the Text

In my other adaptations, I've gone to great lengths to preserve Shakespeare's verse in the original iambic pentameter. In this play, however, the lines seem to read better as prose, so I took out the line breaks for most passages. There's still an iambic rhythm driving the lines, but I think they flow better without the line breaks to trip over (and unlike in *Romeo and Juliet,* there are almost no rhyming couplets to preserve). I also removed many of the contractions Shakespeare used to indicate when part of a word doesn't get its own syllable (for example, he would write *o'er* to turn *over* into a one-syllable word—you could say he was cheating). I believe removing the contractions makes it easier to read without sacrificing the power of Shakespeare's writing.

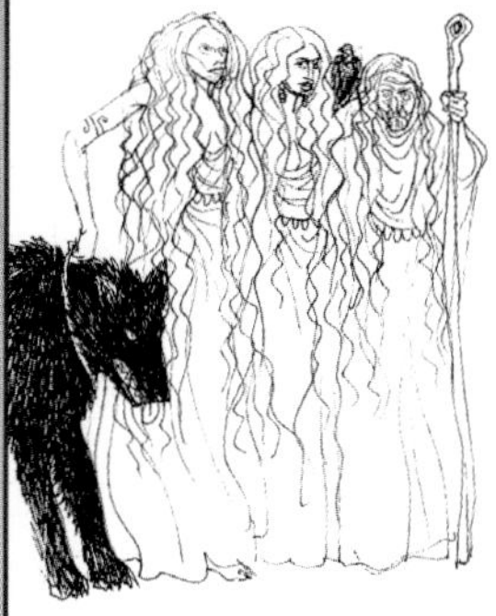

As with my previous adaptations, I've had to remove a fair amount of material from the original play in order to keep the script to a good length for a graphic novel and make the speeches short enough to fit inside comic panels. I try to do this in a way that respects the text and preserves the essential elements of the play. However, a lot of good material did end up on the cutting-room floor, so I highly recommend reading the unabridged play.

In addition to cutting material, I have occasionally substituted a more modern word for an archaic one, when I could do so without disrupting the poetic meter or diminishing the richness of Shakespeare's language. But because meeting both those criteria is not easy, I've left quite a few archaic words in place. Here's one example of what I mean:

In act 5, scene 5, Macbeth exclaims, "Blow, wind! Come, wrack! At least we'll die with harness on our back." *Harness* in this context means armor. Both words have the same number of syllables, so it would be easy to substitute *armor* for *harness* without breaking the meter. But *harness* has other meanings, and if we consider the more common sense of the word (a device to connect an animal to a plow or vehicle), then the phrase "die with harness on our backs" has a powerful extra layer of meaning in a play about fate versus free will. It would also be more colloquial to change Macbeth's royal *we* to *I,* but isn't it more interesting that he could be saying we *all* die with metaphorical harness on our backs? This rich use of language is a big part of why Shakespeare rocks so hard—I mean, is so beloved by scholars.

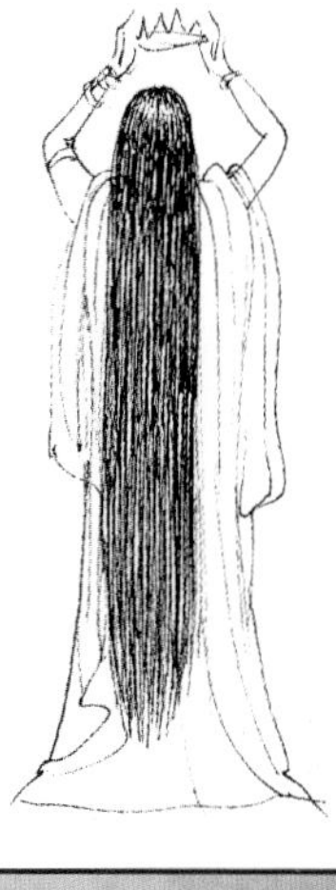

Page-by-Page Notes

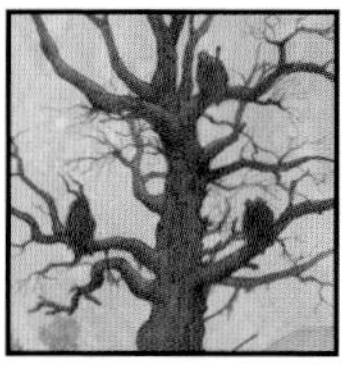

Pages vi–2:
The witches are drawn from my imagination and are not intended to be historically accurate. I wanted one hideous-looking example of a "classic" witch with warts and all, one earth-mother/fertility-goddess type of witch, and one decidedly non-Scottish witch. The witches call themselves "posters" (that is, rapid travelers) "of the sea and land," so I think they must have some power of flight, but I didn't want to show them actually flying because that seemed to depart from historical realism too early in the story. I decided to suggest that they transform into crows in the interval between two panels.

Throughout the book, I use black speech balloons to signify that a character is dwelling on, calling on, or channeling dark forces.

Page 3:

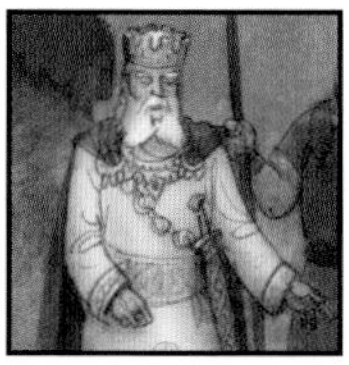

Historically it doesn't seem Duncan was any less of a hard-living, hard-fighting Scotsman than any of his thanes, or noblemen, but Shakespeare made him a very pure figure, so I gave him white hair and robes. However, on page 7, he appears haunted by dark shadows, a visual theme that you may notice I use frequently in the book. See how many creepy shadows you can find.

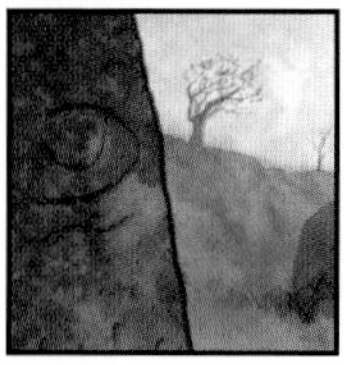

Page 8:
Standing stones with pagan symbols are common in the British Isles. The eye I've drawn on the stone isn't an authentic Wiccan symbol, but eye symbols do show up in many pagan traditions around the world.

Page 10:

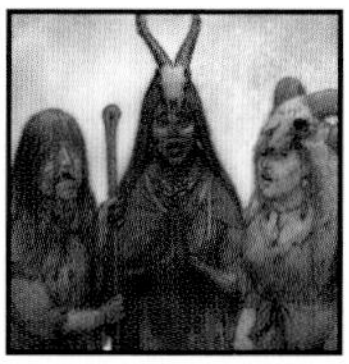

Some of the early Scottish tribesmen were known as Picts because they adorned themselves with body paint or tattoos. While popular folklore has them painting themselves with bright-blue woad, most of my research suggests that it was more likely they were tattooed with dark metallic pigments, so I gave Banquo a swirly permanent tattoo in a dark metallic color.

The witches are wearing the symbols of the mythical Fates—a spindle for spinning the thread of life, a rod or tape for measuring the length of the thread, and a pair of shears to snip it. (The rod would have been more traditional than the tape, but I had already given them a stick that they pass around among them as a walking staff, stirring stick, and flute, so I gave the African witch a measuring tape she could wear around her neck.)

The African witch also wears the skull of an impala (an African antelope), while the red-headed witch wears the skull and fleece of a ram.

The one genuine occult symbol I did use several times is the pentacle (usually a five-pointed star inside a circle), which indicates that the witches are summoning dark, otherworldly forces.

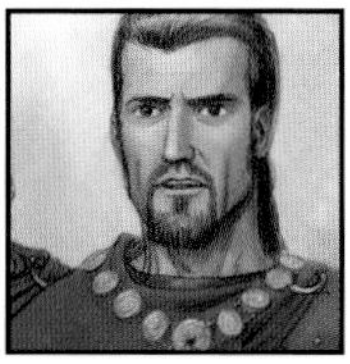

Page 15:

It's not easy to keep all the thanes, or noblemen, straight in this play, especially as Shakespeare barely mentions their names. I added the line "Ross and Angus" here to help readers identify the characters.

Chains of office, like the one Ross gives Macbeth here, have been a fairly common way of denoting noble rank from the Middle Ages all the way up to the present. There aren't many good surviving examples from the 11th or 12th centuries, so I'm not sure all the ones I've drawn are completely accurate, but it's likely Macbeth's new rank would have been signified by a fancy chain of some sort, and I've based my designs on examples from slightly later periods of history.

Page 20:

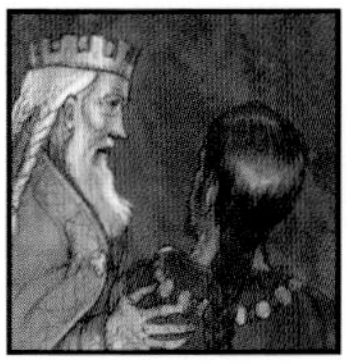

In 11th-century Scotland it was *not* commonly accepted practice for a king to name his heir. Usually when the king died, the nobles chose the next king (ostensibly according to merit). So actually Duncan naming Malcom as his heir is a bigger part of Macbeth's motivation than it may at first seem. He perceives that Duncan is making an unprecedented power grab, thus greatly reducing the chances of Macbeth rising to the crown "without his stir" (as is his hope on page 18).

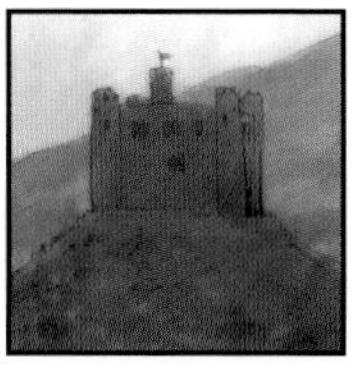

Page 21:

I've drawn Macbeth's castle at Inverness as an early transitional type—a motte-and-bailey fort rebuilt in stone, relatively small and simple, lacking glazed windows or elaborate defenses. For staging reasons, I've given it a more complicated interior layout than would have been common in most early castles. This is mainly because I wanted there to be more places where one or two people could walk around by themselves (to plot murder, for instance!). In a typical castle of this type, there would be only a few rooms and no corridors, so privacy would be almost nonexistent.

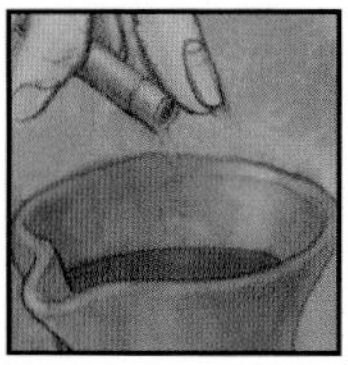

Page 35:

I thought about having Lady Macbeth use a poison ring here to drug the wine, but I didn't want to imply that she poisons people on a regular basis, so I went with a *Princess Bride*–inspired tube. The outline of the inner panels echoes the jug, as well as the iconic stereotype of a female silhouette.

Pages 37–39:

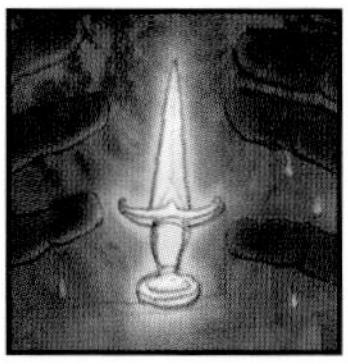

When *Macbeth* is staged or filmed, I generally feel it's best if none of his visions are actually seen by the audience, with the possible exception of the ghost. It's scarier to see an actor's eyes fixed on empty space as he reaches for the nonexistent dagger than to see a special effect of some sort. However, in a graphic novel, where static images have to convey the scene, I think we need to see at least glimpses of what Macbeth sees. Luckily such special effects are much easier to draw than to create convincingly onstage or in film.

Similarly, turning the dagger into a shadow that leads the way out of the scene is the kind of touch I like because it works well in the medium of comics but you probably wouldn't see it onstage or in film.

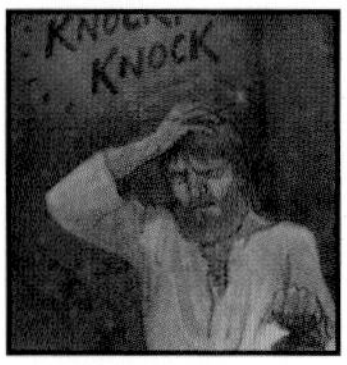
KNOCK

Pages 46–48:

This is one of the few passages of genuine comic relief in an otherwise dark and claustrophobic play, so I wanted to give the Porter his full due. His monologue is quite long and a bit difficult in places, but it becomes much easier to read once it's broken up into logical chunks. Speaking of chunks, did you get the joke at the bottom of page 48?

Page 50 and pages 58–59:

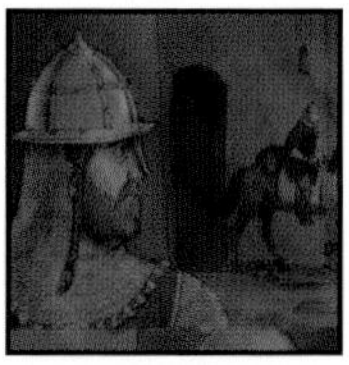

I chose not to illustrate all the wild supernatural happenings described here, because they take away from the more realistic and psychological horror of the murder itself. Still, I like the idea that nature itself is responding to the "unnatural" deeds of Macbeth, and it's a theme that comes up again later.

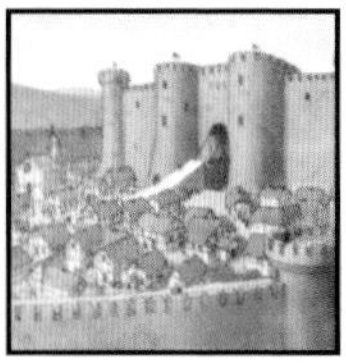

Page 61:

The royal palace at Forres is a classic 12th-century castle with typical features such as a church-like grand hall, an inner and outer curtain wall with a bustling town between them, a moat, ramp, drawbridge, and portcullis.

Page 62:

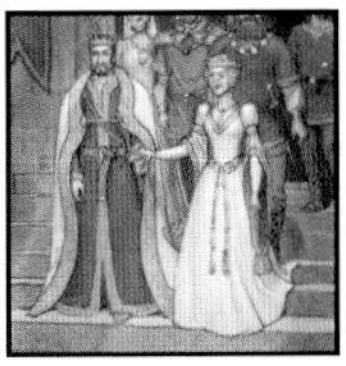

I chose to show the newly crowned King Macbeth wearing the same royal robe and crown as Duncan, but with the robe looking a bit stiff and confining on him. I wanted the crown to look like the crenellations on a castle turret, and the whole effect to subtly suggest a chess piece (without putting a big cross on his head, which seemed like the wrong image for him). Lady Macbeth's crown is more explicitly reminiscent of the crown on a queen chess piece.

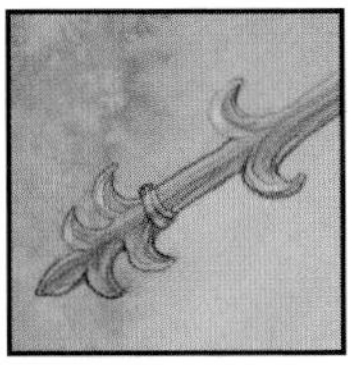

Page 64:

Macbeth's fleur-de-lis scepter of office is based on several drawings of early Scottish kings but owes its finer details to a statue of Saint Margaret of Scotland in Farm Street Church, in London. In addition to being an important Scottish saint, Margaret was the wife of Malcolm, so it seemed appropriate to use her scepter as reference.

Page 70, panel 4:

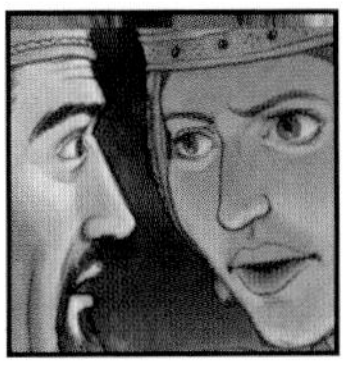

The play's original line is "Come, seeling night, scarf up the tender eye of pitiful day." "Seeling" means sewing or stitching, and this is a powerful, disturbing image I didn't want the reader to miss, so I recast it to "Come night, sew up the tender eye of pitiful day."

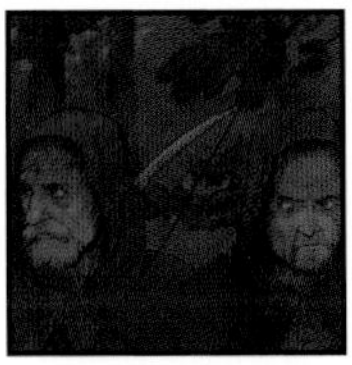

Pages 71–74:

Shakespeare doesn't say who the third murderer in this scene is. Some directors make him a stranger; others use Seyton or one of the thanes who are loyal to Macbeth. I chose Seyton.

I've seen some very cool ways of staging this ambush, but for some reason the murderers almost never use bows, which seems to me like the obvious weapon of choice for a stealthy attack against a strong mounted foe.

Pages 75–77:

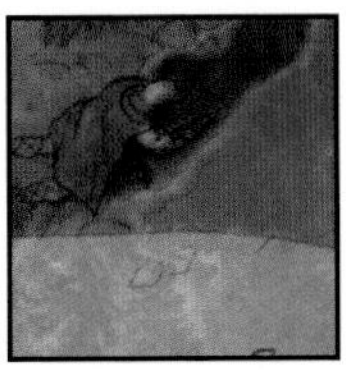

This is a subtle device, so in case you missed it, the ghostly borders indicate that this section is seen through the eyes of Banquo's spirit as he rises up from his body and seeks out Macbeth in the great hall, after which he manifests as a shadow and then as an increasingly gory ghost.

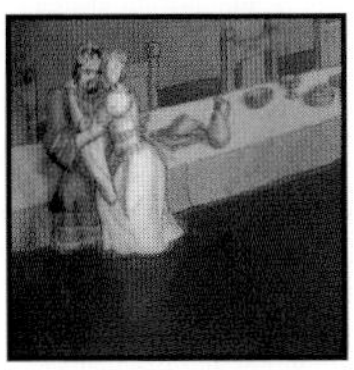

Page 87:

The pool of blood is an image that I first thought might be too literal, but as soon as I tried drawing it, I loved the way it worked.

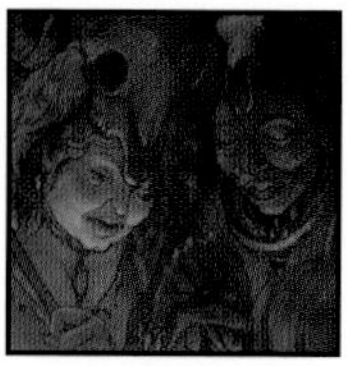

Page 89:

I removed from this scene the appearance of the witch-goddess Hecate. Many Shakespearean scholars believe she was written in by a later playwright. I tend to agree, and more important, I don't think she adds anything to the scene.

It wasn't until I decided to illustrate the ingredients of the witches' potion in their entirety that I noticed "witch's mummy" was an ingredient in the spell. Pretty dramatic, in the midst of a bunch of animal parts! I decided the witch would be mummified in a cross-legged position, as though she had died while performing some meditative ritual.

Page 92:

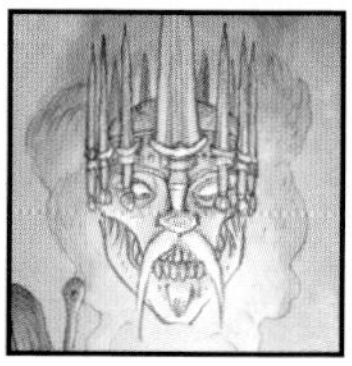

The first apparition is described by Shakespeare as an "armed head." Usually scholars and directors interpret this as "armored," that is, wearing a helmet, but I tried to picture how a disembodied head might actually be *armed*. This crown of daggers is what popped into my mind. Although the head is almost totally fleshless, the jaw shape and facial hair are suggestive of Macduff.

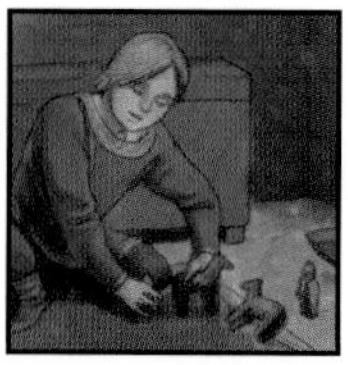

Pages 98–99:

I cut much of the scene between Lady Macduff and her son. In the original, they have a rather charming conversation, which seems intended to make the reader fond of them (especially the kid) before they are murdered. This is a clever device, but I don't think getting to know the two of them is actually necessary to feel the horror of their murder. The best part of their conversation is as follows:

Son: And must they all be hanged that swear and lie?
Lady Macduff: Every one.
Son: Who must hang them?
Lady Macduff: Why, the honest men.
Son: Then the liars and swearers are fools,
for there are liars and swearers enough to beat
the honest men and hang up them.

Ross also appears in the original scene, but I removed him because he delivers no important information except to remind us that Macduff has fled the country. He does have an interesting interaction with Lady Macduff at the end of the conversation, in which it's hinted that they may be attracted to each other, but that possibility has no bearing on the plot.

Page 100:

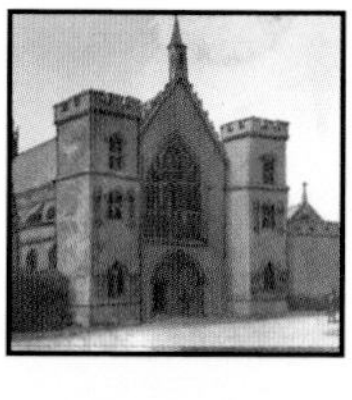

The building shown here is Westminster Hall, the only part of the Westminster complex that dates back to the original palace built by

William II in the late 11th century. I removed many of the architectural elements that were added later, but some of the details are speculative.

I also removed a large portion of this scene — in the original, Malcolm "tests" Macduff by pretending to be a depraved wanton unfit to rule. Then Ross arrives and tells Macduff his family is safe before telling him, no, actually they're dead. It seems to me that both of those bits are unnecessary and confusing.

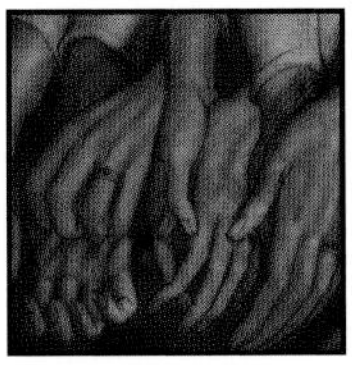

Page 104:
I wanted to capture the frenetic motion of obsessive-compulsive hand washing by filling the page with hands. I also like the idea that her hands are actually getting worse because she's scratching them.

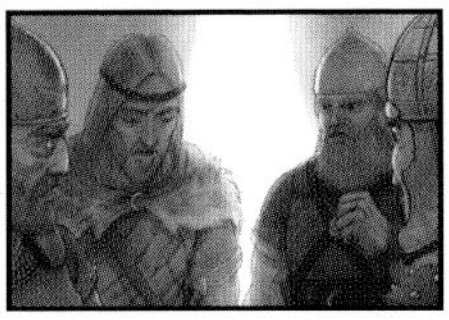

Page 106:
The characters depicted here are (left to right): Menteith, Caithness, Angus, and Lennox.

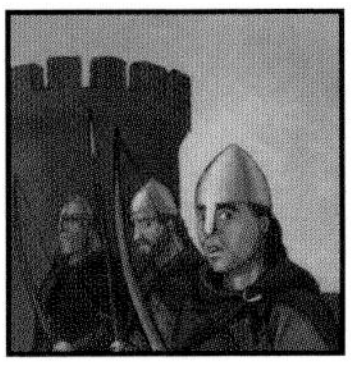

Page 107–end:
Dunsinane castle is quite similar to Forres, but gloomier and plainer. Although Macbeth is said to be strongly fortifying it, I chose not to cover the battlements with wooden hoardings (as was often done prior to a battle), because that would have obscured the action.

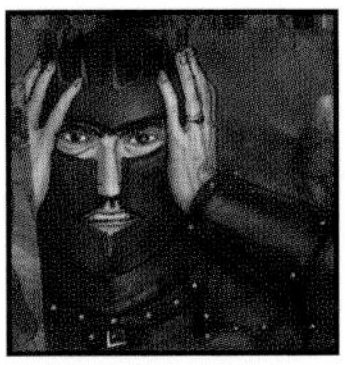

Page 111–end:
The armor Macbeth dons for the final battle was an interesting challenge. Visually I wanted him in heavy black armor, and I was inspired by a suit of black plate mail I saw in the Musée de l'Armée in Paris a few years ago, but full plate armor wasn't in use in the 12th century. They did, however, use some fairly elaborate leather armor, so I went with a black leather scale hauberk (coat) topped with black and brown leather arm and chest plates, plus a helmet similar to the one I saw in Paris.

The flanged mace was only just beginning to appear in the 12th century, and I'm not aware of any historical record of a weapon quite like the one I've given Macbeth in act 5, but his line "give me my staff" on page 111 inspired me with the idea that Macbeth might have had his rod of office replicated and enlarged as a weapon. It speaks to his desire for power, as well as his paranoia and constant need to defend his title, and it makes for some cool dynamics in the final fight scenes.

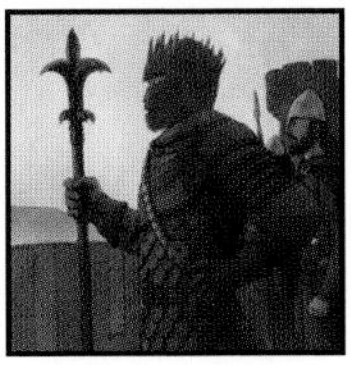

Page 113–end:
In the original text, Macbeth states his intention to stay inside Dunsinane castle, but shortly afterward he appears outside on the battlefield. Changing his mind like that is perfectly in character for

him, but I (and many directors) have chosen to keep him within the castle walls. Some directors have Macbeth's henchmen desert him entirely and lay the castle open with no resistance. I preferred to have a large, but brief, battle. When Macbeth says Dunsinane will "laugh a seige to scorn," he is not taking into account that his foes are so numerous and his allies so demoralized that the castle can be swarmed and taken with little resistance.

Where, then, would he make his stand? I like the idea that a combination of grandiose, fatalistic, cowardly, and tactical impulses would have him defending the top of the tallest tower against all comers — so I placed him on the turret as a kind of extreme "king of the hill," if you will.

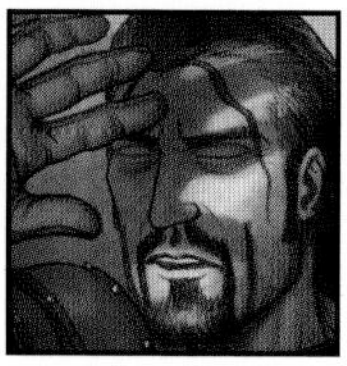

Page 115:
If you're interested in shadow imagery, here is Shakespeare's ultimate statement on the subject: "Life's but a walking shadow." He may have been referring to Plato's classic philosophical metaphor of the firelit cave, suggesting that everything in the world is a shadow of a more perfect, abstract, *ideal* form.

Page 134:
I removed the final two lines of the play, because I've always been bothered by such a dark story ending on an awkward rhyme and the word *Scone*. But now I'll end with those lines, in an attempt to make Shakespeare's ghost happy.

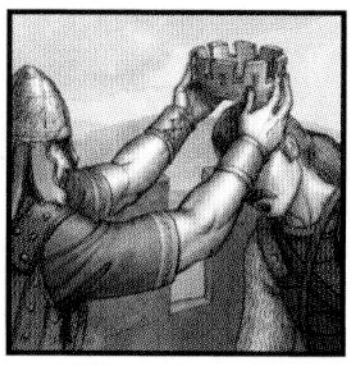

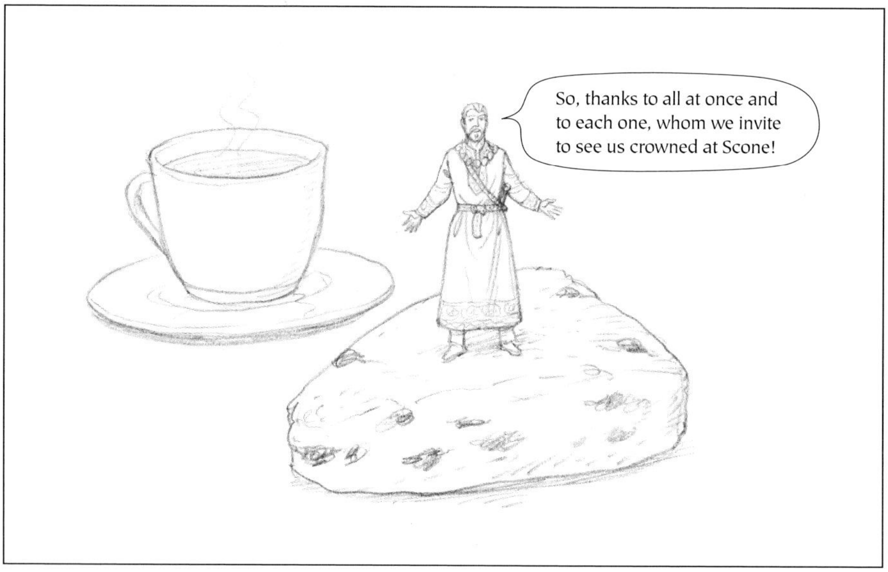
So, thanks to all at once and to each one, whom we invite to see us crowned at Scone!

ACKNOWLEDGMENTS

I'd like to thank the entire team at Candlewick, especially "my" team, for their efforts on this book: my editor, Deb Noyes, with additional editorial help from Carter Hasegawa; design by Lisa Rudden; art direction by Sherry Fatla; technical production by Gregg Hammerquist; final production by a large and detail-oriented team headed by Amanda Bellamy; copyediting by Hannah Mahoney, with Emily Quill and Martha Dwyer as proofreaders; also the marketing efforts of Laura Rivas, Jennifer Roberts, Sharon Hancock, Anne Irza-Leggat, Andie Krawczyk, Alex Nash, Regan Castle, and many others behind the scenes. Thanks also to the always-cheerful head of sales, John Mendelson; the head of legal, Becky Hemperly; and the excellent team at Walker Books U.K. who handle all things international.

I would particularly like to thank my beloved wife, Alison Morris, who provides my first line of editorial feedback. Her unflinching honesty, her deep knowledge of the book industry, and her eagle eye for detail, continuity, likeness, expression, and emotion are absolutely invaluable. My early readers were Mat MacKenzie, Judith Hinds, and Steve Hinds.

Karen Green, medievalist and graphic-novel champion at the Columbia University libraries, was generous with her help on several questions I had about the historical period of Macbeth.

In memory of a great teacher
and friend, Les Kanturek

First edition 2015

Library of Congress Catalog Card Number 2014939338
ISBN 978-0-7636-6943-0 (hardcover)
ISBN 978-0-7636-7802-9 (paperback)

14 15 16 17 18 19 TLF 10 9 8 7 6 5 4 3 2 1
Printed in Dongguan, Guangdong, China

This book was typeset in Tiepolo.
The illustrations were done in pencil, ink wash, and digital media.

Candlewick Press
99 Dover Street
Somerville, Massachusetts 02144

visit us at www.candlewick.com